THE WIZARD'S NEMESIS

VOLUME III OF THE WAR OF THE DRAGONS

ALSO BY DAVE SMEDS

The Sorcery Within

The Schemes of Dragons

Raiding the Hoard of Enchantment

Piper in the Night

Embracing the Starlight

X-Men: Law of the Jungle

Swords, Magic, and Heart

THE WIZARD'S NEMESIS

†

VOLUME III OF THE WAR OF THE DRAGONS

DAVE SMEDS

BOOK VIEW CAFE

LAS VEGAS, NV

Thank Riv
CILENDRODEL
Old Stump
Yent
Eruth
Garthmorron
DRAGON SEA
Dragonsdeep
ELANDRIS
Firsthold
THIAGRA
MOIN
Lealin
T'jet
SIMORILIA
TAMISAN
Tazh Tah
ANRAHOU MTS
Tira
TAREZAD
AHIRINAR

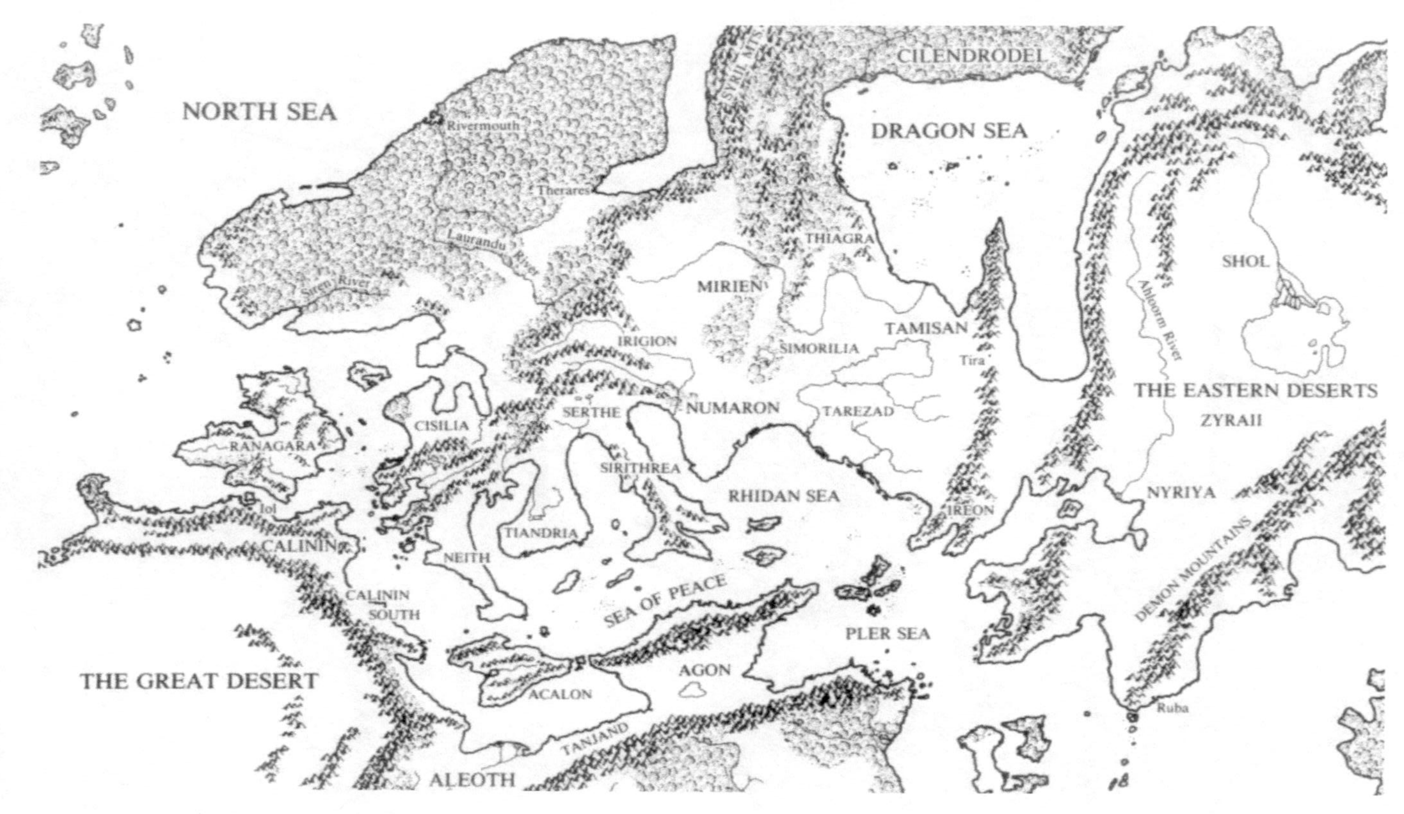

NORTH SEA
Rivermouth
Therares
Laurandu River
Siren River
CILENDRODEL
STRIL MTS.
DRAGON SEA
THIAGRA
MIRIEN
SIMORILIA
TAMISAN
Tira
THE EASTERN DESERTS
ZYRAII
SHOL
Ahloorm River
IRIGION
NUMARON
SERTHE
TAREZAD
IREON
NYRIYA
DEMON MOUNTAINS
CISILIA
RANAGARA
SIRITHREA
RHIDAN SEA
Iol
TIANDRIA
NEITH
CALININ
CALININ SOUTH
SEA OF PEACE
PLER SEA
Ruba
THE GREAT DESERT
ACALON
AGON
TANJAND
ALEOTH

Arrogant dragon will have cause to repent,
for what is at the full cannot last.
—*I Ching*, First Hexagram, Sixth Line

FIFTEEN HUNDRED YEARS AGO

DAREL'S HUT STOOD AT the very edge of the Dragon Sea, along a strand where only hardy tufts of sea oats could prosper. The old sailor sat on a makeshift stool of driftwood near the door flap, casting weatherwise glances at the clouds over the waves to the north. Cured and seasoned over the years by the wind and water and salt, he resembled the desiccated husks of the sea creatures that dotted the beach along the high tide mark.

As he repaired a net, Darel carefully marked the progress of the three people approaching along the shore from the west. Behind them in the haze, the city of T'jet was strewn across the hills, near enough that on days when the wind poured off the continent, the reek of open sewers and crowded humanity would settle over his shack, and Darel would take to his boat for relief. As a young man, he had vowed that when his fortune was made, he would move to a better place — perhaps across the gulf to Anrahou, where the sand was stark and clean, and the shoals full of fish.

The strangers' clothing gleamed. The fabric was unmistakably fine quarn silk. Embroidery decorated cuffs, lapels, collars. Nobles. Why here? Why no guards or retainers?

The newcomers stopped a few paces away. Darel kept his eyes on his work.

"Is this how you greet your betters?"

It was the youngest of the group who spoke, a stripling who had yet to fill out in girth or beard. Beside him stood another man and a woman, more mature than the lad—a dusting of grey in the man's beard, a few nascent wrinkles at the corners of the woman's eyes—but still unfaded by Darel's standard. Dark-maned and brown-eyed, the pair had obviously sprung from the same sire and dam.

Darel cinched a last knot and stood. "Beg pardon, young lord. A man of my station has to keep to his work or he goes hungry."

Darel straightened fully, and the youth's eyes widened as he saw how the fisherman towered over him.

The older man stepped forward. "Are you Darel?"

He was short and slight. The fairness of his skin demonstrated how seldom he ventured outdoors. Yet he exuded an aura that said Darel did not have the means to intimidate him.

"At your service," Darel replied.

"My name is Alemar, Consul of Moin. This is my sister, Dame Miranda. Perhaps you have heard of us."

The sound of the man's voice overcame the crash of the breakers in a manner Darel could only call eldritch. At close range, Alemar still appeared as relatively young as he had seemed at a distance, but Darel now knew that was an illusion. Darel was an infant by comparison.

"I know of you, yes." Darel's voice gave out before the sentence was fully spoken. The moisture in his mouth had fled.

"I need a man familiar with the Dragon Sea, to sail with me, to be my pilot," Alemar stated.

Darel dug out a flask from his mending basket and fortified his courage. He could tell he was not going to be told anything he wished to hear. "Ackusso the Cripple has served as pilot of the Moin consulate these past twelve years."

"Indeed. But he declined to take us where we must go."

"And where is that?"

"The Lost Isles."

A sudden, mewling cry came from within the shack. A woman's

voice overlaid it, uttering words of comfort in low, soothing tones, as if she were speaking to an infant. Darel stopped short of throwing aside the door flap and rushing inside. He faced the consul, forcing himself to keep a respectful tone.

"I beg of you, do not speak of that place here!"

"I take it you do not wish to come?"

Darel laughed, but the lack of air in his lungs made it a nearly soundless thing. "Since you ask, no."

Darel braced himself. When a man of Alemar's station and power desired service, he was indulged. It could not have gone well with Ackusso when he had chosen as he had; at the least, it must have cost the peg-legged navigator a position he had worked toward for twenty years, a job that had given him the wherewithal to buy four of his children houses as they came of age.

All Alemar said was, "I think I can convince you that it is in your interest to accept the commission." Spoken without threat.

Darel sighed. "What did you have in mind?"

"Let me see your son," Alemar said.

Darel swayed. "No. No, I don't want that."

"Let me see him," Alemar repeated.

Because the sorcerer's voice was paternal, even gentle, Darel yielded. Wearily he beckoned the others to the shack. The noises from within had faded to whimpers. A small mercy.

Darel entered first and held up the flap. On the far side of the low, dim, single room, Darel's wife Neena combed her fingers desperately through her stringy hair, attempting without hope of success to look presentable. She moved her bulk behind the chair in which sat her son Vonni, eyes vacant, drool staining the front of his shirt.

As strangers always did, the visitors winced as they caught sight of Vonni.

Darel coughed. "Here you see what happens to a man who ventures into dragon country."

At the mention of "dragon," Vonni emitted another strangled outburst, and shuddered so violently it seemed certain he would splinter his frail bones. His mother rushed to pour tea into an earthenware cup. The aroma of dreamcress and honey wafted up, tempering the hut's pervasive atmosphere of soiled clothes.

Vonni let the tea be poured into his mouth. He swallowed automatically. The act seemed to engross him, cutting short his panic.

"He remembers how to drink and eat, if we fill his mouth." Darel found it difficult to speak loud enough to be heard. "Sometimes he will sleep if we lay him on his mat. He is capable of little else."

The young stranger grimaced, but the two magicians simply nodded. "Let me approach him," Alemar requested.

Neena shook her head, silently begging. Darel made her let go of Vonni's shoulders. She allowed her husband to move her back, but she kept her arms extended, reaching for her boy.

Alemar knelt and lifted Vonni's head gently by the chin. He whispered a few words too low for Darel to hear. Vonni's glance ceased wandering. The longer the young man studied the wizard, the more his mouth and cheeks and brows lost their wax-figure stillness. His expression began to hint of coherent emotions, evolving from fear to calm to curiosity. Finally Vonni turned to his father. He whispered three hoarse, but clear, words.

"Go with him."

Darel's eyes widened. Neena gasped. Alemar rose and turned to the sailor.

"You toy with us. You put the words in his mouth," Darel claimed.

"The words were his. I cannot promise to make him capable of sustained speech, but I can make him more whole than he is now. Come with me and I will do what I can to heal him. That will be your reward. Along with this, of course." Alemar tossed Darel a sack purse. "I am paying you in full in advance."

Darel poured several large-denomination coins into his palm. He had only to heft them to calculate that he had been paid an amount at least triple the usual sum to hire a pilot for the season. As for receiving it in advance, Darel took it as an acknowledgment the wizard was aware the voyage would probably end in all their deaths. It was a widow's legacy.

"What will you do about the dragons?" Darel asked.

"I will kill them," Alemar replied.

Darel nodded slowly. "You will have to." He put the coins back in the purse, put the purse in a small chest, closed the lid, and locked it. "You have charts, I expect."

"You will not lack for the necessities of your trade," Alemar promised. "Our ship is at the long wharf. Report at tomorrow noon. We leave in three days on the morning tide. Bring your son along."

Darel regarded Vonni. No trace remained of his momentary lucidity, but the room still echoed with those three, clear words.

"Aye, m'lord. I will be there," Darel said.

— o —

The drizzling sky hid the smoke until they crested the ridge. Polk himself did not notice it until Larkmeadow, his father's head ranger, stiffened in the saddle and pointed.

Down in the little valley, a farmhouse was smoldering, its thatch roof consumed, its wattle-and-daub walls crumbling into piles of char.

"Two scouts to each flank!" Polk's father commanded. "The rest, with me." He drew his sword.

As bidden, two sets of men-at-arms sped off to right and left to check for lurkers, mud flying up from the cloven hooves of their oeikani. Everyone else galloped with the marchwarden straight toward the ruined homestead.

Polk rode at his father's left, two lengths behind, where he could keep watch on his little brother. With all the heedless enthusiasm of a twelve-year-old, Kihen was riding as hard as his elders, even though he should have allowed the trained fighters to take the lead.

The hilt of Polk's sword jostled in his palm. His father's blademaster had promised him that with enough practice, the weapon would feel like an extension of his arm. At age fifteen, he had yet to experience that sort of unity. Like so many young men raised on the wolds of Moin, he was an archer first. If not for the moisture coming from the sky, he would choose to be an archer now. But his bowstring was in his saddlebag, sealed away from wetness, and his quiver was hooded.

As they crossed the outer pasture, Kihen's well-trained doe proved its worth, slackening its pace despite its rider's signals. Polk came even and shook his head at Kihen. With a sigh, the youngster accepted his restrictions.

The party, ten strong even without the four who had gone to check the flanks, did not rein up until they reached the yard between the house and barn. Or what had been the house and barn. What portions remained had survived only because the rain had discouraged the flames.

Polk's father and half his men dismounted and stalked through the debris, checking possible hiding spots—a well, a root cellar, the privy, the lee side of an overturned cart. Polk and the others stayed on oeikaniback, gazes pulled inevitably toward the bodies.

Polk counted five dead. In the pigsty lay what had been a young man, at most a year or two older than Polk. Two arrows sprouted from his back. No marks of struggle showed in the mud and manure around him; he had been dead by the time he keeled over. Probably first to die, before the family knew it was in danger.

An outdoor oven stood on the side of the house where the kitchen had been. It had survived the attack with no harm. The two women propped against it had fared worse. The cord used to garrote the farmwife was still wrapped around her throat, bloating what had already been a round, plump face. Polk suspected she had been a person who often smiled. That was bitter to ponder, yet it was worse to look at her companion, an elderly woman whose skull had been beaten flat.

In the front yard was the corpse of the farmer. He had been a balding, stout fellow. The rain had rinsed the knife cuts on his arms, but the dark stain in his shirt remained, covering the whole width and most of the length of his torso. Here was the only heartening part of the scene, because it was plain he had managed to fight back. The last corpse, which lay face down near the farmer, was that of a wiry man with a thick braid of red hair, runic tattoos flowing down the length of his arms. Dirt encrusted his fingernails. A foulness rose from him that made Polk wave his hand in front of his face. It was not the stench of death, but the intrinsic ripeness of someone who had not had a bath or a swim any time in a season or more. He was dressed in raid tradition—that is, not at all, save for a loin clout. Dark, clotted blood plainly marked the deep slice in the side of his neck. His weapons were missing.

"It's a reaver!" Kihen cried. "Look! Even his arse is tattooed!"

Heronmarsh, one of the veterans of the escort, chuckled at the sight of the dead marauder. "He underestimated that farmer. Got himself cut in the wrong spot. Then his so-called friends took what he wouldn't be using no more."

"Come away," Polk urged his brother.

"But—"

"Come away," Polk repeated.

They circled the house and came back to the front yard. By then, the flankers had returned, and all of the men-at-arms sat or stood less tensely. Most had sheathed their swords. Larkmeadow knelt beside the dead farmer. He lifted an arm. An impression of gravel remained in the underside of the corpse's chill, doughy palm.

"The attack happened near dawn," Larkmeadow said. "The hog-lickers must be halfway to the Thickwood by now." He had barely finished the sentence when his glance locked on the muddy puddle just beyond the body. He reached into the water and lifted out a girl's harvest smock. Polk could see at once it had been worn by someone more petite than either of the dead women by the oven. Shreds dangled where the garment had been torn off its owner.

Polk's father stalked from the ruin of the house. He kicked the lintel, which lay as charcoal over the front entrance like a second threshold. The force of his blow shattered the piece into fragments, knocking sparks from its still-burning core. "This steading was on the main road!" he growled. "Rangers pass this spot three times a week!"

Everyone understood. If raiders could strike a freeman's property as secure as this one had seemed to be, next they would be harrowing the crofts of the great manor houses, killing the peasants, raping their daughters, stealing their iron. Already in the fringe lands near Thiagra, farmers had taken to working in pairs — one to stand guard while the other tilled. Harvests had grown meager. Taxes and tithes of grain could not be collected.

Once, garrisons of the Calinin Empire lay in place to prevent such problems. Once, legions would have been dispatched across the border to hunt down reavers who grew too bold. No more. To all intents and purposes, Moin itself now lay outside the empire. Exposed.

"Bury them," the marchwarden commanded. "It's all we can do for them now."

"We could go after the girl," Polk suggested. "The ground is muddy. We'll be able to see which way they went."

His father returned a withering stare. "They have too much head start, and we have a rendezvous to keep."

Polk said no more. He knew it wouldn't do any good.

Kihen, though, didn't understand. On other occasions, their father had been relentless in his pursuit of those who encroached on territory under his protection. "I want to chase them," the boy protested. "I want to rescue the farmgirl."

The marchwarden smiled. "And that is proper and noble of you," he said indulgently. "But I have spoken."

The journey resumed an hour later, once the bodies of the local folk had been put in the ground, with a cairn of fieldstone over each grave to keep wild animals from them. The reaver's remains were simply tossed in the pasture for the vultures and crows.

As they wended their way along the trade road, getting closer to the river, the hedgerows grew thicker, the clumps of marsh reed grew more dense, providing more potential hiding places. The rain ceased, but drips fell from branches onto leaf mulch, making enough noise that it could be concealing the tread of human feet darting from one ambush point to another. The men often checked behind them.

They kept their eyes on the periphery, letting their mounts pay attention to the road.

Shortly after midday they reached the landing. A customs house stood on the nearer bank, protected by its palisade of sharpened stakes and a barracksful of sentries. A ferry stood idle on the far side. On the near side waited a barge. Stevedores were loading the last few barrels and bales of goods. The barge owner and a customs official stood on the dock, arguing the final particulars of tariffs versus services.

The marchwarden and his men dismounted. Larkmeadow strode up to the barge owner, spoke to him briefly, and handed him a purse of coin. The man nodded.

The arrangement was now sealed in full. For the next several days, this barge would be Polk's dwelling, as it progressed downstream to its final stop at the river mouth, far beyond the borders of Moin.

Larkmeadow retreated with the other men to the corral, where the oeikani were being fed, watered, and combed down. Only the marchwarden and his sons remained at the verge of the river.

Polk contemplated the gap between the dock and the edge of the barge. One step and he would be aboard.

"Must I go?"

His father's eyes narrowed. "I have explained myself on this matter already." The answer was not just stern, it was angry. The man had not wanted Polk to raise this issue.

It was true that he had explained. Polk had heard the words very clearly, standing by the great fireplace of the manor house, seventeen days past. "Until our lands are safe," the marchwarden had said, "I think it wise to put one of my heirs out of harm's way. Your eldest brother must stay, of course, to be my right hand. And Veram is your uncle's steward in training. Meanwhile Kihen is too young to go. So it falls to you. I have arranged for you to join the retinue of Lord Alemar, our consul in Tamisan. You will travel to T'jet within the month."

There had been more to the speech. More about how important the treaty with Tamisan was, how the river was Moin's vital link to the civilized kingdoms now that overland caravans were so often attacked by reavers. More about how Polk would learn useful skills he would not acquire if he stayed, and how he might develop important relationships among the increasing population of Moinese who had sought the safety in the consulate enclave, beyond the reach of barbarian hordes. But Polk had only heard one message: He was being exiled.

Polk had hoped when the moment of leave-taking arrived, things might be different. The marchlord had more than once declared what he intended to do about something and done otherwise — or done nothing — when the time came to put his words into action.

"Let *me* go," Kihen urged, tugging his father's sleeve. "You promised one day I would see the ocean."

The marchwarden smiled at his youngest child. "And so you shall. One day. For now, you must stay with me."

Kihen sighed, gazing at Polk with undisguised envy. To the boy, Polk's departure was the beginning of an adventure.

Polk embraced his brother, then stepped back to shake hands. Like men. They remained that way, sharing a farewell moment.

Kihen had his father's olive complexion and short fingers, as did Polk's older brothers. Polk gazed down at their clasped hands and was reminded once more that his own skin had the bronze tone and his fingers the slenderness and length that resembled Sir Trennec, the marchlord's master archer in former days. Trennec, who gossips said had been much admired by Polk's late mother.

Polk did not have Kihen's privilege — to go home. He would never have that again. His choice was only between resenting what the trip downriver represented, or embracing it as the beginning of something grander than he had known.

His father shook his hand as well, but did not linger at the touch, nor did moisture brim on his eyelashes.

Polk stepped aboard. A man strapping down cargo jutted his chin at a place to sit. It was in the gap between a pair of large crates, where Polk would be shielded from any reavers' arrows that might come sailing from the trees should the barge drift too near the wrong bank during the journey.

Polk's last glimpse of his family members—Kihen standing on the dock, waving to the last, his father already turned and checking to see whether the oeikani were ready for the return ride—was lost in the glare of sunlight on the water.

—o—

Born and raised far from the coast, the ocean's immensity had dismayed Polk when he had first encountered it. Now he never truly slept well unless lulled off by the caress of wave upon hull. He treasured the times when he could wrap himself within it and explore its vastness firsthand.

Tilting his head upward, the young nobleman was drawn to the sight of fish swarming to the scraps a crewman had just thrown overboard. They were no longer the denizens of the murk they seemed to be when observed from above. Their argent bellies shimmered, renewing the sun's light, mimicking the sheen of the waves. To the fish, the trait was the protective camouflaging that helped them survive; to Polk, it was a manifestation of beauty.

He swam on, taking in as much of his surroundings as he could, while he could. He had no need to rise to the surface to fill his lungs. Over his face he wore a transparent membrane stretched around a framework of golden wire. He simply breathed as he would when not immersed. The membrane magicked the air he needed right out of the water in front of his face.

Profuse growths of coral thrust toward him from below. Even here, well beyond sight of the coast, the sea was shallow, as it was across most of the great gulf people called the Dragon Sea. Polk weaved through it, catching glimpses of squid, shrimp, and octopi, along with dozens of types of fish.

Kihen would have loved being here, sharing this moment.

To think of his younger brother was to picture him as he had been on the day Polk had seen him last, vanishing into sun glare much like the brilliance above him now. Had it already been three years?

A small cascade of ballast gravel, tossed overboard in his vicinity, pulled him from his reverie. The gravel was the agreed-upon signal to him from Scab, the cabin boy, to inform him the wind had returned. Polk needed to rejoin the ship or be left behind.

He rose to the surface and climbed the rope ladder. A hand reached for him. Polk accepted the assistance climbing over the rail.

"You look like a demon of the Eastern Deserts with that on, young warden," Darel said.

Polk removed the mask. Tilted it this way and that, letting the sun's rays scintillate on the framework. "You haven't tried one yet?" He knew that Darel had been present when Alemar urged all of the crew to make use of the opportunity.

"If man were meant to swim like a fish, he'd have been given gills," the pilot said.

"But we have, thanks to Lady Miranda. Gills that serve when needed, and can be set aside when not." Polk stowed the airmaker beside its mates in a trough of salt water near the mast so the open air would not dry and crack the membrane. Then he gestured at the array.

Darel merely closed the lid on the trough, hiding the devices from his view. "It's sorcery. Best leave that to dragons."

"So some would say," Polk replied. "Not I."

"Which is your right. My lord." He gave Polk a salute and turned away to resume scanning the waters to the south, off to starboard.

Polk went below deck to change into dry clothes, but the way the conversation had ended troubled him. Despite the nods to etiquette, it was as if he had been dismissed.

He couldn't have that. On this voyage he was next in command after the sorcerers. What was it Lord Alemar always said? *"Speak as if you know people will listen, and they will listen."*

He put on the best of the outfits he had brought. He combed out the tangle the ocean had made of his hair. He emerged through the hatch with chin up, spine straight.

He deliberately did not glance toward Darel at first. He

observed the crew at work, the idleness gone now that the sails had filled. He nodded as if giving his sanction to their actions. Only Scab nodded back. Polk was reminded that rank or no rank, he was the youngest person aboard other than the cabin boy.

Darel was standing near the prow, a small foldaway workstand in front of him. Having apparently sighted something, the pilot picked up a chart case, unrolled a map, and made a small mark.

Here at sea, Darel was transformed. He was in his element. He knew what needed doing. Every man of the crew saw it.

Just what *was* he doing? Polk knew if he couldn't answer that on his own he would condemn himself as naïve. That would make his approach pointless.

Ah. The color of the sea had deepened. The ship was crossing one of the infrequent regions of deeper water. So Darel had been noting the feature on his chart—perhaps confirming the position of an undersea bluff he had expected to reach at just this point in the voyage.

Leagues from any sight of land, the man knew where he was.

Enough. However intimidating the pilot might seem now, back at the beach he had been little more than old laundry wrung out and hung on a stick to dry. Polk headed straight for the man.

"Something I can do for you, Wold-Steward?"

Polk cleared his throat. "I cannot say as I blame you for hating the sort of dark working that was inflicted upon your son. But you seem to mistrust all manner of sorcery, even that wielded by men."

"I see no reason to worship a force so few control."

"It's a force with many uses. Good can come of it."

Darel rolled up the map. He ran his fingertips over the texture of the woven hemp. "You say it as if you have something particular in mind."

"This voyage, of course. If wielding sorcery saves an entire people from destruction, would you not call that good?"

Darel frowned. "The people of Moin, you mean?"

"Did you think we were challenging dragons for amusement?

My homeland's salvation is at stake."

"Is it?" Darel asked. "I don't deny you Moinese seem to have a deckful of broken spars to deal with these days. I've spent many an evening in the harbor taverns, sampling a brew with those who've had to flee. They deserve a happy life as much as any. But this voyage? All that will come of it is a few more deaths. That's not much in the way of salvation."

"What would you have us do?"

Darel stored the chart case in the small oak chest at his feet. "Stand firm. You may no longer have the Calinin legions at your call, but you have your own men and swords. Give a few extra tithings to whatever gods might grant your people a little luck. Things may get better."

A gull swooped for a bit of bread flung by a crewman. The wind brushed a curl of Polk's hair across his temple.

"You've no idea how bad it is," Polk said.

Darel seemed to see Polk for the first time. "Begging your pardon for speaking, Wold-Steward, but it's from the heart. You've seen some things, young as you are. I can see that. I think you'd agree I've seen some things, too. Trust me when I say you've nothing to look forward to in the Lost Isles. All that grows in the old gardens are piles of bird guano."

"It once was a rich place," Polk argued. "Elandris, they called it. It means Sea Haven in the Old Tongue. It had copper and tin. Quarries of the finest marble in the known world. Amath pearl oysters. It was founded before the Calinin Empire—even before the Igitians had shaken off the yoke of the Shagas. The first human-led civilized land north of the Great Strait."

"That was then. This is now. Why not pick another place?"

"Another place would not have the same history. The same meaning to us." Polk said.

"Eh?"

"Moin was founded by those who fled Elandris when the dragons came. In taking them back, we take back our forefathers' domain."

Darel burst into laughter.

"What's so funny?" Polk demanded.

"I see how they snared you. They found the right story."

"It's the truth. Moin was founded by refugees from the Lost Isles."

"I have no doubt it is true, as far as it goes," Darel said. "The rest of what I've heard is no doubt the truth as well. The sorcerers mean to build cities beneath the sea, covered by domes of vartham glass."

"Yes," Polk admitted. "That is the plan."

"They'd have to," Darel said. "There isn't enough arable land in all the islands that would take up more than a fiefdom of Moin. I don't wonder that the Council of Marchlords gave those two enough tar and oakum to caulk their boat. It must have sounded like they couldn't lose. Either the mages die in the attempt while the Marchlords have time left to weigh other options, or the two of them succeed and the people of Moin have a new home."

"Where is the problem? Lord Alemar..."

"*Lord* Alemar. Yes, that's just it, *Lord* Alemar. He's already become a noble of Moin. Most realms have laws against sorcerers reaching so high. Imagine what will happen when everyone is tucked into domes, able to go out only with those demon masks in the trough there?" He flicked a hand at the container of airmakers. "It will be a realm where those two are *indispensable*."

Darel waited, but Polk did not reply. He was too busy recalling conversations with Miranda and, less often, with the consul himself. One or the other had described how they would teach lesser magicians how to draw gold from silt, would show weavers and glassmakers and brewers ways to make their wares superior to anything the civilized lands had to offer — until traders would have no choice but to make the new realm a destination, bringing money and commodities aplenty. It had never sounded anything but reasonable.

"Don't let the gale darken your horizon, young lord." Darel shrugged and waved his hands. "Nothing I spoke of matters. The dragons will kill us all. Fretting over what may happen in ten or twenty years is battening the hatches before you've even built your ship."

"If you're so certain of that, why did you accept the commission? Are you eager to die?"

Darel tilted his head down. Polk saw he was gazing in the direction of Vonni's quarters, below deck. "Death comes anyway, sooner or later. I *do* believe the dragons will win. But the wizard may hurt them before they suck the meat off his bones. That I would like to see."

—o—

Miranda's eyes burst open. Lantern glow and broad shadows danced on the ceiling above her berth. What time? Immediately she thought in nautical measures: watches and bells. She guessed dawn was still far off, but there was no doubt of it—despite her intentions, she had slept.

She rolled onto an elbow. Across the chamber, Alemar sat on a stool opposite the idiot, a small table between them. Both men stared straight at the other, hands resting on the table fingertip to fingertip. Vonni was slumped. Drool trickled off his lips. Alemar sat straight, mouth closed, but had the same bird-bright cast to his eyes as his companion. The pair were in the same positions they had occupied when she had gone to sleep.

Miranda hurried to her brother's side and seized his upper arm.

He did not react.

She formed a tendril of energy and flicked it along the flows of his aura.

He jerked. Blinked. She saw the glow around the two men begin to disentangle. Tears began to stream down Vonni's face. He whimpered. Alemar inhaled sharply.

Abruptly Vonni sobbed and fell off his stool. He remained in a quivering heap. Alemar drooped onto the table, barely managing to support himself with his elbows. Five breaths, then the last of the trance dissipated.

"What were my instructions?" he demanded.

She pointed to the windows, to the positions of Motherworld and the moons.

He grunted. "That long?"

"Yes."

"Forgive me," he said. "I didn't realize."

She poured them cups of cold tea. Uncovered the bread on the sideboard. Cut slices off a haunch of salt pork. Peeled two oranges. Alemar gathered himself while she worked. By the time she set the platter on the table, he seemed composed. He had pulled Vonni off to the side. Other than an occasional twitch, the pilot's son was sleeping soundly.

Her brother winced as he reached toward the food. He aborted the effort. His eyes were so bloodshot she found it hard to look at him.

"Time and again, I felt as though I had only to look a little deeper, sort through one last tangle, and I would perceive just how the dragon did what she did. But it was almost as if the beast were still alive inside him. A second consciousness. If I came near, she would hide. When I would force my way past some barrier she had set up, I would find that she had built a new one to detour me again."

He reached again. This time he succeeded in spearing a small slice of orange. He draped it over a bite-sized block of bread, and raised both toward his mouth.

"I do not believe I was in danger."

"I did not say you were," she replied.

"Yes, you did."

Yes. She had. It was all she could do not to tremble. She had seen her brother in trances before, but not like the one tonight. He had looked *dead*.

But he was alive. He chewed. Swallowed. Seemed surprised at how fine a thing it was to consume food.

"Did you learn what you needed to know?" she asked.

"Some."

The disappointment in his tone said it had not been much, but she knew she would not get him to admit the probing of the pilot's son had been an unwarranted risk. And perhaps he was right. Even a small measure of insight into the dragons' abilities might influence their fate for the better.

She gestured at Vonni. "What about him?"

"I did what I could. He may be able to eat without help now. Keep himself clean. Not that he will care. All he wants is release."

"You would think he would have long since killed himself."

Alemar made a noise in the back of his throat, as if clearing something disgusting he did not want inside himself. "Even if he could control his limbs enough to raise a knife to his throat or reach for a bottle of poison, the dragon has left a compulsion inside him that prevents him from following through. She wanted him to suffer as long and as thoroughly as possible. Thirty, forty, fifty years."

"All because she felt the vessel he was sailing upon encroached upon her territory?"

"Only that. I believe Triss regarded the shaping of him as an example of her art."

Miranda shivered.

"She is stronger than I estimated," her brother admitted. "Faroc might be stronger still."

"But still you say we go forward."

He squeezed her hand. "I promised you one day we would live in a place where we belonged. The stronger the dragons are known to be, the mightier our reputations when we slay them. We'll be able to get everything we've worked toward."

Miranda regarded Vonni, still moaning on the floor. There lay a tangible example of the price of underestimating dragons.

"I'll fetch crewmen to take him back to his father," she said.

Alemar put his open palm in her path. "You keep picturing what will happen if we are defeated," he chided. "What you put in front of you, you move toward. We *will* win, Miranda. Let *that* be what you envision."

She swallowed hard. "I will picture you, strong." That much she could do. That much, she believed.

—o—

Polk stood next to Darel, who manned the helm. The young man felt the tension among the crew. Gone was the cheer of the first few days, when the invigoration of being on a grand quest overwhelmed its distant danger. Now everyone cast wary looks at the northeastern sky, and held their breath every time a large sea bird appeared over the horizon.

"Yellow kelp," Darel muttered, pointing at segments of seaweed boiling up beyond the rudder.

"What's it mean?" Polk asked.

"It grows near the Lost Isles. Some say the dragons mark the edge of their domain by how far out it grows. When sailors on these waters see yellow kelp, they change course."

Polk nodded gravely.

Darel spat over the side. "To stand here now takes all the salt I have in my blood." He waved at the other men. "Those bilge drinkers are the lucky ones. They won't really understand what we're up against until they see Faroc or Triss with their own eyes."

Darel had not spoken so unguardedly with Polk since their argument nine days back. The young man decided to ask the pilot a question that had been nagging him ever since. "Have *you* seen them? The dragons? With your own eyes?"

Darel hesitated. "I have seen Triss," he responded at a volume so low Polk could just manage to hear him. "So close that my clothes were rippled by the force of her breath. She landed next to my hut when she returned Vonni to me."

"She *returned* him? Brought him back herself?"

"Yes."

"I don't understand. Why would she do that?"

"To make an example of him, as a warning to others."

Both men turned to look at Vonni. The imbecile was sitting midship, his spine braced against a hogshead barrel of drinking water, his legs sprawled on the deck. He was turning a short piece of cord over and over. Twice in the past hour he had started to make a knot. Polk had often seen young boys at the docks practicing the dozens of ties and cinches all sailors' sons should know; he had learned a few himself. Vonni had not managed yet to complete a single example, but he did seem to know what it was he was striving toward. Whatever the wizard had done, it had given Vonni back that much of himself.

Improved though he was, the mere sight of him was still enough to bring a caring man to tears.

"Vonni wasn't even the one responsible for the trespassing, you know," Darel said. "That was his captain—a fool trader who thought he could cut a few days off a voyage to Cilendrodel to take on a shipment of quarn silk and make it back to T'jet in time for The Heir's nuptials. The lords and ladies were paying their tailors prices as high as the clouds to get new finery for the occasion, and there wasn't enough quarn to meet the demand by half. The merchant saw his chance to make a career's worth of profit in one trip. He plotted a straight course, meaning the ship was to pass west of the Lost Isles. Not within sight of land, he was quick to tell Vonni. And barely in the waters the dragons patrolled. He also swore the beasts were known to hibernate at that time of year. His tale smelled rancid to me, but Vonni kept lusting after all the things he was going to buy with his share." Darel was gripping the wheel so tightly he was distorting the shape of his fingers.

"I'm sorry your son had to pay a price another should have," Polk said.

"Thank you for that, but the truth is, it went the way the dragon wanted it. Had she done what she did to the trader instead, it would not have been as frightening. She wasn't interested in justice, you see. She just wanted to show she was strong and cruel and that no one should annoy her."

Darel studied his chart. The pilot mumbled, and turned the wheel, shifting the prow a few points to starboard. "What is it, my lord?" Darel asked as the silence grew too long. "You're going to tell me your master will pin the dragons by their tails? That he's the answer?"

"I believe he will put an end to them," Polk replied. "But there's more. Imagine a world full of dragons."

"Now why would I want to think of that? Even one dragon is a plague."

"I do not want to think of it, either, but I've forced myself to. When Lord Alemar began making preparations for this mission, he gathered all the lore about dragonkind that he could. I have read some of those scrolls. Do you know how many dragons there are in the world today? Thirteen. Fourteen if you count the Dragon of the Firelands, but that beast has not been seen in over a century."

"And that means...?"

"That's fewer than the number that came through the portal from Serpent Moon, all those thousands of years ago. If they had multiplied as other creatures do, by now they would be overrunning the known lands. Instead, we have only thirteen. Why?"

"They're killing each other off," Darel said. "Everyone knows they don't get along with one another."

"It goes beyond that. They're barely breeding. No new dragons have been born since ancient times. Does that strike you as natural?"

"No," Darel admitted. "All creatures want offspring."

"As you say. I believe I know the answer. I found it in a particular scroll written by a monk of a minor temple in Headwater, in Serthe. He claimed to have spoken many times to one of the original dragons who escaped from Serpent Moon. Asked it questions, if you can imagine that. The dragon told him that on their home world most of their kind is made up of a type unknown here. Not male. Not female. Neuter. They don't have the hot-bloodedness we think of as being part and parcel of every dragon. The fertile ones are needed to reproduce the race, but it's the neuters that run the society, raise the young ones, keep the wild kind in check. The bunch that jumped through the portal were renegades. For them, raising families would be acting like the slaves they used to be. They've kept to themselves. Rarely taken mates. But now..."

"Faroc and Triss are mates."

"Yes. The only ones in all Tanagaran. Do you realize what that means?"

"I believe I do," Darel said softly. And his gaze drifted until he was staring beyond the prow of the ship, beyond the horizon, as if at a land of plenty or a beautiful woman he had never thought he would be fortunate enough to lay eyes upon. "But I dare not utter the words for fear a lie will pass my lips and the gods will frown at me. Say it for me."

"If we kill Faroc and Triss," Polk said slowly and emphatically, "or even if we kill only one of them, we will have destroyed the last set of dragon parents in the world." Polk stretched out his arms and traced a huge arc in the air over his head, suggesting the beginning and end of something immense. "Eventually no dragons will be left to make anyone suffer the way Vonni has suffered."

There were times when Darel, tall and ropelike as he was, seemed on the verge of being blown overboard by a gust. The effect had never seemed stronger than it did just then. Polk was even beginning to think the pilot might crack a smile. A real smile, not as part of mockery or a jest, but to show joy. Years seemed to melt from him. The jagged contours of his wrinkles eased.

Then the radiance winked out, replaced not just by the skepticism and fatalism he had shown before, but by suspicion. He coughed a plug of phlegm into his spittoon. "You've travelled in the wake of those sorcerers too long. You've picked up their tricks. Dangle my heart's desire before me? Make me believe in you?"

Polk's jaw dropped, and blood began to pound in his temples. "I'll not have you speak so to me, Navigator. I showed you nothing but good will."

"Is that so? Is it my friendship you wanted? Or my admiration?"

Polk scowled. "What are you on about?"

"You need me the way your master and mistress need you. Do you not see that's why they brought you along? Where would they be without a witness of their grand deed? When they present themselves back at court with claims of victory, will it not help that a member of a Moin high house, son of a member of the Council of Marchlords, can bear testimony that their tale is true?"

"I—" Fury choked off the rest of Polk's reply.

"Spare me your tasty bait, Wold-Steward," Darel went on, his voice warbling with emotion, "I want no more disappointments."

"And I want no more of your broken spirit," Polk snapped.

The young man stalked away and took up a spot near the door of the magicians' cabin. He refused to look at Darel for a full hour. When, however, a giggle from Vonni—who had at last managed to form his cord into the most basic of slipknots—caused Polk to look in the general direction of the helm, he noticed that Darel was uncharacteristically oblivious to his son's glee. Instead the pilot was again gazing sightlessly over the horizon, his expression full of fathomless, desperate hope.

—o—

The next day, they came to the reefs.

At the worst point, Polk looked around and saw choppy water in every direction, a precinct of extreme shallows. In some spots, rock outcroppings jutted well above the waves, and now that the tide was ebbing, coral poked up as well. Elsewhere menace lurked just low enough to remain unseen.

Every member of the crew, from Darel at the helm to young Scab up in the rigging serving as their lookout, kept grips locked on rails or other convenient moorings. Whenever anyone moved from place to place, they never released both hands at the same time. Instead they shifted rather than walked, always at least partially secure, continually braced for a possible impact. They would not risk being knocked overboard. Some of them could not swim. Polk had been astounded to learn how common that lack was among sailors, but as explained by sailmasters Coller and Rand—two members of the expedition who *did* know how to swim—men often thought it better to go down at once with a ship if it sank than to tread water for their last few hours, knowing that exhaustion would eventually set in and they would end up rotting on the sea bottom just the same. It was an attitude they refused to set aside even in the presence of magical airmakers that would buy a shipwrecked man much more than a few hours. A sailor loved his vessel all the more if he believed it was his last and only hope of survival.

For the first time, the wizard himself had found it necessary to stand on deck, reinforcing by his presence that, no matter how much it might seem otherwise, their safety depended upon maintaining the course he had set. For the first time, Polk wondered if the consul's powers of intimidation would be enough to keep the calm. The crewmen's fear of the dragons was, in its way, too removed from their experience to confound them, but the prospect of ruinous holes below the waterline was a nightmare that had plagued their sleep many a night of their lives.

Polk suspected what truly kept each man at his station was Darel. The pilot did not panic. He kept the ship on clean, straight tacks and gave plenty of warning when the next adjustment would come, showing that he had studied the relevant charts and that he knew the vessel's exact position. From time to time he called for the results of soundings. He nodded as Scab made out one distinguishing feature after another and called down his discoveries. Such features included high points of major sections of reef, or an atoll and its lagoon, or one of the increasingly rare channels of somewhat deeper water.

Finally came a moment when, at Polk's side, Rand leaned over the side and studied an undersea wall as it slid past not a mast-length beyond the gunwales. Several of the formation's protrusions were stout and jagged enough to puncture clear through the hull if struck at the wrong angle. The crewman let go a hoarded breath.

"That's the worst one," Rand said. "Old Barnacle-Skin might get us through after all."

"Land ho!" Scab called.

Polk, Rand, and those whose duties allowed it began to crowd toward the prow, anticipating the moment when they could have their own look at what the youngster had glimpsed.

Gradually a series of rocky spires began to jut above the horizon, remnants of some buttress of rock that had otherwise long tumbled down into the sea.

"I don't see reason to make a fuss," Polk complained. "That's not enough 'land' for a goat to live on."

"You're seeing through farmer's eyes, Wold-Steward," Rand said. "Those pillars are outrunners of the Lost Isles. Small or not, the dragons claim them."

—o—

Faroc watched the ship sail into his domain. The dragon remained as still as the weathered crag he perched on, seeming to be an extension of the rugged stone and guano. Only his whiteless eyes moved. It had been years since any men had dared to come close enough to his dominion that Faroc had been inclined to roast them. It had been decades since one had sailed directly toward the isles.

He could smell the sorcerer, faint though the scent of human magic was compared to that of his kind. Languidly he remembered the last wizard who had tried to match powers with him. Faroc had found him to be just as combustible as any other man. Such beings could not hope to develop enough power in their ephemeral lifetimes to pose a real threat.

But this adept was at least a decent strategist. He was adhering to a course that kept his ship over thrijish coral. Intoxicating as its emanations were under normal circumstances, thrijish could sap a dragon's magic if perverted by spells. Faroc would have to keep his distance.

To kill them, he would have to be creative. How entertaining!

—o—

By early afternoon, the ship had passed within a few bowshots of the rocky pillars and was proceeding in the direction Rand stated would take them into the heart of the Lost Isles. The sea began to deepen ahead.

Polk left the rail in search of the midday meal, a need he had postponed while the vessel won through the zone of reefs. He saw Alemar spin about and stare hard at the spires.

"Do you sense it?" the consul blurted to Miranda.

Miranda's eyes went wide. "Yes. On the highest crag."

"Lower the sails!" Alemar shouted to the crew. "Drop the anchor!"

The men hurried to obey. Polk stared at the indicated pillar and, to his frustration, could detect nothing.

"Is it a dragon? Where is it?"

"We can't see it, but we know it's there," Miranda explained. "It revealed itself to us."

She had barely finished speaking when the top of the crag shimmered and its features changed in the peculiar way that told Polk what he had been seeing until then was illusion. Even so, the great beast perching on its top was difficult to discern until its head rose atop its towering pedestal of a neck.

The crew scrambled to seize the bows and arrows they had cached at various locations around the deck. Then, ever so gingerly, they broke the seals on several small crocks and eased off the lids, revealing brown, viscous unguent. The men began dipping their arrowheads into the substance.

An appetizing aroma wafted over the vessel, suggesting bread fresh from the oven, lathered with butter. How odd, thought Polk, that so sinister a concoction should smell so appealing. Fellit, sometimes called dragonsbane, was a poison of the highest order. A batch could be years old and a trace of it in a gash—much less a full smear delivered deep beneath the skin—could kill a man in moments. To ensure the same outcome with the dragons, this supply had been freshly made only a few days before they had embarked.

Polk anointed his own arsenal and placed his quiver on his back, attempting all the while to keep his hands steady and his demeanor resolute, as befit a peer of Moin. He worked as quickly as he dared.

Time, however, seemed to be ample. Up on the height, the dragon had not roused itself further, save to rub its chin against a convenient knob of rock. Then it yawned. Polk used the delay to prepare Alemar's arrows, as he had been assigned to do.

For weeks Polk had been worried that he would be rendered witless upon encountering the first dragon. It was not so. True, his heart was slamming against the inside of his sternum. He was sweating so much beneath the armpits he would soon be able to wring drops out of his tunic. However, his thoughts were clear and well-schooled, and his body obeyed him. Like all the crew, Polk had rehearsed his role over and over both during and prior to the voyage; he knew where he should be and what he should be doing.

He took a position near a pair of large crates, his bow strung and an arrow nocked. Miranda had settled into the gap between the crates, a well-protected spot that would at the same time give her a full view of the battle once it was engaged.

Miranda reached up, and squeezed him on the hip. He wanted to turn and acknowledge her with a glance, or even a smile, but he was finding it to be hard enough just to keep down the contents of his stomach. He was suddenly glad he had not had the chance to eat the meal he had been seeking.

"Eighteen months ago I made you a promise," she said. "This hour I make good on it."

"I never doubted you, my lady," Polk replied.

As much as they could be, everyone aboard was now braced for what would come. But to their consternation, the dragon did not stir.

Alemar gave a grunt of disgust. He strode to the very middle of the ship. The rest of the crew moved away, leaving him prominent, a target for their opponent's attention. Short though he was, he laid claim to his arena like a champion accustomed to humbling his foes.

"Dragon!" the sorcerer stated in normal tones, "I am Alemar of Moin. My ship lies in your waters. Have you no greeting for me?"

To invite a conversation in this way had not been part of the rehearsals. Polk didn't see how the creature could hear the question.

Then Polk's head seemed to burst. Around him crewmen clutched their scalps. Even Alemar and Miranda winced.

Words formed *between* Polk's ears, a roaring that left him so dazed that the meaning came through many moments later. *"I am Faroc. Why do you trespass?"*

"I came to destroy you," Alemar replied.

Polk had the uncanny feeling that it was he who was laughing, because the mirth intruded full blown into his mind. Even after he managed to mute the dragonspeech, he could not control the quiver of his muscles.

"I thought as much. I suppose I must test your mettle."

No sooner had the dragon spoken than his wings flashed out to either side like great sails, and he launched from the crag top.

Polk gasped. The full awesomeness of their enemy was revealed. The dragon's broad, batlike wings were five times the length of a man. His body was long and sinuous, two pairs of legs hanging slack in flight, tipped with huge talons. But the most frightening aspect was his head—narrow, pointed, thick with fangs.

"Light the shield flames!" Alemar commanded.

Despite their shock, crewmen had remembered their duties and were already doing what he asked. They struck sparks into the oil reservoirs of a series of shoulder-high torch sconces that had been bolted to the gunwales at intervals of every five paces or so. A ring of flames immediately outlined the vessel.

And then Faroc was upon them, far quicker than a living beast had a right to travel. The old scrolls had told many fanciful things about dragons, but one tale was apparently all too accurate—their kind did not ply the skies solely on the power of their wings. They used magic as well.

The monster belched a narrow gush of brilliant heat as he bore down upon the ship. Most of the men dodged for shelter or threw their arms up to cover their eyes, and did not see, as Polk did, how the bolt abruptly splattered into thousands of fiery fingers.

For a moment the ship was enveloped in a shell of incandescence. Then the torches flared like suns, casting the enchantment back to the skies. The crew instinctively shrank away from the sconces, but they did not need to do so. The heat, unlike the brilliance, had been negated as Alemar funneled the force through the talismans.

The view cleared. Polk scanned about and found that Faroc was already distant, and beginning his circle back.

"Remember to use your arrows!" Miranda pleaded.

Her voice, full of fright, lacked volume. Polk took up the call. "Lord Alemar's protection is working! You can see for yourselves!" he shouted. "Stand fast and prepare to shoot next time the creature comes within range!"

Climbing to an altitude three times higher than the rock pinnacle, Faroc settled into a level glide. The beast seemed unperturbed that the initial attack had failed. Alemar, by contrast, was stiff and teetering as he edged from mid-deck and took hold of the mast for support.

Polk swallowed hard, pointed his arrow upward, and struggled to banish the mental image of being laid down upon his father's doorstep, in the same way that Vonni had been delivered to Darel. Did Faroc engage in the same cruel games as his mate?

Uttering a trumpet that made Polk's knees weaken, Faroc folded his wings and hurtled straight down at them, spewing an outpouring far thicker than the first. When it struck the wizard's barrier, the torches blazed higher than the windfeather. The entire ship was pressed into the sea. As the craft popped up again, Polk maintained enough presence of mind to shoot his arrow, but between the dragon's speed and the impossibility of bracing himself against anything steady, the projectile streaked wide and tardy.

"Good!" Miranda blurted. At the relief in her voice, Polk saw that he had not been the only archer. Coller and Rand and one or two near them had managed to shoot. Others were shaking off their disorientation and picking up the bows they had dropped. "Keep trying!" she urged.

The sorceress was shaking and pale. Polk found it disconcerting to witness someone with her powers in such a state, even though she had warned him she might react this way. Far more alarming was the sight of Alemar, shuddering against the mast and blinking to try to focus his eyes.

"My lady. Your brother—"

"I can't help him. You know that."

"But it's worse than he described!"

"I must keep to the battle plan." She was weeping as she said it.

Polk could not stifle his dread. The plan had been made without any direct experience with dragonflame. They knew that the beast should have no more than five or six bursts until his fuel was spent. Alemar had been certain he could endure that much. But Alemar had the look of a man who had already been assaulted with as much force as he could handle.

Miranda's contribution might be essential. Polk could sense her thinking that very thought, and weighing the options. But she remained huddled where she was.

For the third pass, Faroc zoomed at them from the port side, gushing a bolt as strong as his last one. The barrier deflected the energy, but the craft slammed to starboard, gunwales dipping into the sea. Two men, caught unprepared, flew over the side and were left dangling from their safety ropes.

Faroc circled and dived again, and again, and again. Some men continued to freeze in place each time they heard the dragon's roar, but an increasing number were remembering to be archers.

Alemar had kept his eyes closed for the last two passes. Now he sagged to the deck, into a puddled kneel. Only when Faroc failed to attack again did he rouse and look up.

And he grinned.

Belatedly Polk realized that the last three surges of dragonflame had been progressively weaker. The wizard had done it!

The dragon screeched and dived again. But this time he belched nothing.

"Archers!" Miranda cried.

Arrows flew. Polk's was among them. He deliberately waited until the final moment, and then shot as well as he ever had. His missile flew true straight at the beast's throat.

But the metal tip stopped a few inches away from the hide, its momentum thwarted. The shaft hung in midair for an instant, then fell. Faroc veered off, blowing a foul wind over the deck.

Alemar stood up, swayed, and took up his own bow.

Faroc returned to his crag. His deep rumbles echoed off the waves.

Alemar panted, chest heaving, but even breathless, his voice demanded an audience. "Dragon! What's wrong?"

"I salute you, wizard. Another wingspan closer to the thrijish and I could not have warded the arrows. I smell the fellit. You have prepared well, and you are strong."

"Strong enough to destroy you."

"I think not."

"Come for me then."

"You think taunting will make me stupid? No, dragonsbane is not for me. I will stay here. Though I cannot touch you, neither can you touch me. Sooner or later, you must leave or starve. If you leave, sooner or later you will sail away from the thrijish. Then I will have you, if not before."

Alemar did not answer.

As before, the dragon let anticipation gnaw at his opponents' composure. When nothing seemed to be happening, the men began to let go of some of the extreme tension they had endured during the assault. Those who had dropped their bows retrieved them. The two individuals who had been flung overboard were hauled up. Scab emerged from behind a barrel. His pants were stained at the crotch, but no one mocked him for it.

Finally Faroc sprang from his perch. He held a huge chunk of rock between his forelegs. He hovered directly over the ship, well out of arrow range, and let it go.

Alemar raised his arms in a fending motion, even as members of the crew scattered. Two men, in their haste, actually went over the side, including one who had just been retrieved. Around the ship, a bubble of green radiance outlined the sphere of protection. More radiance flowed from Alemar's hands, bolstering the ward at the point where it would be struck.

The impact knocked everyone to the deck. The rock shattered, raining huge shards into the ocean. A splash soaked Polk and Miranda.

Faroc trumpeted gleefully. *"And just to keep you from resting, I'll do that every so often."* The dragon scribed an insouciant loop before returning to the crag.

Alemar staggered to his feet.

"Are you well, Lord Consul?" Polk asked, lending support.

The wizard sloughed off the arm. "Leave me be!"

Polk backed off. Other crew members hauled aboard the two men who had leaped over the rail. They hung their heads like wet cats, casting apprehensive glances alternately toward the wizard and the dragon. When Alemar roused from his daze, he strode to them.

"I should have made that rock fall on you!" He passed his hand in front of them. Steam burst from their shirts. They yelped, faces flushed scarlet from the heat. "Desert your posts again and it won't be the dragon you have to fear!"

Polk noted the overly bright cast in Alemar's pupils. Nearby, Miranda let out a gasp. The pair of chastised men cowered, mumbled weak apologies, and quickly backed away from Alemar, bowing. The sorcerer relaxed his stance very slowly. Eventually he walked back to the mast and sat with his spine to the timber, gaze fixed up at Faroc.

Miranda wobbled over to her brother. She didn't speak, but Polk could sense the question in her mind, and although Alemar never looked toward her, the youth could see acknowledgment in the wizard's expression.

Finally Alemar said, "I am well."

Miranda began to breathe again.

"We miscalculated," the sorcerer confessed. "But I have the strength to do what I need to do. And so do you."

Miranda bowed her head.

The wizard sighed. He reached out and squeezed his sister gently on the shoulder.

"You can do it. I know you can."

Color returned to Miranda's cheeks. She nodded. As Alemar resumed staring at Faroc, she retreated toward the stern, where she clutched the rail and appeared to be attempting to avoid heaving the contents of her stomach over the rail.

Polk followed, standing in such a way that her distress was hidden from the majority of the crew.

"Please do not stare at me," she murmured.

He swallowed. "Lady. You are one of those women all men stare at, as often as they can manage to do so."

The compliment worked. She recovered a trace of poise.

"You are better to me than I deserve right now."

He stepped nearer. "When is a better time to tender aid, than when someone needs it?"

"You don't want me to need aid now," she replied, still in a near-whisper meant for him alone. "You want me to be formidable."

"I—" He rubbed at a raw place on his thumb, where he had chafed it in his hurry to draw the bowstring to shoot at the dragon. "Yes."

She took his hand and gave his injured thumb a kiss. "I am what I am. Come nightfall, we will see if that is enough to keep us alive."

—o—

Faroc wondered if he should drop more rocks. He had dropped two since the first. Both had shattered on the ward, rocking the ship and obviously costing the human energy, but doing no permanent damage. Faroc thought perhaps the sorcerer was nearing the limit of his endurance. Certainly if enough stone were dumped on him, he would succumb, but that would be dull. Therefore Faroc waited to see what tricks his opponent had other than thrijish and wards and dragonsbane. All that was needed was to watch the vessel very carefully, and sit safely inside his own ward. Patience would cost him nothing.

Afternoon dwindled into dusk, twilight into full night. The glow from Motherworld dominated the scene, keeping the starlight faint. The ship remained easily visible, though the men aboard were reduced to undulant shadows and huddled smudges.

A flicker in the ward's intensity caught Faroc's attention. The dragon tensed, weighing whether to launch from the crag. But the ward blazed back to life at once, so briefly interrupted as not to matter.

Gradually, Faroc became aware that something had changed. The resonances of the human's magic wafted differently through the air. It was a thing easily explained by a recasting of the protection spell to relieve points of fatigue in the earlier weaving, but Faroc's suspicions were aroused. He watched the ship all the more closely, and the waters between it and the shore.

— o —

Standing precariously on a rugged ledge, Alemar focussed his concentration upon the rope between his fingers. He murmured words to it long forgotten to anyone but the sorcerers of Acalon, causing it to climb tenuously upward. If he could get the rope to tie itself around a protrusion of rock, he would be able to reach the top at last. But before he could fasten the knot, a gust distracted him and the rope fell into a limp coil at his feet.

His head swirled from the amount of power he had been forced to expend that day. Scalding those two fools had been a mistake. He should have hoarded every particle of his reserves. He flexed his aching arms. A sorcerer could scale a crag like this in a quarter the time it would take a normal rock climber, but that did not mean it was easy.

Some time before, he had heard the sound of a boulder crashing upon the ward and, reassuringly, the hum of the ward deflecting it. Soon after, the thud upon the crag had told him that Faroc had landed again. The plan was working. Miranda was maintaining the ship's defenses adequately, and the dragon had not attempted a significant assault, nor had he flown around the back of the crag closely enough to notice a small, camouflaged figure clinging to the rock face.

An airmaker had enabled Alemar to swim to the rock

undetected. He had left Miranda dressed in his cloak, her long hair concealed. He had descended the far side of the hull, gone right to the bottom, and circled far around before coming up on the side of the islet opposite the ship. A simple tactic, but those were the best kind. Faroc had no reason to believe humans could swim so far without surfacing.

That he had a chance to ambush Faroc might seem too great a bit of fortune to expect, but Alemar had manufactured his luck. His studies of dragon lore had told him that the creatures did not think as men would. They fought their own battles. It would not occur to Faroc to enlist Triss's aid now that the contest was underway. By the same token, it was in the dragon's nature to conclude he was facing only one magician.

But dragons were far from witless. Alemar could not help but entertain the possibility that when he reached the top, instead of reaping the reward of all his planning, all he would find was a looming monstrosity grinning down at him.

On the fourth try, he succeeded in taming the rope around the rock. He wiped the sweat off his palms, took a breath, and scaled the final distance to the top.

The sweet stench of dragon hung in the air, so overwhelming Alemar feared Faroc had changed positions and was now too close at hand. But as he eased his head around the last angle of stone, he spotted his quarry on the far side of the flat-topped spire. The beast was actually leaning partially over the edge in order to improve his angle of view of the ship.

Quiet was Alemar's watchword. The sorcerer squirmed onto the flat and silently unhooked himself from his rope harness. Pulse pounding, limbs shaking, he clambered and crawled toward his opponent. His efforts brought him halfway across the crag top, to such a proximity to Faroc that the dragon could send him flying off the heights with one swipe of that tremendous tail—a nerve-wracking prospect, but he needed to be that close to do what he intended.

He freed his bow and strung it. Faroc did not stir. Still a chance, still a chance.

He withdrew a special arrow from his quiver. The point was a razor-edged barb, the shaft extremely true, made especially for Alemar by the master fletcher of T'jet. Painted along the shaft were delicate runes, each of which had taken hours to apply, for the process had required far more than brushstrokes. This arrow, and its four mates, represented the final element of Alemar's strategy.

Despite the barb's sharpness, it would never penetrate the dragon's hide by itself. At the moment, no ordinary weapon could touch Faroc, safe as he was inside his ward. In flight, in attack, the dragon could not always maintain his defense because of the concentration it required, but here, on the crag, there were no such distractions. To thwart the obstacle, Alemar had spent days in the creation and magical treatment of his arrows. If he were enough of a mage, if he had used the correct spells, if Faroc did not become aware of him and muster his ward to guard a specific area, then the shaft should penetrate. There would be no second chances.

He loosed the arrow.

Faroc screamed, swinging his head around and biting the shaft that protruded from his haunch. The point had driven only a finger-length into the skin, but it was enough.

The dragon searched for his attacker, but Alemar had scuttled behind a boulder. In the next moment, the creature began to writhe. His tail jerked spasmodically, jarring loose chunks of stone. Flame coiled out of his mouth, directionless.

"Alemar! Your name is cursed to the last generation! Beware my spawn!"

Faroc did more than utter the curse; the dragon made his mental shout into a weapon. As if hit by a physical blow, Alemar pitched forward, landing in the open where the dragon could see him.

Faroc arched as if to strike, but could no longer control his great body. Through blurred vision, Alemar watched as his opponent convulsed, teetered at the edge of the precipice, and fell.

On the way down, Faroc produced one last scream: "*TRISS!!!!*"

The wizard sprawled on the stone, unable to rise due to the aftereffects of the dragonspeech. His ears rang, denying him the satisfaction of hearing Faroc crash. Crippling pain coursed from his spine to his extremities, echoes of the dragon's last conscious sensation. Alemar fought it back. There was no time to be weak.

Faroc had called Triss.

Triss inhabited the northern half of the Lost Isles, leaving the southern half to Faroc — for it seemed that even mated dragons seldom associated with one another. Alemar had never heard that a dragon could communicate with another across dozens of leagues, but now, aching with the savagery of Faroc's death thought, he knew Triss had heard the summons. He had at most a few hours to get himself and the ship to safety — wherever that might be — before she would arrive.

He struggled to his feet, carefully making his way to the edge. Faroc lay on the rocks and shallow water below, bones shattered and body pulped by impact. His dwindling throes were sending dark, swamping waves toward the ship. Miranda's ward took the brunt of the initial surge, but in the dim light the sorcerer could make out dim shapes of crewmen toppling. Others were already sprawled on the deck. They were as numb from the dragon's mindshout as he was. His sister was a slim silhouette, still upright when he spotted her, but then she crumpled to her knees.

The ward burst.

Unprotected, the ship swayed alarmingly, but Faroc was growing quiet. The choppiness was no longer as formidable. Fellit was a quick, thorough poison.

Alemar's disorientation faded. He turned and ran toward the rope, intent on getting back to the ship.

A shadow passed in front of Motherworld.

—o—

Vonni was the first to sense her. And Darel, alerted by the change in the pitch of his son's strangled cries, was the first to glimpse her speeding across the night sky.

Initially the old pilot, his cheek bleeding where a snapped

halyard had struck, assumed that what he had witnessed a few moments ago had been a lie — that Faroc had not truly fallen to his death, but had risen and taken flight. But it was not the same dragon. The beast's scales cast back the ochre glow of the giant planet in a different pattern and with a heightened sheen. And then there was the size. This was a bigger dragon.

Darel recognized her.

Triss hurtled straight for the crag. Swooping low above the water, she nearly brushed the waves as she inspected her mate's body. She did not linger or land, for that would have cheated her of the advantage her momentum provided. Brief glimpse or not, Darel knew she had seen what mattered. As she pumped her wings and regained altitude, a prolonged keening poured from her throat.

Oh, yes, she had seen, thought Darel, licking lips that had suddenly gone dry. He bounced up and down on the deck, smiling so much he stretched the laceration on his cheek and worsened the bleeding. But the pain of the wound vanished. Triss's wail brimmed with grief. It was a song Darel had dreamed of hearing.

Then the dragon fell silent. Her flight took on an efficient, no-wasted-motion aura of purpose. She swung past the crag, hissing as she spotted what could only have been the sorcerer. She did not land there. She headed for the ship.

Larger and larger she loomed. Darel heard his companions scrambling, ducking behind cover, jumping. The lid of the airmaker trough clattered as it fell closed, the gear having been distributed to those who could use it. From either side came the sound of splashes.

Triss opened her maw. Darel remained at the helm, facing her. As the spear of brilliant fire accelerated toward the heart of the vessel, he laughed as deeply and mockingly as he could.

— o —

Atop the crag, Alemar watched helplessly as the dragonflame struck. The ship exploded, sending flaming shards of deck and cargo — and crewmen — in every direction. The sconces withered like grass consumed in one of Moin's infamous prairie fires. The hull dissolved into the sea.

Triss chose a spot over the site of the wreckage where the smoke would not rise into her face, and hovered there. She belched a wide, leisurely band of flame, which sprawled over the surface of the water, transforming the area into scalding death for any man who surfaced. She continued as long as her fuel lasted, altogether a span longer than any man could hold his breath.

Alemar saw something that gave him a shred of hope.

As fast as he could, he dumped out his quiver and seized his two remaining pair of rune-scribed, ward-piercing arrows. Two more such arrows had been on the ship. Now he wished he had arranged to manufacture dozens, in spite of the difficulty. He had assumed it unlikely that he would get more than one shot per dragon. A total of five arrows had seemed to be an abundance.

He hauled up his rope, tied one of the special arrows to the loose end, and flung the combination back over the edge. He checked and saw that the line played out fully, leaving the arrow dangling a few feet from the shallows at the base of the crag, at the point where his climb had begun.

The second arrow he nocked against his bowstring. Squatting down where the shelter was best, he arranged his other arrows — of the standard type, but at least coated with dragonsbane — at his feet, where he could snatch them up as quickly as possible.

Then he waited for Triss.

She finished her grisly work by diving to pluck one of the corpses from the ocean, and carried it with her in her talons. As she approached, Alemar loosed his dart. As he feared, she reinforced her ward, and his precious shaft broke into slivers. He nocked one of the lesser arrows, but had not finished pulling back the string when Triss was upon him. She blew him over with a single flap of her wings, sending the bow tumbling off the pillar.

She landed gracefully on three legs, balancing the dead man's body in her right foreclaw. Though her trophy was heavily charred, with hair and clothes completely burned away, Alemar recognized

Darel. The dragon ripped the pilot into convenient-sized pieces and ate him.

Alemar had seen many grisly things in his day, but this vied for the worst. He closed his eyes, only to hear the nauseating crunch of bone, and to feel the splatter of blood against his brow, lips, and neck. Finally he looked, only to see Darel's head, pallid from blood loss and freakishly unmarked by the flames, disappearing down Triss's gullet.

A rictus of delight was frozen on the old sailor's face. The sight gave Alemar the courage had been struggling to find.

"Whatever you do to me won't bring Faroc back to you," the wizard taunted. "He is gone."

Triss seized him. He waited for her to squeeze the breath out of him, or to burrow her talons into his flesh until he perished of blood loss. Or to eat him.

But her grip was unaccountably gentle. She brought him close and studied his features.

"You look no different than others of your race. Yet you have accomplished something none of them ever have. Before I am done with you, I will know how you managed it."

A crackle of magic haloed her head, and an ethereal tendril reached out and thrust into Alemar's skull near his left temple.

The insertion was not painful. In some ways it seemed that Triss was doing nothing at all. But then the wizard's muscles went slack, and he understood how quickly she had established control.

The dragon's pale skin blurred in front of his eyes. The sound of the ocean beating against the crag stilled to a whisper. Lines of thought unravelled. The only constant was a great, gnawing background presence, a sense of alienness, an Other. What Alemar thought, it would think; what he felt, it would feel. Soon it was taking his mind where it willed....

— o —

The blood flowing from his forehead made little Alemar close his eyes, but he could tell the rocks were still being thrown at him and his family by the sound of them whisking past or hitting their mule's panniers.

"Leave off!" he heard Father bellow. "We don't have the sickness."

"Maybe you don't. Maybe you do. We'll not take the chance!" replied a gruff voice.

A cloth dabbed at Alemar's wound, and soon he peeked out with his least afflicted eye. He saw first his mother, bending over him, hissing in concern at the swelling. She rounded to face the attackers.

"Enough! We're going! Must you attack children? He's only five!" she screamed at them.

The rocks kept coming. Perhaps the projectiles were smaller in size after her outcry, but they still came.

Mother bustled his sister and him toward the direction they had so recently come from, along the rutted road toward the stone bridge. He stumbled, but found his balance at once, worried that if he seemed to be having trouble walking, the onlookers might think he had the plague after all.

Father had told the truth. They didn't have the plague. The plague was gone. For the last few months of their journey, they had seen no piles of rotting bodies waiting for burning, nor been assaulted by the odor of burst bowels. That was why the family had dared to venture off the main road and approach the hamlet. By now, landholders should be ready to welcome newcomers. As Father said, it was time to rebuild, time to find replacements for the neighbors that had died in the previous waves of the disease.

But it was plain that here, the people were still unwilling to believe good tidings. After three awful years, they would not trust strangers and what they might be carrying.

Father hurried to catch up, hampered by the pace of the ox. The animal dragged its hooves across the hard-packed clay, abrading the fringes of the ruts. It bellowed plaintively.

Alemar knew what the ox wanted. It had smelled other livestock in the stables at the edge of the hamlet. It was lonely. Father had to beat it hard with his willow switch, and tug cruelly on its halter. He struck and pulled harder than he needed to, but Alemar understood that, too. Father couldn't hit the people that had thrown the stones at them. So the ox got more than it deserved.

Alemar felt sorry for the beast. All it wanted was to be home. That's all any of the family wanted.

The villagers still clustered in the road, filling it from verge to verge, rocks still clutched in their grips. Glaring. They didn't seem to relax until, ox and all, the fleeing family reached the bridge and turned back onto the king's highway.

Mother tied off a bandage around Alemar's brow and went to check the nicks on Father's arms, where he had fended off the brunt of the first salvo. Irritated, the man batted her hands away.

She bent her head down and took her place one step behind him. She gestured for Alemar and Miranda to keep up.

Alemar's knees and ankles ached from all the keeping up he'd been doing lately, but he didn't complain. The family didn't have much food left. They'd have to reach the next settlement soon.

Behind them the road vanished into a dimple in a line of low hills. It went on and on in that direction. Alemar knew because he had walked every footstep of it, all the way from the coastlands of Neith. They weren't even in Neith anymore. Days ago they had crossed the border into Serthe, past an abandoned royal outpost.

The whole way, the road had been lined with communities where the plague had either made the people as fearful as this last group, or had deprived the farms of so much manpower that the harvest had been meager, and no additional mouths could be fed. Or both.

"It was a pretty place, Mama," Miranda said. "I wanted to stay."

"They didn't want us there," Mother replied. "We'll have to keep looking."

"How long?"

"As long as it takes. It can be hard to find a place where you belong."

Triss was studying the incident, drawn to its vividness. Alemar had not realized how keenly he had recalled the details until the dragon had dredged them up.

The burrowing continued....

The potion vendor was a fat woman well past her childbearing years. She smelled like cheese even over the aroma of the incense with which she sweetened her market stall. She narrowed her eyes first at Alemar.

"How old did you say you were?"

"Eight."

The woman jutted her double chins at Miranda. "And her?"

"Eight. We're twins."

"Are you now? And you've no mother?"

"She's dead."

"Father?"

"Drunk, mostly. If we spend our days serving you, he won't care."

The woman poked Alemar in the ribs. "Doesn't feed you much, does he?"

"No."

"Your bellies won't go empty here, and you'll have a little coin, too, if you're not fussy how you earn it. That's assuming what you've told me is true—that you have the Talent." She drew her hand out of one of her pockets and turned it palm up. She was holding what appeared to be an ordinary stone the size of a hen's egg, perhaps a cobble drawn from the Slip River. "Show me."

Alemar touched the stone with a forefinger. It darkened, shifting from the color of sand to the color of mud, as if he had dropped it in water. But the stone was as dry as ever.

Miranda repeated the demonstration. She couldn't make the color as dark, but the potion maker nodded.

"Yes. I can make use of a pair like you. Mind that you do as I say. Mind you work hard. Otherwise I'll chase you off and you'll have no one to look after you but that father of yours. And I don't imagine you'd like that."

She fixed her eyes on Miranda, who shook her head solemnly and tried not to weep. Alemar's temper flared—he couldn't abide anyone manipulating his sister to tears—but he kept his tongue. The twins needed the fat woman. They would have to search long and hard in their borough to find another magic worker, even one of such modest skills as she, who could cultivate the spark they had discovered in themselves.

"The tricky thing about magic," the potion maker warned, "is knowing what it can do to change your life, and what it can't. I'll expect you to remember your bounds."

Memory after memory was laid open. Those that Alemar most wanted to keep to himself were the ones Triss wanted most. Inevitably she forced him to reveal the one he was guarding more closely than any other.

The blow knocked Alemar to the floor. His father had used his fist, not his open hand. Thirteen years old and still much smaller than his sire, Alemar knew the stupidity of attempting to retaliate. Instead, he crab-walked backward, out of range, ending up in the corner where Miranda cowered. Their parent, already well into his second jug of the day, was swaying too much to lunge after either of them without risking an embarrassing tumble. The man chose instead to straighten and loom large, shaking a heavy purse.

"You've been holding out on me!" He upended the purse. A rain of copper pennies, a lesser quantity of silver fourths and bits, and two whole silver crowns, clattered onto the rough-hewn dinner table. "I put a roof over your heads, and this is how you treat me?"

The roof was that of a shanty left empty in the wake of the plague. It had cost the man nothing. The immigrant quarter of Headwater was infested with hovels of its sort, there for the claiming. All Kobos the Mason had ever given his son and daughter was a heritage that yoked them, for so many landless and desperate folk from Neith had settled here in the previous decade that they were the city's lowest caste. Life had beaten Kobos down until all he thought about was how much more he deserved. What he could get his hands on, he kept for himself. Now that he had ferreted out the trove beneath the floorboard, he would spend it all as if every piece came from his own hauling of marble blocks up the heights of the nobles' district.

The money would vanish. The man would spend it on drink, whores, and gambling. He had done as much with Alemar's earnings, on the occasions when he could convince an employer to hire a brick boy so small in stature. Alemar and Miranda had needed five years to accumulate it. The first of it had come from shavings off the pittances the fat woman handed them, when she was inclined to pay in anything other than food or lessons in sorcery. The bulk they had made running errands or, lately, by selling potions of their own making. The hoard was their means to leave this city, go where they might have some real chance of making a home.

"Where's the rest of it?" their father growled. "Show me, or you'll have my boot in your balls this time."

There was no more. But Alemar, rubbing his throbbing cheek, knowing the bruise would be even bigger than the one that had just finished healing, said, "Inside the ram's horn."

Their father hurried to the mantle. Upon it lay the one possession he prized — the one item Alemar had known he would not pawn or sell as he had nearly everything else of value the household had once contained. Big enough that a toddler could use it as a stool, the curved horn had come from a rare cliff sheep Kobos had killed as a youth — his one accomplishment that was truly, fully his own doing and worth the tale. A hunt of four days. The souvenir held a place of honor in the hovel, and the children were forbidden to touch it. The suggestion that they had not only handled it, but used it as a hiding place, made their father bare his teeth at them. Holding off on their punishment for the moment, he picked up the horn and peered in.

A searing gush of eldritch energy fountained out of the horn, slamming Kobos in the face. He pitched backward and landed hard on the wooden floor, the back of his skull colliding with the foot of one of the table legs and leaving a visible dent. The center of his face was a blackened ruin. He had no nose; it had been burned away.

For a brief time, Kobos's limbs twitched. Blood oozed from the back of his head. A whisper of air drifted out of his open mouth—none could pass through his nostrils. Then he went completely still.

Alemar crawled forward. He pressed on his father's neck, feeling no pulse. He peeled back the man's eyelids. A few specks of soot—the remains of eyelashes—drifted onto the bloodshot whites, but the eyes did not blink.

He began gathering up the litter of coins. Miranda wobbled over from the corner and held open the purse for him. Neither of them cried.

They were orphans now. And better for it.

Triss liked this memory. She studied it again.

"This happened centuries ago," she said. "You have stretched your years somehow. I will see how that was done."

She renewed her probing.

—o—

The bow dangled from Faroc's wingtip, having become snagged there when it had fallen. Polk had missed seeing it at first in the dim murk of the night, thinking it to be part of the creature's limb. Making sure that the dragon showed no signs of reviving, he eased from one slick rock to another until he reached a spot in the very shadow of the wing. He slipped on the last perch, and was forced to reach out and brace himself against the corpse. Shuddering, he caught his balance as quickly as he could, and removed his hand.

He had estimated he might be too short to reach the bow, but his fingers brushed the tip after all. By straining and clutching, he finally seized enough that the weapon slid off the projection of flesh and into his grasp.

He puffed in relief. The bow was undamaged. The string had been moistened by the spray and would not be as responsive as one that had remained fully dry, but it had not snapped, nor had it been submerged. It would serve.

Polk began to retrace his steps. As he passed a shadowy cleft, he noticed what he had missed earlier—a half-submerged human body caught in the rocks.

The char, the bloating, and the missing limbs saved him from recognizing which of his shipmates it was. A quintet of forearm-sized, lamprey-like scavengers was clustered around the fringes of exposed flesh. Feeding. With a snarl, Polk picked up a stone and flung it. It struck one of the creatures a glancing blow; within moments, it was back. The rest did not even pause in their gorging.

Moaning, the young wold-steward rushed on. Had the corpse been that of someone he knew? Had it been Vonni, his life stripped away by Triss for a second time? Polk had to concentrate to keep his gaze on his footing, his mind's eye too full of recollections of Darel's son as he had been only two days before — beaming in triumph as he succeeded in tying a knot. When Polk reached the tidal shelf that fringed the base of the crag, he dropped to his knees and sobbed.

Vonni. Darel. Scab the lookout, barely twelve years old. He saw face after face, and hated himself when he realized he could not put a name to some of those who had voyaged with him.

So many dead. The ship destroyed. This was not how he had imagined the quest would go.

Gaining control did not come quickly, but eventually he rose to his feet and continued around the pillar. He found Rand and Coller where he had left them, standing guard over Miranda, near the dangling end of the rope her brother had used to scale the height.

Only they four had survived the onslaught of Triss's flame. When Triss had suddenly appeared in the sky, they had been the first to grasp that they had to don airmakers and dive as deeply as possible. Even so, they had all been scalded red as cooked crabs.

The two men brightened at the sight of the bow. Coller held the enchanted arrow they had found dangling at the end of the rope. Now they had the means to deliver it.

"It's Lord Alemar's bow," Polk said. "All of ours must have been destroyed with the ship."

The sailmasters inspected the item, as he had, to be sure it was sound. Both nodded.

Through it all, Miranda remained huddled against one of the

few dry rocks, shivering, head down.

"My lady," Polk said. "We must go up."

She whimpered.

Polk knelt down, force of habit urging him to offer comfort, but the impulse died. It was not sympathy he was feeling. For an instant, her wretchedness had beguiled him.

And that had been the way of it, had it not? In one manner or another, she had beguiled him time and again. Seduced him, literally and figuratively. He had been a part of her plans for so long that he was no longer sure which life ambitions were genuinely his own, and which had been instilled in him by her. He remembered the lure that had hooked him most deeply, the promise, eighteen months back: *You will be part of it. You will be one of those the tales will speak of.*

He had been part of it, indeed. A part of pain, loss, shock, failure. Witness to dismemberment. And still to come was his own likely death, for to prevent it, they must kill Triss.

She owed him more than this.

"Up, woman!"

Coller and Rand stepped back in surprise. Miranda jerked, and looked up, wide-eyed.

"Sit there and you doom us," he growled. "The arrow is useless without a magician enlivening its charm. So up with us you will go. You will do your part. Good men have died furthering your schemes. I do not intend to join them."

She quivered, looking small in her soaked garments. She maintained the forlorn look for the length of time it took a wave to crash against the rocks and subside. Polk only glared back.

She stood. She reached for him.

He stepped back, and gestured toward the rope.

—o—

The ache inside Alemar's head was merciless. He opened his eyes. He was still in Triss's grip. Dawn colored the horizon. Triss had not moved, but he knew much more time had passed than had seemed to. He knew she wasn't done. She was still seeking a place in him that would yield permanently. But for a moment, the mind contact had ceased.

He was left with a disturbing sense of twoness. He strained to identify which thoughts were his own and which were those of the dragon. The creature had become his intimate. Bits of her consciousness lingered in him, unveiling her thoughts concerning him. He was startled to realize her primary feeling toward him was no longer anger, but something bordering on admiration.

"You should have been a dragon," she said.

—o—

Dawn turned to sunrise as the survivors climbed. No sounds came from the crag top. They began to wonder if the dragon were really there at all. The ascent probably took only an hour or so, but to Polk, it seemed endless. The pillar was steep and treacherous, their progress methodical even with the aid of a well-anchored rope. Twice they had to rest on ledges, taking miserly sips from their only flask of water. Polk was the first over the crest.

The dragon loomed on the far side of the rock. She was unnaturally still. Alemar, held securely in her talons, was much the same, with only occasional shudders proving that he was still alive.

Gingerly the would-be slayers climbed onto level footing, aware of their exposure, trying to exploit what little cover existed. The two sailors murmured curses under their breath.

Miranda blanched. "She is dragon-touching him," she whispered. "We cannot kill her. Their minds are mingled."

"He's doomed anyway," Polk said. "She will squeeze him to death during her final throes. We have to save ourselves."

He presented the arrow to her. In the morning light, the painted runes gleamed.

She gazed at it with hatred. Then she sighed and turned away.

"I do not need to rouse its hex," she whispered. "Triss thinks herself safe. She has put up no ward."

Polk knew Miranda could have chosen not to disclose this fact. She could have said the ward was present, and then refused to clear the way for the arrow. It seemed she had accepted what had to be. Stiffly, she turned, clear-eyed, and gazed at the soft spot behind the dragon's front limb, which they had earlier agreed was the thinnest part of her hide. The target.

Polk took the bow, nocked the arrow, and faced his prey.

He took a step, then another. His knees would scarcely hold him up by the time he had taken the third. He hesitated, breath tight, saliva gone. He *could* make the shot from here.

It would be stupid to miss, he thought. Abruptly he strode forward until he stood less than a man's length from Triss. Then in one smooth motion, giving himself no time to let hesitation spoil his aim, he released the arrow.

The projectile buried itself to the feathers in Triss's side. Polk leaped back, anticipating a violent reaction. He ducked behind a boulder. He heard his companions gasp.

The only indication that Triss had felt the attack was a spasmodic fluttering of her many-layered eyelids. After many agonizing moments, she stunned all the watchers by releasing her captive. Alemar flopped onto the stone like a cloth doll. As for Triss, she simply closed her eyes and went slack. A final breath rattled out of her, ruffling Alemar's clothing and hair.

When he could summon the courage, Polk eased forward. Twitches rippled across Triss's form, but they were just lingering habits of life. Polk grabbed Alemar and dragged him to the lee of the boulder.

The sorcerer was pale. He looked decades older than he had the day before, hardly the imposing leader Polk had journeyed with across half a sea and almost into death. He did not respond to prodding. His chest, however, rose and fell with regularity.

Miranda rushed forward.

"He's alive," Polk announced.

She gathered him up in her lap and arms. Polk stepped back, rejoining his two other companions, letting her tend to her kin.

The observers stared at the dragon. "What do you make of *that*?"

Rand said, wiping the sweat off his face.

—o—

The vigil lasted hours. Polk spent the interval pacing the crag top and gazing at the vista of open sea, at the shards of the ship lapping against Faroc's body, and at Miranda, who still sat with Alemar's head in her lap.

Rand and Coller, meanwhile, rappelled down the precipice. From time to time Polk could see them sorting through driftwood, collecting burned ship planks and scraps of cord from the rocks and the tidepools. When they had enough, the two sailmasters began assembling the material into a crude raft.

The blur on the northern horizon was one of the main islands of the Lost Isles archipelago. Food and fresh water waited there, along with trees for a substantial, truly seaworthy raft that could convey them to the nearest civilized shore. Even without the sorcerers' aid, survival was in their grasp. With that assurance went the dregs of their fear of imminent death. That concern had been replaced by the ache and annoyance of hunger, thirst, and battered flesh.

Polk knew he could benefit from being down there helping deal with the group's practical needs. The task would distract him, keeping his thoughts away from all that would stem from this voyage.

But he had to stay. He was the witness.

Darel had called him that, saying it in cynicism. Had painted him as the convenient noble of Moin, brought along only so that he could swear that great deeds had been done in the way the sorcerers claimed had been done.

The old pilot had not been wrong. Polk intended to fulfill that role. He would testify that the dragons had died, and recommend that his people fall in step with the grand scheme to reclaim the Lost Isles. Alemar and Miranda had, after all, succeeded in doing what they said they would do. The new haven was waiting.

But Polk was not the same untested youth who had set out on this voyage. He took a longer view now. A wizard powerful enough to kill dragons? A witch who could make talismans that would open the sea bottom to human settlement? A pair so persuasive in manner that they rose to the nobility of a country foreign to them, despite the bigotry that came with their profession? What sort of realm would they craft?

It *could* be a great land. If Polk didn't believe that, he would pick up one of the poisoned arrows scattered about the crag top and stab Alemar with one right now. It *would* be a great land. The people would thrive.

He would make sure of it.

— o —

At first, whenever Polk passed by, Miranda stiffened. The young wold-steward had shown her a new side during this night and morning. She didn't know what he might do. Once, she even saw him bend down and examine one of the arrows lying near Alemar's emptied quiver.

As the day wore on and Alemar did not awaken, she recalled the eagerness of Polk's caresses on those occasions when she had allowed him in her bed. She remembered his admiring smile when she painted pictures of bright futures. Ultimately, when he drifted near for the twentieth time, she lifted her hand up.

"Please," she murmured.

He continued pacing.

— o —

She would not leave him. As Alemar fumbled to sit up, bolstered by hands other than his, he struggled to cast the dragon from his mind. But she clung, leaving him with a double perception of the people around him, the crag top, the scent of the salt air. Questions were being asked of him, but it was as if he had never heard the language. On the third repetition, he understood. "Alemar! Can you hear me?"

Miranda. Sister. His only lifelong companion. In a rush, he reoriented himself. He knew his own name, where he was, how he had come to be where he was, what he had done, and what had been done to him.

Or did he?

He clambered free of the nest of her arms and began to crawl toward the edge of the precipice.

"Alemar! No!" she called out. "It's not safe!" She snatched at his ankles, and missed. Polk was faster. He seized Alemar firmly and kept him from advancing.

"I have to see."

"There's nothing left down there." Polk's voice was hoarse. "The ship is burned."

"*I have to see.* Take me to the edge."

Alemar struggled. Eventually Polk let him move forward.

Alemar peered down. In the late afternoon light, the sea was crystalline, revealing coral, fish, sand, seaweed.

And there, crowded near the lee of Faroc's corpse, swam dozens of eel-like shapes.

He had hoped it had been a nightmare Triss had tried to thrust into his mind. But they were real.

"What—what are they?" Miranda asked.

"The babies," Alemar answered.

"Babies?" Polk asked.

"Dragon babies."

His head filled with a searing white flash. He heard himself groan, felt his companions lifting his head from the stone where it had dropped. He had no memory of collapsing, but he knew a few moments had passed that were not his to recall.

The infant dragons were now darting away from the islet, fleeing in every direction. Within moments, they had vanished into the shimmer of the swells.

He would never be able to track them all down. Not even half. They would take refuge in the Deeps east of the Dragon Sea, down at depths beyond the reach of men with airmakers. They would survive. They would grow. They would remember who had killed their parents.

"What have you *done*?" Polk hissed.

Inside, the ghost of the dragon laughed. She was fading, but not as if dying. More as if retreating to some den deep within him.

Alemar crawled back to the corpse. He seized handfuls of Triss's slack, pliant wing flesh and clung there, half-upright, too spent to kick her, too spent to dig his nails in.

He felt Polk's gaze boring into the back of his head.

"We just wanted a place where we belonged," Alemar murmured.

He hung there until the sun drowned, leaving only the wan light of the Sister and the other stars. When twilight was full, Rand and Coller declared that the raft was as ready as they could make it. Alemar was too weak to rappel down the crag, so the others lowered him. Once everyone was aboard, the three able-bodied men raised a makeshift sail. A breeze filled the tattered cloth.

CHAPTER ONE

THROUGH THE VEIL OF years and distance, Alemar heard his teacher's voice: *Find the pain. Go to the source. Do what you can.*

How simple it had been, that first time. A few steps on his part. A shifting of sand along the slope of a dune. And there—a tortoise with a thorn in its neck. He had done what he could, and it had been enough.

There was sand here, too, not a piece of context painted by memory but actual grains, dislodged from the crevices of the thatch roof by the ocean breeze and powdering his hair. He brushed his head off. It was not the sand of the Eastern Deserts. Gast was not here, not available to step in when he failed.

The lesson here, this day, he did not want to learn.

The person beside him was Toren. He had no Hab-no-ken lore to offer. Just a cup of water from the crock. Alemar ferried it to Treggei's lips, supporting his comrade's head so that he could drink.

Treggei sipped. That much he could still do. But no sooner had he swallowed than he lapsed back into his fevered monologue.

"Left onto Sailmaker Lane. You'll see the fountain..." He coughed.

"The fountain with the whale fluke," Alemar prompted.

"...the whale fluke. My great-grandfather knew the sculptor."

Another cough. This one triggered a groan. "Choose the uphill way..."

"Uphill. Count the houses," Alemar said.

"Count..."

"Twelve houses. Yes."

"Twelve. Then the downhill way. Ten houses...turn right..."

Toren stood up, doing it too suddenly, apparently having forgotten the low clearance of their shelter, bumping his head on the hanging lamp. "I'm going out to the cistern." He grabbed the kettle and stalked out. The door, a rectangle of weighted canvas, slapped violently against the frame when he let go.

Alemar was grateful for his absence, and not just because of the anger. Toren himself was a distraction. His presence lured Alemar's focus back to that first conversation they had shared when they dragged themselves out of the sea and into the confines of these bamboo walls:

"The Dragonslayer and Struth are one in the same?" Alemar didn't mean it as a question, but it came out that way.

"I am certain of it," Toren said. "We were sent by the wizard himself."

Alemar might have laughed were he not trapped within the joke. A dragon pretending to be a god turns out to be a sorcerer pretending to be a dragon. Illusions within illusions, carried on for what must have been centuries.

"How could he live so long? He founded Elandris fifteen centuries ago."

"If Miranda survived, the Dragonslayer must have survived as well."

"I know," Alemar murmured. "But how?"

None of those questions mattered in the here and now. Treggei was what mattered. Treggei and his pain. *Find it. Do what you can,* Gast had taught him.

Sand shifting. Gulls crying. The huff of the wind.

There. There was the pain. He followed it.

Eyes unfocussed, his perception went where actual vision would have failed him. The interior of Treggei's abdomen was rendered as an ethereal portrait. The wrongness that had once been a small foothold of infection along the track left by the crossbow bolt had become a burbling mass, foamlike and dark, evil to contemplate.

The magic that allowed him to see what was wrong was not the same as the magic that would let him assuage it. No healing energy stirred within him, no upwelling to consolidate and direct at the places where Treggei's body's native defenses were being overwhelmed. Not one pulse.

"Ten houses, then turn right," Alemar said, voice cracking as the words came out. "That's Oysterman's Way."

Treggei's eyes remained shuttered. He spoke so faintly Alemar could barely make out what he said as the wind pestered the thatch overhead and wormed between the stalks of bamboo. "Yes... Oysterman. No signposts. If...you're not sure...don't ask anyone. You'll...only prove you're a stranger...to the city. Everyone knows Oysterman's Way."

"Nyorette sold flowers on Oysterman's Way."

"That she did. I first met her on...Oyster...man's..."

Treggei lost consciousness again. Alemar reached out, intending to jostle him, but in the end, held back. Instead he rose, teetering, too hampered by battle soreness to unfold completely. He raised the door flap and hobbled, crablike, through the opening.

Glare assaulted his eyes. He tried to raise his left arm to forehead level, forgetting until too late how much that sort of action made his elbow throb. He raised his right arm in its place.

The islet unfurled around him, surf lapping on its shore fifty paces to the south, bamboo grove swaying half that distance to the north. Aspects the walls had blocked—the emeraldine hue of the water, the gritty kiss of the wind, the meditative percussion of the waves—were restored. He was reminded that he would have liked to dally upon this mote of land if only he were visiting it under benign circumstances.

Toren lay on his stomach on the rim of the catch basin, reaching down with a dipper almost to the full length of his arm. He transferred the water he brought up to the kettle. He did not glance in Alemar's direction. Alemar did not expect that he would.

Up where the islet gathered to its lone, runtish peak, Geim was where he was supposed to be—tucked into the clump of dune bracken in the shade of the coconut palms, systematically gazing in every direction, ready to sound the alert if anything other than a bank of clouds or a pod of pelicans rose above the horizon. Alemar trudged up the path, massaging his elbow, grateful the incline was so mild the wind at his back all but floated him along.

Geim made room for him in the sentry post he had constructed out of bracken fronds and driftwood.

"Has he passed out again?" the Vanihr asked.

"Yes. I'll rouse him when I go back. By then perhaps he'll have recovered a bit of strength."

A furrow deepened down the center of Geim's forehead. But he wasn't Toren. The emotion he exuded wasn't outrage. It was compassion.

"Has this not gone on long enough?" Geim set two fingers on the hilt of his knife. "I can be the one, if you prefer. I only met Treggei a few weeks ago. You have known him for years. You should not be the one to have to do it."

"He still has time left. Important time," Alemar replied.

"You must know what it's like to die as he is dying. Surely you must."

"My mother died that way."

Geim closed his eyes and bent his head down. "Oh."

"This is Treggei's choice," Alemar added. "This is what he asks of us."

"Is he in his right mind, to know what he wants?"

"It's been hours since he was in his right mind. Nevertheless. Thank you for the offer, my friend, but I have to decline."

The furrow in his brow remained, but eventually Geim nodded.

"I came up to look at your leg," Alemar said.

Geim rearranged himself. Alemar unwrapped the bandage from his companion's thigh. The redness had diminished along the sword cut. The temperature of the flesh was no longer elevated.

If the palace guardsman's jab had been a bit to one side, Geim might have been unmanned. A bit in the other direction, an artery would have been opened and he would have bled out during the battle. But neither of those things had happened. Now, ugly as the sutured gash looked compared to the small punctures in Treggei's torso, Geim was likely to recover. All Alemar had needed to be a healer was to apply ordinary measures. Clean the wound. Sew it closed. Wrap the leg. No sorcery. Geim's body would take care of the rest, just as Alemar's own body would deal with his wrenched elbow and assorted bruises and nicks.

"We'll leave the bandage off. Let the air get to it."

"As you say."

Alemar headed back down the knoll, into the wind now, but downward, so once again his battered body was able to cope with the journey. His heart and mind, though—that was another matter.

The islet was one of a thousand flyspecks of territory strewn across the reaches of Elandris—and it was south of Dragonsdeep, not north where the search would be concentrated. The hut belonged to a reef forager. Such a man tracked down prey and articles of value by walking and swimming along the sea bottom wearing an airmaker, operating from a base such as this for several days or even a week until his brothers or cousins—fisherman of the usual sort—came round with their boat to take him to another outpost. This particular shelter had been restocked in the recent past—the larder held three jugs of cooking fuel, hogsheads of flour and potatoes, and even a jar of coffee beans—yet Alemar and his companions were unlikely to be disturbed. The cistern was depleted. Until a good storm or two came along to fill it, the hut's owner would postpone any reoccupation he had in mind.

They had, therefore, found themselves a proper sanctuary—a place to rest, have meals, tend to wounds. Alemar knew how lucky he and his companions had been to stumble across the place. He knew they were lucky even to be alive to make that discovery. But he didn't feel lucky. He was stiff and numb and reeling from the ordeal of their escape from the palace and their headlong rush away from Dragonsdeep and the settled parts of Elandris.

In their wake, a dragon lay dead. Two of her teeth were in Alemar's backpack—the trophies he had promised to deliver to Elenya. Also dead was the Ril wizard and the cadre of guards that had attempted to prevent their escape. By some measures, they had done the impossible. How little that mattered.

They'd had a mission, and that mission was a failure.

Alemar lifted the door flap and ducked inside. His eyes adjusted. Toren was re-lighting the burner stove, having already refilled its reservoir of alcohol.

The Vanihr was partially in the way, but he did not shift. Alemar stepped around him, soreness making it an ordeal, and settled into his place next to Treggei.

He squeezed his friend lightly on the wrist. He got no response, though, until he bore down with his nails.

Treggei opened his eyes. "Stay clear of the Trade Hall," he said as if he had been speaking all along without interruption. "Money going in and out all the time, so it's where the pickpockets loiter."

"And that means city watchmen," Alemar said.

"Yes. And bodyguards. All in all, too many people making it their goal to study whoever's around."

"Very good. I won't forget."

For an instant, Treggei seemed pleased. Relieved. Then he frowned and met Alemar's gaze. "What was I saying?"

"Avoid the Trade Hall. Too much scrutiny."

"Oh, yes. You'll also need to be sure to..."

—o—

Treggei rallied another four times over the next few hours, to murmur directions, instructions, advice, but increasingly the words sank into a snake nest of coughing, gasps, and moans that could no longer be suppressed, and what intentional sounds escaped were not always decipherable. Veins blackened within the pallor of his skin.

He was fading out again when abruptly he opened his eyes, reached out, and touched Alemar on the upper arm. "You remember the place you showed me near Eruth? Where the moths come?"

"Of course." Treggei could only mean the grove where the silk moths gathered to lay their eggs on the biggest, most verdant trees, sometimes collecting in such numbers that the trees seemed to be adorned in wings, not leaves. Alemar had been pleased to share that marvel of Cilendrodel with his Elandri-born comrade.

"I went back last season on my own, just to see it again," Treggei said. "When you can, go there for me. A thing like that should always be witnessed."

"I will," Alemar promised.

Treggei turned to the Vanihr. "It was a privilege to fight beside you, if only for a little while."

"You have no children to remember you," Toren replied. "But I will remember."

Treggei managed half a nod, then his moment of clarity was done. His eyelids went slack. His breathing, so tortured all day, became an almost imperceptible expansion and contraction of his chest.

Alemar took his friend's hand before it fell limp, and held it. One last time, he tried to call upon his power. As ever, the well was empty.

A minute or so later, Treggei's breathing stopped completely. Nature had taken the pain away.

Little though it may have been, Alemar had done what he could. He had *listened*.

—o—

The three survivors dug a grave near Geim's lookout post. Twilight enveloped them while they worked, though it was not as dark as their moods thanks to the half-bright, half-shadowed orb of Motherworld directing her muddy gleam upon them.

They made sure the hole was deep enough the crabs would be reluctant to tunnel down for a carrion feast. They laid the remains in place as gently as they could manage given the unsteady footing. Once they had backfilled, they scattered driftwood and other debris in a random pattern, disguising the fact that a burial had taken place.

No marker. Alemar consoled himself with memories of the

Eastern Deserts, where the dying and the dead were consigned to the sand, and the only memorials were the words spoken by those who remained.

He hoped one day he could speak of Treggei at a time and place when the words would matter.

"Was it worth it?" Toren demanded, as Alemar had known he would. "All those hours? Did you learn enough to make a difference?"

"I don't know. I only know it was all he had to offer."

Toren shook his head and turned away. "We'll be waiting on the beach." He headed down the slope, Geim limping along a few paces behind.

Alemar knelt by the mound and bowed his head.

He stood. He knew he shouldn't delay further. He'd taken the moment. He and the other needed to be on their way. As they had done on their journey to the islet, they would travel at night, the better to avoid the gaze of dragons or of lookouts in crow's nests. Nevertheless, he couldn't help but look to the north.

The leagues between him and Cilendrodel expanded even as he tried to consolidate the distance in his mind—make it manageable, take the sting away. His wife's smile filled the darkness on the horizon, chin ever so slightly padded with the bounty of pregnancy. He reached out, only to lose the portrait, unable to sustain the mirage no matter how much he needed it.

Wynneth was now impossibly far away. And the birth that he vowed to himself he would witness? That was not to be one of those memories he would be able to cherish in the years to come.

Before he could go north, before he could return to his homeland and to his wife, he would have to go northeast. Back to Dragonsdeep.

The mission had failed. But the goal had not changed. Gloroc had to die.

He stalked down to the beach with a tread that hurt in every part of his body, letting the discomfort fuel his rage. He joined Toren and Geim at the water's edge. They waded into the twilit shallows and recovered their airmakers from the coral formation where they had stored them. Alemar took out the ring that Obo had given him, raised it to his lips, and whistled. Three dolphins soon answered the summons.

Each man took hold of a dorsal fin. Within moments they had left the islet behind.

CHAPTER TWO

As Elenya watched from her hideaway, the fleet began to protrude above the horizon. It was still far from shore. All she could make out was a line of soot marks: masts and yards and sail tops silhouetted against salt blue sky. The rest was still hull down.

Beside her, Dalih raised the spyglass. Elenya waited with arms folded.

Eventually he spoke. "More than fifty. Some of them are dreadnoughts."

Dalih's naval lore was expanding every day. He had not let being a desert man stop him from learning what types of sea vessels an enemy might use in an attack.

It was every bit as bad as their spy had predicted. Fifty ships. Another ten thousand of the Dragon's soldiers in Cilendrodel. The ones in the dreadnoughts would be battle-hardened veterans. The Dragon was taking no chances. The rebellion had been gaining momentum since Alemar and Elenya's defeat of Lord Puriel and then of Omril. Gloroc wanted to quash the threat before it grew stronger still — even if it meant diverting forces from his campaign in the west.

The twitch was there in her sword hand: Let them come. She would fight them. And if she died, what better death could there be than by the sword, defending a cause? But the feeling was the old

Elenya trying to manifest. Merely an echo. She was not that person anymore.

Even so, here she was placing herself in the Dragon's maw. The only thing that had changed was the reason. Where once the thrill — and the rage and the hate and the wish to die — might have led her to this spot, now she came out of responsibility. Her brother was gone to Elandris. The other rebels looked to her to determine how to meet this threat. The decision was not one that could be put off until his return. *Would he return? Had he survived?* The fleet's arrival alone was almost enough to win the war for Gloroc. Few men would pick up swords and bows in the face of hopeless odds. The rebellion might collapse unless she somehow tipped the scales.

She had spilled blood many times, but not in the way she would cause it to be spilled today.

She took the spyglass and scanned down the line until she made out the flagship. As she expected, it bore an extra flag. She had tossed such a flag on the bonfire at the fortress of Lord Puriel. The fleet had come with its own wizard of the Ril.

The magician was the greatest of the complications she would have to deal with today, but if he was anything like Omril, she knew how to bait him. She only wished she could fight him with steel rather than magic. She never doubted herself this way when the hilt of a blade was in her grip.

"Let's go," she told Dalih. "They'll be at the right distance by the time we get back to town."

She and Dalih slipped further into the wind-sculpted brush of the promontory. Dressed as common Cilendri fisher folk, their weapons hidden or absent, they looked the part of a pair of locals, though the Surudainese was obliged to keep his hat low so as not to call attention to the fact that the shade of his complexion was natural, and not a consequence of sun exposure. Soon the terrain eliminated their vantage of the approaching enemy — but also the ability of that enemy to glimpse them in return. When they came to the trail, they walked openly along it, as if they belonged there. The route took them along the curving edge of Hole Bay. They soon were passing the first outlying huts of the community of the same name.

Hole Bay was the best harbor on the Cilendri coast. Whatever had fallen from the sky in ages past had slammed down right along the coastline, leaving a hollow of deep water ideal for berthing even the largest of vessels. So much of the ring was intact that the harbor was spared the wrath of all but the fiercest of storms.

Hole Bay was the ideal beachhead for a large invasion. The Dragon's forces had every reason to make their initial thrust here, and little to gain by doing so elsewhere. Even before the spy had brought his warning, Elenya and her friends had expected the landing would happen here, and had made their plans accordingly.

As they reached the town, it was bustling. The harbor watch had spotted the fleet and the news was spreading from wharf to tavern to pickling shed. A number of boats were setting out, one of them the harbormaster's sloop. Elenya and Dalih went unnoticed as they threaded through lanes and alleys and came to a chandler's shop on the inland edge of the merchants' quarter.

They entered. The chandler recognized them; he gave them the All Clear. Elenya and Dalih slipped through the curtain and through the stock room and its miasma of scented tallow and wax, and into the chandler's living quarters.

The chandler's wife and children were gone, having fled early that morning at Elenya's urging. Now the main room of the dwelling held only fighting men.

And one other, tied to a chair in the center. A man who had once been not only a wizard of the Ril, but nearly the mightiest of that exclusive cadre.

"Hello, Omril," Elenya said, lifting his head by the hair to gaze into his eyes. He returned the same vacant regard as ever. Drool fell from his chin, adding to the wetness drenching the front of his shirt. "A friend of yours is coming to see you. I am going to give him the greeting he deserves."

The men surrounding her waited in silence. They were all

comrades she had known for years. They had fought beside her. Trained with her. She had even bedded a couple of them before her attachment to Milec had bloomed. They would follow her lead without question—and so it was up to her to voice the question they all had the right to weigh.

"Do we do this now? If any of you wish not to be part of it, you still can leave. I will think no less of you than I do now." *Perhaps I will even think more.*

If they had doubts, they kept them to themselves.

So be it.

Dalih set an empty chair behind the sorcerer. Elenya sat, placing her hands on Omril's shoulders. She closed her eyes and began to concentrate.

—o—

The coast loomed nearer, revealing itself to Enril. *Green as Cilendrodel,* so the saying went. And green it was. The forest blanketed every part of the terrain except where held back by the steepness of cliffs or the battering of ocean surf. All very pleasant, the sorcerer admitted—or it would be if not for the certainty that enemies were hiding within all that cover.

The flagship came even with the gap in the bay's promontories. Enril spotted the harbor on the distant shore. Several local vessels were setting out from the docks. All of them were small. None of them were warships. No warning beacons were being lit. Even the weather was benign.

"What do you think, Auntie?" he asked the bird on his shoulder.

"Land ho. Land ho," muttered the nag parrot, fluffing its buttery plumage. "Watch the rocks."

"Quite so."

The creature was Enril's only companion on the quarterdeck aside from the helmsman and a pair of signalmen. Admiral Handett was down on the main deck conversing with his junior officers. To what purpose Enril wasn't sure—to show solidarity? To give advice? Or just to stay away from Enril? Throughout the voyage Handett had been uncomfortable with the presence of someone who outranked him. A pity. Enril could make friends with almost anyone given a fair chance. Even Gloroc liked him — a distinction only three other living human beings could claim.

The spotters in the rigging scanned incessantly for indications of the enemy on land and peered down at the depths for possible saboteurs wearing airmakers. Handett studied them as if expecting them to shout and point. Clearly the fleet commander did not trust the tranquility, either.

Enril sensed the wizards aboard the dreadnoughts awakening their various talismans, though not yet putting them to use. Unlike him, they were not so adept they could channel power from a standing start.

Finally the admiral joined Enril on the quarterdeck.

"Not quite what we expected," Enril commented.

"No."

Auntie tugged on Enril's earlobe. The sorcerer gave her a raisin.

"I suppose if I were the rebels, I wouldn't want to confront us straight on, either," Handett ventured. He moved a bit to the side so that Auntie was hidden behind Enril's head and hat. Enril suppressed a smile.

"What say you, then?" Enril asked.

"We will find what we will find," Handett replied. He raised his arm and let it fall. The klaxon sounded.

Throughout the fleet, the last of the sails unfurled. The wind was already in their favor, ideal for a straight run toward the harbor, and now they would consummate the potential. Enril sensed the storm callers in the nearest dreadnought applying their skills.

Wind was elemental. It resisted taming. But the one thing any decent storm caller could do was make a steady breeze stiffer. Soon the fleet was speeding into the bay itself as fast as ships of battle could travel.

The color of the sea began to change ahead, growing darker.

"What's that?" Enril asked.

"Giant kelp," Handett replied. "There are beds of it all along this coast."

The admiral's tone said he shared Enril's dubious opinion of its presence. Things could be hidden in a forest of kelp that would be far more apparent in open waters. Soon the entire fleet was over the darkened depths.

The back of Enril's neck suddenly tingled. "Sorcery is being cast," he told the warlord. "It's strong."

He was just beginning to divine the type of spell when it became apparent to anyone with a pair of eyes. A dreadnought veered to port, its rudder hard to the side. The helmsman and another sailor tried to force the wheel back to its correct position but no matter how much they strained, it did not budge.

The afflicted dreadnought struck its neighbor. The sound of colliding timbers reverberated across the water.

Handett hissed through his teeth.

The spell evaporated. The helm and rudder resumed normal behavior. The damage of course was already done.

Handett turned toward Enril. "Can you keep that from happening again?"

"In time. I have to study the magic before I know how to counteract it. That burst didn't last long enough."

Another outpouring shot across the waves. Again a rudder slammed sideways, sending a dreadnought off its heading and toward an adjacent transport.

The results were less severe. Having seen what had happened the first time, the crews loosened sheets and brailed sails to spend wind, reducing the momentum of their vessels until the contact, when it came, was only glancing, and certainly not enough to crack a hull.

The fleet's haste had become its prime liability. Handett did not wait on Enril. He barked orders to his signalman, who immediately began waving his semaphore flags. The storm callers ceased their work, and all along the line, vessels made adjustments to slow their rush.

A third burst issued from the shore. It had even less effect. More than that, it lasted long enough that Enril managed to sample its flavor. As he had noticed at the start, it was powerful. Surprisingly powerful. And he couldn't help feeling that it was woven in a way he recognized, as if the enemy magician was someone he had encountered in the past.

He set up a counterspell he was sure would be effective and stood poised to bring it to bear.

But when the next surge of power shot out from shore, it was not not the same sort of magic. Instead it was a salvo of twenty or more thin slivers of energy. They were too feeble to do anything as assertive as divert a rudder, much less harm the vessels in any other way. The entire episode ended in a heartbeat.

What had the point of it been? The threat seemed little worse than a razor wielded by an angry grandmother. Not a single tentacle had actually touched a vessel, probing instead into the waters just ahead of the fleet.

Enril frowned.

"What is it? Did something happen?" Handett asked. As a non-magician, he had not even been aware of the salvo.

"There," Enril said. Oil was welling up, staining the surface of the sea. Soon the circles began merging into a vast slick, just as the fleet began to proceed into it.

So that was it, the wizard realized. Their opposition had hidden bladders or kegs of oil inside the kelp—oil that had been released by the slicing action of the salvo of energy.

Handett cursed.

Enril took hold of the pouch of metal spheres that hung in front of his chest, concentrated upon the iron one and threw up a ward around the flagship.

He acted just in time. Another salvo of energy came from the harbor. This time it was the most basic of all such attack castings—fire.

The oil slick ignited. The fleet was suddenly enveloped in a conflagration. Flames reached hulls and began igniting seams caulked with oakum and tar. Crewmen began tossing bucketfuls of bilgewater at the hot spots. Others rappelled down on ropes to slap burning ship parts with wettened canvas. Burning sails were cut loose. The only vessels spared were the flagship and the eight privileged dreadnoughts, protected by wards, and a handful of supply ships holding off farther out to sea.

"Enough of this!" Handett shouted. "We never should have slowed down!" He barked orders to his executive officer and to the signalman to reverse the measures they had just taken.

Enril did not try to interfere. For one thing, the commander had made the right decision. If the fleet lingered, it would remain in the midst of the burning slick. For another, he had his own responsibilities to worry about. Maintaining magical protection while the ship was moving was a challenge, and the faster they went, the more that was the case. A wizard of the Ril should not be seen doing a poor job at anything. He focussed first on one talisman and then another in his pouch—the iron then the gold then the copper then the electrum and on through the rest of the twelve and bolstered the sphere of protection he had wrought.

Even as he performed that labor, he reserved a measure of his concentration so that he could attempt to fend off whatever additional measure of sorcery might come from shore.

None did.

Strange, Enril thought. Was the sorcerer exhausted? Surely there would be more. It wasn't as though the rebel effort had done much true damage. Not a ship had been lost, and he doubted any would be. Already the flagship and a few of the dreadnoughts were beyond the oil slick and were passing the inland limit of the kelp beds, entering the clear waters of Hole Bay itself.

The enemy hadn't so much hurt them as spat in their face. Provoked them.

Perhaps that was the point.

Enril went to Handett. "Warlord," he said firmly. "Scale back the assault."

Handett's brows rose. He almost scoffed. "The enemy has engaged us. We will beat him down, sir."

"If you were hanged for your sense, you'd die innocent."

Handett blinked. He made one reflexive flinch toward the hilt of his sword before he recalled just who it was insulting him.

"Explain," he insisted.

"I think you will find few traitors in that harbor," Enril said. "If anything, you'll find this to be the sanctuary of those who are most loyal to the Dragon. Kill as few as possible. Do so only if they resist. Put nothing to the torch."

The admiral hesitated. Enril allowed him that. It was hard to control bloodlust. He knew that as well as any man.

"You do recall the story of how I acquired ownership of this bird?" he asked, nuzzling Auntie's neck with a finger.

The color drained from Handett's face. "I meant no offense, Your Eminence."

"Then by the authority given to me by the Dragon himself, you will obey. If there are negative consequences, let the blame be mine."

The warlord turned and began spitting out new orders to his underlings.

—o—

The orders reached all parties in time. The longboats were not sent rushing headlong to shore. The last ships were outside the area of the slick by now and even the slick itself was barely burning. No further magical attacks arose. The only activity on shore consisted of villagers gathering to watch the fleet approach.

The flagship eased up to the end of the long wharf and was moored. Two gangplanks were lowered and fighting men disembarked. After the vanguard had taken up positions Handett crossed over. He was surrounded by an honor guard of a dozen of his best men. Enril came next. He had only half as many guards. Even that was more than necessary. He was his own best defense.

Just beyond the land end of the wharf stood a cluster of about thirty men-at-arms. On their vests was the Dragon's red-and-black insignia. Their swords lay on the paving stones in front of them and their helmets were held at their sides. Standing in their midst was a trembling man in a well-tailored quarn-silk tunic and hose of the local fashion.

Handett's men jogged in formation until this greeting party was surrounded three deep by warriors of the fleet. They showed no resistance. Handett and his guards came forward. Enril and his escorts followed right behind.

"My L-L-Lord Admiral," the civilian stammered. "I am Harbormaster Faml. On behalf of the port of Hole Bay, I tender greetings to you and your fleet."

Handett gave the man the tiniest of nods. "And you?" he demanded of the officer at the front of the thirty men.

"Captain Ressem. We are the local garrison of Our Lord Gloroc, Dragon of Elandris. Welcome to Cilendrodel."

"Why are there so few of you?"

"Months ago High Sorcerer Omril ordered all available forces to head north with him in pursuit of the Elandri rebel prince and princess. I held back only these few. And they were enough. Hole Bay is secure."

"You are telling me this place has not fallen to the rebels?"

"No, Warlord. Until that, um, *display* out on the water today, we had seen no hint that any rebel had come within many leagues of Hole Bay in all the time since Governor Puriel was killed."

Handett frowned. "Then who attacked the fleet?"

"I don't know, sir. All I can say is that whatever rebels may have hidden themselves among us cannot be great in number."

Handett spat on the paving stone in front of his feet. "You will understand if we insist you stay here while the town is searched. If it is as you say, you'll have your swords back. I would ask you to help us search but I find I have no confidence in your ability to sniff out rebels."

The captain bowed.

Handett gave his orders. The search parties, their responsibilities already determined before they had dropped anchor, set out into the streets and alleyways. The process was loud but, Enril noted, orderly and non-destructive.

"You have matters to deal with, Admiral," the wizard said. "I have one of my own."

Handett nodded. Enril beckoned and a contingent of men followed him—his six personal guards plus another twenty regular soldiers.

Ever since setting foot on land Enril had been able to sense the direction and distance of the source of the flavor he had detected out on the bay. He threaded without hesitation through the warren of lanes until they arrived at a chandler's shop near the outskirts of the community.

The wizard turned to Lhan, the grey sergeant who commanded his six. "Listen to me carefully. No mistakes. Surround the shop. When you are in place, rush in. I want anyone you find in there taken alive if possible. Are we clear?"

"Alive. We are clear," Lhan replied.

Lhan, three others of his group, and the extra twenty men took up their positions. At Enril's nod, they charged forward, breaking down doors in front and back. Crashes and banging issued forth for several seconds. No screams. No shouts. Just sounds of cabinets and trunks being opened to look for anyone trying to hide.

Shortly after the furor had faded out, Lhan emerged through the front door. He grimaced. "We found one man. He put up no fight. He's alive. I think."

"Show me," Enril said.

Lhan led him through the shop into the back room. There on a chair in the middle of the space was a sorry figure of a human being tied into a sitting position in a chair, so vacant of affect he gave the certain impression he would flow into a lump on the floor were it not for the bindings.

It was as bad as Enril had feared.

"There were others here," the wizard said. "I believe you will find they have fled into the forest. Check for signs. If they were careless enough to leave a trail you can follow, pursue them with every breath you have."

The twenty men departed, leaving only the six. They stood in a circle around the drooling man. More than one of the men waved hands in front of their noses, trying to disperse the reek of urine and stale spit.

"What is going on?" Lhan asked softly. "Who is this?"

Enril almost couldn't say it. "This is Omril."

He knew the guards to be as stoic as any men of their profession, but even so one gasped, and Lhan glanced at the floor.

"Uncle," Auntie chirped, and flew across the room to begin nibbling affectionately at Omril's left earlobe.

Omril gave no indication he was aware of the bird. Nor did he give any sign he knew people were in the room.

Enril turned aside, hiding his expression from the men. He carefully picked up an empty crate from a corner and set it on its side on the chandler's work table, moving deliberately and slowly so as to disguise the trembling of his hands.

Gently he removed Auntie from Omril's shoulder. He placed the nag parrot in the crate.

"Stay," he commanded. He placed a tablecloth over the crate, cutting the bird off from the view of the room.

"Night night," Auntie muttered unhappily.

Enril sighed. Was he ready for this next part? He had to be.

"I'm going to place my hands upon him," Enril told his guards. "I will enter a trance. If you see me twitch or shudder in a way that doesn't seem right to you, pull me loose from him. Use force if you must."

"As you say," Lhan responded.

Enril stood behind the chair and set his palms against Omril's temples.

He felt no resistance to his probing. It should have been difficult.

All entities resisted intrusion into their thoughts. So immediately did Enril pass into Omril's mind that his entry was like a plunge into a well, taking him far deeper than he meant to go. A chaos of sensation enveloped him, seeming to come from all around and from within. Sounds. Sights. Aroma. Heat and cold. There was no directed mindfulness here, only disintegration. The one remnant of coherency was foreign, not part of this "place" at all. It was the impression of a young woman, dark-haired, short of height, with a physique as supple as a dragon's tail. She was whispering, guiding, injecting her will even while somehow managing not to be overcome by the sheer formlessness of the environment she was intruding upon.

Enril found himself sprawled on the floor, nauseated, head throbbing, panting hard. He had no idea how long he had been there. The guards regarded him impassively, not daring to show amusement though he must have looked ridiculous. The flesh over his collarbones ached in a way that said someone had just gripped him there hard and then flung him to the floor.

"You did well," he said. "Now help me to my feet."

Lhan grasped him beneath an upper arm and by the wrist and did as he was asked. He held on even after Enril was upright, and not without reason. The dizziness took its time to fade. Finally Enril signalled and Lhan let go. The wizard swayed but did not fall. The contents of his stomach stayed down. The colors of the objects in the room, though still too bright, no longer swirled through a rainbow of hues.

"Send for the admiral. He will want to hear what I've learned."

Lhan dispatched a man at once.

"The rest of you wait in the other room. I need a few moments alone with my colleague."

They filed out at once.

Enril removed the covering from Auntie's makeshift enclosure. She fluttered up to her usual place on his shoulder. Together they contemplated the wretch in the chair.

"Uncle," the nag parrot repeated. Softly. Sadly. With a question mark.

"I'm afraid not," Enril murmured. "Not anymore."

The real Omril was gone. This was only a fragment. This was what was left after the Elandri bastard prince had delved into him. But what the prince had done was the minor part of the story — that could be reduced to something as simple as two mages battling until one was left victorious, the other maimed. In a way, Enril could not blame the prince for his actions. What the prince's twin sister had done, though, was an abomination.

Just enough of Omril remained that he could be used as a talisman. During the attack the rebel princess's magic had flowed through him and been amplified, reaching a level well beyond what the whore could have managed on her own. Omril himself had played no active part. He was incapable.

This was not the first time in Enril's life he had seen someone who had been dragon-touched. But until now he had only seen people whose minds had been delved by Gloroc. Humans were not dragons. When they made use of such magic, the practitioner was likely to emerge from the process as afflicted as the subject. It was a tactic of desperation — and of frightening boldness. This princess had courage.

And she had ice in her heart. Enril had not expected that. The woman had been prepared to let a harbor town be ravaged. A town of Dragon sympathizers, true, but Enril knew perfectly well that had he not restrained the admiral's rage, discipline would have vanished and the men of the landing force would have raped shopkeepers' wives. They would have hacked down old men too slow to get out of the way. Babies would have burned in cribs in dwellings set to the torch. The princess had been willing to incite that carnage in order to cast the Dragon's forces in a bad light.

Enril was impressed. It was what he would have done.

He had thwarted her gambit. He would make sure she continued to fail. He would explain to Admiral Handett the strategy that must be pursued. They would make the most of this turn of events. If they capitalized on what they had gained here, then the rebellion in Cilendrodel was already half quenched.

There was only one way in which this day had not been a victory. Closing his ears to the whimpers, ignoring the redolence of urine, Enril caressed Omril's cheek with the back of his hand.

Omril's twitching eased for a moment. Some part of him was in there, after all.

"I will track her down, Beloved," Enril promised. "She will suffer for what she did to you."

CHAPTER THREE

FROM THE DEEP PLACE inside Toren's mind where they dwelt, his Fhali ancestors were generating a litany of pleas and reprimands. As he had not done in weeks, he loosened their gags and let the babble swell. Judgmental they might be, but they spoke in what had once been the only language Toren had ever known. Their presence reminded him of childhood, of sweet shade and babbling brooks, of drunken laughing on feast days, of swinging from branches with friends.

Not to mention that much of what they said sounded right.

This is not our home. It is a realm of cheli. There are no trees. There is no open air. Vanihr were not meant to roam here.

How could he argue? Vanihr did *not* belong in Elandris. Yellow hair, golden skin, and beardless faces marked Toren and Geim as strangers to the undersea kingdom. Yet here they were, about to venture into Dragonsdeep. Alemar could amble down the streets unchallenged as long as no one noticed how well he matched the description of the bastard son of Keron the First, the exile king. The two southern warriors would have to remain hidden or disguised at every juncture.

The three men were huddled at a point so close to Gloroc's capital its great dome occupied the entire horizon in front of them. A coral formation screened them, but its shadow would weaken once

Motherworld rose and began to cast its glow. Soon they would be irreversibly committed to the plan as it stood.

Toren's ancestors urged him to turn around while it was still possible.

You have come this far only because you are not yet within the walls, his great-great-grandfather Koipen warned, his tone tinged by his contempt of enclosures made of materials that did not come from a forest. *Do not go forward. Do not let yourself be killed to no purpose. Do not cheat your son of the chance to receive your totem.*

The other voices tumbled over one another to give their own opinion. Some berated him. Some tried to persuade rather than demand. Somewhere within the din a few conceded that Toren and his companions had done well thus far to thwart detection. And well they should. It had been no small achievement. Days had passed since Toren, Geim, and Alemar had left the islet. In that span, they had hung on to dolphin fins until their fingers cramped. They had slipped between search parties, thrown sea dogs off their trail, and as they had reentered the immediate vicinity of Dragonsdeep, had escaped detection by sentry charms laid by the Dragon and his magicians over the past many decades.

All members of the totem — even Toren's father, who had known him in life and whose pride in him was the most personal of all the entities inhabiting him — agreed that Toren and his party had come as far as was safely possible, and should now back out.

Even if you make it in, even if you succeed in remaining hidden at first, all you will have done is let yourself become surrounded by tens of thousands of enemies. You will not be able to fight your way out of that. Again, it was his great-great grandfather who spoke.

You are right. There are too many to fight, Toren admitted.

Then why do you take the risk?

I would rather go forward than go back. Alemar sees a way to do that.

Why should you be the follower? This foreign prince has no chance unless you contribute to the cause. Turn aside, and he must turn aside with you. The decision is in your hands.

To Koipen, life was simple. What the strongest warrior decided was what would come to pass. He had been a renowned modhiv in life. His voice had been the one Toren had most often heeded since his totem had been planted inside him. Back in The Wood, Koipen's advice had often served him well. But what he was going through now was nothing like what Koipen or any of his other ancestors had dealt with while they were alive.

Koipen was right about one thing—Toren, not Alemar, had the controlling choice. Only Toren could open the way into the city.

Directly ahead lay one of the main undersea gates into the dome. It was a threshold designed to thwart infiltration. Not far inside loomed a barracks of the city garrison. At the moment four of the resident guards, well-armed and well-trained, stood sentinel at the access point. They could summon the rest of their comrades at a moment's notice. A sentry enchantment lay on the whole vicinity. Once an intruder was detected, a barricade of impenetrable vartham would block the threshold.

The story was the same all around the perimeter. Guards. Strength. And in the wake of the recent sneak attack, a high level of vigilance, both mundane and magical.

What are you going to do? Koipen demanded.

I haven't decided.

Koipen was pleased by the answer. He took it as an indication Toren was still in doubt. Koipen attacked that doubt. The other ghosts followed suit.

Toren sloughed off their pressure. *Enough. I will decide in a few minutes.*

You do not have a few minutes.

Actually, I do.

Ignoring the cacophony, Toren reached out and touched Alemar's sleeve. The prince, who had been regarding the array of ventilation and trade towers at the top of the dome, turned and met his gaze. Toren nodded. Alemar nodded back.

Moments later, Alemar and Geim slipped away into the murk,

moving away from the dome. Toren remained.

That man has infected you with his madness, Koipen muttered, as if he could point to the departing figure of the prince with his own hand.

Toren tried to keep his reaction private, but that was always a difficult prospect when it came to his totem.

You see it, too! Koipen proclaimed. *The cheli has gone insane.*

What I see is a possibility, Toren replied. And how could he not? In the past few months Alemar had been through ordeals enough to wrench any man's mind up by the roots: The loss of his healing power, the capture of his pregnant wife by an enemy sorcerer, the face-to-face confrontation with Gloroc. Perhaps it had been too much. Insisting that Treggei must suffer to the last moment, denied the mercy a knife would have brought—that decree not only continued to infuriate Toren even now, but made him worry his companion's grasp upon reality had dissolved. Had he set them all upon a suicidal course?

That is it, Koipen said. *The man is battle-touched.*

Toren lowered his hands to his belt. The gauntlets hung there. He wore them only when he had to. Putting them on activated their magic, and required him to concentrate in order to keep their emanations in check.

A sensible man would listen to his elders. And it wasn't as though he had no other honorable paths open to him. If they retreated from this spot and fled back to Cilendrodel after all, there would still be opportunities to prove their honor, and the fights there would be engagements that could be won. There would be allies, and high ground, and fewer of the enemy. In place of brine and sharks, there would be solid earth and trees. And beneath the boughs of those trees, Deena was waiting for him.

Yet when the moment of decision came, he slipped his hands into the gauntlets.

His ancestors were stunned to silence—not by his defiance, but by the intoxication of the sorcery. They had never felt it before. Toren had never before allowed his totem to be active while he wore the talismans. So for the first time, they shared the glory as Toren's perception of the world expanded. They observed with awe as the power surged and became part of him.

Well? he asked. *Now what do you say?*

Koipen remained mute, too affected to respond. It was Toren's father's spirit who said, *Show us more.*

So Toren did. He proceeded with the spell Alemar had requested of him.

Within moments, it was accomplished. He swam out from the coral formation, stopped in mid-depth, and waited. A short time later, a school of fish tried to swim through the place he occupied. The creatures scattered in panic as they bumped into his very real and solid — but completely unseen — body.

Matters would have been much easier if he could have made Alemar and Geim invisible at the same time. Unfortunately that was beyond him.

Toren drifted toward the perimeter, but he did not directly approach the portal. He waited until five members of the Dragon's garrison swam into view. Groups such as this patrolled the outside of the dome at all hours. Their shift having ended, this set of five were headed back to their barracks and would be making use of the gate.

The quintet passed within three body lengths of Toren and did not see him. He propelled himself after them. Within moments, whatever slight turbulence his swimming created was subsumed inside the wake of his unknowing escorts.

Now came the hardest part. The rest of the way in, he had to focus intently in order to simultaneously remain invisible and thwart the sentry enchantment.

The magic flowed as it should. Even Koipen complimented his handling of the challenge.

In due course, the five patrollers slipped under the rim of the dome and emerged into the bubble of the guard station. Toren clambered onto the platform with them in the midst of the splashing and noise. Then he retreated a step and waited so as not to bump anyone while they made for the smaller aperture that led into the main dome.

Only two of the men went on. The other three gathered near the opening to listen to an animated discussion taking place between the gate's guards. As chance would have it, they stood in a cluster that occupied the narrow place so fully Toren decided it was too risky to attempt to glide past. Inevitably, his attention was drawn to the conversation.

" — rather be in the West, would you, huddling on some patch of ground with only a bit of hard biscuit and the dregs from your waterskin to give you comfort? The war is going well, they say, but don't you be clam-headed enough to think there'll be anything for the likes of us on the front but the chance to be gutted by a royalist pike. It's not our sort what gets the glory and the spoils."

The speaker was a short, scarred older warrior with the ends of two fingers missing from his shield hand. A younger, jittery comrade kept shaking his head throughout the speech. "I still say we're not as cozy and blessed as you make out," that one said. "They say the Dragon hasn't come back to his palace even now. I say anything that makes him that careful is not an enemy I want within a hundred leagues of me."

"The Dragon has his reasons for — "

Toren had already determined that the Dragon was not in residence. With the gauntlets on, he would have known whether Gloroc was near. But he was intrigued to learn that the great serpent had not returned at all during the days and nights since the assassination attempt.

The patrollers continued on. Toren quickly shadowed them. Invisible he might be, but he was leaving drips and wet footprints on the tile. By moving on at once, these signs merged into the traces left by the trio.

The men made straight for the barracks. As they entered, they peeled off their airmakers and left them in a trough by the door among the dozens already there. Toren followed suit. Many of the devices bore identifying marks, but one extra amid so many was unlikely to draw attention.

They went to the changing rooms. The men stowed their weapons and other tack carefully, but simply stripped off their patrol suits and tossed them on the floor for some barracks squire to deal with later. Toren stood near the pile so that any dripping he did would blend into the puddle flowing toward the drain.

The men put on street clothing and departed. Alone now in the chamber, Toren welcomed the opportunity to release the invisibility spell. Only when he had done so did he notice just how much his head had started to throb.

He dried off his gear, including his belt and the gauntlets— slipping the latter off in order to do so. Inspecting the cubbies and shelves, he found what he was looking for: freshly laundered uniforms. The barracks served not only the men who patrolled outside the dome, but those who patrolled within. The livery of the city watch was an excellent disguise in which to roam the streets. Once he had found pieces that would fit, he stripped off his wet clothing and hid it at the bottom of a refuse container, glad to say farewell to it.

Once he was arrayed in his pilfered ensemble, he evaluated the effect in the mirror. As long as he kept the gauntlets unobtrusive within the cloak, he scarcely needed to resort to the invisibility spell again—save for his hairless face, his unusually blond hair, and the burnished tones of his skin.

There was an answer even for that, once he reached his next intended destination.

He gathered up two sets of uniforms he estimated were the right size for his companions, then he slid the gauntlets back on.

The throbbing in his head remained, but it ceased to trouble him, overlaid now as it was by the sweetness of the flow of energy and the heightened sense of his surroundings. He almost laughed out loud. He was Struth's candidate—the Dragonslayer's candidate. He felt as though he could do anything.

At the moment, what he needed to do was make the uniforms in his hands invisible, as they had not made the shift along with his flesh and his own attire. He held the bundle closer and increased his focus.

There. He checked the reflection in the mirror to be sure. That had done it. He did not like how hard the effort had been, though.

At the barracks' exit, a recruit was shining an entire row of officer's boots where the fumes of the polish would not disturb his sleeping comrades. The young man was working with a lackluster air, but his task kept him occupied enough that he did not react in the slightest as Toren slipped past.

—o—

It was an hour before Toren reached the place he was seeking. At least it seemed like an hour. Back at the islet, he had listened to nearly all of Treggei's description of the layout of the city, and since then he and Alemar had gone over it again. Toren knew the journey should have taken an hour, so it must have. And yet it seemed later. When he had first left the barracks, the lanes had been busy with early-evening human activity, requiring Toren to navigate carefully in spite of his invisibility. Now only a few locals were still out. And that glow above the dome — surely that was Motherworld, already risen.

Motherworld should not have risen yet.

Rubbing his aching head, he studied the building. He had never seen a theater before. The closest the land of the Fhali had to such a thing was the Ring of Giants where some of the sacred rituals were conducted, and that was not a building but a granite clearing surrounded by ancient trees. He understood its function: A place where members of the community gathered in large numbers to watch lengthy and sometimes elaborate performances. He even understood the concept of a stage play, because Obo had loved them. The more Toren stared, the more certain he was that Obo had known this very theater, back in his youth when Dragonsdeep had still been Wizardsdeep.

Toren found a hiding place near the rear exit and waited. A short while later, a middle-aged man emerged. He padlocked the wrought-iron gates and ambled off down the alley.

Once the man was fully gone, the modhiv crossed to the gates. The padlock was strong, but not robust enough to withstand the tug he could apply while wearing the gauntlets. After he had entered, he rearranged things so that only a close inspection would expose the damage he had caused. Satisfied, he ambled up the curving ramp to the backstage doors.

Once he was around the first part of the curve and out of sight of the alley, he finally let go of the spell. The release made him stagger. To his surprise, his knees buckled, his body failed to correct itself, and he crumpled against a wall.

His ancestors chided him in various ways — for keeping the spell going so long, for being here in the city, for falling over like a toddler. Exasperated, he applied the technique he had learned at the Temple of Struth and muffled them all. But without their whispers, he was alone in a way he had not been since entering the city.

The stage doors were unlocked. He found a lamp on a small table and lit it at the same time that he shut himself inside.

He soon found the dressing room of the male performers, and on the shelves and tables found what he needed, just as Alemar had said he would, and just as Obo's memories said he should — cosmetic face paints and wigs. He filled a satchel with a suitable variety.

It took him longer to find false beards of the type he needed; that is, the type that went over smooth faces rather than those that clipped onto existing facial hair. He found what he needed only after he ventured into the female dressing room.

Given how he had stumbled while coming up the ramp, he wanted to limit further use of the invisibility spell. Now he had the means to do that. He sat down in front of one of the mirrors and set about making his face resemble a native of Elandris, not a denizen of The Wood.

— o —

Some time after midnight, so he calculated, he arrived at the very front of the Dragon's palace.

The main entrance was the best choice. The doors were open even at this hour, accommodating the few who still had reason to be going back and forth. A half dozen guards stood along either side of the portal—a pair for each level of the great steps. Toren, invisible for one last interval and able to stifle the sentry charms as soon as they reacted to his incursion, strode straight up the middle of the steps and slipped over the threshold without so much as causing a hair to flutter.

In the grand foyer, he was confronted by a bizarre spectacle. Suspended from the ceiling and hanging just above the height of anyone who might pass through the chamber was the preserved remnant of a man.

Toren could not have guessed how tall the man might have been in life. The poor wretch had been...reduced. The head was intact, but the spine had been removed at about the level of the chest, leaving just enough structure around which to craft a torso less than a quarter the size the person had possessed in life. A set of short, almost flipperlike arms hung from a false and minimized set of shoulders, and two narrow and ludicrously small legs dangled below—the arms adorned with the full-sized hands, the legs ending in the full-sized feet. The figure had been left unclothed, conspicuously revealing the absence of genitals, and not even a seam to show where they had been.

All of it had been crafted out of the original flesh. Toren could detect no lingering trace of spellcasting. A faint whiff of preservative chemicals and lacquer reached his nose. The specimen had apparently been created by the science and methods of a taxidermist. Grotesque as it was, it was artwork.

The head was arranged so that it regarded palace visitors as they came in. Its glass eyes shone with a startling degree of liveliness. Anyone who had known the man in life would recognize him. He wore an expression of pure horror, as if he were looking in a mirror at what had become of him.

Toren found the spectacle particularly unnerving. No one could see him, so no one stared at him. But this dead man seemed to.

He hurried on, almost forgetting to tiptoe.

—o—

The ache in his head was driving him to distraction by the time he arrived at his final destination. He had been able to let himself be visible as he walked along deserted corridors, but the palace was riddled with small enchantments meant to alert the guards to the presence of an intruder. Some were woven with dragon magic. Under normal circumstances, no human sorcerer could have negated them. But the gauntlets were meant to thwart dragon magic. He had succeeded, but the process had been an ordeal.

He strode out to the middle of a chamber almost as large as the great hall where he and Alemar had killed Gloroc's sister. From it a great shaft rose up, extending well beyond the city's main dome, and further still until it broke the ocean surface.

It was the Dragon's own door.

Once, the shaft had been the most central of the city's ventilation towers, designed to bring fresh air directly into the palace. It still served that function, but its role had multiplied in the last few years. The Dragon was too large to enter and leave the city through the usual gateways. The shipping bays could accommodate him, but here was the best solution. The grillwork across the top of the shaft, originally designed as a fixed barricade to thwart entry by any attackers who might succeed in capturing the outside of the tower, had been divided down the middle to make semicircular flaps that opened on hinges. Gloroc could fly in and out of the palace at his convenience.

It occurred to Toren, as he stood there in the circle of moonglow shining down from the opening, that if Gloroc happened to choose this very hour to reappear, things would suddenly grow very complicated.

He tossed down the coil of rope he had brought. It had come from the storerooms near the kitchens. Every palace this size needed rope to secure casks and barrels and crates in its storage areas. The Dragon's residence was no exception, though Toren had not been pleased at how much time had been consumed by the search. The worst part was, now that he saw how high the shaft was, he wasn't sure he had enough.

Only one way to find out.

He wove the magic as he had been taught back in the Temple of Struth. Janna had said—no, *Miranda* had said—that the Dragonslayer had used the same rope-taming spell to climb to the place where he had slain Faroc. With the gauntlets, she said, he would be able to put it into effect far more easily than the wizard had been able to do on that legendary day.

Miranda may have lied about some things, but not about the spell. He held one end of the rope so that the gauntlets made plenty of contact, whispered the words he had memorized, and the other end rose straight upward.

The rope made it all the way. It was long enough with a few feet to spare. Getting it to tie itself into the grillwork took all of his attention, but in the end he managed it on the first try. He gave his end a yank and the knot cinched tight.

He released the line, letting it dangle. He needed all his talents and all the advantage of the talismans for his next feat. He closed his eyes and listened to the music of the enchantment the Dragon had laid upon the hinges and the gears of the door. And of course, to the music of the locking charm.

When the design revealed itself to him, he laughed softly. So simple, really—for a dragon. Almost primal. Easy to subvert. The Dragon hadn't bothered with anything elaborate. Something more complicated would only have made it harder for the beast himself to open and close the grill.

"Open," he murmured. Not that he had to say it aloud, but it helped him focus.

The two sections of the grill parted, each side raising up. The edges, when fully open, did not quite extend to the top of the shaft.

He climbed hand over hand, as he had climbed a thousand vines and ropes back in The Wood. When had he first gone up a rope? The Fhali liked to joke that their children learned to climb before they could walk.

Along the rim was a walkway built to accommodate a squad of defenders should invaders ever try to storm the tower from boats. Not a likely prospect. Mostly it was just a place for seabirds to shit. Guano rose to the height of his knees except where the Dragon's comings and going had knocked off the accumulation. Toren picked his way around to the spot he desired.

In the distance rose other ventilation towers. The ones along the city edges in the distance were manned by live sentries, but their attention was directed outward at the open sea, the only direction from which enemies would be expected to come. No need to resort to the invisibility spell again. The darkness would cloak him enough.

Except that the stars, already rendered faint by the glow of Motherworld, were vanishing from the east.

That was not possible. Surely dawn was hours away. Toren could not account for the passage of so much time.

He threw the rope over the side. He saw the end splash down. It was just long enough to reach the sea with maybe a man-length to spare.

He knew he had found the right spot, but he saw no one in the water. Was he too late? Had Alemar and Geim noted the imminence of the dawn and fled while they still had the cover of darkness?

No. There they came, up from the water, discarding their airmakers as they cleared the waves.

Toren grimaced. They were too slow. While they might be little more than shadows from the vantage point of anyone on the other towers, all it would take to ruin their luck was for a lookout to grow suspicious and raise a spyglass. Alemar's swollen elbow was hampering his ability to climb.

Toren took hold of the rope and began pulling. He eased into it so as not to surprise the climbers, but ultimately he was pulling as fast as he could. The gauntlets gave him such strength it was as though he were a boy pulling up a snare's worth of pond fish. Alemar and Geim soon were clambering over the rim.

"What took so long?" Alemar asked.

"You're here. That's the important thing," Toren snapped. "Now let's get down before anyone sees us." He dropped the rope through the aperture and rappelled down while they were catching their breaths.

By all rights, he should be the one catching his breath after pulling them up, but he felt fresh. He was ready to do it all over again.

He reached the bottom and steadied the rope while Alemar descended. His comrade had to pause and rest his elbow halfway down, holding himself in position with his feet while he did so. But eventually he made it down to the floor without slipping.

He regarded Toren intently, a frown furrowing his brow. "Are you all right?" he asked.

"I am doing better and better all the time," Toren declared. He was feeling so...light. He tilted his head in the direction of the bundle of guard livery and the satchel containing the cosmetics he had taken from the theater. "Look at what I found. I think you'll be pleased."

Alemar slowly went over, picked up the satchel, opened it, and studied the contents. By the time he returned to Toren's side, Geim reached the bottom and got his feet beneath himself, his injured thigh stealing away the grace he usually displayed.

Toren sent a tiny burst of energy up the rope that caused it to untie itself. As soon as it had fallen to the floor, he began coiling it up. He would tuck it somewhere out of the way. No use leaving in plain sight evidence that demonstrated the Dragon's palace had been breached.

"There's something I think you should see," Alemar said. He pulled out the small mirror Toren had included with the items in the satchel. He turned it so that Toren would see his own reflection.

What Toren saw made no sense. He saw no wig pulled down over his own hair. No false beard covering his lower face. No make-up disguising his Vanihr complexion.

What he did see was a man whose face was painted with a traditional Fhali deathmask — the same design he had placed there on the day that Geim, Deena, and Ivayer caught up to him and made him their prisoner.

"I think it's time for you to take the gauntlets off," Alemar said.

"I am fine," he insisted.

"Toren. Take the gauntlets off."

That sounded like a command. Toren did not like that, but as he opened his mouth to retort, his tongue went numb, his knees softened like beeswax near a flame, and his vision faded to grey —

And then to black.

CHAPTER FOUR

THE CITY BREATHED.

Geim had no better way to describe it. Dragonsdeep was alive. All along the base of the dome, giant airmakers lured fresh drafts of atmosphere out of the sea water. The currents warmed and rose until they escaped through ventilation shafts such as the one he, Toren, and Alemar had come down. Breezes flapped flags, stirred branches, cooled sweat from the necks of laborers, just as they would in any city built on land. And it was a breeze rich with the aroma of grass, of flowers, of crop soil recently turned.

There was rain, too. It had come in the late afternoon, and even now the pavement beneath his feet was wet, the trickles running off into gutters.

It was not at all what Geim had expected. He had seen many cities since leaving The Wood. Cities made him restless. He was a creature of the forest. Yet this was a city he could live in.

"What *are* you looking at?" Alemar demanded.

Geim gestured around. "All this. It's magnificent. Why would Gloroc leave it standing? Why wouldn't he tear it all down? It's the sort of thing dragons *do*, isn't it?"

"What he's done is worse."

"How so?"

"Look at the *people*."

Looking at the people had been something Geim had been trying *not* to do, for fear it would invite them to stare back and spot some inadequacy of his disguise. The cosmetics only did so much. His false beard kept shifting upward. His wig...looked like a wig.

But he did as Alemar suggested. On the other side of the avenue, an elderly man and woman were passing by. Their chins were down, their vision directed at the bases of the buildings, away from the street. A minstrel emerged from a tavern side door; he clutched his lute tightly to his body and hurried off, checking to be sure he was not being followed. A cobbler was closing the front door of his shop, securing it with three separate locks.

No one — no one at all — spared them more than a glance, and all of those, every last person immediately turned their head away as if to pretend they had not looked.

A leaf wafted past them, skittering down the avenue and into an alley. Geim understood Alemar now. The inhabitants of Dragonsdeep resembled that leaf, blown adrift, headed for a fate no better than to land in a puddle and dissolve.

Toren plodded along between the two of them. The glassiness of his eyes showed he was failing to take in any aspect of their surroundings, whether it be the magnificence of the city's engineering or the woefulness of its residents. As long as Geim and Alemar kept hold of his elbows and surreptitiously urged him along, he continued to put one foot in front of the other, but he was lost within himself.

Even that much was something to be thankful for. When Toren had first slipped into his personal murk, he had gone stiff as a length of polewood from the River Sha. Geim and Alemar had been forced to carry him like that out of the great chamber and down the palace corridors until they found a storeroom devoted to what must have been an obsolete set of dishes and tableware, judging by the dustiness of the items on the shelves. Had his condition not changed, they might be hiding in that uninviting set of quarters even now, wondering how to deal with him. They could not have carried him through the streets without calling attention to themselves. But bit by bit over the course of the day, the unnatural tightness of Toren's neck and elbows and knees had dissipated. He had even curled up, closed his eyes, and seemed to sleep for a few hours.

Geim had slept a little as well, while Alemar kept watch. And then Alemar had slept while Geim kept watch. Their luck was decent enough that none of the servants passing back and forth in the corridor sensed them there just one thin door away. Eventually Toren had stirred—in a manner of speaking: His eyes opened. He drank water when a cup was lifted to his lips. He didn't interfere when Alemar wiped the Fhali death mask off his face and applied the thespian make-up properly, nor did he struggle when he was wrapped in a cloak to hide the gauntlets.

At the end of the day, they had departed the palace as part of the intermittent trickle of servants heading out for their evening entertainments, the twilight helping to hide the oddities of their appearance.

They came to another intersection adorned with one of the sculptures made from human remains, this one differing from the other two they had seen in that it was the remnant of a woman. It no longer had breasts nor genitalia—these had been eliminated so thoroughly and artfully that it appeared the living being had never owned such attributes—but the face was beardless, the features feminine, the hair arranged in a way typical of the women of the city. One arm pointed at the direction straight ahead of them, the other pointed along the cross street. Each arm was tattooed with the name of the relevant thoroughfare.

When Geim had first spotted one of these macabre memorials, he assumed they were evidence of a special punishment given to a chosen few. But this was already the fourth he'd seen. They were obviously a feature of the city, their existence an indication of how Dragonsdeep differed from the Wizardsdeep of old.

"Not far now," Alemar said. Only once had they been forced to backtrack in order to determine the correct route. Geim had not listened to enough of Treggei's deathbed litany to contribute to the navigation effort, but Alemar had committed everything to memory. The one place they had gone astray was due to the absence of an alley that must have existed back when Treggei had lived here, but that had since been filled in.

Soon they turned off the public lane and headed along a stone walkway through a garden plot. The aroma of edible crops wafted up—the saltine musk of hair melon, the sweet tang of ripe tomato. Layered over that was the fragrance from the hedge of incense herbs along the path. Geim's empty stomach rumbled.

The residence lay in the midst of the lot, its size ample but far from the largest they had seen during their walk, perhaps the dwelling of a moderately successful merchant. Here in Dragonsdeep one did not have to be a nobleman to own a house with landscape around it. In every neighborhood space was devoted to gardens, shrubbery, compost heaps. Some of the parks even had ponds with live fish and sedge flats full of tiny but exuberantly loud frogs.

They approached a front door that was bracketed on either side by a pair of laceleafs. The specimens must have been growing there for centuries, for their crowns rose higher than the ridgeline of the roof and their trunks were as thick as a fat man's belly.

Toren stopped walking.

It was the first thing he had done all day of his own volition. Alemar and Geim waited to see what else he might do. Eventually they were rewarded by the sight of their companion tilting his head back and gazing at the canopy of branches. As far as Geim could tell he was not looking at anything specific, unless it was the miniscule turtle beetle crawling along the smooth bark, but as a Vanihr, he knew that some part of Toren was thinking: *Trees!*

Meanwhile Alemar pulled the cord of the chime.

The door was answered by a balding, middle-aged man whose beard betrayed all the absent tugging it had endured.

"Master Quandai?" Alemar asked.

"Yes."

"I am Alemar Olendim. I am the natural son of Keron, King of Elandris."

Geim blinked. Had he actually said it so bluntly, to a man he had just met?

The blood drained from Quandai's face. "Get inside. Quickly," he squeaked.

Alemar strode across the threshold. Geim nudged Toren, who fortunately was willing to be drawn away from the trees. Not quickly, though. Quandai danced on his heels at the delay. He puffed in relief once they were in far enough within that he could close the door.

"What are you doing *here*?"

"Forgive the intrusion," Alemar said. "I understand your support for my father's cause has been discreet. I'm sure you want to keep it that way. We will be gone by tomorrow if you can put me in contact with others in Dragonsdeep who can help me."

Quandai hesitated. "How do I know you are who you say you are?"

"You know I am who I say I am, or you wouldn't have let me in." But Alemar opened Toren's cloak, exposing the gauntlets. The knuckle gems coruscated with green light. "The Dragonslayer made these talismans. A few days ago, we used them to snare Gloroc himself. He escaped. His sister did not."

Quandai...wobbled. "We've been hearing rumors of an attack on the palace. Everyone has noticed the search parties going out. This was hardly the time for you to come back!"

"That may be true, but here we are."

The man didn't take his eyes off the gauntlets until Alemar closed the cloak over them. He kept shaking his head. "You really killed Gloroc's sister?"

Alemar removed the dragon's teeth from his pack and held them up.

Quandai took a step back.

"So I see," he whispered.

Geim heard a sharp intake of breath. He turned. A young

woman was standing in the doorway opposite the one through which they had entered. She stared with wide eyes at the dragon's teeth.

"My niece," Quandai explained. "Solia."

"Hello," Alemar said.

She came out of her daze faster than her uncle had. "Welcome to our home. You look like you could do with some food."

Finally, thought Geim, *Someone who knows what's important. Perhaps I should marry her.*

"Yes," Alemar answered. "But first, if we could have some soap and water and bandages?"

"I'll see to it."

When she was gone, Alemar waited until Quandai made eye contact before he said, "Can you help us or not?"

"O-Of course," Quandai sputtered. "Forgive me. I know just whom to turn to. I will send my nephew with a message. Meanwhile let me show you to the guest room."

Quandai gestured to the hallway on the left.

Alemar put away the teeth. Geim tugged at Toren's elbow to get him moving. He was even slower to react than he had been at the front door. His eyelids were drooping.

"What's wrong with him?" Quandai asked.

"We need to remove the gauntlets," Alemar explained. "It's easier said than done."

—o—

Leaning back on pillows upon one of three narrow beds in what must have been a servants' suite before the war had emptied homes like this of their domestic staff, Geim wasn't certain he was going to be able to rise any time soon. His boots were off. Alemar had removed the sutures from his leg wound and applied a numbing salve. Geim was as comfortable as he had been at any point since the battle with the dragons, and now had little means left to ignore just how weary he was in a general way.

He sipped more tea and sampled another wafer with some of the delightfully spicy jam Quandai's wife had brought. It was the matron's own recipe, made with gnarlpepper and some sort of tree fruit Geim had never before tasted. His stomach was still full from the meal he had eaten, but he couldn't help having a little more. The memory of hunger was fresh. Rations had been minimal since they had left the islet.

Alemar was rubbing liniment on his elbow. The joint had been improving but the climb up the tower had caused the swelling to reassert itself. Toren was lying quietly on the center bed, staring at the ceiling.

Geim regarded the trophies mounted on the wall. One was an octopus, its tentacles poised. Another was an eel with an extraordinary frill of multiple colors. Both were so lifelike they seemed to be in the water, going about their lives.

"The craftsmanship is extraordinary," he said aloud.

"Not surprising," Alemar replied. "Quandai is the Dragon's taxidermist."

Geim abruptly sat up. "Treggei told you that?"

"Treggei spoke to me of Quandai a number of times over the years — the last time back in that hut. You were standing sentry at that point."

"You mean Quandai is the one who made those signposts?"

"Yes. Gloroc enjoys having the remains of enemies hung up where their friends and loved ones can see what happens to those who oppose his rule. I have no doubt that had our attack on the palace gone wrong, our bodies would have found their way onto Quandai's worktable."

Suddenly the food no longer rested at ease in Geim's stomach. There had been no way to retrieve the remains of their dead comrades when they had fled the palace. "Ebben was obliterated by dragonfire, but what about Match? He was strangled by the spell."

Alemar lowered his arm as if the pain in his elbow had flared. He set a cloth on his lap and awkwardly wiped the liniment off his fingers. Finally he shook his head. "Quandai hasn't been given Match's body. If he had, he would already have known the attack on the palace was more than a rumor."

Geim agreed with the logic, but that didn't quell his unease. "This isn't what I imagined when Treggei said you had allies inside Dragonsdeep."

"This is a stop along the way," the prince said. "Treggei knew where Quandai could be found, and that Quandai could refer us onward. It may be it was the house, more than the person, that made him tell us to come here. Treggei spent some happy times here."

"How so?"

"This is where Nyorette lived. His sweetheart. I have no doubt that bench we passed when we walked through the garden was the very spot she and Treggei used to sit while he was courting her."

"You don't mean Quandai is her father?"

"No. When Nyorette and her parents were discovered to be royalists, they were taken to the Dragon's dungeons. They were all executed. They came for Treggei as well, but he managed to escape to Cilendrodel."

"I see."

"Treggei said it comforted him to learn the house had later been given over to Quandai. The joke was on Gloroc. The Dragon imagined he was installing a loyal servant in the home. He didn't know his own taxidermist was even more of a traitor than those who'd been caught."

"I'm not sure how much I trust Quandai. He's jittery as an Ijitian tax collector."

"I agree. But we won't have to depend on him long. We'll have other help soon."

"I hope so. We'll need even more help than we planned for, as long as Toren stays as he is."

As if the sound of his name had triggered something, Toren stirred. Unfortunately, all he did was roll onto his side, curl up, and close his eyes.

Alemar went over to him. He reached out. A ward formed, keeping his hand at bay. The situation was the same as it had been in the palace. Alemar couldn't take hold of the gauntlets whatsoever, much less remove them from Toren's hands.

The prince leaned down. "You need to take them off," he murmured. "You'll die if you don't."

Toren just lay there. The only improvement was that at least now, in the new position, he seemed to be in the midst of a natural sleep.

Shaking his head, Alemar returned to his spot.

"I thought he could get us into the city without harm to himself. I thought using the gauntlets was the safest option."

"At least he ate the food," Geim said.

"Yes. But I'm not worried he'll starve to death. The talismans will kill him more directly than that. They don't supply energy. They transform strength that's already there. They keep siphoning no matter how little the wearer has left to give."

Geim was glad Alemar did not apologize for pushing Toren beyond his limits. Things were far from ideal at the moment, but they had to keep taking risks.

Struth was a lie. Janna was a lie. But what they were trying to do now in Dragonsdeep was an honest quest. Geim needed that.

"The only approach I have yet to try is to break the enchantment by force," Alemar said soberly.

"That doesn't sound safe."

"It isn't. The process may kill him. May kill me as well, for that matter."

"So you will only do it as a last resort."

"Yes."

The door opened, preceded by a soft knock. In came Solia carrying a bucket of steaming water, clutching fresh washcloths in her left hand. She set the items on the sideboard next to the basin of bloodied water and the linen they'd already used.

"I thought you might want more." She nodded at Geim. "You still have some of that make-up on your neck."

"Thank you," Geim said. He had just been noticing how sticky the remnant felt. He hoped he wouldn't have to venture out again this evening. He preferred letting his skin feel like skin.

Solia gazed at the pack on the floor. "I want to see the dragon teeth again. I want to touch one."

Alemar hesitated.

"It's the least we can do," Geim said.

"I suppose you're right." Alemar gestured at the pack. "Go ahead."

For an instant Solia just stood there with her hand over her mouth, then in a rush she knelt down and opened the flap.

She lifted up a tooth to the lamp glow, turning it round and round.

"It's so light," she whispered.

"Yes," Alemar said. "As firm as a tooth usually is, but somehow not as dense. I suppose heavy teeth would make it harder to fly."

"I saw her fly."

Alemar leaned forward. Geim did not, as it would mean leaving behind the comfort of the pillows, but she certainly had caught his attention.

"When was that?" Alemar asked.

"About a fortnight ago. She and the other one flew in together. The High Chamberlain issued invitations to about two hundred common citizens to come up to the observation tower and witness the arrival."

"The *other* one?"

She nodded. "The male."

"Gloroc has a *brother*, too?"

"Yes."

"How long have you known this?"

"Since the day it happened. There hadn't even been any rumors before that. All these decades Gloroc has been the only dragon anyone had ever seen. The other two were kept hidden until they became airbreathers and began to fly."

"Where is the brother now?"

"He left the next day for the battlefront."

Alemar went silent. Geim did not have to struggle to guess why. The prince was thinking of his father.

"I'm sorry," Solia said. "I didn't realize you didn't know, though of course you wouldn't. I'd find it hard to believe if I hadn't seen it. I'm sure that's why the High Chamberlain assembled the witnesses."

She ran her finger up and down the length of the tooth. "You can't imagine what this means," she added.

"It means all sorts of things. None of them good," Alemar said.

"On the contrary. You being here? Just when it seemed like Gloroc was in complete control, you proved otherwise."

She carefully — reverently — placed the tooth back in the pouch.

She stood up. "You asked my uncle to send you on to others who could help. Don't go. Stay here."

Alemar searched her eyes. "Why?"

"My uncle has a good heart, but sometimes he needs help to stiffen his courage. If you stay, you can be sure he won't let word slip to the Dragon's men, because if they find you here, he would have to explain how you came to be guests in his house. I doubt he could give an answer that would save him from the inquisitors in the dungeons."

"So this is the safest place to be?" Alemar said.

She nodded. "For now. Stay. Recuperate. You have plenty of challenges in front of you. Finding a place to sleep and eat shouldn't be one of them."

"Thank you."

Solia picked up the basin of old water and used linen and made her exit.

"*Her* I get a good feeling from," Geim said.

Alemar was gazing at the spot Solia had occupied. He seemed as lost in himself as Toren was.

Well he should be. How many dragons were they up against?

CHAPTER FIVE

"THERE THEY ARE again," Enret said.

Keron wished he could keep his eyes level. But how could he not look up?

Two dragons glided high above. So high, in fact, that at first glance they resembled a helix of carrion vultures. Yet no birds ever boasted such batlike wings, stretched broad as sails. No birds had such long, serpentine bodies.

Two dragons. Treynaf had predicted it.

Treynaf had also seen a dragon dead in a palace beneath the sea. Keron had hoped it meant the mission to assassinate Gloroc would succeed. He didn't know what to think now. Toren and Alemar should have reached Dragonsdeep six, seven, or even eight days back. And yet one of those dragons up there *was* Gloroc. Keron had seen him enough times to recognize him, even in silhouette against the bright sky.

He certainly wasn't dead.

One of Keron's escorts became so distracted his oeikani bumped the broken-down wagon they were navigating around. Cheeks reddening, he tugged the reins and slipped back into formation.

No one scolded the man. They were all feeling it. The dragons weren't doing anything but passing by overhead, but that was enough to churn the bowels of every person touched by their shadows, be they Keron and the men of his party, or the soldiers of the encampment they were threading their way through.

Everyone knew the beasts could do far more. Four days ago, they had. Keron and his forces had been chasing the Dragon's main army across the war-torn fields of Simorilia. The enemy had not expected to be harassed in such an all-out fashion. Treynaf's advice for once had been as sound as it could be: "March to Elandris! Do not wait for the dawn!"

They had hurt the enemy. Oh, yes. They had struck the hardest blow of the entire war.

And then the dragons had appeared. The mere sight of multiple dragons was itself enough to disrupt the charge. Their bombs of oil and their flames had done the rest. What could have been a decisive blow by Keron and his allies was thwarted. On the other side of a freshly created no man's land of smoke, char, and roasted bodies, the fleeing army had reached its goal, a set of fortifications erected earlier in the war. The disorganized retreat had turned into an increasingly stout defense of that line.

Keron had experienced frustration at many points during the war, but none as sharp and deep as he was feeling now. The enemy was still vulnerable, but each day that grew less true. They were digging in. They had to be attacked soon. But Keron didn't have enough men.

He should have, but he did not.

When Keron had launched the pursuit, the army of the Calinin Empire, under the command of Prince Fanhar, had supposedly been only a day or so from joining them. If those reinforcements had arrived as promised, he might have now been pressing on to the coast, harrying the heels of the Dragon's shattered regiments.

Fanhar had not come. His army had reached the fields outside Tazh Tah on schedule. There they had remained, a dozen leagues from the fighting.

Keron would know the reason for that.

The dragons glided on, scribing a huge circle that enclosed not only the entire army encampment, but all of the city of Tazh Tah. When that was complete, they headed back to the east, as if satisfied that nothing was going on that required their active discouragement. They had disappeared beyond the horizon by the time Keron's party reached the picket line around the royal pavilions.

The captain of the guard placed himself in the path of the visitors. "Halt and be recognized."

Keron sloughed off his travel cloak, revealing the insignia on his breastplate. "The King of Elandris wishes to speak to your lord."

The captain did not bow. He saluted. Keron took it for the sign of greater respect it was, and saluted back.

"If it please your majesty, your men can take their refreshment by the tables there." The captain pointed to a nearby area where members of the honor guard were sitting in canopied shade having their afternoon water break. "The grooms will see to your oeikani."

Keron understood it was a requirement, not an invitation. He nodded to his men, who handed over their mounts and headed off. Only Enret remained at Keron's side. The captain led the two of them on toward the main pavilion.

They were met outside the flaps of the sumptuous main tent by a herald. The captain of the guard all but sneered as he regarded the man's gold-threaded livery and elaborately braided hair. The herald in turn frowned at the captain's scarred and callused hands. Keron wondered if they played out this exchange every time they had a new audience to witness it.

"Your Majesty honors us," the herald said. "But it is my master's pleasure that you remove your footwear before entering."

Removing boots in what was supposed to be a battle camp? Keron regarded the herald until the man blinked. But he decided not to make an issue of something small. He tugged off his boots and set them aside. Enret did the same.

"I will announce you now," the herald said, and slipped through the flaps.

Keron heard himself introduced. The herald came back out and held up a flap. Keron and Enret stepped within.

The rug was a seduction of cashmere layered over pads of goosedown infused with dried rose petals. The design, the colors, the loomwork were equally glorious, but Keron ignored all that.

The man on the dais, nestled in cushions, was not Prince Fanhar.

"Who are *you*?" Keron demanded.

"I have the honor to be Mahosh, Lord of Thickreed, Legate of Emperor Iristhene, Revered Be His Name. You are no doubt startled to see me here. Rest assured it startles me as well."

"Explain."

"To answer that, I must tell you something known only to myself and these four guards." He gestured Keron and Enret closer and cupped a hand beside his mouth.

"Prince Fanhar is dead."

"What?!" Keron blurted.

Mahosh's brow furrowed. "Your Majesty, you must keep your voice down."

Keron stifled the urge to do just the opposite. "How did it happen?"

"Fanhar had a courtesan with him for the campaign. Sleek otter of a girl. His favorite. Two nights before we reached Tazh Tah, he had her brought to him. As always, the guards—the same ones you see here, the best personal sentinels a prince could wish for—remained at their posts, but naturally they turned their backs to the bed, and the prince closed the veil for his privacy.

"The guards heard a sigh. Then silence. They deserve credit for understanding at once that this was suspicious. The prince was not a man to fall asleep after his moment of release. The guards opened the curtains, and there was the prince and the courtesan, both dead."

"How?"

"Throwing stars laced with murk eel venom, as deduced from the stain at the wound sites and the speed with which the poison killed. Thrown from above. The guards looked up. They saw a shadowy figure climbing out through the ventilation hole."

Mahosh paused and gestured proudly at one of the guards, a supple, long-limbed fellow. "Stolio is very good with his throwing knife. He had no time to aim, but he hit true. Down came the assassin. Unfortunately his blade was a little too true, so there was no chance for questioning. But I believe we know the answers. The killer was female. No bigger than a child, really, and a scrawny child at that. She was so agile and strong for her size she managed to crawl up the sides of the pavilion like a monkey and lower herself on a cord far enough to fling the stars with accuracy. And she did it so quietly she nearly made good on her escape before anyone was the wiser."

"Tressya of Pearl Reef," Keron said. The Claw was a faceless cadre for the most part, but anyone familiar with the exploits of the Dragon's assassins knew that name.

"It must have been. We do not doubt it. She had the guild mark tattooed right over her heart."

"Why are you keeping this a secret?"

"You need not be so vexed, Your Majesty. I did it for *you*."

"For me? How so?"

"Well, to be fair, I did it for Prince Fanhar. I know how much the campaign meant to him. I am trying to see it through, in deference to his wishes."

"And yet you've not ordered your army to reinforce mine," Keron said.

"Again, I do not think you realize how much I am a friend to you...."

Mahosh went silent as a servant girl slipped into the tent bringing a tray of pressed wafers and a bowl of tiny, nearly transparent fish eggs. Judging by the brand on her flank and the lack of any clothing other than a loincloth, she was a slave—something not often seen in the New Kingdoms, a reminder to Keron that by crossing the threshold into the pavilion, he had ventured into a world with different rules than his. He had seen too much of that world on his trip to Xais.

Mahosh waved the girl away when she began preparing the

wafers. He picked up the mother-of-pearl spoon, added a thicker layer of roe, and began nibbling.

"Would you care for a bite, Your Majesty?"

"I am not hungry," Keron replied. "I will ask one more time. Why did you not come to my aid?"

"Because of this." He opened the dispatch case and pulled out a scroll.

Keron took it. He saw the emperor's seal, already broken. The scroll was addressed to Prince Fanhar. He opened it and read the message. It was brief. It was abominable.

Mahosh winced. "According to that, as you can plainly see, the emperor ordered Fanhar to turn around, withdrawing his support of your cause."

"When did this arrive?"

"Two days before the assassination."

"You believe this is real?"

"I believe it probably is not. Fanhar declared it to be a forgery. He set it aside and we continued marching toward Tazh Tah."

"And there you stopped."

"Yes. When Fanhar was killed, we stopped. Because, you see, I am in a most difficult position. I do not *know* the dispatch is a forgery. It certainly *looks* real. And you must know the emperor's support of you has wavered more than once."

Keron pressed his jaws together so hard his teeth hurt. He wished he could deny what Mahosh had said.

"It was Fanhar who believed in you. It was Fanhar who persuaded his father. But now I fear the Dragon may have offered enough opposing persuasion to change the Exhalted One's mind. You know this is possible."

"Yes," Keron growled.

"I saw those dragons in the sky just now. I heard what they did to you these past few days. You see my problem. I could have ordered the army into that chaos, but then what if the dispatch was not a forgery? And even if it is, the emperor could still be whipped to a fury if he learned his legions were roasted to slag just to push back the Dragon another few leagues toward the coast. Prince Fanhar could take risks. His father always forgave him when he overstepped. But me? I am only a grandson of the emperor's youngest uncle. Call down the emperor's rage upon myself and I would be lucky to keep my head, much less my lands and position at court."

"In what way is this being my friend?" Keron asked.

"Because, Your Majesty — the army is still here. The Dragon does not know his assassin succeeded. He will be concerned you will be reinforced after all, with Fanhar and all his passion leading the charge. Meanwhile, I have sent a courier to the emperor to ask him his true wishes. I for one will be delighted if he commands me to do as Fanhar would have done. Until then, I fear I can do no more for you."

Keron did not know what to say.

"Please," Mahosh said. "You have been fighting for days. I am told things are finally at a lull. The royal guest pavilion is next to this one. Take your ease. Think about what I have said. We can talk again this evening."

—o—

Keron was offered an elaborate meal, but he insisted upon field rations: Oaten porridge, a ladle measure of beans, and a cup of weak ale with which to wash it down. He did not believe a leader should indulge himself amongst men forced to endure the privations of battle camp.

He pictured Legate Mahosh garnishing his wafers. That had been glass caviar. No other kind of roe was so transparent. It could only have been harvested from icefish taken from the high lakes of the Syril Mountains, transported at considerable trouble, and probably escorted by a courier gifted enough in sorcery to be able to preserve the freshness.

"What did you make of him?" he asked Enret. The other men had given Keron the isolation they knew he needed, and now the only person close enough to hear was his old comrade.

"I wonder if we were to pull off his robes, whether we'd find any balls tucked below that dangling belly."

Keron held up his forefingers and thumbs, indicating two objects the size of pomegranate berries.

"He was everything I've heard people say about the high house of the Calinin," Enret continued, "except when they were talking about Fanhar."

Keron recalled what Struth had told him, that the prince was of better blood. "Yes. If Fanhar had been alive when word came that we were pursuing the Dragon's army, he would have swooped in like a gale of The Deeps to join us in time to make a difference."

"I don't think we will get much out of this one."

Keron nodded. "I fear you are right, but I couldn't read him. Oh, he's a pampered, selfish ass, yes, but he didn't strike me as a liar. He said he sympathizes with our cause. Perhaps he meant it."

"It's possible he's just a very *good* liar."

"As you say. In any case, he hasn't turned the army around. That does have value. Perhaps we can persuade him to do more."

"A bribe?"

"Mmm. The question is, what do we have to offer that would tempt him?"

Enret began to suggest something, but the words were drowned out by the clanging of a bell.

Both men rolled backward and came to their feet, daggers drawn, so smooth in their action their food remained undisturbed on the small folding table.

"That's coming from Mahosh's tent," Keron said. He rushed outside, scooping up his sheathed sword and its belt along the way. Enret followed at his heels.

They were among the first to reach the pavilion. The sentries on duty had already thrown aside the hangings over the entrances, rushed inside, and were now standing there, swords drawn, trying to understand the tableau within the tent.

Legate Mahosh and his four personal guards lay sprawled. Blood was still draining from them, ruining the rugs. Standing by the klaxon, holding the chain but no longer ringing the bell, was a trembling slave girl. The horror and uncertainty on her face was so profound it took Keron a moment to recognize her as the same server who had brought in the tray during his conversation with Mahosh.

Shaking off their surprise, the sentries bent down and lifted the eyelids of the slain. Not one of the five showed any sign of life.

"The Claw again?" Enret murmured.

"They're usually more subtle," Keron said. He stepped inside, gesturing for Enret to be allowed to enter with him. Boots on. The sentries did not stop the two of them, though they did bar the way of the growing herd of onlookers.

"These men were all died by sword," Keron declared after a quick study of each body. "Look how they fell. Mahosh was killed from behind. Two others were taken by surprise. Then these two faced one another. They both thrust. Their blows were both mortal. It was all over within moments."

Keron pressed his boot into the ribs of one of the corpses. "This one must have been the assassin. Look at all that spatter on his tunic. That's not his blood."

There seemed to be no need to search further for a killer, but the herald did so anyway, methodically checking the few hiding places the pavilion afforded. He turned finally to a large chest. Keron assumed he'd saved it for last because, after all, who could hide in it and then strap it shut from the outside?

The herald unfastened the strap, opened the lid, and gasped.

"My prince!" he blurted.

Keron rushed over. There in the chest, bound and gagged and propped with bolsters and pillows so that he could not shout or wiggle or otherwise call attention to his presence, was Fanhar. Alive. Eyes open.

"Prince Fanhar," Keron said. "It is so very good to see you."

The sentry cut the gag loose.

"Keron of Elandris," Fanhar wheezed. "It is good to be seen."

"Bring the flesh mender," the herald commanded. "And drop

those walls."

The pavilion dimmed as the flaps of the entrances were lowered, closing off the view to the crowd. A pair of sentries cut the bindings around Fanhar, lifted him out of the chest, and laid him down on an unbloodied rug.

Fanhar tried to unfold. He groaned and gave up.

By chance, he had been placed near the body of the man Keron had labelled the killer of the others.

Fanhar pointed at the man. "He was no assassin. He reconsidered his loyalties and acted to save me. I suppose I should be wroth with him that he helped betray me in the first place, but I confess if he weren't dead, I would kiss him right now for helping get me out of that box."

Fanhar was naked save for the swaddling cloth wrapped around his crotch. Keron gave him his privacy while attendants cleaned him up and slid a light blanket over him.

The flesh mender arrived. She was another slave, but adorned in the khaki livery of the Healers Guild and with glyphs shaved into her close-cropped, steel-grey hair. Her social status was therefore higher than the freeborn sentries, whom she brushed aside. She knelt beside the prince and began massaging him. She began with the largest muscles, those of his buttocks and thighs—the ones that had suffered most from the confinement.

Some flesh menders could summon a bit of magic to help them. Others depended upon nothing more than their hands and their skill. Keron couldn't tell what type she was, but she was good. Fanhar began unfolding. When he spoke again, his voice was far less strained than it had been.

"Pour my bath," he told his attendants.

While the hot water was being brought, Keron squatted down near the prince.

"Mahosh led me to believe you were dead."

"Apparently I was supposed to be, but Mahosh tried to play both sides. He kept me captive instead. He intended to ransom me. To which buyer, I'm not sure."

"He showed me this." Keron unrolled the scroll showing the emperor's order to turn around.

"Pay no mind to that."

Keron smiled.

The sentries were placing Mahosh's body on a litter to carry it out. The captain removed the signet ring and gave it to the prince.

"I underestimated him," Fanhar murmured to Keron. He wiped a bit of blood off the sigil of the royal house of the Calinin. "He was an unlikely enemy. I wouldn't have guessed he could show so much initiative. I won't make that sort of mistake again."

"Indeed."

Keron stood. "I should leave you until you've been tended to."

"As you wish. Come back within the hour. You came here with urgent needs. We'll talk as soon as I'm presentable. Perhaps you would share some caviar and wafers with me, Your Majesty?"

Keron chuckled. "It would be my pleasure, Your Grace."

CHAPTER SIX

DOGS SOUNDED ON the other side of the ravine. The Ril wizard's trackers had found their trail again.

"May your next lovers be pisshole chiggers," Elenya muttered.

She had with her a set of confederates thoroughly versed in woodcraft. They knew this particular terrain well and had been moving fast from the start, not aiming for subtlety, not slowing down to set traps. They were just trying to get away. They should have been able to. Yet none of their tricks had worked.

The wizard—Enril was his name, assuming her spies were correct in which member of the order the Dragon had been dispatched to replace Omril—was coming for her as if it mattered to him. As if catching her were personal. It must be, though she wasn't yet sure what she had done to earn that vehemence. She might be the leader of the resistance for the moment, however odd that felt, but in the end she was just one swordswoman, not a general. Killing or capturing her would not in itself stop the rebellion. Others would carry on in her place. The main thing the wizard could do was to continue the theme displayed at Hole Bay—show up with overwhelming numbers of fighting men, fully organized and fully supplied, and methodically secure the strategic locations where the rebels had established a level of control.

Part of that overwhelming force, a key part of their arsenal, was the Ril wizard himself. And yet here he was separating himself from the main force, seemingly repeating the mistake that Omril had made.

It wasn't the same mistake, of course. Elenya had no delusions about that. By the time Omril had tracked down her brother, Alemar had already had enough time to gather his strength. And Alemar had been able to call upon the Dragonslayer's gauntlet—and the help of the rythni, for that matter. Enril was not in danger in the same way now. Nevertheless he should have stayed with the campaign, lending his advice and his power to the larger battles.

Relentless, she thought. *He is relentless.*

She weighed her options. For the first time, she considered the tactic she had rejected thus far, which was to use sorcery to disguise their trail. Perhaps she could do it artfully enough that Enril would not detect the traces.

No, she decided. He was surely an adept the equal of Obo, and Obo had always seen through any of the illusions she tried to craft, except that one time when she had slipped out at fourteen to kiss the potter's apprentice—what had that lovely boy's name been? No. Magic had a tendency to complicate things. She needed them simple: Run. Get away. Hide.

The others waited for her order. Eighteen men counting Dalih. One other woman—Slees, the rope tamer whose skill with snares and treetop rigging made her as valuable as any three of the warriors.

"Divide again," she said. "My group to the west."

Elenya's half continued on more or less in the same direction they had already been moving. The rest angled off to the right, making for the northeast.

They had already divided three days earlier, splitting the few dozen comrades who had come with her from Hole Bay. They had hoped to split the pursuers equally as well, but no such luck. The main cluster of trackers had continued to—literally—dog their trail.

Slees vanished into the trees with the northeast-bound group. Elenya was the only female left in a company of men. How often had that been the case in her life? Not as often here in Cilendrodel as in Zyraii. Still often enough that it felt normal. Nevertheless, she would miss Slees. Her skills were a meaningful advantage.

Right now it was important that the other group have those skills. They would need them.

As for her group? Well, they had *her*. Let the hunters catch her, and they would see if that was really the outcome they would enjoy.

At the next ravine, they came to a creek whose waters eased down a gentle slope over boulders and logs. They did not cross right away. First they went upstream, hopping from rock to rock and even up onto the bank on the side from which they had originated. They came back downstream doing the same, until any group of hounds would be presented with a multitude of interruptions in the trail of scent, and no footprints would remain for men to see.

They exited the creekbed by clambering up a hanging vine one person at a time, and then pulled up the vine and hid it so that no one would suspect it had recently hung down over the stream. They crossed from that tree to the next to the next to the next before coming to ground, and then they jogged away single file, each person's feet landing in the same spots as the person ahead, leaving only one set of tracks, and that set was rarely upon ground soft enough to leave impressions.

They had used such tactics often in the past days. Somehow they had not worked. But they only had to work once, and the pursuit would fall too far behind to catch up.

The trees thickened again up ahead. She saw a route that would take them through the middle canopy for two, three, perhaps even four bowshots of distance.

They picked the easiest tree to climb and began clambering up.

They had climbed repeatedly during the chase, and now here they were doing so again. Her arm muscles throbbed. She envied the men their upper body strength, but she uttered no complaints. Every one of them had more weight to lift than she.

She reached a thick lateral branch. She was winded, but not so badly she had to catch her breath. She raced off horizontally, leaped to a slightly lower branch of a neighboring tree, and continued on. She did not look back, trusting her companions could do the same, trusting that none of them would fall.

—o—

No one fell.

And no one slowed down. When dusk came upon them, the ten members of their party were far from the place where they had first heard the dogs.

The dogs were still sounding, off in the forest. It meant they were still finding scent, and still bragging about it. But the noise filtered through the foliage so faintly it wobbled against their eardrums, clear one moment and then almost inaudible the next.

Abruptly, it stopped.

No one spoke. They all listened.

And heard only noises that belonged: Insects in the bark. Birds jostling leaves as they chose where they would roost. The warble of the brook where the group had just filled their water flasks.

Elenya glanced at Veyrenn. He had the keenest hearing. He signalled All Clear.

"We'll camp here for the night," Elenya declared. "Mildo will take the first watch. His choice who takes the next."

The pursuers knew better than to risk coming after them in the dark, and Elenya and her men knew better than to keep running in the dark if they didn't have to. They wouldn't get as far as they could during the day, and then when the day did come, they would be even more exhausted, and less able to use the good hours to make speed.

So. One more night. That was not a resolution, but at least it was a respite.

Not that they would let down their guard.

Bainne found some sweetcress near the brook. He handed out fistfuls to the group. Elenya chewed, working the tart juice out of the stalks before spitting them out. The acidity cut through the brackish film on her tongue and the insides of her checks. Her mouth was foul after running all day, even though she had managed, for the most part, to breathe through her nostrils.

She dug into her cache of nibblenut and hunter's gnaw. She craved something softer, fresher, wetter, but nothing beyond more sweetcress was near at hand. The creek had fish and Negg had a seine net in his pack, but they'd have to cook anything they caught or risk gutworm, and building a fire was not something she would allow.

Dalih returned from his good long piss and sat beside her, mimicking her repose, relaxing against a fallen log.

And it *was* relaxing. She could tell that, like her, he was letting his tension go. They were in danger and they were warriors. Both knew that resting as profoundly as possible when those moments presented themselves could be as critical to survival as the thrust of a sword or the release of an arrow.

"There were dogs in the merchant quarter where I grew up," he commented. "I never paid much attention to them. Most of them were there to be eaten, and I didn't care for the meat. Too stringy. Not enough fat."

Elenya had nearly eaten dog herself while living among the Zyraii. She had been handed a skewer straight from the cookfire and if the strip of meat on it had been cool enough, she would have taken a bite before she knew what it was. When she handed it back everyone there had narrowed their eyes at her, but she had not let that sway her. Her choice simply became another of the many ways she had not fit in while dwelling in the Eastern Deserts.

Dalih had paused. She knew he was waiting for her to signal that she was in a mood for talk — and further, talk in the language of the Zyraii, the challenge of using the High Speech being an ordeal for him in his weary state.

"Go on," she said.

"When I was eighteen, I lived with the marshfolk in the delta north of the Sea of Azu. That was where I first saw dogs like those you have here in Cilendrodel. That is to say, dogs allowed to hunt like dogs are meant to hunt. Running and running, wearing out their prey.

Not many creatures use that method. Dogs. Humans. Also a strange species of spider you might have seen when you lived in the desert."

"The scurry-spiders. I had forgotten about them."

"Ugly things. At least they get out of your way fast. My people called them dog spiders. It wasn't until my time in the delta that I understood why men of old decided to give them that name."

An owl hooted. It was louder than it should have been, and too much like a human imitating a birdcall. But a moment later, the owl itself launched from a branch and glided off into the canopy on the other side of the brook. The group resumed taking their ease.

"The trapper I lived with had two mature dogs plus a young male he was training. He was the one that taught me I could feel affection for a dog. Sometimes on a cold night, it was me he would curl up against. He would beg me for morsels."

Dalih chuckled, holding his hand out as if dangling a scrap of meat.

"We were hired to find and kill a bog panther that had been marauding the flocks along the western edge of the delta. Now that was a hunt that took the right kind of dogs. Bog panthers will thwart ordinary trackers. Those cats, even when they don't know they're being followed, they'll behave just the way they would if they *did* know. They go up rock faces no dog can manage. After they've made a kill and eaten their fill, they don't stay near the carcass for another meal. They never use the same lair twice in a row. And they like to swim.

"We found that panther's trail in the first hour. To corner the panther itself took almost a fortnight. We went way up into the canyonlands, then back down the main river, and all the way across the delta to the eastern edge. How many leagues, I don't know."

Elenya knew what he was getting at. "The dogs never gave up."

He nodded. "Somehow they always found the scent trail. Unless ordered to stop, they never would—you could see that in the old dogs' focus. They didn't react when a pheasant or a rabbit would bound away as they came near. They kept their noses sniffing the ground. They didn't wag their tails. They saved their strength for following the spoor. After three days, the young dog was so excited he became just as hard to distract. He tried his best to imitate what the senior dogs were doing. After a week, if a bitch in heat had passed by, I think he would have ignored her."

Elenya swallowed her last mouthful of nibblenut and washed it down with a long pull from her water flask. She dug her dew blanket from her pack and spread it over her legs in the hope that her calves would not ache so profoundly if they cooled off in a more gradual progression.

"How many dogs do you think they have?" Elenya asked.

Dalih gazed back in the direction where they'd last known their pursuers to be.

"Four. Unless there are some that are staying quiet. I heard baying at four different pitches. Two of them are big. Hate to imagine the jaws on those two. The others are leaner. They're the fast ones."

"See you in the morning," she said, tucking her pack beneath her head as a pillow.

"I miss that delta pup," she heard Dalih murmur as she sank into sleep. "Even if he wasn't really mine."

—o—

They woke refreshed and set out as soon as the shadows succumbed to the dawn.

At first, they could hear the baying of the dogs, but the noise grew fainter and fainter. It had a tentative, confused quality to it. Soon they reached a point where even Veyrenn could no longer hear it.

Three hours later they had a bit of decent luck when they accidentally encountered a long-abandoned syrup-maker's cottage and vathouse. The buildings were little more than ruins. The garden was likewise nearly reclaimed by the forest. Yet where the arbors had once been, several thick mosh vines stood tall, too thick now and treelike to fall over. They brimmed with ripe fruit. The fugitives ate some right away — it was worth the extra heaviness in the gut to have the sugar and the refreshing aftertaste to speed them on their way. They tucked more into their packs to have when evening came.

Three hours after that, Elenya was beginning to believe they might finally have won free, then her group reached the apex of a small ridge just as a contingent of Dragon's men reached it from the other direction.

Both groups were clad in forest colors. Both had been moving silently. Elenya had only to see the expression on the face of the man closest to her to know that the enemy, however much they may have been trying to find them, had not expected to find them right then and there, already up so close.

She did what instinct told her to do. She charged.

Only as her body was hurtling forward did her mind become conscious of the strategy she was employing. She drew her rapier. The man in front of her—the patrol leader, from the alertness in his eyes— drew his own blade in time to parry. If he had been slower, she would have sought an immediate kill. Instead she deflected his weapon away and brushed past him. She slashed backward after she was clear, aiming without looking at his hamstring. She felt the blade cut deep.

She did not turn to reengage. She sprinted past and reached her true goal—the pair of archers toward the back of the squad.

One had finished stringing his bow, but was still pulling an arrow from his quiver when her blade plunged into his throat. Bright arterial blood spurted out, splattering her as she engaged the second man.

Her target knew it was too late for arrows. He left the string loose and swung the bow like a club. He caught her on the wrist of the hand she raised to fend off the blow. Before he could land another, she thrust.

And missed. He was quick-footed, and knew how vulnerable he was with no proper weapon at his command. He had dodged just as she committed to the attack.

He glanced behind her as if one of his compatriots was about to blindside her. She wasn't fooled. She did sidestep—just in case—but only to put herself in the right spot to thrust again at the archer. As he swung the bow again, she dropped to the ground. Her blade snaked upward and plunged deep into his groin.

As any man would at such a time, he curled into a ball and flung himself back. She sprung in, staying close. She had missed the femoral artery; she needed to deliver a lethal wound.

And she did, right below the sternum and into the huge vein below the heart, but as she did so, he kicked. She flung her leg out of the way, but not soon enough to avoid contact. The blow rendered her shin as numb as her wrist.

He kicked again. It was a death spasm. She dodged it, but fell over when all of her weight ended up on her injured leg.

She rolled, partly from momentum, and partly as a defensive tactic.

No one was coming at her. The archer's glance had indeed been an attempt to fool her. She took a moment to test her leg. The cramping was fading into mere twinges. Good enough. Her wrist was better as well.

She had no time to add up a tally, but she could tell with one scan from left to right that her group was not outnumbered. All across the crest of the ridge, where one of the Dragon's men was to be found, one of hers was engaged with him.

Dalih was immersed in an exchange with the patrol leader. She had not hamstrung him after all. He did have a deep cut on his leg. It was limiting his footwork. But he was good with his sword.

Elenya trusted Dalih to take care of himself. She turned to the right, just in time to see a burly swordsman bury his sword point in Veyrenn's midsection. Veyrenn collapsed into a patch of ferns.

The burly man turned to meet Elenya's charge. His first swipe had no finesse, but it didn't need to. She had to spring back, forced to execute a complete backward roll.

Her opponent pressed in quickly. But not foolishly, despite his size. He avoided her counter.

And so the bout began in earnest. He was the best of them, she could tell. Better than the patrol leader.

She felt slow. She had so often worn the Dragonslayer's gauntlet in recent years that she had grown accustomed to accentuated speed. Three times her rapier darted in toward an opening in her foe's guard. He deflected the first two thrusts, and was barely pinked by the third.

When he countered, she moved back so sluggishly — by her former standards — that she nearly lost her sword hand.

But she was still Elenya of Garthmorron Hold. Still the former student of Troy of Calinin South. Inevitably, the big man did what big men always did when fighting her. They assumed they could overcome her with strength instead of technique.

His thrust whisked past her chest an instant after she had turned out of its way.

Her simultaneous thrust went right into his mouth and into the stem of his brain.

She spun in a circle as she retreated, taking in the whole tableau. She had no need to fight on. The battle had turned. Three of her men had won their bouts. They cut down the remaining enemies from behind. It was the point when honor leaves the field. Elenya did not intervene. They weren't in a position to leave alive men who would worsen the odds of escape.

As expected, Dalih had been victorious. He was wiping off his blade on the dead patrol leader's tunic. Six others of her group had survived. Nyor was lying supine on the leaf litter, unmoving, a gash in his right eye explaining what had eliminated him from the fight, and from the chance to walk away from it.

Nyor had been young. He was one of the rebellion's newest recruits, joining after Alemar and Toren and the others had departed for Elandris. Elenya regretted she knew almost nothing about him.

Veyrenn groaned.

She knelt down in the ferns beside him, opposite Bainne, who was applying pressure to the wound. Blood seeped through Bainne's fingers despite how firmly he was bearing down. Veyrenn's face was growing more pale by the moment.

Elenya took the stricken man's hand and held it. They had no time for words. His eyes closed. When he let his next breath go, he drew no more in to replace it.

Elenya let go. Bainne lifted his hands away.

She rose. Dalih was standing there watching.

She saw that two others of her men had sustained cuts, one on the upper arm, one on the forearm. Comrades were cleaning the slices and preparing to stitch them with catgut. The pair would have trouble if more tree-climbing became necessary, but they were fully able to run.

Two fatal casualties. The enemy had lost eleven. She supposed that was a victory. But the enemy could afford to lose eleven.

They had been lucky. They would not fare as well if the main force caught up with them. The men they had just fought had removed all their armor in order to move quickly and relatively soundlessly. They had been meant as a flanking force, trying to trap Elenya and her group more than to clash with them outright. The larger group would not be as lightly outfitted.

Dalih was still beside her. Finally she noticed his expression. His slumped shoulders said he was properly aggrieved at the losses they had suffered, but he gazed at her with a bright regard.

"What is it?" she asked.

He answered in Zyraii. "I have finally seen you in battle."

Her brows rose. "And?"

"You were the wind that flattens the tent. As he said it would be."

The pain in her wrist and her shin throbbed a little less sharply. "Thank you," she replied. At least she still had that. When things came down to swords and blood, she knew what to do.

Dogs sounded. The baying came distinctly through the forest and up the slope to the ridgetop. It originated from a spot no more than a league away, right where they had been no more than an hour earlier.

Relentless.

"Get those wounds bound and let's move," she ordered, trying not to sound as aghast as she felt.

CHAPTER SEVEN

QUANDAI PACED IN the front room until he could no longer cope with the wait. He did what he usually did when he was unable to calm himself. He sought out the company of his wife.

Brikka was no longer in the kitchen. He found her in her alcove, knitting. He collapsed into the other chair.

"Remm's not back yet," he said.

"It could be that Stamren and Amdres were out for the evening," she suggested. "Remm might still be tracking them down."

"Maybe," he conceded.

"There's no need to worry yet," she said.

He said nothing.

"I mean it," she said. "I'm sure he'll turn up any moment. The strangers will be out from under our roof, and we'll be back to normal."

Again, he said nothing.

She lowered her hands to her lap, letting the knitting needles fall idle. "You're troubled in a way I've not seen."

He and Brikka had been married a long time. Many times over the years he had been troubled. But she was absolutely right.

"It doesn't really matter whether the strangers take shelter with Stamren or Amdres or at any other safehouse we can find for them," he said. "They've brought the war to Dragonsdeep."

"The war has always been here," she argued. "Since we were babies in our mothers' wombs."

"This is different," he said somberly.

She placed a hand over his. "My dear. One thing at a time. Tonight we send them away. Whatever troubles come later, we deal with later."

It was the first time in more years than he could recall that Brikka had failed him. She was offering a means to bottle his fear. That was no good. He *needed* his fear. He needed to make it his elixir and drink it. Otherwise how was he to make the right choice?

The door chime sounded. He nearly leaped out of his slippers.

"You barred the door," Brikka reminded him. "Remm's key isn't enough to let himself back in."

"Yes," Quandai said. "Of course."

He hurried toward the front of the house, shedding some of his gloom as he went. It would be good to see Stamren's face. Stamren might be elderly, but he could take charge of a situation like a man in his prime. Often Quandai felt his own steadiness emerge in the presence of that sort of example.

He unbarred the door and pulled it open.

It was indeed his nephew, though he was nearly obscured behind the looming figures of the two men on the stoop.

Oh, no. This would not do *at all*.

"Tollvar. Clavos. You shouldn't be here."

"But we are. Let us in and be quick about it, Quandai," said the man in front.

Quandai had little choice. He didn't dare let these two be seen standing around outside his front door, out where an informant might spy them. He stepped aside. The newcomers marched on past. They left their cloaks on.

Quandai gripped Remm by the collar as the youth attempted to follow in their wake. "What have you done? Where are Stamren and Amdres?"

"Never went for them," Remm admitted. "I spent the whole time finding Tollvar."

"How did you even *know* where to find Tollvar?"

"Solia knew. It was her idea."

"Of course it was." Quandai sighed. "Did you have to go along with it?"

He released his hold on his nephew's shirt and hurried on into the front room. He found his fool of a niece there, and she had brought Alemar with her. The prince and the two interlopers were facing off from opposite ends of Brikka's prized Iridainese carpet.

Tollvar and his compatriot were cut from the same cloth. Both muscular. Both tall. Clavos's features were marred by a knife scar that ran through one of his eyebrows. Tollvar bore a similar battle vestige across the back of his left hand. Quandai supposed men who had never met them before might suspect they were brothers. He knew without a doubt that *women* who had never met them before would see Tollvar and not even notice anyone was beside him.

Tollvar gazed down at Alemar. Down being the only way to describe it. Quandai had not really noticed before how short Alemar was. Then again, Tollvar could make any number of men seem short.

"Apparently you were invited here," Quandai said. "Surely that wasn't a good enough reason for you to be out and about on the streets."

"We were careful," Tollvar said. "No one saw our faces."

"If they had—"

"I don't answer to you, Quandai. In fact, no one does. Not even your own nephew and niece."

Clavos chuckled at that. Heat rose up Quandai's cheeks.

"Did you really think I could hear such news and stay tucked in a hideyhole?" Tollvar asked. "The first dragonslayers in fifteen centuries? That's something I had to see for myself." He peered past Alemar toward the doorway to the guest quarters. "The other two are shy, I take it?"

"It's hard work, killing a dragon," Alemar quipped. "They need their rest."

"A Cilendri accent. So it's true. The king's by-blow steps foot inside Elandris at long last."

"I'll not have you behave so in my house," Quandai interjected.

"We'll be gone soon enough, signpost maker. I'm here to see for myself if this fellow has something to offer to make up for the trouble he's brewed."

"Sorry about the trouble," Alemar said gruffly. "I was trying to win a war."

Tollvar nodded. "That much I appreciate. But you didn't succeed, and now I'm left with the aftermath."

"And who would *you* be?"

"I lead the resistance here in Dragonsdeep."

Quandai cleared his throat. "I would put it differently."

"Spare me," Tollvar said. "Who else could make the claim?"

"It's not the sort of thing to lay claim to. It only makes you a target."

"The people don't want conspirators working from the shadows. They want to follow someone whose name they've heard."

"Well, *the Dragon* has certainly heard your name," Quandai allowed.

"He has indeed. I don't consider that a mistake."

"Are you actually *unhappy* that my companions and I killed Gloroc's sister?" Alemar asked. "Oh, and we killed a wizard of the Ril during our escape. I suppose you're displeased about that as well."

Tollvar shrugged. "Vanril? He was scum. Glad he's dead. But thanks to your *activities*, the city is on high alert. The plans I had in motion are piss in the pot. And now we've word that Leyaril the Poisoner is on her way from Firsthold. She's worse than Vanril. If you're that good at killing Ril wizards, tell me how you plan to get her out of my way."

"I wouldn't get her out of *your* way," Alemar said. "I'd get her out of *my* way."

Tollvar folded his arms. "Dragonsdeep is *my* city."

"I'm the son of the king."

"You think your father has any authority here? You think we ever *want* him to?"

That hit home. Quandai could tell that particular thought had not occurred to Alemar. He watched closely as the expressions evolved on the young man's face. Surprise? Yes, that was one of them. Fury? Quandai expected it, but he did not see it. What he saw was someone adjusting his shoulders to take on more weight when he was already bearing a load so heavy he might buckle.

Alemar took a step toward Tollvar. "There are three men in this house who've defeated wizards of the Ril. My friend Toren, he's the one who killed Vanril. My friend Geim, he chopped off the head of a fellow over in Irigion whose blood melted the sword that made the cut. Don't know who that one was. Perhaps you would. Any of the order gone missing?"

"Hadradril," murmured Quandai, more to himself than to answer the question. He wondered how many companions Geim had lost in that altercation. Hadradril had been the most junior of the Ril, but he could not have gone down easily.

"As for me," continued Alemar, "I sat nose to nose with Omril, and when I was done with him, he was no longer a threat to me nor, far more important, a threat to my wife."

Tollvar still had not broken his stare off. "And?"

"A Ril witch on the way to Dragonsdeep? Why don't *you* have a turn? See how well you fare. Perhaps you can charm her into submission."

"Stop it!" Solia blurted. "This isn't going how this meeting was supposed to go!"

"I'll stop any time," Alemar told her.

Tollvar spread his arms wide. "I do not serve you. I do not serve the House of Olendim. I serve the people of Elandris. I welcome your help in freeing them from Gloroc's reign. When we see each other next — if that day should come — be prepared to show me we fight for the same cause."

The two visitors pulled their cowls over their heads and marched out.

Belatedly, Solia rushed across the room, but the door was closed by the time she reached the foyer.

Chin down, shoulders slack, she shuffled back. Quandai could not recall seeing her so deflated since, at age seven, she had finally accepted that her parents' ship truly never was going to make it back to port, and she and her brother really would have to live with him and Brikka for the rest of their childhood.

"You and your brother need to learn when to involve a man like that, and when not to," Quandai told her. He was shaking. Sweat was beading on his forehead. "Go back to your rooms now. We will speak in the morning. *At length.*"

He waved toward the family living quarters. Solia did not try to argue. She and Remm followed Brikka out of the room.

Quandai dabbed his forehead with his sleeve. "If that halfwit is seen before he makes it back to his hiding place, he'll have cost himself his life just for the chance to wave his baton at you."

"How can a man like that have any status at all within the resistance? Or was he simply lying about that?"

"He does have his faction. It's as he said — his name is known. He was arrested about a year ago. He managed to escape. Two days later, he led a successful assault on the dungeons and freed some of his comrades. It's been a year now, and the Dragon's security forces still have not caught him. That makes him a figure of admiration, particularly to the younger generation. When you live in a city that has been occupied as long as Dragonsdeep has, you take your heroes where you can find them."

"What about the men you sent your nephew after? The ones you mean to summon?"

"Good men. The best of men. You would have been safe with them."

"But they're not leaders?"

Quandai sighed. "Not of the sort it appears you came hoping to find. I'm sorry. Dragonsdeep has been breathing Gloroc's fumes for many decades now."

The weight became an almost visible thing on Alemar's shoulders. He slumped down on the main sofa.

Quandai took a place across from him on the smaller couch. "It's as I said to you at the door. You should not have come back. Even now your best course is to slip out of the dome and keep going."

"I can't do that," Alemar said.

"That sounds like pride. Careful or I won't be able to tell you apart from Tollvar."

"You think I want to be here?" Alemar asked. "I have a wife and baby. I was on my way back to them, but my instincts and my reason say the best chance I have to keep them safe is if I make my moves here, now, inside this city."

Quandai tried to smooth the wrinkle on the back of his left hand. "I am sorry about your wife and child. I understand you better now. Nevertheless my advice is the same. I think you are mistaken. I don't think you can do much here."

Alemar sighed. "You are not the man Treggei described."

Quandai hesitated. "What do you mean?"

"He said you were a man of resources."

"He gave me too rich a compliment."

"He said you saved him. Got him out of Dragonsdeep when the Worm's garrison was coming for him."

Quandai's heart began to pound. This was turning into the very sort of conversation he had wanted to avoid.

"Is that true or not?" Alemar asked.

"That was a different me," Quandai said. "A younger version of me."

Alemar chuckled softly, almost to himself. "I've had the privilege of studying under two especially wise men, one in Cilendrodel, and one in the Eastern Deserts. They both told me that people become more like themselves as they age, not less. What kind of man are you really, Quandai? I don't need advice, however sincere it is. I need your *help.* Have you any to give?"

Quandai was glad he was already sitting down. He tried to conceal the shaking of his bones.

"I *am* a man of resources. That much I admit."

"But you've held back. Why? You know I'm the son of Keron. You've been a royalist all your life. Are you unsure of me?"

Quandai's mouth was dry, making it hard to speak. Things were moving too quickly. He was never comfortable with fast-paced developments.

"Yes, I *am* unsure," Quandai found himself saying. "Of you? I don't know. Of me? Yes. I am contemplating what my role should be."

"Would you help a friend of Treggei?"

The question brought Quandai up short. "I..."

"Forget the issues of dynasty. Keep it personal. Would you help the friend of someone you once knew as a friend? Would you help that man help *his* friend? It's not wrong to say it's as simple as that."

Quandai was surprised to find he was no longer shaking and his heartbeat was slowing back to normal.

"You have given me something to think about," Quandai replied.

"Good."

Quandai stood up. And once up, found himself to be steady on his feet. "May I ask that we revisit this in the morning? I've had a long day, and you have been through an ordeal."

Alemar shook his head. "I'm afraid I'm not likely to get much rest tonight. My friend's condition is dire. Within a few hours I will have to...tend to him."

Quandai hated to see the pain in his guest's expression. "That sounds ominous."

"I fear it is. I don't think I have any way to save him. If what I try goes wrong, he will die."

"And if you don't try?"

"He will die."

"I'm sorry," Quandai said. And somewhat to his surprise, he found he couldn't just leave it there. "May I see him?"

Alemar hesitated.

"You know the sort of work I do," Quandai added. "The mortal remains of many a man or woman has passed through these doors. By the time I receive them, the only sentiment I can extend is despair. It would do me good to view your companion while he still breathes. There is still hope, I trust?"

"Yes. Of course."

"For once, I would like to feel some of that."

They went back to the guest quarters. They found Geim leaning over Toren. The latter appeared to be as absent from the normal world as he had been before, but Geim's eyes shone bright.

"He spoke," Geim said.

"What did he say?" asked Alemar.

"Couldn't quite make it out. It was murmurs. His eyes stayed closed. I think he was arguing with his grandfather's grandfather."

Quandai's brows drew together. "Fever dreams? He's that far gone?"

Alemar explained. "It's something that Vanihr of the Far South can do. The memories of their ancestors can be written into their minds. They call it their totem. It can feel as though the ancestors are actually alive within them. Sometimes they carry on conversations. Of a sort."

A memory rose up with such power it left Quandai blinking. "I may have something that can help! I'll be right back."

He sped from the room, letting himself be guided by recollections he'd not revisited in years—not since the Dragon's chamberlain had awarded him this house, and he had gone about putting his things in their places within it.

The larder. Yes. He lit a lamp and slipped into the narrow space. Brikka kept it well supplied. He barely could find clear areas of floor on which to place his feet.

Now where...? Yes. Behind the harrow root. Not a spice often used. Only at the winter solstice, because of the tradition. He moved aside the sealed jar and worked free the loose brick in the wall behind.

He was almost surprised to find what he was after. It was not often he thought of it.

He pulled it into the open: A small stone reliquary case. Clutching it with care, he rushed back to the guest room.

"This might be what you need," he said. He blew the dust off the case, lifted the lid, and pulled out a bracelet.

Its gem was blue. A light was coruscating within it, as if it held something alive.

"Whuh," Geim blurted in surprise.

"You've seen this sort of talisman before?" Alemar asked.

"I would never have thought there was more than one of *those* in existence."

"And?"

"Quandai is right. He may have brought us something that can help Toren."

CHAPTER EIGHT

WHEN THE BLACKNESS lifted from Toren's mind, he found himself sitting cross-legged on a granite outcropping in a beautiful forest glade, where a stream flowed down into a small lake. He knew this place. It was near the heart of his tribe's territory. At certain times of the year women of the Fhali would gather and use the natural hollows of the granite to grind meal out of acorn or cone nut or sweetgrit.

Toren had occasionally come here within his own lifetime, but it was his grandfather Neppen who remembered it as a favorite place. As a small boy, Neppen had often sat beside his mother, savoring the caress of direct sunlight, laughing inside at the way his adolescent sisters went on and on about the boys they imagined had noticed them. Later in childhood Neppen would enter the sphere of his father and uncles and his elder brother. That was challenging and exciting and joyful in its own way, but here, within this glade and among his female kinfolk? This had been a refuge unlike any that came after.

And so it was a refuge for Toren now. That was one of the blessings of carrying a totem within oneself. One could retreat into a thousand special memories. One could pause and examine every detail—or at least, every detail that had managed to catch the attention of the ancestor who had been there in the flesh. Just as Neppen had once done, Toren studied a snail as it navigated through the itchberry bramble at the edge of the outcropping. He watched his aunt—Neppen's aunt, that is—lift a milk-laden breast to her new daughter's mouth, and gasp as the baby latched on. He helped fetch a netful of shelled acorns from the stream where they had been leaching—his mother tasted one, spat it out, and had him restore the batch to the water. All of these experiences felt as though they were happening right then, to Toren himself. And yet he could also hold himself back, aware of who he actually was, aware that many years had since passed. That was the best part of all, because he knew, as Neppen could not have, that nothing bad was going to disturb this scene.

He adjusted the way he inhabited the memory. The women, the maiden girls, and the other little boys faded away, leaving him alone on the granite amid the trees beside the lake. He was now more Toren and less Neppen. As Toren, he could savor the setting not just as a manifestation of his grandfather's nostalgia , but appreciate how wonderful it was just to be home.

He couldn't entirely remember what had happened to him in whatever place his body currently occupied, nor where that place was aside from the fact it was not in any part of The Wood. He chose to leave that setting at a distance. He didn't want to be there.

He sensed the murmur of the many consciousnesses embedded in his totem, but faintly, unobtrusively, as if ducks were splashing and chattering among themselves on the far side of the lake. His ancestors were not intruding. He had privacy. That was the way he wanted it. That was what he needed. This glade might exist only by means of summoning it up from Neppen's memory, but that didn't mean Toren wanted Neppen's presence and his commentary.

He stood. As he did, he grew until he was no longer a small boy, but full-sized, clad in his true shape, with long legs and the physique of a well-conditioned modhiv. He jogged across the outcropping, past the itchberry bramble and into the forest.

The shade embraced him. He was even more at home beneath the canopy of the branches, darting around hanging vines, filling his lungs with the fecund aroma of log fungus and trefoil and mulch wort.

He came to a broad tree and found it arrayed with hammocks. Another memory. This was where his fifth-great-grandfather Bost, a hunter, had spent so many nights. The game was always plentiful here, so he and his comrades returned again and again, lounging and drinking *chotji*, knowing that other hunting bands of Fhali in other parts of the forest were still out stalking prey, bellies empty.

He jogged further. The scene transformed again, taking him to the secluded niche in the bole of a fatflower tree where his great-great-grandfather Koipen had once found both of his lovers waiting to welcome him.

And so it went, from one place to the next, from one memory to the next, from one generation of his ancestors to another.

From time to time a peculiar whisper rose up at the edge of his hearing. The voice did not belong to any of his ancestors. He knew if he tried, he could identify the owner, but he wasn't going to listen to any person that called to him from *that place*.

He had no idea whether he slept or not. The scenes evolved. He even spent a few moments deep in the territory of the Amane, a place Koipen recalled as the setting of an exciting confrontation with the cannibals, and at another point, he saw the volcanic peaks of the Firelands in the distance. He enjoyed it all.

Finally his surroundings shifted in a way they had not done until then. The trees dissolved away. The sun emerged. He was ambling through a landscape of rolling hills and meadowlands. In the distance were cultivated fields.

He stopped.

The Flat. It must be.

That meant this was sure to be a memory of his ancestor Naemor. Toren had seen The Flat with his own eyes only once, and only from its edge. Naemor on the other hand had penetrated deep into the realm of the Alahihr many times, reconnoitering for the tribe, taking revenge twenty or more times for his murdered brother. He had died in The Flat, his luck finally running out the year after he had passed his totem to his son.

Very well. Toren would explore The Flat. For some reason the relentlessly open sky and the vista of croplands did not perturb him. He couldn't recall why he found them unthreatening, but it was so. With no obstacles to navigate, he slipped into an easy, loping run—a warrior's pace, meant to chew up distance without stealing away the vitality he might need should he have to fight.

He ventured up a slope. Cresting the top, he saw a small valley in front of him. It contained a farmhouse and barn and a few small outbuildings.

The Alahihr did not build structures of this sort, with walls of wattle and daub and roofs made of thatch. They used lumber. They used shingles. It was part of their perversion, killing the sacred trees of The Wood and rendering them into shapes nature did not mean for them to have.

This was not The Flat. This was not Naemor's memory.

And yet it felt like a memory. It was as familiar as lying in a hammock as a boy, watching his mother preparing the evening meal—slipping a snake onto a skewer and positioning it over the cookfire before going back to grinding sweetgrit with her mortar and pestle. He was seeing this small farm through the eyes of someone who had once seen it. Someone who wished he could forget.

Suddenly he was in the middle of the farmyard, without having descended on foot from the ridge. The clear blue sky had vanished. A drizzling rain was falling, but not hard enough to quench the odor of smoke. He could see now that the farmhouse and barn were only shells, the heart of each reduced to ash and charcoal.

A young man lay dead in the pigsty, two arrows jutting from his back. The bodies of two women were sprawled against the outdoor oven, a garrotte left in place around the neck of the middle-aged one, the skull of the crone smashed in.

In the middle of the yard, not far from where Toren was standing, lay the farmer on a large patch of bloodied ground. A warrior clad only in a loin clout was crumpled nearby, face down, runic tattoos running down the length of all four limbs and even up onto the cheeks of his buttocks. This last corpse reeked with a peculiar foulness — not of death, because none of the slain had been dead long enough to decay.

A reaver. Why did he know that word? A reaver of...Thiagra.

Then he saw the girl's harvest smock in the mud.

This was not a memory he wanted to be in. He didn't understand how he had been steered into it. He had no intention of staying.

He turned, chose a direction at random, and rushed forward, willing the scene to change. He deliberately pictured a grove in The Wood near his home village, a place he personally knew, and that most of his ancestors had visited many times, including his father.

But when his surroundings completed their rearrangement, he was not in The Wood. He was on the top of a crag in the midst of an ocean.

He sensed human presences around him, people who had been there when whatever happened here had happened, but Toren refused to let them manifest. He turned to choose a different direction, gathering his concentration to force another shift.

But when he completed the turn, he was confronted by the sight of a huge dragon. It lay crumpled on the rocks, eyes closed, an arrow buried so deep in its flesh only the feathers showed.

"No," Toren said aloud. He turned away.

A voice called, "What have you done?" It was a voice he had never heard before, but it was as familiar as his own.

Toren was now standing at the edge of the crag. Down in the waves a horde of eellike creatures were darting away from the corpse of yet another dragon, heading out to the open sea.

One of the creatures paused and stared up at him. Stared with the regard of a sentient being.

Another of the things swam up to the staring one. As its head lifted from the water, Toren made out a discoloration on the side of its head, a birthmark of sorts.

He knew that marking. He had seen it on the side of the face of a dragon. A dragon as dead as the one behind him now. That distinctive pattern had been right in front of him as he reached into that dead dragon's mouth and broke off a pair of her teeth.

He was now more determined than ever to get out of there. Belatedly he realized he knew a sure way to do so, and was angry at himself for failing to think of it earlier. All he had to do was do something that no one would do if they were there in a real place and time.

He flung himself off the precipice.

Instantly his environment changed, and this time it changed according to his desire. He landed on a path in The Wood, a path along the edge of Fhali territory that he had patrolled as a scout, a path along which he had proved himself a worthy member of his tribe.

His knees nearly buckled from the impact, and the joints complained as he set off at a full run, but he knew it was illusion. His true body had sustained no harm.

He ran until he was breathless, concentrating all the while upon keeping himself surrounded by his beloved, familiar trees and ferns. He ran until he reached a set of piled stones near a towering fissurebark tree. The pile denoted the edge of his people's lands. He stopped.

"Did you really kill her?" The voice was the same as the one he had heard on the crag. "What about the other one? The one that stared back so hard?"

Toren whirled around. A few paces away, standing in the dappled light, was an elderly man. Hair grey. Beard white.

The setting was still The Wood. Toren did not have to brace against a stout ocean breeze. No sulfurous fumes were leaking from between the lips of a dead dragon. The only thing out of place was the old fellow. No denizen of The Wood would ever wear quarn-silk robes of office, embroidered in gold thread, bearing the sigil of Elandris. No denizen of The Wood, for that matter, possessed a beard.

"What are you doing here?" Toren demanded.

"I would have thought you'd know more about that than I. You are obviously a member of the Vanihr race."

"But you are not my ancestor."

"I'm sorry to hear that. I believe I'd be proud to have you as a descendant. I didn't mean to intrude. My being here is a surprise to me."

"You're saying you had no part in it?" Toren asked.

"A part in it? Well, I suppose I had a role in the sense that I willingly placed myself on a bed and let a spell be cast upon me. I did it with the understanding that the enchantment would craft a replica of my memories, and that someday that distillation might be placed inside another person and become manifest. I see that the process must have succeeded. Miranda and the Vanihr shaman she hired seemed to think it would."

"If you're a friend of Miranda, I don't want you here."

The old man blinked. "Friend? No. I wouldn't use that word. I only call someone a friend if I trust them to do as I would do. But I was acquainted with Miranda. Over the long run I stayed on good terms with her. It was *important* that I stay on good terms with her."

"I am *not* on good terms with Miranda," Toren declared.

"She used you?"

"Yes."

"I know the feeling."

"What about you?" Toren challenged. "Are you using me right now?"

"Not by intention. Though I can see why you would feel set upon. You were forced to witness what I went through. My memories of that awful day. It's bad enough I had to live through all that. Now it's as if you had to do so as well. I'm sorry. If anyone had asked me, I would have spared you."

"Who *are* you?"

"I'm not anybody anymore, I expect. I'm sure I've been dead for quite some time. Strange, though. I feel quite like myself."

"Answer the question."

"I am—I was—Polk, First Steward of Elandris."

At first, the name meant nothing, but Toren had the sense that he should know it. He calmed his mind and let the answer surface. And yes, the answer was there, embedded in the fragments of memory he had absorbed from Obo during the language-lesson trances at the temple of Struth. Obo was a devout scholar not only of magic, but of the history of the kingdom he served.

"The dragonslayer."

The stranger frowned. "There aren't many who call *me* that. It's true that I shot the arrow that killed Triss, but I'm not sure I had any more say in the event than the arrow did."

"You mean to drag me back there," Toren accused.

"Back where?"

"To Dragonsdeep." He remembered now. He remembered it all—his journey to the northern continent, the assault on Gloroc's palace. The only vague part was what had sent him into his totem memories. The last he could recall, he was striding invisibly through the streets looking up at the dome, wondering if he would ever reach the theater.

"Dragonsdeep is not a name familiar to me," Polk said.

Toren wanted to call him a liar, but if the man inhabited him the way his true ancestors inhabited him, he couldn't lie to Toren—unless somehow he were lying to himself at the same time.

"It used to be called Wizardsdeep," Toren said. "The last of the Dragonslayer's sixty cities."

"Sixty? The Elandris I knew contained considerably fewer cities than that. Is that where you are now? Your body, I mean?"

"Yes."

"Can't say I want to go there. I like *this*. Sunlight shining through leaves instead of vartham glass? I never had the chance to venture as far as The Wood while I was a living man. It's even better than I imagined. What is that wonderful aroma?"

Toren waved at the vines crawling up the trunk of the fissurebark tree. Bright yellow-and-cream flowers adorned the climbing strands. "Lovers woodbine."

"Ah. We had something like that on my father's estates. It was called moist maiden. I suppose that's because it gave off its best scent at night."

He went to the nearest vine, plucked a bloom, and held it up to his nose.

"Wonderful," he murmured. But then, still carefully embracing the flower in his thumb and finger, he turned over his hand and regarded the gnarled flesh and mottled coloration. "Shame I have to smell it with such an old nose. You'd think with a lifetime of memories as reference, I would wear the shape of my younger days."

"That's not how it works," Toren said. "Whenever my ancestors speak to me as you are doing now, I see them at the age they were when they put themselves in the totem."

"Is that how it has to be, or do you make it so?"

That was a question Toren had never contemplated. He thought of the memory he had so recently been wrapped within — the memory of someone barely into his adulthood. Suddenly the man standing in front of the woodbine was young and fit.

Polk regarded his supple, smooth, blemish-free hands. He held a strand of his long hair in front of his face and smiled at the rich auburn hue.

"Outstanding. I'm liking this place more and more."

Toren concentrated again.

"Now what are you doing?" Polk asked.

"Trying to make you disappear."

"I don't think you should be alone right now. Not with *those* on your hands."

Toren blinked. He raised his hands. They were enclosed within the Dragonslayer's gauntlets. The talismans had not been there when he had first manifested in Neppen's memory of the granite glade by the lake. At what point the gauntlets had reappeared, he wasn't sure.

"Those are *his* work, aren't they?" Polk asked.

"The Dragonslayer? Yes."

"Must have taken quite some sorcery, and quite some time, to manufacture those. That's just like him. Putting his effort into things instead of people. My advice? Take them off."

Toren clenched his fists, anchoring the gauntlets in place that much more. "You're trying to trick me."

Polk sighed. "You're not the type to trust people at first, are you? They have to prove themselves to you. You're a lot like him. I imagine that's why you would be able to wear his talismans in the first place."

Toren said nothing.

"Keep them if you want," Polk continued. "Apparently they haven't killed you yet. I suppose that's a good sign."

"I want you to leave," Toren said.

"How? I don't know how it is that I arrived, so I certainly don't know how to leave. Besides, as I said, I don't think you should be alone."

"I'm not taking them off," Toren insisted.

"You've said as much. I have a counter-proposal. Why don't you show me around this beautiful forest of yours? We'll talk. We seem to be stuck with one another. We might as well fill the time."

Toren almost said no simply because he had not been the one to suggest what they would do, but the fact was he was desperate to be moving again. Movement provided some relief from the sensation that he was caught in a snare. So they set out down the path. Toren made Polk walk beside him where he could keep him in sight.

The transitions behaved themselves. Their surroundings blurred. They came to a stream. This was a spot where as a youth, Koipen had enjoyed swinging on a rope from bank to bank. And sure enough, the rope was hanging from the tree. Toren made his companion take the first turn. Polk hesitated, as if struggling to shed the notion that he was a very old man, but then performed the crossing itself with grace and coordination. Toren followed. Side by side they slipped into the thick woods beyond.

Things shifted again, bringing them to a destination Toren had not anticipated: the interior of a tent. He recognized the furs on the floor, the gourds of steaming water, the lacemoss for sopping up blood. This was the tent in which his son Rhi had been born, looking just as it had on the day of that birth, except for the lack of a woman in labor and her attendants. Not a fragment of his totem, then, but a personal memory, one of those he hoped to pass down to Rhi in due course. He hadn't known it was possible to revisit his own experiences in this way.

He lowered himself to the place beside the furs that he had occupied on that precious day. Polk settled where the elder midwife had sat while supervising her apprentices.

"Something you said has been nagging at me," Polk said. "You referred to Miranda as if she's alive."

"Yes. She is alive."

"Does that mean *he* is alive?"

"Apparently so. Though that's something I learned very recently."

Polk studied his youthful hands again. "That dragon you killed. It was an adult?"

"Recently fledged, but yes, she was an adult."

"I know something of dragons, and how long they take to mature. So it's been far more than just a century or two since my memories were plucked from me and preserved."

"Elandris was founded about fifteen centuries ago, so I'm told."

"How is it the Dragonslayer is still alive? When I last saw him, he was already running out of ways to rejuvenate. I can't believe he could have found anything new to try."

"It was done with dragon magic, I believe."

"That's an approach I wouldn't have expected. What dragon would possibly have helped him?"

Toren may not have asked for Polk to be there with him, but by now he was willing to concede that it wasn't Polk's idea. He was perhaps not an enemy, nor a spy. In any case, telling him the story didn't seem as if it would cause any harm.

So Toren did. He told of being kidnapped and taken from The Wood to the temple of Struth. Of meeting the being he thought was an ancient, decrepit dragon. Of the retrieval of the gauntlets in Cilendrodel and the mission to Dragonsdeep, and the slaying not of

Gloroc, but Gloroc's heretofore unknown sister.

Polk was quiet. He was passing his hand over the steam rising from the gourds. Had this been a real setting, where time passed according to its rules, the water in the containers would long since have cooled.

"I'm so very sorry you were caught up in their schemes, Toren," Polk said at last. "I know better than anyone how you must feel."

"I see that now. I have a question for you."

"Yes?"

"You realized how high the cost was of tying your life to them, and yet you continued to stay by their side," Toren pointed out. "You helped them build Elandris. Why?"

"I didn't stay for *them*. I stayed for Elandris."

As he spoke, the years bore down upon Polk once more. He lost his youthful face and supple body and transformed back into the older version Toren had first met.

"They hooked me with the right bait," Polk went on. "I wanted to help my people. The people of Moin. That didn't change because of what happened on the quest. It just let me know that the process was going to include keeping watch on those two. When I was an old man and lay down to let my memories be cast into a totem, I was still observing that vigil."

The light in the tent grew dim—just a soft glow from the wick burning in the oil in the vessel of bear tallow. That was how it had looked after the birthing was done, and Toren had sat there watching his newborn son and his mother sleeping off the exhaustion of the ordeal they had both been through.

That was too private a memory to share. Toren stood and slipped through the tent flaps. A rustling noise told him Polk had followed.

He took a few steps into the trees. Contemplated what Polk had said.

"Do you have laceleaf trees in The Wood?" Polk asked.

Toren frowned. "In places. Mostly near the coast. Why?" He

turned to find Polk gazing off down a well-maintained garden path.

"Nice bench," Polk commented.

Toren looked up. Where the gaps in the foliage should have displayed only stars and the glow of Motherworld, he saw a dome of vartham glass.

"It's not my doing," Polk assured him.

"I know. It's *my* doing. I have things I have to do here."

"I see. Can I help?"

"Actually, I think you can."

Toren placed his left gauntlet within the grip of his right. And pulled.

CHAPTER NINE

AUNTIE WAS ENJOYING the forest. The nag parrot cruised ahead whenever the patrol encountered a fruit-bearing tree, scattering whatever lesser birds and insects might be feasting there. She never ate pristine berries or drupes. She was too smart for that. She let herself be guided by the example of the creatures native to the area, sampling whatever they had found to be fulfilling. She never gorged. She only tasted. Then she flew away, waiting for the smaller birds to return, and flew back, cackling as they again dodged madly out of her way.

The men of the patrol tried to pretend they weren't watching. They chopped vines to clear the trail. They adjusted the loads on the backs of the oeikani. They wiped sweat from their brows. Inevitably their gazes would drift up to the bright yellow blur of activity. When they thought the parrot had noticed their scrutiny, they glanced down with a suddenness that brought a smile to Enril's face.

The detachment wended its painstaking way along. These wilds were roadless. Of course. The fugitives they hunted had chosen the hard paths, the ways that made following difficult, especially for a company such as theirs, of eighty men, dozens of pack beasts, the cook's wains, and the anguish cages — the latter, alas, still empty. Enril did not let himself be annoyed by the pace. They had all they required to keep going for weeks. They had the numbers to swap out the runners of the squads who hounded the heels of their prey. The forces of the Dragon therefore remained fresh while his opponents were being driven to a paralyzing weariness.

The land grew level and the trail widened. Enril eased his oeikani back until he was beside the wain that carried Omril and his nurse attendant.

Omril was sitting on the bench that had been built into the wain for him. The padded straps — meant to hold him in place if need be — were loose and lying at his feet.

"He has not tried to climb out again?" Enril asked.

"He has. Twice," the attendant reported. "But he stopped as soon as I put a hand on his shoulder."

"Good."

Enril wished the straps were not needed at all. Perhaps soon they could be stowed away. His beloved was improving steadily. He no longer drooled. He no longer stared without blinking. Holding a bowl and eating from it was too still too much for him, but he could sometimes hold a flask and drink from it unaided. He cooperated when the attendant washed and dressed him.

If only he would speak.

At the moment, Omril had his head tilted back. He was peering at the crown of one of the giant trees as if he expected the Dragon himself to land there and summon him to the roof of the forest.

Omril did not look at Enril. He seldom did. But Enril knew his beloved was aware of his proximity. He saw it in the way the elder wizard sat still without twitching, how he breathed evenly rather than panted. For the most part it showed most clearly in reverse. The farther off Enril went, the more agitated Omril became.

Enril reached out and placed a hand on the top of the wain's side rail. How he wanted to do more — to touch Omril himself, to feel the warmth of his flesh. But even this minor gesture of attentiveness had drawn a glance from the guardsman walking on the other side of the wain. After a moment, Enril withdrew his hand. He tried to find contentment simply riding beside the conveyance while the terrain still allowed him to do so.

In every realm across the face of Tanagaran, there were men who shared their beds with other men, and women who shared theirs with other women. In some places, this was seen as a perversion, bearing risks as severe as flogging, castration, or even execution. In other places, it was tolerated as the way things were. But nowhere in all the lands Enril had visited — and he had visited many — had such men and such women been applauded for their natures.

Powerful men could do what they wanted. Enril was a powerful man. Omril had been powerful as well. Back in Elandris, they could have let their bond with one another be openly known. None would have dared to speak against it. But even there, they had been discreet. And here on this journey, the attendant shared the tent, and it was the attendant who laid hands upon Omril when it was time to change his diaper or rinse the grime from his beard.

Men would always obey a wizard of the Ril, but it was best if they *wanted* to obey. He let these men — especially Grey Sergeant Lhan, the next in command of those he travelled with — see only the sort of leader they wanted to see.

That was the first great lesson Enril had taken from Gloroc: Do not depend on power to solve every goal. Make those closest to you believe in you. Wise words. Yet every day since their departure from Hole Bay, he had found it increasingly difficult to maintain the façade.

Auntie had vanished, exploring up ahead. She came fluttering back sooner than he anticipated. She landed on Omril's shoulder, but did not nuzzle his ear as usual. Enril understood at once she was simply using the shoulder as a perch conveniently near Enril.

"Dead dogs," said the parrot.

A moment later the twitter of a scout's whistle filtered out of the trees ahead. Enril was already off his oeikani and jogging to the head of the group. Lhan fell in with him, as did a dozen of the select fighting men. The drivers and tradesmen remained with the gear and supplies, the remaining soldiers taking defensible positions around and among them and readying themselves for a possible ambush.

Enril soon saw the point man. He was standing in the open, beckoning.

Along the trail lay the bodies of two dogs. They were the leaner pair, the fast ones who tended to range ahead while the large ones remained with the men. Arrows jutted from the carcasses.

"There's a lot of trampled ground from here leading onward," reported the scout. "Our men were charging."

Lhan gestured and the group moved along. It was as the scout said. Deep footprints and scattered leaf litter proved how suddenly the warriors had been moving. A bit farther along they came to a clearing where nearly all of the bracken had been trampled or otherwise violently crushed.

The other two dogs lay there, along with broad scattering of human bodies.

Lhan had his men check to be sure the area was secure and confirm that there were no survivors. Enril was already certain there were not. The mephitis of death hung in the glade like swamp fog, the aroma a mixture of the sourness of decay and the metallic tang of spilled blood. Ants were crawling over every corpse, so much so that the flies and carrion gnats could barely find places to land.

The grey sergeant finished counting. He winced. "It's all of them. All of ours, that is."

Enril had guessed as much. That made twelve dead, to go along with the eleven men of the other advance party they had lost four days back. And it was all of the dogs.

The squad had not gone down without inflicting damage. Over to one side, the bodies of four rebels had been carefully arranged in a row, lying as if asleep, hands upon their torsos, holding sprigs of flowers. The fugitives had not been able to afford the time to bury their comrades. By now the flowers had wilted and the ants were crawling over them just as enthusiastically as if the slain had been left where they had fallen. Even so, the gesture had been made.

There was no woman's body there in the row. Enril reflected

back upon the story he had recently heard of the rebel princess at the sack of Puriel's castle. *Hard to kill, that one.* Indeed.

Two scouts came up to Enril and Lhan, having examined the tracks heading off into the forest. "Four rebels left," announced the senior of the pair. "They've been gone at least a day."

"Still able to move at speed?" Lhan asked.

"It seems so."

Enril knelt down where the spoor was clear in the dirt between the stalks of the bracken. Judging by the modest size and depth of one footprint, it had been left by the princess herself. He placed the fingers of his right hand in that print. From his pouch of talismans, he selected the sphere of copper, palmed it in his left hand, and slipped into a trance.

His opponent had been smart throughout the chase. She had not cast any spells. Active magic would have been a beacon. Enril had hoped for that, these past many days during the chase, but she had not indulged him. Still, now that the dogs were gone, he had to try.

The trance distorted the passage of time. Enril opened his eyes and saw that the main party had caught up. Off to one side, away from the stink, the cooks had hung pots and were beginning to gather deadfall for the porridge fires. Tents were being raised. Graves were being dug.

He stood. Took a deep breath. Waited for the disorientation to fade.

Lhan approached and stood at attention.

"As you were," Enril said. "We'll return to the coast. We'll have to find another way to bring our target to us."

The grey sergeant passed along the order that the group would spend the night there. He did it quietly, going to the quartermaster, the head cook, and his squad leaders and speaking to them individually and privately. He knew the protocol Enril preferred — failure did not warrant a loud announcement.

Many of the members of the patrol walked with a light step as they set up hammocks and tents. They tried to avoid displaying their ease to Enril, but he saw it anyway. He understood it. The grueling pace was now a thing of the past. These men were on the verge of heading back to the safety of territory where the Dragon's forces held sway.

Auntie landed on Enril's shoulder. She rocked back and forth. "Uncle," she said. Following the hint, Enril turned and found that Omril was standing unattended over by the cooking area. He was once again gazing at the crowns of the trees, oblivious to the activity around him. He had managed to put himself in the way of the men trying to arrange the camp in its proper tactical order.

The workers went about their tasks without disturbing Omril, giving him plenty of clearance even when often it required them to detour. No one glared at him. No one muttered a complaint loud enough for Enril to hear. They knew better.

Enril went to Omril, took him by the elbow, and guided him to the mage tent. The laborers had already assembled the frame and had secured it to one of the giant padleaf trees. Now they were fastening the canvas. Inside, the nurse attendant was arranging the cots and the clothing chests.

The attendant looked up and saw Enril standing there. His cheeks reddened. Before he could babble apologies, Enril gestured for him to continue with what he was doing.

Finally Omril glanced down from the treetops and saw the familiar structure, which he and Enril and the attendant had shared since leaving the harbor. He grunted.

Enril couldn't be sure Omril had actually recognized the tent, but it was the right reaction. Enril gave his beloved's arm a surreptitious squeeze.

And then he immediately turned back the other way as if to show Omril wasn't the person he most wanted to linger with. He spotted someone who was taking no pleasure in the moment. He was a pudgy man with a bird's-nest beard. Not a warrior. Not a cook, either. It took Enril a moment to place him. Ah, yes. He was the dog trainer. During those times when the dogs had been out actively hunting the fugitives, they had been managed by one or more of the fighting men. The trainer was part of the rear echelon, there to keep the dogs content, to feed them and nurse them during rest periods, and to remind them which handlers they were to obey.

Enril remembered now. The trainer was a local man who had bred the dogs himself, had raised them from the litter to adulthood. He'd been paid well for their use, and had already been assured that if the dogs died while serving the Dragon's cause, he would be paid further—an amount more than sufficient to purchase new dogs of equal or better quality. Those considerations did not seem to matter to him just now. The man was somberly digging out a grave large enough for the four slain animals, whose carcasses he had brought to a peaceful spot in the lee of a boulder. He had dealt with the tree roots and had already created a trench deep enough to serve, but he kept tidying up the sides of the pit with his spade, as if he were deliberately delaying what had to come next. Finally he lowered the bodies into place. No sooner had he done so than he paused once again to gaze at the remains, holding back on covering them.

The remains were a pitiable sight. Rodents had gnawed on them during the night. Better not to remember them this way, thought Enril, but the trainer nonetheless waited. Only when the other gravediggers began covering the human dead did he begin doing the same for the dogs. He used his hands, not his spade, to move the dirt atop them.

Enril walked over, knelt down beside the trainer, and began gently pushing dirt into the trench.

When he realized who was beside him, the trainer wiped sweat from his tangled-lint eyebrows and made sure what he was seeing. Then he shifted a little to the side to allow Enril more room to help.

Make friends, Enril thought. *Make friends when and where you can.* The last thing he wanted was for this fellow to believe the sacrifice of his beasts meant nothing to the person who had put them at risk.

Soon the trench was full. As Enril slapped the dirt from his hands, it became his turn to be surprised.

Omril knelt down beside him. He placed two large stones upon the loose soil: The beginning of a cairn. Without one, scavengers would dig up the dogs as soon as the men departed the area.

The trainer nodded, stalked over to an even larger rock, and began rolling it toward the grave.

The two wizards helped until it was done. The nurse attendant and one of the soldiers came over as if to assist, but Enril waved them away.

Enril was not accustomed to manual labor, but he put himself into the effort, lifting stones that strained his capacity. He had nearly given up hope that he would ever again see what he was seeing now — evidence that Omril had produced not just a coherent thought, but a *new* thought.

The Omril of old would not have cared about dead dogs, certainly not dogs that belonged to a commoner of Cilendrodel. Helping carry cairn stones of his own volition meant he had grasped that Enril was trying to build trust among the locals, and it had occurred to him what he might do to contribute to that goal.

That was real thought. That was conscious thought.

"Thank you, m'lords," the handler said.

"I am sorry we could not do better," Enril replied.

It was his greatest hope that Omril would add something, but his beloved began staring into the treetops again. The attendant came forward with a washcloth, moistened with hot water from one of the kettles, and cleaned Omril's hands before he could wipe them on his mouth or his clothing. Omril paid no notice.

He *had* been there, for a moment. Enril tried to preserve his mood of hopefulness. Mostly, he contemplated the reason why the real Omril could be with him so incompletely and so briefly.

He would still track down that sword-witch of a princess. And he would make her suffer.

CHAPTER TEN

KERON HAD ALWAYS assumed the great strength of an army lay in its cohesion: A hundred men fighting in tandem were worth more than a hundred men fighting a hundred individual battles. But gathering together in large numbers was not how to fight an enemy that could attack from the sky.

Clad in ordinary infantryman's garb and gear to make it harder for the enemy to notice that he, the king, had approached the zone of active conflict, he surveyed the scene.

Sunlight blazed down on the ruptured pastureland. Smoke still wafted upward from places where the dragons had dropped great sacks of oil and then lit the soaked landscape with stiletto-thin bursts of flame. As he watched, the skeleton of a burnt wain crumbled into a pile of charcoal. Elsewhere a raven landed on a soldier's corpse, only to hop away when it found the flesh still too hot to stand upon.

The dragons were gone. They had done their damage in the morning, while traces of fog still puddled in the riverbottom. The great beasts needed that moisture in the air, or their magic was weaker than they liked. Now it was mid-afternoon, and not a cloud stalked the sky. At such a time, Keron was of the opinion Gloroc and his brother might not be able to fly at all, their bodies too massive to remain airborne without the assistance of sorcery. They had retreated east, toward the coast. They were unlikely to return again this day.

And so, at last, the dispersed troops could recombine into a true army, and aim at a goal. The sun was conveniently at their backs, and would be dipping even lower to shine straight into the eyes of the men they were to attack. Time to press forward.

A week earlier, his and Fanhar's army had finished whittling away the Dragon's stronghold at Herd Ford. Two days back, the Dragon's stronghold at the village of Softgrass had fallen. Now the battlefront had shifted to the low ridge ahead.

It was an unnamed spot, as far as Keron knew. Just a fault-line wrinkle in the landscape, all too commonly seen in Thiagra, significant now only because it was the nearest high ground and the Dragon's forces had dug trenches and stationed a rear guard within them. Once the fortifications had been overwhelmed and passed by, this would again be a nameless place. But at the moment, it was what stood between Keron and the eventual liberation of Elandris.

If Keron's forces could reach the top of the ridge decisively, they would make quick work of the defenders. They had the numbers, thanks to Fanhar. The problem was how to initiate the engagement. A charge by the cavalry was out of the question. The opposition had dug pitfalls, set trip cords, embedded pointed stakes in clumps of grass. The ground between the combatants had to be crossed slowly and attentively, or too many mounts would be lost, and not a few riders as well. Yet a surge by foot soldiers had the great disadvantage that the men would have to spend too much time subject to a rain of arrows from the heights.

There was no avoiding the problem. He and Fanhar and the commanders had however agreed what set of tactics might improve the odds of success. That strategy would have to do.

Abruptly a lone rider came forward from the Calinin divisions and moved out into the buffer zone. It was unexpected. Not part of the plan. Keron was shocked to see the rider was Fanhar. The prince was not wearing armor. He was not accompanied by his bodyguards. Clad in mere leathers, bereft even of a helmet, he was light in the saddle and his lively, gracile-bodied oeikani was therefore exceptionally quick on its cloven feet. That, as far as Keron could tell, was the only advantage Fanhar had.

Fanhar proceeded at once to a swath along the base of the slope that was well within the arrow range of the enemy. And indeed, arrows began arcing down.

Fanhar wove his buck closer in and farther out, spun it and reversed direction, varied its pace. Any one archer might be thwarted by those measures, but there were many. An arrow whisked by his head, nearly shaving off a lock of his hair. Another glanced off one of the oeikani's antlers, leaving a white mark of exposed bone.

Keron was aghast. What was his ally thinking? The man was too valuable an asset to risk in such a way. But Keron's own men were too far away to intercede. Those close by were all Fanhar's own, and clearly they had been told not to act. At most, there was a battle wizard or two serving as protection, but that was scarcely a factor. The arrows were coming too quickly and too numerously to divert by magic. All a defensive battle wizard could do was sense whether an offensive counterpart was attempting to guide an arrow to its target, and interfere with the spell. That did nothing to counter an arrow whose flight was naturally accurate.

Fanhar let go of the reins, spread both arms out to the side, and rode in a straight line, guiding his animal with his knees, essentially daring the archers. The archers redoubled their efforts. Keron saw a veritable curtain of pointed shafts come down toward the spot where Fanhar would momentarily be.

And yet he rode on. Not one arrow found its mark. Fanhar remained unhurt. His oeikani was unperturbed.

Shouts broke out in the distance. Here and there along the ridge, fighters were clashing.

This *was* part of the plan. Two squads of Keron's men, his son Val's hand-picked best, had come up the back side of the ridge, camouflaged and getting as close as they could in secret. Thanks to the distraction provided by Fanhar, they had obviously been able to get very close indeed. The battle had begun.

Keron signalled his men to attack. They surged forward, most of them advancing in groups of one or two or three, but a few arranged in phalanxes, shields touching. The individuals and small groups dodged the traps. The phalanxes paused just long enough to neutralize them before proceeding on.

The Calinin forces moved forward in tandem. Fanhar was soon surrounded by them and ceased to stand out so perilously.

Keron set out in the wake of the main charge, advancing steadily, his guards on every side. He was not the sort of king who led from the rear. At the same time, he was too valuable to place at the forefront. His compromise was to take the middle. That way his men knew he was with them, and he was able to stay close enough to the main action to directly weigh the progress of the battle.

On several occasions during the war, he had become embroiled in the thick of the struggle. His sword had claimed many lives, and he had the scars from the occasions when his opponents had bloodied him. Today his personal safety was more or less assured. True, a stray arrow might descend in his direction, but he had a spry young lookout on either side of him tasked to watch the sky, and either raise a shield or knock him out of the way if he should come to be threatened in that fashion.

At first, too many men died before they reached the top, felled by sabotage or by the archers. But an even greater number did make it, and each one, even if he did no more than keep a defender occupied, eased a comrade's journey upward.

This was the thick of battle, the part Keron hated the most. War in general was awful, but at least the early phase of a battle was a matter of strategy and possibly ingenuity, when choices could be made. And afterward, there was the satisfaction of a job done, or at least the relief of survival. This middle part was just doing what had to be done, and hoping the process did not last any longer than it had to.

Immediately above Keron's position, the conquest was finished within the first hour, the last handful of Dragon's men throwing up their hands in surrender. Keron reached the spot, congratulated the victors, and ordered the prisoners into shackles.

The remaining concentrations of violence were all well away from him now. The need to conceal his identity and position was moot. When Enret rode up, bringing along a spare mount, Keron vaulted into the saddle and together they picked their way carefully up the slope, alert for danger to their oeikani, letting the animals judge for themselves that each step they took was a good one. Before long they reached one of the ridge's prime vantage points.

By now the Dragon's side no longer had any advantage of high ground whatsoever. In the east, down in the lowland, Val rode in command of a hundred cavalrymen. They kept away from the slope and away from the active combat, but their presence denied the enemy any real hope of retreat.

The clang of sword against sword, pike against armor, still rose from some of the trenches. A hand flew up into the air, still clutching a dagger, followed by a spurt of arterial blood. Moment by moment, more attackers — a combination of Keron's infantry, Val's specialists, and the southerners who had come with Fanhar — were jumping in to reinforce their comrades. The fight was becoming a slaughter.

Only at the northern end of the battle were the shields still up, and arrows still flying, keeping those emplacements stout. A burly officer with the Dragon's sigil on his breastplate was standing in the midst of that resistance, stoking the courage of those under his command with shouts and the waving of his well-blooded sword. Suddenly an arrow sprouted from the left eye hole of his helmet, and he keeled over.

That was enough for the defenders. Those actively engaged with the enemy could not turn away, and fought on. But those who could, chose to attempt escape. Leaping out of the trenches, they fled down the slope toward the northeast, the one direction where they had not yet been blocked off. For the most part, they kept ahead of the attackers who tried to reach them. Some of the pursuers fell, foiled by hidden pits or trip hazards that the retreating men knew to avoid. Several dozen of the craven-hearted made it to the flat and spread out in singles and pairs, hurrying off as fast as their lungs and legs would allow toward the distant hedge of reeds and willow and deer scrub that fringed the desiccated streambed at the valley's crease.

A cadre of cavalry veered off at Val's signal. The foremost rider closed in upon a runner, threw his spear, and down the man went. The rider dismounted, finished his target off completely, and climbed back on his oeikani to continue the chase. Keron estimated that most of the deserters would come to a similar end. Not all, though. Night would soon fall. A few would find places to hide, would wait, and slip off under cover of darkness to the next fortified line.

Keron looked beyond. His spot on the ridge, and up in the saddle, allowed him to fully assess how much territory they had won. It was not much. The valley was no more than a league across. Its eastern edge was a bluff—a steep one, and over twenty feet high. It was not the sort of incline an army could charge up, whether mounted or on foot. It would have to be scaled.

But raising his spyglass, he saw what he had hoped for. The gleam of sunset made the details especially sharp. The emplacements along the top were incomplete. So the answer was yes. The price had been worth it. Had he and his allies conquered the ridge in a less bloody and less abrupt way, the bluff would have become a theater of siege, not assault. That was a critical difference. A protracted engagement at this place and time would have been just what Gloroc's generals wanted.

It remained to be seen whether his side could push the enemy all the way back to T'jet and deny the Dragon the use of his main port and staging ground—the key to nullifying the invasion. But for now, for tonight, they stood on a victory ground. Minor victory though it was, after the many setbacks he had endured in past years, he would savor it.

"Didn't even have to draw my sword," he told Enret.

Enret took off his helmet and wiped the sweat off his bald head.

"I suppose that had to happen one of these times. Are you complaining, Your Majesty?"

"No."

They grinned at one another.

"What about that Fanhar?" Enret said. "Never thought I'd see something like that from a Calinin emperor's son."

"Are *you* complaining?"

"No."

They grinned again.

—o—

As dusk deepened into twilight, the clean-up of the battle was left to the rank-and-file. Keron's pavilion was quickly erected—it had stayed down during the day so as not to be spotted by either dragon and recognized as a prime target—and he met with his senior commanders. Val was present, as was Fanhar. Over a light meal, they all discussed how to proceed in the morning—how best to deal with the disadvantage the bluff represented. Keron made his decision early. Enret and the other officers departed to relay the orders. As soon as the servants finished removing the food, plates, and utensils, the space was inhabited only by royalty: Keron, Val, and Fanhar. The latter had sent away his attendants, even his cupbearer. It was he who set out a trio of mugs and filled them with pear cider.

Fanhar raised his mug in salute. "To archers with bad aim. My thanks."

Keron drank. He wished for something less tame, but it was his own policy not to allow consumption of alcohol the day before a battle.

"Where did you learn to ride like that?" Val asked. "It looked like your oeikani could read your thoughts."

"My tutor was a Zyraii," Fanhar replied. "Committed some sort of infraction back in the Eastern Deserts. Not sure what. Those people seem to have a lot of rules, and whatever one he broke? I think the penalty would have been castration. In any case, he made his way to Xais and eventually taught riding skills at the royal stables. This one time..."

Fanhar went on, describing not just his Zyraii trainer but half a dozen more of the characters that inhabited his father's palace and sprawling estates. Val listened avidly. This was no surprise to Keron. Val had never seen the wonders of the Old Kingdoms. His childhood had been spent entirely within Elandris, and ever since, his life had been circumscribed by his role in the war effort.

Finally the southern prince clapped his hand on Val's shoulder and said, "Enough of this dull talk. Get back to your tent, my boy. I'll send you a bedwarmer from my comfort flock. That's how a young war commander should celebrate the sort of day you had."

Val looked at his father. Keron shrugged, and nodded. Any of them—or all of them—might be dead tomorrow. A reminder of why it was good to be alive was appropriate.

"Be sure you bathe," Fanhar added. "Expectations, you know. Every one of them is highborn. Give yours something to boast about when she's back among her sisters."

Val nodded, ducked under the flap, and was gone.

"That was kind of you," Keron said.

"You are invited to do likewise."

"I'm still so sore from Herd Ford and Softgrass that I'm having trouble lifting this mug," Keron said, though in fact his hand was perfectly steady as he downed another swallow of cider. "What about you? If I were your age, I'd go off with two and welcome the challenge."

"I've made my arrangements, but I have opportunities of that sort whenever I like. On the other hand, I rarely have an occasion to enjoy such company as yours, Keron of Elandris. Allow me to bide here a while longer."

"Of course."

Keron was surprised by Fanhar's choice. The prince of Xais was infamous for his sexual appetite. Keron would have expected him to be eager to assuage it. He was glad it was otherwise.

"Truth be told," Fanhar continued, "I was troubled by how long the two of you had been here occupying the same stretch of carpet.

The hour was up. Don't you think?"

Keron couldn't argue. Given an enemy that could drop firebombs, given the number of assassins constantly trying to infiltrate the camp, his policy was to keep his heir away from his immediate vicinity most of the time. But he missed his boy. And tonight, they had in fact needed to assemble to discuss strategy.

"He's a fine young man. A proper scion," Fanhar said. "A critical thing to have at this time."

"I know," Keron replied. "Yet be that as it may, when I look at him, I don't see what comes from me. I see his mother in him. It was the same when last I set eyes on my other two."

"Your Cilendri twins."

"Yes."

"You must have loved the mothers very much."

The tent seemed to dim, as if the roof canvas had sagged halfway down. Keron hated that Fanhar had used the past tense. Yes, Lerina was dead. Nanth was dead. Yet he had not seen either one die. Usually when he thought of them, he imagined each woman full of breath, heart beating, skin warm against his. That's how he preferred it.

"One I couldn't help but love. The other I loved as best I could. Either way, our offspring remind me of what was remarkable in both of them. I don't know that they get enough from me to make up for the burden my heritage lowers onto their shoulders."

"Give yourself more credit," Fanhar insisted. "Through you, they're a part of something extraordinary. A single dragon might live seven thousand years. What have our civilizations and empires shown that compares with that? No wonder Gloroc laughs. Even Xais had four dynasties before the Calinin came, and there have been seven since, no matter how much the noble houses try to argue otherwise. But Elandris? Every ruler from the Dragonslayer on down has been a direct descendant along a male line, and every generation legitimate. I would hate to witness the end of that."

"Strange to hear you speak so about a kingdom you've never

even seen with your own eyes."

Fanhar chuckled, and refilled his mug. "I am not saying I am not devoted to my father's empire. But I am a second son. My older brother has three sons by his chief wife, one son with his second wife, and two more with his third. And all three wives are pregnant again. I have no likely chance of ever taking the throne. If I am to cheer on a ruler for the sake of cheering, why not *you*? Especially if the alternative is cheering on that giant turd I grew up with? His one accomplishment is managing to emerge from my mother's womb a few years before I did."

Keron could not avoid smiling. He had after all met Fanhar's older brother.

"You could easily have died out there today," Keron said. "Not that I didn't appreciate your effort, but there were other ways we could have distracted the enemy. I nearly lost you and your support once already. No need to make it real."

Fanhar shrugged. "No matter what we do, life is short. I am young, you say. So it may be. All too soon, I'll be dust. Today I saw a way to make a difference. I acted. I am not sorry for that. If I see another chance to help, I hope to have the courage."

The conversation went on, shifting to less dire matters. Keron regretted having to call an end to it after an hour. He'd not had a peer to talk to in a long time. If the war ever ended, if he and Fanhar both survived, he would be sure to arrange another session, but without a curfew, and with something more than cider to drink.

CHAPTER ELEVEN

ALEMAR WOKE IN as leisurely a fashion as he had experienced in many weeks, transported benignly out of a dream of a rambling, pleasant conversation with Wynneth. His wife's voice became a whisper, then an echo, and then was gone altogether.

He heard a sound so subtle it was barely more than a moth flutter, but it was a noise of the waking world. He opened his eyes. Geim was sitting on the other bed, rubbing the bracelet with a parchment-thin square of pillow leather.

"Didn't mean to wake you."

"You didn't," Alemar assured him.

Geim resumed polishing. Already half of the links were brighter than when Quandai had pulled the item from its reliquary. It looked less like an artifact of a forgotten age and more like the potent talisman it was.

Toren was lying on the center bed, eyes closed. Alemar went to him. He laid two fingers on the side of his neck. Leaned down. Sniffed. Toren's pulse was faint, his skin clammy, and his breath stank of fungus.

"I changed his swaddling cloth when I got up," Geim said. "Nothing solid, and not much urine, either. I got him to suck down some water. I'll try again in a few minutes." The Vanihr tilted his head in the direction of the sideboard. The pitcher of water was still three-quarters full. A moist sponge lay in a dish beside it.

Alemar frowned. He knew it had been the right thing to put the totem into Toren—and for what it was worth, the process had been seamless. Following Geim's instructions, Alemar had managed to activate the talisman on the first try. The energy had flowed from it into Toren, pouring out in tendrils like an octopus wrapping itself around his chest. In the thirty-some hours that had passed since then, Toren's eyes had often moved rapidly from one direction to another beneath the closed lids, and the muscles of his arms, legs, and jaw had twitched. *Something* was going on in there.

Whatever was happening, it was taking too long. When they had first come to Quandai's house, Toren had chewed and swallowed food when it was put into his mouth. He had reacted in small ways to his surroundings. Now he just lay there, getting weaker.

Alemar almost felt guilty that after a night and a day and another night of rest, he was all but restored. His elbow was still stiff, but no longer sore.

"Stretch your legs if you like," Geim suggested. "I'll let you know if anything happens here."

Virtually all of their waking hours the day before had been spent at Toren's bedside in the expectation that he might break out of his trance. Quandai's guest room was beginning to feel like a dungeon cell. Even the fantastical preserved specimens on the walls seemed less like decorations, and more like guards. Stepping away was an excellent idea.

"What about you?" Alemar asked.

"I went out earlier. I had quite a nice conversation with Solia and her mother in the kitchen. I hope to continue it later. They've gone to the market."

"Very well, then." Alemar took his leave.

After washing up, he went to the kitchen and had a small serving of porridge and a cup of tea. The latter was as restorative as that first cup he'd had, the evening of their arrival at the house.

Brikka and Solia did not put in an appearance, so Alemar went exploring. Having already seen the entry lane and its garden—and wishing to avoid being spotted by passersby on the street—he went to the large courtyard in the rear.

Soft but bright sunlight beamed down upon the rose bushes and perfume hedge, the scents wafting toward him on a lively breeze. Bird chatter and wind-in-leaves noises drifted over from the tall trees on the neighboring parcel. Geim had remarked upon the wonder of Dragonsdeep when they had walked through the city. Finally Alemar let himself appreciate it. In so many ways, the city did not resemble a place confined within a domed enclosure beneath the sea.

A large shed occupied the very back of the property, its walls made of masonry brick, its tile roof festooned with multiple chimneys. The barnlike door was open.

As Alemar stepped across the threshold, the bouquet from the flowers and fertile soil was overcome by the taint of preservative elixirs, tanning acid, and hide glue—along with a whiff of dead flesh too reminiscent of the atmosphere within the tunnels of Setan. That was not a memory he wanted to invoke. Fortunately the stink was somewhat tamed. It consisted only of the vestiges escaping from sealed caskets, covered vats, stoppered bottles. Even the buckets had lids.

Quandai was sitting on a stool, his apron freshly laundered but teeming with the stains of previous work sessions. A cadaver lay on the platform in front of him, already reduced to dwarf size, the flesh already treated to thwart decay, the arms already tattooed with street identifications. However, along the seams some of the stitching still showed, as it had not on the specimens hung in the intersections of thoroughfares or at the entrances of the city parks.

The subject was face down, the feet hanging off the edge of the platform. The feet were, in fact, the very thing Quandai was working on. In one hand he held a small paint brush, which he dipped into a pot of lacquer.

The lacquer was almost as clear as water but it clung to the brush with the intimacy of honey. Quandai held the brush over the mouth of the pot until no more was likely to drip off the end.

"I'm afraid I can't step away just now. Did Brikka not tell you?"

"She's out, along with Solia," Alemar explained. "Your nephew is gone as well."

"Yes. He'll be out all day."

Alemar continued to observe as Quandai dabbed the resinous substance between the cadaver's toes, smoothing out each drop until it was thin as sweat. He lightly blew into the crevices until the application ceased to glisten. The skin took on a soft, natural quality. It didn't look painted. If anything, it looked *alive*.

"Is your friend's condition unchanged?" Quandai asked.

"I'm afraid so."

"I'm sorry. Did you sleep well, at least?"

"I did."

"I envy you that. I've been up for hours. But this helps." He posed the brush in front of his face. "Keeps my hands busy. Distracts me."

"Would you prefer to be alone?" Alemar asked.

"You are welcome to stay. Though I warn you this is one of the least gruesome things you might see."

"I understand. Nevertheless, I'll stay."

"As you wish."

Quandai began brushing the soles of the feet, heels first. The calluses required repeated attention, but Quandai did not lather on a large amount all at once. He applied one thin layer at a time, making sure the substance fully absorbed into the flesh before he dipped his brush into the pot again.

"Don't ask me how the concoction is made," Quandai said. "The supply was obtained years ago by my predecessor. It came from the Embalmers Guild in Xais. It takes magic to make it, I suppose, but I don't know for certain. My specimens last so long people assume I'm some sort of necromancer, but the truth is, I haven't an ember of magic in me. I cut and sew and glue and paint. I have always wondered — if

I can practice my profession without the casting of a spell, could it be the journeymen of the Embalmers Guild can say the same?"

Quandai turned the mannequin over. He examined the feet, nodded, and began adding another thin coating to one of the insteps.

Now that the dead man was face up, Alemar couldn't avoid studying the grotesque ways its natural state had been perverted. Inevitably his gaze was drawn to the crotch. All Alemar saw was a featureless triangle of skin, the pubic hair having been removed along with everything else.

Quandai noticed where Alemar was looking. "It is Gloroc's express wish that they be like that. He regards his own sexlessness to be a mark of his superiority. The trophies declare the sexless will reign over Elandris, right down to presiding over the street crossings."

Alemar noticed Quandai called Gloroc "he" even while commenting on his lack of gender. It was the same for him. His experience as a boy watching the livestock at Garthmorron Hold had taught him a castrated goat or ox or oeikani behaves mildly compared to an intact male. Gloroc was not mild.

"Dealing with this set of remains is easier than some I've had on my work table," Quandai said. "He was no one to me. Just a criminal."

"Who was he?"

"A senior quartermaster of Gloroc's army. He diverted too many of the supplies that were supposed to go to the front. Not to help the rebel cause, you understand. Just fattening his own purse. If he'd been less greedy, his crime would not have been discovered."

"I see. But I take it there have been times you've known the deceased?"

Quandai's expression had already been somber. Now he exuded the aura of a man who has not smiled in years. "Yes. Four times now. Once quite recently."

Alemar held back a follow-up question. He simply observed. Quandai put away the pot of lacquer, placing the brush in a glass with a measure of mineral spirits. Going to a shelf, he lifted down a case of polished stagwood inlaid with amath nacre. When he set aside the lid, the light shone in upon two dozen eyeballs nestled in felt beds, the irises ranging through the various colors and hues found in human faces.

Alemar knew the eyeballs must be glass, but they were so realistic the sight of them raised hair on the nape of his neck.

Quandai consulted his notes, then chose an eyeball with a medium brown iris. This he placed in the left eye socket of the mannequin. He fixed it in place with a few quick dabs of glue on the eyelid and along the base, behind the bottom lashes.

Then Quandai made things even worse. He poured a measure of some sort of clear oil into a cup, pulled a pipette from a drawer, and placed a drop on the eyeball. This created the illusion of moisture, as a living eye would exhibit, and it became almost impossible to believe the eyeball was artificial.

Quandai fetched a second case, much like the first save for the pattern of the inlay. It also contained a set of eyeballs arranged by iris color. But Alemar knew these were not the same as the first. Not at all.

"You feel the sorcery?" Quandai asked.

"Yes."

"I'm not able to. I consider myself lucky in that respect."

"They're talismans," Alemar said. "Why?"

"One of the original Ril wizards created them. Danril. He's been dead for twenty years, but he made so many the supply has yet to be exhausted. Every signpost I've made has contained one. Any of the Ril order, using an apparatus Danril created, can gaze through them to spy on what's happening throughout the city."

Alemar took a step back.

"No need to be concerned," Quandai said. "As you may have gathered from what Tollvar said, there are no Ril wizards in Dragons-deep at the moment. There won't be until Leyaril the Poisoner returns."

Quandai ran his finger along the array of eyeballs until he found one with the same hue of medium brown that he had already selected. This he installed in the right eye socket of the mannequin. He gave the glue a moment to establish a grip, then he added the drop of oil.

Alemar could not shake the impression that he was being stared at by a dead man. He shifted away to the side. He half expected the eyes to turn and follow his movement.

"Eventually the oil hardens," Quandai said. "Then the eyes look like glass again. Lifelike enough for mundane trophies, but Gloroc wants better than that. About once a month, Remm and I make the rounds of the city, adding a fresh drop to each and every eye. We usually hire helpers, because there are one thousand, seven hundred twenty-one pairs of eyes. This fellow will make it one thousand, seven hundred twenty-two."

Alemar had seen his share of bodies. Some of those remains had belonged to people he himself had killed. He had witnessed the transformation of a person from a vital, animate presence to mere meat. But seeing Quandai manage a sort of reversal of this—changing the dead into something that all but drew breath—made him glad he had eaten so little for breakfast.

"How do you bear it?" Alemar finally asked. "Week by week, as part of your trade?"

Quandai placed the pipette in the cup. He closed the lids of the cases of eyeballs. "To be honest, I don't know. I have been there when family members have been forced to witness their loved ones being hung up for the Dragon's lackeys to mock. After an occasion like that, I find it especially hard to go back to work. But somehow I manage it. I suppose I do it by reminding myself of the benefit."

"Which is?"

"I have access to every part of the city. Even the palace. I am a trusted servant of the Dragon. That means from time to time, I am in a position to do some good."

Quandai pulled a hood over the head of the mannequin. Alemar was embarrassed how grateful he was for that change.

"You didn't come out here to see all this," Quandai said. "You've been wondering about me. Your first impression of me was not what you had hoped."

"Treggei spoke favorably of you. I confess I wondered if he had even met you."

"Treggei's father and I grew up together. It's true I helped the boy escape Dragonsdeep, but my part was small, all things considered. A few words in the right ears."

"Actually, I'm beginning to think the praise was deserved."

"If so, I'm glad. Solia confessed to me that she told you I was not brave. She was correct. I am not brave. I was horrified to find you at my door."

"What has changed?"

"What do you mean?" Quandai asked.

"You're calm now."

Quandai lifted the mannequin down and placed it in one of the morgue niches in the back wall. He faced Alemar straight on.

"Until now, every contribution I have made is from the shadows. It even seemed possible I might grow old and die a painless death without ever having reveal myself as Gloroc's enemy. Now I understand that's not the way it will be. I am calm because I no longer have to wonder what I will do when I face the test. The test is here. *You* are the test."

"You will help me, then?" Alemar asked.

"I will do all I can. My prince."

Quandai had not addressed him with an honorific at any point during the past two days. He wasn't using one now because he had to. He had chosen to. Alemar stood a little straighter.

Rapid footsteps scuffed the flagstones outside. Solia abruptly appeared in the doorway, panting slightly.

"Your Highness — your friend is awake."

— o —

They found Toren on the bench in the front garden. The gauntlets lay on the paving stones by his feet. Geim was sitting beside him. Toren's head was down and he was rubbing the back of his neck.

"He came out here on his own," Geim reported. "He sat down. He pulled off the gauntlets. And when he saw me, he said my name."

"I would rather have seen Deena's face beside me when I looked up," Toren said in a surprisingly lively voice for someone who only a short time ago had seemed as though he would never wake again. "But you know, Geim's not as ugly as I remember."

"You see?" Geim told the others. "He has come to his senses."

The two Vanihr grinned at one another.

Toren rubbed his belly. "Not everything's quite right, though. I feel like I could eat a whole sheep."

Quandai frowned. "My wife is back and I know she's been planning to serve something substantial, but I doubt it's lamb or mutton."

"It was another joke," Geim explained. "In the Far South, only the enemies of his tribe eat the meat of animals who graze in open fields."

"Oh."

"It wasn't entirely a joke," Toren said. "I am incredibly hungry."

"Why don't you all retreat to the front room?" Quandai suggested. "I'll fetch something to nibble on while we're waiting on the full meal."

"I take it you're the fellow whose house we were supposed to find?"

"Yes. I'm Quandai."

"Toren."

"Pleased to meet you properly. Welcome to my home."

"You have nice trees."

"Thank you."

Alert as Toren was, his weak condition was obvious when he tried to rise. Geim had to help him make it upright.

Toren left the gauntlets at the base of the bench. Alemar gathered them up.

Once the visitors reached the room where Alemar had endured his confrontation with Tollvar, Toren needed further help to sit down. Other than that, he genuinely seemed fine. Alemar stopped short of examining him. The best thing for them all right now was to try to relax.

And eat. Now that the crisis was over, Alemar realized how

inadequate the serving of porridge had been. He was famished.

Quandai soon brought in a pair of well-stocked trays and set them down on the center table. They proceeded to nosh on day-old bread and olive oil, on oranges, on morsels of a crumbly sort of cheese Alemar had never sampled before and which he doubted came from any sort of mammal milk, but which pleased his palate nonetheless. Toren ate in a deliberate fashion, taking small bites, chewing thoroughly, sipping copious amounts of tea, but continuing the process for quite a long time. Aside from the occasional scratch of an itch or shifting of a sore muscle, he did nothing but eat and listen. Alemar used the interval to summarize what Toren had missed while he had been lost to the world outside his skin.

Finally Toren set down the remnant of a slice of bread. He jutted his chin at the gauntlets, which Alemar had placed on the table right between the trays. "Thank you for getting those things off."

"I can't take credit for that." Alemar replied.

"Yes, you can. You're the one who understood how much danger I was in."

"I suppose that much is true."

"I can't ever wear them again, can I?"

"Not even for a few moments," Alemar confirmed. "They'll take control of you again. The good news is, if you keep them off, I believe you'll recover as thoroughly as you could hope for."

"How fine that would be," Toren said. "You mean my health will recover, but even if I stay away from every talisman the Dragonslayer ever made, I'll never be the same person I was back in The Wood."

"I'm troubled by the way you put that."

"Don't be. My way is forward. I accept that."

"If that's the case, I'm pleased to hear it," Alemar said.

"It is easier than you might think. My new ancestor has a way of helping me to put things in perspective."

"So he did manifest within you? You remember that life?"

"I remember his lifetime as I remember those of any of my other ancestors. More perhaps. Polk lived here in Elandris, and before that, in Moin. What he experienced is so different than what my blood ancestors went through, it stands apart. Easy to distinguish."

"And the two of you...get along?"

"We're learning to." He laughed. "We are, after all, two of the same rare type. We are both dragonslayers."

"Fair point."

"He's a little pesky at the moment, though. He has so many questions I am unable to answer. Perhaps you could speak with him directly."

"That's possible?"

"I believe so." Toren closed his eyes, held them shut, and when he opened them again, his manner had shifted in an eerie way.

"I feel as though we should introduce ourselves," Alemar stated.

"No need. I am aware of who you all are. The challenge is to remember who *I* am. Please, for the next few minutes, call me Polk." The voice was still Toren's, but it was more evenly modulated and at the same time, had acquired an accent. Toren spoke the High Speech as perfectly as anyone—his gift from Obo. Now his way of speaking was not the same. It wasn't that it sounded foreign as much as it sounded antiquated.

"Polk it is," Alemar said.

Quandai cleared his throat. "That's too informal for me. I would prefer to call you First Steward. Or Founder, if you like."

Polk/Toren turned to Quandai and gave him a friendly, open smile. "You are the one I'm most curious about. You had the relic. The one I last saw in the grip of a Vanihr shaman. How did you come to be its custodian?"

"It was passed down to me, as it has been passed down for centuries."

"So the Order of Watchers still exists?"

"Yes."

"What is that?" Alemar asked.

Quandai indicated with a small bow of the head that Polk

should answer. The latter shrugged.

"It's there in the name," Polk said. "Watchers. Of all the people on the scene when Elandris was founded — who do you suppose bore watching?"

"Weren't you their ally? Their partisan?" Alemar asked.

"Next you'll be calling me their lapdog."

"I did not mean to imply that."

"Before the voyage to slay the dragons, before I saw what I saw on the day Faroc and Triss were killed, I was much as you imply. But I learned better. From that day onward, I kept close to Alemar and Miranda not out of devotion, but to be in the best position to mitigate the damage they might do."

"You tricked them?"

Polk chuckled mirthlessly. "Of course not. They knew I didn't look at them the same way. They let me do it. They understood they needed someone like me. We found our way. They had achieved their greatest goal — they had a home where no one could say to them, 'Enough. We're done with you now. You have to leave.' They made it a realm where even *breathing* depended upon their genius. Meanwhile I did what I knew had to be done."

"You took care of the people," Quandai gently interjected.

Polk nodded. "I set up systems of administration. Filled posts with the most sensible and fair bureaucrats I could find. Listened to complaints from every faction and tried to provide solutions."

"You ruled," Alemar concluded.

"No. *They* ruled. I governed."

"I see. And the Watchers?"

"I grew old. I handed off my official post to a successor. He turned out to be, in my judgment, an even better administrator than I had been. As much as possible, I retreated into the background. But I found myself worrying about the long term. Alemar and Miranda were still finding ways to prevent themselves from aging. I knew one day I'd be gone and they'd still be there. Handling those two took a special sort of finesse and I knew at some point they would grow unhappy with whatever steward held the staff of office, and that man would be dismissed. I wanted some means to mitigate the damage those transitions would cause. If a steward fell out of favor, it was vital his replacement be the right sort of man. So I founded the Watchers."

Polk turned to Quandai. "What I never imagined was that the Watchers would still exist after all this time. People who shape a realm tend to have too much ambition. They want power for themselves. It's hard to find worthy men."

"The society nearly died out a number of times," Quandai replied. "Precisely for those reasons. But when Gloroc took control of this half of Elandris, more of the right sort of men came forward. There aren't many of us, but we are here."

"To guide the resistance," Alemar said.

"No. Most members of the resistance aren't aware the Watchers are among them. We aren't watching Gloroc. We're concerned with what happens after Gloroc is defeated. We have faith that day will come. What then? Will your father and your half-brother still be alive by then? If not, who will rule? Will it be someone worthy?"

Alemar was dumbfounded to realize he had never truly considered what Elandris's fate might be if both Gloroc and the royal family were obliterated in the war. He almost forgot to ask the question he'd been waiting to bring up: "Preserving the memories in the bracelet. The Watchers arranged that?"

"That was Miranda's idea. There were times when she...leaned on my counsel. Since I was not a magic-wielder, there was no hope that immortality spells would work on me. But she wanted a way to perhaps be able to talk to me again some time. I agreed. She recruited a Vanihr shaman. I lay down on a couch one evening. And now at last, here I am, manifest and able to glimpse what came after my natural lifetime."

"Not at last," Quandai interjected. "Again."

Polk turned to him. "You mean this is not the first time someone's had to put up with me knocking around inside their skull?"

"Three stewards of Elandris were hosts of your memories. All three times were long ago, when the Dragonslayer and his sister were still here to guide the process."

"I don't recall those times."

"No, I'm afraid you wouldn't. Miranda and the Dragonslayer needed the help of another shaman to try adding to the original set of memories. They never found one. But they did realize that when the memories were drawn from the bracelet, they weren't transferred; they were copied. The talisman continues to hold the original set. It's possible it could be used again. Toren may or may not be the last in the line, only the last for the moment."

"I see. Well. I hope I was helpful, those other times."

"You were. Your advice was what convinced the Dragonslayer to let his great-grandson Imt take the throne."

"And Imt was a good choice?"

Quandai smiled. "Imt was the best king Elandris has ever known."

Alemar thought back to the lessons he'd had in Elandri history in the library at Garthmorron Hold. "Imt was not the heir apparent, as I recall."

"No. He was a younger son of a younger son. Sixteenth in line for the throne at the time. His uncle and cousins and older brothers did not appreciate his elevation. But he was the right choice."

"I am glad to hear this," Polk said. "But I would like to move on to the present." He faced Alemar. "I am able to review Toren's memories just as he can review mine. You had a plan in mind that brought you back to Dragonsdeep."

"Yes," Alemar confirmed.

"It's a bad plan."

"You have a better one?"

"Not yet. But I know the one you have is not good."

"What would you have me do?" Alemar asked.

"Get more information. Then make a new plan."

"And where would I get more information?"

Polk gestured to the side. "From Quandai, to start with. Tell him what you have in mind."

Quandai found himself at the center of everyone's gaze. He blushed.

Alemar sighed. "I suppose it wouldn't hurt to get another opinion. Here is the gist of it," he told the taxidermist, "you remember I told Tollvar I defeated Omril?"

"How could I forget," Quandai said.

"I didn't just defeat him. I delved him. Polk can see Toren's memories. Well, I got a good look at Omril's. He has a cache of talismans in his suite inside the palace in Dragonsdeep. That includes some of the Dragonslayer's talismans. That was one of Omril's functions within the order of the Ril. He studied the talismans. I mean to take possession of that trove. We came back to do that. Once we obtain that arsenal, I think there will turn out to be something useful there."

"But you intended to accomplish that with Toren's active participation," Polk said. "Using the gauntlets. Which as you said earlier, he can no longer use without plunging into a trance and dying."

"I can still use one gauntlet," Alemar said. "And we're already inside Dragonsdeep. All I have to do is get to that room."

"I can get you into the palace," Quandai said.

"There you have it," Alemar told Polk. "Is that the plan you feel is bad?"

"Yes," Polk said. "It's the sort of step you can't take back. I doubt it will take long before someone notices Omril's quarters have been pilfered. After that, you'll be on the defensive. I believe you should learn more about what you may find there."

"From whom?"

"From Miranda, of course."

"From —" Alemar blinked.

"She's alive. That much is clear. And you have the means to consult with her."

"I do?"

Polk nodded. "It's right there in Toren's memories. When you and he and the others infiltrated the palace, while you were waiting for the moment to spring the trap, he sensed that there was an oracle chamber within the palace."

It was Quandai who responded. "Yes. There is. He's right. There were several oracle chambers built, and one of them is in Wizardsdeep. Gloroc's masons sealed up the main passageway after the conquest, but there's another way in."

"How do you know?"

"The palace architect was a Watcher."

Alemar sat back and let the prospect sink in: Talk to Miranda.

"Obo told me of the time my father consulted with Miranda. The process took many hours."

"Your father is not as strong in magic as you are. And as you pointed out, you have a gauntlet at your disposal. Surely it will be easier."

Alemar looked at the right-hand gauntlet, the one he had worn so often during the previous four years.

He already knew he was going to do it. Now all he could think about was precisely what questions he would ask.

CHAPTER TWELVE

HIGH IN THE crown of a perfumeblood tree, Elenya scooted out on a branch until she could see the entire outpost through a gap in the leaves. She knew the place. Knew how the residents should behave if they were going about their normal routine. She studied for signs that Dragon's men might be lurking.

The denizens here were quarrymen. They had been here for two generations, chiselling away the hillside's deposit of tawny granite. They might be here for another two generations before the site was exhausted. A steady living. A good living. Cilendrodel had plenty of wood and silk, but a civilized realm needed stone, too. The demand was always enough to keep half a dozen families in residence here year-round.

Four burly men were nearly done wrestling a cornerstone up a ramp onto a wagon. The axles groaned, but the vehicle was built for the weight and barely wobbled. The block settled into place. The laborers nodded, clapped each other on the back, and shared a dipper of water from the rain barrel. The teamster gave his oxen one last check. He was using four yoke of them—eight beasts in all, each pair varying in age to ensure the right kind of strength regardless of the curve or grade or condition of the road. He had more than five leagues to travel to reach the river. Elenya wondered if the block would wait in the warehouse there, or be loaded at once onto a barge for the next stage of its journey.

Amid the talus mound of unworked stone newly broken out from the hillside, a lone man tapped a series of wedges, patiently invoking the fracture that would cause a slab to divide cleanly—a process of seduction, not force. The metal-on-metal ping of his hammer blows echoed back and forth across the little canyon. Elenya's glance returned to him a second and then a third time before she could convince herself the hammer really was as small as it was. Were she not seeing it in action, she would have assumed the tool had been forged for a woman or a child. She supposed if one had to tap spikes into rock all day long, it would be easiest to do so with something that would only lightly tax the muscles involved.

Women were hanging laundry to dry in the breeze. Two boys were fetching water from the well. A long-whiskered man, body too wizened and bent to pursue his craft, sat on a bench in the shade of the engraving shed, smoking a pipe as long as the arm that held it.

For a sweet moment, Elenya was reminded of home. There had been a quarry inland from Garthmorron Hold. Seldom in use, it had been one of the spots Master Troy would take her and his other pupils so that they could hold practice duels, learning to cope with terraced levels, uneven surfaces, and loose gravel.

During one season of training, she had been there when stone was being harvested. But that had been limestone. The workers hauled their wheelbarrow loads to the ovens and when the rock was fully cooked, they crushed the brittle result into mortar. Her grandfather had sent the men there. Lord Dran allowed petty lawbreakers such as them to perform useful labor in the open air and sunlight. They all understood this was better than being confined in the dungeons with the bandits and smugglers or subjected to the gallows like the rapists and murderers, but few of them exhibited enthusiasm over their situation. The labor was still drudgery.

Here, in this little canyon outpost, it was different. The sort of stoneworking done here was a calling. A source of pride. A way of life.

Enough. She made her decision. She clambered down the tree and slipped back into the forest.

Her band of followers looked up expectantly. Two dozen sets of eyes. The remnant of her cadre of forty had reassembled within the past two days. They still had a long way to go before they reached the bulk of their forces in the western part of the province, but at least things were not as desperate as they had been.

Things had been so *very* desperate. Reduced to only four survivors, all wounded, they knew they had only one hope. They did not try to disguise their trail. They did not set traps. All they did was run, as steadily and as far as they could manage. They had run and run until finally they simply collapsed, their legs refusing to work any further until they had rested.

They had waited for the hunters to catch up again. Elenya was sure Enril had at least one dog left, and perhaps many. She fully expected them to end up like the fallen comrades they'd abandoned among the trampled, blood-spattered ferns.

In her sleep she could still hear hounds baying, and probably would for many nights to come, but actual hounds, along with their masters, had not appeared.

"Looks safe," she said. "We'll give our plan a try."

She reached out. Korri, her coinkeeper, tossed the last of their purses to her. The contents barely jingled as she caught it. Not much there. Might be too little to be persuasive. Even so, she tied the pouch to her belt.

She took along only three escorts. The rest of her companions waited where they were, close enough to be summoned but hidden for the time being. Elenya had no wish to intimidate the quarryfolk by a show of numbers.

Dalih was one of those who remained behind. He would not be a comforting sight to strangers, head bound as it was, holding toge-ther the flap of scalp that would otherwise be hanging down past his ear. Bainne and Urrus—the other two survivors of the last skirmish—

were bandaged on torsos and arms as well as heads, and both were still so stiff from the run they walked like men who had no knees. Instead her companions were Slees, Rhete, and Oloro. She'd chosen them carefully, Slees because including her meant that half the party consisted of small women and therefore might make them seem less threatening, Rhete and Oloro because they were from this part of Cilendrodel. The pair looked as though they might be kinfolk of the people here, right down to the freckles.

They went to the wagon road and approached the outpost in the open. A boy with a bucket saw them first, but Elenya did not wait for him to shout.

"Halloo!" she called.

The workers paused at their tasks. One last ping of the wedge hammer resounded off the canyon walls.

Elenya and her companions stopped short of the main yard and waited. As mothers gathered youngsters and took them back toward the cottages, the head quarryman and his strapping young son came forward.

"Master Thrend?" Elenya began, hoping she had remembered the name right. "I am —"

"I know who you are," the headman replied. His tone was not hostile, but it was not welcoming.

"You and your folk have been a help in the past," Elenya said. "We need food. Bandages. Willowbark powder. And a place to rest."

Thrend's brow wrinkled, and he did not speak.

"We will pay, of course," Elenya added. She rubbed the knot that held the coin purse to her belt.

The headman's expression clouded even more.

"I will not have it said I took money from you," he said forcefully.

Elenya was sure he would turn them away. It caught her by surprise when he sighed and beckoned her toward the shade of the engraving shed.

"Have a smoke with me," he said.

That at least was a good sign. Each settlement here in the inland fringes of Cilendrodel grew its own strain of pipe leaf. Some outposts even took their names from them: Sweetsmoke, Oldleaf, Aleweed. If a headman shared a pipe with a visitor, it meant as much as the breaking of bread did in the ancient Calinin Empire.

They walked together across the main yard. As they reached the shed, Thrend gestured to the long-whiskered man on his bench, who handed over his pouch of leaf. Elenya interpreted the silence of the exchange to mean the old fellow was deaf.

Thrend picked up a kettle from the steeping stand and poured his four visitors cups of fragrant tea along with a fifth cup for himself. He picked up a smoking pipe that lay on the main work table, filled it with two generous pinches from the pouch, lit a long straw at the steeping stand, and then lit the pipe. His movements were precise and almost ritualistic and—Elenya was sorry to see—not at all relaxed despite the routine nature of what he was doing.

Thrend indicated that Elenya and her companions should arrange themselves on the stools. His son selected a spot near the old man and stood watching them all closely, arms folded across his broad chest.

Elenya took the pipe as soon as it was offered and dutifully filled her lungs, held the smoke in, and let it out slowly, allowing proper time to savor its character. Like anyone raised in Cilendrodel, she smoked leaf from time to time but not as often as most did. She had to concentrate not to cough.

She decided she might have made a habit of leaf had she grown up near this quarry. The aroma reminded her of freshly-turned compost, full of manure. She was soothed despite her worries— though perhaps some of that came from the potency.

Rhete and Oloro took their turns. Slees had difficulty dealing with the length of the pipe but finally managed to get a good draw. She swayed on her stool as she handed the pipe back to Thrend. She smiled like a maiden who had just seen a handsome man—not at Thrend as far as Elenya could judge, but just because she couldn't avoid pleasant thoughts.

Thrend took another long pull. He seemed to need it.

"I met your brother," the headman said. "The healer. He came here, much as you have today. He asked little enough, and paid in good coin, and I gave him what he asked for."

Elenya nodded.

"Your brother helped my family." Thrend looked over at the old man. "My da had become a stone split cross the grain. Couldn't get a good night's sleep, having to get up every hour to empty his bladder. Elixir of pisswort hadn't helped. Your brother's magic, though—that fixed him. He sleeps half a night now. Sometimes a whole night. He's still old and he's still deaf, but he's at peace. Gets to watch us work. Gets to smoke. It's what I wanted for him. My ma died when I was five. My aunties did well for me but it was my da that kept me right."

He sipped tea. Elenya had forgotten about it. It was part of the ritual and it was important to do likewise. The brew tasted of peach and ginger, not a combination she had ever had before. She would have to try it again some time when she could appreciate it.

"I will not dishonor that debt," Thrend told her. "We'll give you the supplies and let you rest here. But I'll only let you stay one night. I won't risk more than that. I am sorry, but the Dragon's men have been through these parts too often of late."

"Thank you."

"There are more of you?" Thrend guessed.

"Yes."

"Bring them in. I'll let my wife know to pull out the big cauldron for tonight's supper." He shrugged, the first remotely casual mannerism he'd displayed. "She's been wanting an excuse to throw a certain cantankerous hen in it."

—o—

Elenya did not quite fetch all of her company. She left four men in the woods, their presence undisclosed to the quarryfolk. They were the least weary, the ones least likely to mind missing out on a night within walls, in beds instead of hammocks. Elenya had fought this war for too many years to ever leave herself totally surrounded by strangers.

Not that she distrusted the headman. Had Thrend been eager to help them, her suspicions would have spiked, but as it was, she believed his word was good. He had determined to what degree he would help—and would not help—and he would abide by that position.

The men were quartered in the bachelor's barracks and the hayloft of the barn. Elenya and Slees took over the little cottage behind the headman's house ordinarily occupied by two widowed sisters of his. The sisters took the displacement in stride. They apparently regarded having visitors as a refreshing change. They peppered Elenya with questions about the customs of the Eastern Deserts while they heated water, filled a bathtub, and fetched towels. Fortunately they left her in peace when they grasped how profound her exhaustion was.

After they had each bathed, Slees rubbed salve into Elenya's cuts. Elenya was the least wounded of the four who had survived the final encounter with the Ril wizard's hunters, but she had not made it through unmarked. One opponent had given her a slice along a wrist. Another had pinked her in the shin as he went down. The damage was to the same wrist and the same shin injured in the previous skirmish. She knew she must be leaving herself open in a way she needed to correct, but she hadn't had the chance to puzzle it out yet.

Slees slipped a fresh bandage under Elenya's arm. She frowned at the cut before she began wrapping it.

It was healing well enough, but it had needed stitching. It still hurt. It would leave a scar. Elenya had been lucky over the years to have her brother and his magic so often at hand. Otherwise she might not have been able to move from all the scars she would have had. She had enough as it was.

"*One* night," Slees complained. She rubbed the rope burns on her palms.

"Better that than none," Elenya scolded.

Slees sighed.

They said nothing more for the time being, just enjoyed the

sensation of being clean, and wrapped in soft linen while their garments hung from the laundry lines outside. Elenya knew Slees was only trying to commiserate with her, but Elenya would not give her disappointment an airing. It was real enough already. Putting it to spoken word would only make it worse.

They were losing the support of the common folk. A year ago if she had turned up here in identical circumstances, Thrend and his people would have sheltered them as long as they needed to heal up and regain their strength. Everyone across the length of Cilendrodel had known what a tyrant Puriel was, and had quickly learned how sinister Omril could be. The quarryfolk had, in their quiet way, been part of the rebellion.

But this new adversary, Enril, was not making the same mistakes. When Thrend had spoken of Dragon's men, he did not sound frightened of them, he sounded *frightened of displeasing them.* That was a dire difference. It said the headman believed he and his people would be left unmolested as long as they cooperated with the Ril wizard and the new governor.

The locals were imagining it was possible not to choose sides.

She wished Alemar were with her. He might have some notion what to do. Her greatest skill with people was inspiring them to fight, but that only worked with those willing to pick up a knife or an ax or a bow.

It could be worse, though. She was best off following the advice she had just given to Slees.

And so an hour later she made it a point to appreciate the comfort of slipping into a clean tunic. That evening she savored her bowl of chicken and potato soup, her hunk of fresh brown bread, her cup of chewy red wine. That night she burrowed into the blankets and let her head relax into the goosefeather-stuffed pillow. Tomorrow the discomforts would resume. No use feeling cheated until then.

Needing the recovery so much, her stomach finally well filled, her senses so seduced by the potency of the after-dinner smoking of more leaf, she fell deeply asleep. When a sudden weight clamped down hard on her and a cloth soaked in a soporific potion was forced over her nose and mouth, she did not even manage to thrash before she collapsed back into unconsciousness.

CHAPTER THIRTEEN

FOR A QUARTER hour, rain spattered hard on the leaded glass windows of her state cabin, but the squall was in a hurry to cross the Dragon Sea. By the time Leyaril ventured up top, the curtain of precipitation had moved past, lured away to the skies over The Deeps. The last rivulets were draining through the scuppers.

To the southwest, the towers of Dragonsdeep rose from the ocean like phalluses, vartham shafts leading up to fattened caps of brick or hewn stone, colors muted by the cloud shadow. Atop some of them, sentinels stood at the parapets, observing the approach of her ship.

The great square platform of the quay loomed in the nearer distance, its warehouses shut, its cranes idle, the stevedores and inventory clerks tucked into their quarters until such time as she had been given her courtly welcome. Already the other vessels in port had been moved to berths along the other three sides, leaving the west pier ready to receive her frigate.

The ceremonial platoon was waiting along the dock, all thirty guardsmen arrayed in their best armor, standing straight and manly, though she knew rainwater must be trickling down their woolens and puddling in their boots. Off to the side stood High Chamberlain Guestis in his robes of state, hand atop the shoulder of one of his attendants in order to brace himself. The wind was having its way with him, buffeting his whip-thin body and ridiculing what scant hair he had left.

Poor Guestis, she thought. He was such a fish-in-a-bucket anywhere but in the palace. She would have spared him the insecurity of open skies and the insult of rain on his silks, but that was not her indulgence to offer. High as his rank was here in Dragonsdeep, hers was higher still. Protocol was protocol.

The wind sloughed ineffectually off her tall, solid frame. The rise and fall of the deck perturbed her even less. The ship came about into the wind, spent its momentum, and eased close to the quay. Mooring ropes were thrown, caught, and secured over the bollards.

Her footman knew enough not to attempt to aid her as she clambered onto the gangway and marched across. She took four strides onto the flagstones of the quay, gave herself a single heartbeat to accustom her legs to the steadiness of the surface beneath her feet, and she was Arrived.

"Revered Mage," Guestis said, and gave her a precise quarter bow, bending at the waist.

"My Dear Chamberlain," she replied, and gave him an equally precise nod of the head.

"I'm afraid we did not expect you quite so soon," he said. "By your leave, we will not hold the banquet for you until tomorrow evening."

"Quite all right. Mustn't rush those things."

"For now, I have instructed the steward to bring up a bottle of your favorite vintage from Aleoth, and the chef is at work on a few light savories to deliver to your suite."

"Excellent," she said.

They proceeded down the avenue of guardsmen to the funicular platform and entered the coach. She waved away Guestis's attendants and boarded with only him. When the door closed, she and the chamberlain could speak without being overheard.

"Don't add anything to the schedule today," she told him. "I need to see the body."

The chamberlain paled. "As...as you wish."

The coach began its gentle descent down the angled tunnel. Leyaril remained upright. Guestis eyed the seats.

"Don't wobble," she scolded.

He straightened. Tightened his grip on the handrail. But he looked more miserable than ever. "Do I have to go with you to see it?"

"Yes."

"Oh, dear."

"You're afraid of a *dead* dragon? It's the living ones that give *me* pause."

"It's just that it seems so impossible. Gloroc's own sister. Slain, just like that."

"Beyiss," she chided. "Her name was Beyiss." Though even as Leyaril said it, she realized how few times she had ever uttered the name. For so long, the female dragon had been Gloroc's secret, never to be mentioned, not even by the few who knew of her existence. "And it was far from 'Just like that.' As I'm sure you must know."

Poor Guestis. He was a peerless housekeeper. He should not have been the one left to oversee such an inconvenient matter as a dead dragon in the great hall. That should have fallen to Vanril. But Vanril had had the bad grace to die not more than an hour after Beyiss had been slain.

How many decades had it been, she wondered, that Dragons-deep had lacked the presence of a mage of the Ril? Not since Gloroc had named the initial cadre. Not since she had been a maiden, barely aware how to craft a charm or mix a potion, her potential unrecognized by anyone.

The coach emerged from the tunnel into the brightness of the upper dome. Their descent was almost half done. The ascending coach on the other track was fast approaching their level.

She reached out and stroked the wispy strands at the crown of Guestis's head, the remnant of what had once been a forest of curls. "I am here now, Tadpole. Don't I always take care of things? Think of how well it went the last time I came to your rescue."

He did not blush. That told her how genuinely unsettled he was.

"The people are murmuring," he told her. "*My staff* is murmur-ing. Why has our master stayed away? It's as if..."

He didn't say the rest. He wasn't the sort who would.

"Let them murmur." She gave an exaggerated shrug. "Gloroc's plan was to go to the battlefront at this time, and so he has gone to the battlefront. What would he have done if he had detoured back here? I think you know. Would you have wanted to witness his mood? It doesn't pay to be a bystander of any sort when he's in a fury. The slightest wrong word out of your mouth, and you would have been no more than a stain of soot on a wall."

"I suppose you have a point."

She squeezed his shoulder. "It *is* a shock that Beyiss is dead. And Vanril, too. But that doesn't change the fact that the war is nearly won. The enemy has not seen what two dragons working together can do. All we need now is one good rainstorm over Simorilia, then all of Tanagaran will see how unstoppable Gloroc is. Once the armies of Keron and Fanhar are routed, what will murmurs in Dragonsdeep matter?"

"Yes." The wrinkles in his forehead eased. "Yes. You are right, of course."

Leyaril wasn't satisfied. Guestis was still gripping the handrail too tightly. She leaned closer still, and whispered right into his ear.

"Have no concern about what rebels have done or might do. *I am not afraid of them.*"

He turned and looked straight at her. She gave him her little smile. It was the smile that made her enemies soil themselves — but it was also the one that made her friends know they had her protection.

Guestis nodded.

As one, they turned toward the door of the coach. They were almost to the bottom. Rooftops rose to their eye-level. Soon thereafter came the soft bump of the coach settling into its berth.

The doors were opened. Leyaril advanced into the aisle between the waiting guardsmen—another platoon of thirty, even more resplendent those that had awaited her on the quay, the shine of their armor unblemished by weather. Scaffolding had been erected along the lane, and there stood the Witnesses. A full two hundred, as befit her status. Clerks and tailors, street sweepers and barkeeps. Women, men, children. All chosen because they were no one in particular other than denizens of the city, a set of mouths to tell the tale that Leyaril the Poisoner was come to speak for the Dragon, to breath the flame of His law in His absence. She did not actually look at them. Why would she? The point was that they look at *her*. They *must* look at her, if they wanted to keep their heads attached to their necks.

The procession continued down the avenue and up the steps of the main palace entrance, a dozen guardsman serving as the phalanx. Leyaril was positioned behind them in the center of their chevron, but it was she who set the pace with her long, assertive strides. The guardsmen matched her well enough, but Guestis and the attendants struggled not to be overrun by the eighteen guardsmen bringing up the rear.

She proceeded, entering what in any other palace would have been considered a great hall, for it was large enough that even Gloroc had been known to use it as his exit way when he wished to venture out to fly within the confines of the city dome. Here, it was only an antechamber.

One of Gloroc's admonishment relics hung from the ceiling by long strands of tapestry cord. The flesh doll was new to her, made from a corpse of a man who had still been alive back when she had been dispatched to be the representative of the Ril in Firsthold. The ankles were bound, but the knees were splayed wide. The hands were clutched around the neck as if the fool was choking himself. The expression was one of suffocation.

She reached up and gave the left big toe of the dead man a fond little squeeze.

"Marnus. How good you look there. How's the wife?"

She took a moment to admire the quality of the taxidermy. It was one of Quandai's pieces, she was sure. He had shaped the expression to present the late, sadly incompetent minister of the treasury in the manner Gloroc commanded, and yet kept him looking like the man his acquaintances and colleagues knew. Genius.

She continued into the palace, waving her escort off to their normal duty stations. Guestis alone went with her into the royal quarters.

In due course they came to the great audience hall. The Dragon's Den, some called it. Multitudes had been brought within its tapestried walls over the past few decades. Most found it to be a venue of dread. It was not so for her. Leyaril had only ever met with good luck here. Praise. Advancement. Or best of all, tutoring in the methods of sorcery that only a dragon could teach.

The massive double doors were not only closed and locked, but chained. Four guards stood by the servant door. They bowed to her, saluted Guestis, and stood aside.

Guestis unlocked this smaller door and held it open for her. After she had proceeded through, he followed and turned the lock closed again, securing them inside.

"Enliven the lights," she commanded.

Guestis turned the valves and phosphorescence poured into the receptacles in the ceiling. The shadows melted. The dark mass on the floor in the center of the vast room became a dragon.

The air was rife with the fetor of decay, overlaid by the fumes of embalming fluid and of the sealant that had been brushed upon the cadaver's skin. Guestis wrinkled his nose. To Leyaril, accustomed as she was to the miasma of her laboratory, it was a bouquet. She inhaled deeply, using her nose as much as her eyes to assess the tableau in front of her.

Within all the other scents was a whiff of dragonsbane. The crew of undertakers had undoubtedly cleaned away every trace they could find—carefully, so as not to be killed in the process—but a vestige remained inside the sewn-up wounds. The assassins had plunged their weapons deep. The fellit was in the beast's very flesh now, a marinade of poison few could appreciate as thoroughly as Leyaril could.

Leyaril strode up to the head. The crew had propped it upon a dais, as Gloroc's dispatch had ordered them to do, so that as they did the rest of their funereal work, they would have to look *up* to gaze at the face of Beyiss the Magnificent.

The eyes had been sewn shut. The mouth as well. The nostrils had been stuffed closed with dark packing material. The work had been skillfully done, if not as expertly and thoroughly as a craftsman like Quandai could accomplish, given enough time. Viewed from certain angles, Beyiss appeared to be simply asleep.

Leyaril studied the ragged tear in the lips of the she-dragon. The flesh had been sewn up, but to hide the damage would take cosmetic work beyond that the undertakers had been assigned to perform.

"I'm told a pair of teeth were torn out," she said.

The last bit of color drained from Guestis's face. He was ordinarily a pale-complected man. Now he was the same shade as a grub wriggling on a shovelful of freshly-turned soil.

"I don't need to see," she reassured him. "I'm not here for that."

The chamberlain let go of the breath he'd been holding.

Had it been her mandate, Leyaril would not have hesitated to cut the sutures and call in the four guardsmen to stretch open the dragon's mouth for her inspection. But Gloroc had told Leyaril not to touch his sister's body, and she was quite sure that included touch by proxy.

She wondered if Gloroc would in the long run leave alive anyone who had directly handled the body. Gloroc seldom punished anyone who served him loyally and with competence, but perhaps she should get to work on a batch of Sweet Night, in case she needed to offer the wretches a painless demise.

She walked around the body—slowly, absorbing what she was seeing. The situation was all she had been led to believe, but not fully believable until her eyes and other senses confirmed it. When she had last seen Beyiss, she had been vibrant from the metamorphosis, an airbreather at last, as alive as a dragon ever is during the course of its seven-thousand-year lifetime.

The contortions of her death had twisted her tail. Leyaril plainly made out the vulvic seam, still closed by a membrane as thick as leather, the potential of the womb within to remain forever untapped.

Plan ruined. Beyiss would soon have become fertile and Gloroc would have bred her with Aroc. Leyaril knew any babies would have taken the two millennia or more to mature—the same length of time that Gloroc and Beyiss and Aroc had required. She had found it hard to dwell on the prospect, because it was certain never to come to fruition within her lifetime. Gloroc, though, was furious. To him, the matter was immediate and compelling. So much the better that it was she, and not her master, who stood here now.

She completed her circuit to find Guestis waiting expectantly.

She stroked his lightly-whiskered cheek with the back of her hand. "Do you recall when you watched over me in my apothecary keep, that night I tested my version of heartbrace?"

"Of course."

"I need that sort of tending now. Inform the guards that we will not come out for over an hour. Emphasize that we are not to be disturbed."

He did as she asked. Meanwhile she went to the divans along the west wall, fetched several pillows, and lay them on the floor at the base of the dais.

"Sit. Lean back. Let me rest my head in your lap," she told the chamberlain when he returned.

He obeyed. Soon she was stretched out, her head settled upon Guestis's thigh, the tip of Beyiss's snout looming over her head.

"I will seem to be unconscious for an interval. The opposite will be true. My mind will be stretched—so much so that I may fail to pay attention to the here and now. If I convulse, keep me from chewing up my tongue or jamming my elbows into anything hard. Don't let me crawl off anywhere. And do keep me from drowning in my own vomit, will you?"

Guestis hesitated. "Compared to me, you are quite strong. How do I—"

"Don't worry," she said. "When I'm in the trance, I'll have no more strength than a four-year-old."

"Very well then."

"I may utter words," she added. "Try to remember what I say, but do not engage in conversation, even if it seems I am conversing with you. Later, when it's over, I'll ask you to repeat what I said."

"I understand."

"I'm beginning now," she announced, deciding it was best to say that aloud, because he might have been expecting her to bite down on a lozenge or gulp a dose of an elixir, as she might well do were she using her usual sort of magic. But today, she was resorting to a technique Omril had taught her. He was a master of it. Enril, too— perhaps even the best at it of all of the Ril order. The catalyst was not chemical, but a matter of how she concentrated.

She closed her eyes. That was the simple part—removing the distraction of anything in view. Sounds were nearly as easy to ignore. Guestis remained as silent as she had bid him to be. The loudest noise was that of her own heartbeat. Ignoring the fog of strange odors was more of a challenge.

Stage by stage, she slipped into the target goal of mind, opening her mage sense. She no longer perceived walls, objects, or movement. She saw enchantments. Moreover, she saw the *history* of those enchantments. Easiest to perceive was magic that had been cast right there in the chamber, or that had been particularly vibrant, or that had remained in place a long while.

Some of what she sensed was familiar. Gloroc had used his sorcery often in this place. Gloroc was himself a magical creature, and his occupation wrote its own sort of chronicle into the fabric of the tapestries, into the crevices of the masonry. The presence of the portal was of course blatantly clear; it was one of the features that had an actual shape, a rectangle strung across the far end of the room, as clear to her as if it had been activated.

The presence of that portal had been a trap, Leyaril saw. It had

been a means of persuading Gloroc that he was secure while he occupied this chamber, because he could always dive through to elsewhere
at a moment's notice. As indeed he had, when the assassins had failed
to snare him as well as they had meant to.

She studied the tale of the trap, written in the palimpsest of the
spent energies. The magic had been strong, as strong as any she had
experienced, as strong perhaps as human magic could become.

Gloroc had been lucky. He would not have escaped if the spell
had settled upon him alone. But Beyiss had been in the chamber with
him. Two dragons, both struggling for freedom at the same time, was
more than the talismans and their practitioner could deal with.

Her master had been wise not to come back here. His guess had
been correct. The Dragonslayer was alive. The palace reeked with his
energies, and they were not echoes of castings by a long-dead mage.
They were active traces, still bolstered by a connection to a living
source.

"It was here. All around us. All this time," she murmured.

All these decades, Gloroc had lived in Dragonsdeep. In this very
palace. And some of the enchantments Leyaril was detecting now had
lurked there even then. Walls hidden by illusion. Snares set along
secret passageways. A mesh of tiny nodes embedded in the masonry,
designed to amplify the effect of the talismans the assassins had
brought in.

Concealing all that had required its own incredible level of
spellcasting. Leyaril was a powerful mage in her own right, and yet
even she could not begin to say how the Dragonslayer had managed
it. His handiwork was only visible now because the trap had been
sprung, and the seamlessness of the camouflage had been disrupted.

Over the days and weeks to come, she would try to study the
traces one at a time. They were fascinating. Somewhere off in other
portions of the palace, they radiated an immediacy she found compelling, for all that they must be the essence of sorcery wrought ten or
more centuries ago.

In the near term, though, she had determined what needed to be determined. There was no snare awaiting Gloroc should he return. The trap could not be re-set. If anyone tried, they would be discovered in the midst of the attempt.

She opened her eyes.

"All done," she told Guestis.

The chamberlain blinked. "You seemed to be sleeping. Except the one time you spoke." He repeated the words. No surprises there. She had a clear memory of what she had said.

"Hard to predict my body's reaction. Apparently this time I needn't have worried." Then she tried to sit up. She made it only halfway before crumpling so abruptly her head bounced off Guestis's knee.

"Ow."

"Ow," echoed Guestis.

She gave herself several more moments, then tried again. This time she made it, but would have fallen back down if not for Guestis's support. A quarter of an hour passed before she was on her feet, with full control over her body.

"Let's get you to your quarters," Guestis suggested. "I'm sure the food is ready by now."

"That will have to wait a little longer. I have one more room I need to inspect."

CHAPTER FOURTEEN

GEIM FOUND IT remarkable to see the new Quandai. He was no longer the man who had stood in the doorway nearly wetting himself as he realized fugitives of the Dragon had come to his home. The little taxidermist had gone through a metamorphosis.

Geim couldn't help but recall an incident from his boyhood along the River Sha, when he had watched Ellax, his tribe's premier egg thief, engaged in his trade. The Igitians had a superstition that promised great good fortune to any bride who cooked a fresh green-and-gold osprey egg for her husband's breakfast the morning after the wedding night. Ellax had a desperate buyer willing to pay an extraordinary price, and so while Geim and his friend Bullen watched, Ellax climbed to an osprey nest high in a dead river dangler in the hope of finding that rare prize.

Ellax at last found a foothold and handhold that allowed him to look into the massive nest of sticks, moss, and a decade's worth of guano. He smiled. He reached out—

And the long-dead branch broke beneath his feet. The egg sailed from his grip.

Even from the ground, Geim could tell the egg was green with gold flecks, not the common mixture of sienna and cream. It was precisely what Ellax had come for. Yet Ellax didn't attempt to recapture it. The whole treetop and the nest were falling apart. He let himself fall, devoting his attention to the task of determining where the branches further down were. None of those lower branches was strong enough to bear the impact if he landed full upon them, but by momentarily catching hold of them, he slowed the momentum of his plunge. In the end, he landed adroitly on his feet on the rocky bank at the base of the tree, and stepped aside just before the nest made its impact on the same spot.

Ellax was safe. No bones broken. Later in the day, he found another nest and another green-and-gold egg, and fulfilled his contract.

That was the sort of calm Geim was seeing today. Quandai had siphoned out his nervousness and put the jug away in a cupboard. He was behaving as though sneaking a rebel Elandri prince and two Vanihr into the Dragon's palace was the sort of thing he did every day.

Geim was startled to see how unnecessary such things as invisibility spells were. It was not a fortress they were infiltrating. The purpose of the place was not protection. It was the setting from which the daily administration of the empire was enacted. It had many doors. Every day through those doors passed hundreds of menial staff and common functionaries. Quandai knew the routines. He knew the schedules of the maids and cooks and stewards, the guards and ministers and secretaries. And on the inside, he had an ally who could be trusted to leave a service entrance unlocked at the right time.

It helped that the Ril sorceress was due to arrive soon. A day more. Perhaps two. The place was buzzing with the preparations. No one looked twice at a passing quartet of men wearing the livery of palace custodians.

In due course they reached a storeroom in the lowest level — or at least, the lowest level shown in the architect's records. Quandai produced a key. Moments later they were secreted inside.

The taxidermist strode across the chamber, pushed a crate out of the way, and held his lantern up to the lower part of the far wall. Geim saw nothing more there than a discolored brick.

"This is the spot," Quandai said.

Toren helped him move the crate fully away from the wall. They shifted a few barrels so that if any servant happened to visit the storeroom in the next few hours, that person would be unlikely to notice that a section of wall had been deliberately exposed.

Alemar opened the plain workman's sack in which he had hidden the Dragonslayer's talismans. He pulled out the right-hand gauntlet.

He studied it soberly. Geim knew Alemar had often worn the item and used its magic in the years since he and Elenya had returned from Setan, but he had not done so since Toren had laid claim to the whole pair. He slid his hand in with obvious reluctance.

He inhaled sharply. His eyes pooled to black. And then he was steady, as if he had put on nothing more unusual than a blacksmith's glove.

"Yes," he told Quandai. "I see it now."

Alemar placed his armored hand upon the wall, and the shape of a large door was abruptly outlined in a glowing green filament. He pressed the rectangle near the right edge. The section of wall began to swing inward. It did so silently, but sluggishly. Alemar had to exert himself to keep it moving.

Finally it was out of the way, revealing a cobwebbed passageway. Alemar touched the side wall, and the way became lit with the same eerie blue werelight of the tunnel that had led them into Dragonsdeep, back when Match and Ebben and Treggei had been alive to accompany them.

They moved inside. Geim tried giving the door a shove to close it, only to find it was like trying to lift all of Dragonsdeep from its foundation.

Alemar took care of the matter, but again only by straining. In a way Geim was reassured to see how difficult the door was to move, because it meant no one could easily follow them.

They proceeded down the passageway, which soon forked, then forked again. Quandai had indicated they could come up in any of several spots within the palace if needed, but today only the one destination mattered. Quandai consulted the old map he had brought along, and indicated which choices of route to select.

They arrived at another door. Again it took magic to open it, and again Alemar was up to the task. Soon they all stepped into a large pitched-brick barrel vault. Another entrance stood on the opposite side. Geim guessed that had been the main entrance, sealed off by the Dragon's masons. The dust and desiccated roach carcasses on the floor served as evidence of how long ago that had been done.

The vault was an unpretentious, almost utilitarian sort of space with the exception of one feature—a semi-circular dais of polished white stone. The dais took up nearly a third of the floor area, creating the effect of a performance stage, with the rest of the chamber becoming the audience gallery. The illumination falling upon the dais was at least double the amount reaching the walls.

"There you have it," Quandai told Alemar. "Do you see the mechanism? Can you send the summons?"

Alemar concentrated upon the dais, his left hand absently stroking the middle knuckle gem of the gauntlet. Several moments passed before he nodded. "Yes. It's quite straightforward, actually."

"I leave you to it, then. I'll wait over there." Quandai retreated to the dim area near the opening from which they had emerged.

Toren removed his wig and false beard and stored them in his satchel. Even though his complexion was still pale from the cosmetics, he was now recognizable as a Vanihr—and for that matter, recognizable as himself—even at a glance.

Geim left his disguise untouched. "I'm going to wait with Quandai," he said.

Toren understood immediately, but Alemar gazed at him for several moments, sorting it out.

"As you wish," Alemar said.

Geim retreated. Alemar and Toren approached the dais.

The summoning took nearly half an hour. Alemar was cursing under his breath by the end of the interval. Then the glow upon the dais increased and all at once, a woman was standing in the center of the brightness.

Geim knew her, and he didn't. Her height, the curve of her back, her carriage, the songbird sparkle of her gaze—these features he knew because they were indelible facets of the woman he knew as Janna. But she was not wearing the guise of the high priestess of Struth now. She was Miranda.

Geim wished it were not so. He would have liked to regard the face he knew, to help him conjure the temple of Struth in his mind's eye—the one place he had ever regarded as home after he had been forced to flee north. Instead, what he saw was this stranger.

"I am here," she said.

The sound of her voice was faint, as if it had wafted its way around the chamber to reach their ears. It was only one of the ways the magic of the oracle chamber seemed weak. Miranda did not occupy the vault the way someone who was really there would. What had seemed to be a gown of sheer silk was instead made of white muslin, thick enough to serve as outdoor wear. What Geim was seeing through it was the far wall, not skin. He detected none of the small aspects of presence. No perfume. No susurrus of movement as she glided closer to the edge of the dais.

She stopped at the edge nearest Alemar and Toren. She squinted. "Come closer," she told them. "I can't quite see you."

Alemar and Toren took a step forward, putting them fully within the illuminated area. As for Geim, he did just the opposite, fading back until he was leaning on the back wall, farther from her than even Quandai was.

Miranda's gaze paused upon the gauntlet Alemar wore, and then upon the lack of anything covering Toren's hands. "I couldn't imagine who else could be calling out to me from Wizardsdeep, but I could barely believe it's really you. I thought you were dead."

"Half of us *did* die," Alemar said. He did not raise his voice. His tone remained even-pitched—and as cold as Geim had ever heard him adopt.

"I am sorry for that."

Geim was surprised by the sincerity of her tone. He had expected her to deflect blame. But she lowered her glance, posture wilting at the shoulders. "I take it my servant was one of the casualties?"

Geim was relieved when Alemar chose to say nothing about his survival, nor even glance back over his shoulder.

"You owe us explanations," the prince said.

She nodded.

"Did you know you were sending us into a nest of dragons?"

She avoided his stare. "The whole point of the plan was to kill Gloroc when he was the only dragon to be dealt with. We hoped one was all you would find."

"But you knew he had siblings."

"We knew it was possible."

"That was information we should have had."

"Would it have helped to know you might face as many as nine dragons?"

Alemar's mouth popped open.

"That is one of the answers." Miranda held her hand out toward Alemar. "I know you to be a brave man, young nephew, yet what I just said shocked you. Would you have agreed to the mission, knowing the odds might be that bad?"

"There are *nine* dragons?" Alemar asked.

"Possibly."

"How can you know this?"

Her shape flickered, then slowly was restored, shifting from ethereal to faint to a fidelity nearly as distinct as if she had stepped through a portal and joined them in the chamber. She was trembling by the time it was over. When she manifested fully, Geim noticed obvious signs of strain. And not just the ordeal of the moment. Grey flecked her hair more profoundly than it had the time he had first seen her as her true self, back in the temple. The past few months had not been kind to her. The flesh along her jawline was looser. The wrinkles around her eyes had deepened.

"Triss died while delving into my brother's mind. A trace of her was left inside him. Left to torment him. But her presence was useful in one particular way. He could sense her babies. We tracked those young dragons, trying to destroy them all while they were still vulnerable. We cut their number in half before the survivors fled so far into The Deeps we couldn't reach them. We hoped that we had done enough. There were in fact more casualties. Some were killed by predators, or by accidents, or by their own bickering. But then Gloroc assumed control. He formed an alliance with four of his brothers and four of his sisters. It's the pattern back on Serpent Moon. A master dragon forming its cabal. Eventually they discovered how to break the link and my brother could no longer sense them. But at that point, all nine were thriving. We don't know how many are left. All of them? Perhaps. How many dragons did you encounter?"

The question was both reassuring and at the same time, ominous. Geim was relieved Miranda didn't already know all they knew, but on the other hand, it meant she might not have answers they needed.

Alemar quickly summarized what they had found when they reached Gloroc. Miranda did not seem surprised when Alemar described Gloroc's escape. That much she had some way of knowing, even all the way back in Headwater.

"So close," she murmured. "If only we had been able to make the attempt earlier. Even just a matter of weeks earlier, it would seem."

"And why was that?" Alemar demanded. "Why the delay?"

"You know as well as I. We did not have anyone who could use the gauntlets."

"Your brother made the gauntlets. Surely he could have used them. He could have used them half a century ago, when Gloroc emerged from The Deeps."

"That was not possible. Still is not possible."

"Why?"

"We are not the same as we once were. You don't understand what it requires for us just to remain among the living."

As she was speaking, Geim found himself watching Toren. He was holding himself differently. His gaze was centered upon Miranda's mouth, as if he were paying attention not so much to the content of her words, but to the modulation of her voice, like a man walking through a camp would halt and listen when he realized one of the speakers inside the nearest tent was someone he had known for many years.

He was not Toren. At the moment, he was Polk.

"Where is he?" Polk asked.

As had been the case back at Quandai's house, the words came out with antiquated phrasing, but they rolled out with the assuredness that comes of having lived many years and learning precisely how to say what one wants to say.

Tears abruptly welled in Miranda's eyes. "It appears I'm not the only one who has awakened from a long sleep."

Polk, by contrast, showed no visible emotion. "Where is he?" he repeated.

Miranda wiped her cheeks with a sleeve. "He's not here."

"Are you telling the truth?"

Miranda lifted a hand, palm up. "You learned the trick long ago of knowing when I am telling the truth, and when I am not."

"So you say."

"He is not here. I mean that plainly. He is not in the temple. He is not in Serthe at all."

"You made a promise to me, long ago. Both of you. For as long as you lived, you would protect Elandris."

Fresh tears welled onto her lower lashes. "We are doing all we can. *He* is doing what he can. Believe me when I say I wish he were here to speak with you. I begged him to stay. I argued we should try to do as we had been doing these past few decades, and keep to this refuge, where Struth's magic lingers and our strength is at its highest. But he left."

Polk turned aside, brows furrowed.

"You have no help to offer us here in Dragonsdeep?" Alemar

asked the sorceress.

She pointed. "You have the gauntlets, and an adept trained to use them. Providing those took centuries of preparation and planning. If we could have provided more, we would already have done so."

Alemar glowered. "I will not—"

Polk placed a hand on Alemar's upper arm. He leaned in and whispered.

Alemar frowned. He took one last long glance at Miranda, raised his armored hand, and snapped his fingers.

The image of the sorceress vanished. The glow upon the dais faded back to its former level.

Mystified, Geim approached, Quandai at his side. "It's over?"

"There was nothing to be gained by more conversation," Polk said.

"I don't understand," Geim said.

"We have to make our own way," Polk explained. "If anything, it was Miranda who needed our help. It was...a theme I didn't like to see repeated."

Alemar nodded his agreement. "She was terrified."

It was Quandai's turn to be confused. "Was she? She seemed ill at ease, yes, but was it fear? I'm not sure I saw that."

"You don't know her as I do," Polk replied. "The last time I saw her that frightened was right after Triss had killed our shipmates and we had every reason to expect we'd be next. The difference this time is, she's old and weary. I know that feeling. You get so beaten down by the years you don't have the energy to tremble or fall into hysterics."

"So what do we do next?" Geim asked.

Alemar sighed. "Well, first of all, we finish what I meant for us to do. We break into Omril's chambers and steal the talismans."

"Please don't do that," Polk said.

"I'm aware of your reservations."

"There is more I want to say."

Alemar sighed. "Go on."

"What kind of a man was Omril?"

"What do you mean?"

"Was he a good man?"

"Of course not."

"Then ignore whatever he left in his quarters. In my experience, it doesn't pay to use the tools of a bad man to try to further your goals."

"This is not the time for a philosophical debate," Alemar responded. "We need that arsenal."

"I don't agree. Leave it be."

"And do what? Just keep hiding in Quandai's house?"

"I'm saying you don't have to use the Dragonslayer's approach, putting all your hope into spells and weapons and trying to do it all yourself."

"It has come down to me, whether I like it or not."

"Has it?" Polk gestured toward Quandai, then toward Geim, then toward himself. "Are you alone? I realize you feel that way. You're worried if you don't go upstairs and raid Omril's hoard and use what you find to help you stage an attack, the war will fail, your loved ones will die, Gloroc will win. But that's desperation talking."

"What would you have me do?"

"First and foremost, stay alive. That alone is helping to keep Gloroc in check. Think how much more secure he would be if your father and your half-brother fall on the battlefield, and your sister is killed in Cilendrodel, and you throw your life away here? Who will the opposition rally around? Survive, and you give his enemies the hope they'll survive as well."

"Who would follow a coward?"

"I'm not saying cower in a basement. I'm saying choose your fights carefully. Don't assume you have to do it all. Stay alive, and give friends and allies a chance to find their way to you."

"You have a lot of faith in the people of Elandris."

Polk smiled. "Yes. I do."

"Let's say I do as you recommend. I'm not sure what my next step is. Getting to Omril's trove was the 'small goal' I was aiming at."

"I'm not certain either. But tell me, if you weren't embroiled in this war, if you weren't Alemar Olendim son of Keron, what would you want to fill your days with?"

Alemar sighed. "If I could, I'd go back to being what I was. The kind of magician I was."

"And what kind were you?"

"I was a healer."

A brightness welled up in Polk's expression. Geim was struck by how even though the eyes belonged to Toren, the spirit radiating out of them was all Polk.

"Now isn't that interesting? That's not something you ever mentioned before. Here you are, acting like a warrior."

"That's what I've had to be, for quite some time now."

"When you aren't being your true self, you miss things. I ask you, what choice would a healer make here and now? What would your next move be?" Polk reached out and flicked a fingernail at one of the jewels adorning the gauntlet. "Would you really be looking for more weapons?"

—o—

Leyaril wiped sweat from her brow. There. Finally done. She could at last take her ease, have a bite to eat. And a bath. Definitely a bath.

She stood at the threshold of Omril's chambers, regarding the work she had done, making sure one last time that she had not disturbed the existing enchantments. There were many of those. Omril relished snare-setting. Any non-magician trespassing here would quickly die. Even she would have needed hours to neutralize all of the ways she might be captured or killed if she ventured inside. For the sake of caution, she had done all of her work from the open doorway.

Nothing had been disturbed. That was good. Finally she could set aside the worry she'd had ever since receiving the dispatch from Enril, informing her that he had found Omril, and that Omril's mind had been delved. Unlikely though it was that the Cilendri prince could have capitalized upon the knowledge of the existence of the collection, still it was best to be certain the trove was secure. The Cilendri prince had, to be sure, proved he was a resourceful adversary.

In the weeks to come, she would be sure to keep an eye on the chamber. Meanwhile, her hard hours of labor were complete. Now the trove was guarded not only by what Omril had set in place, but by her own extra layers of protection.

She smiled, picturing the fate of anyone who triggered any of her sentry charms. There was good reason she was known as the Poisoner.

She closed the door, locked it, and put the key away. Finally she was able to let go of the strands of energy she'd been keeping in place, and open up her senses to the general environment.

Strange. The palace no longer reeked of the Dragonslayer's magic as profoundly as it had seemed while she was examining Beyiss's corpse. Perhaps she was too weary now to sense it as keenly. Or perhaps she had imagined its potency earlier. After all, she'd had a lot on her mind.

She'd puzzle it out another day. In the meantime, she set off in the direction of her suite.

CHAPTER FIFTEEN

IT WAS THE shivering that woke her—that and the daylight filtering through her eyelids. Elenya knew the room should be dim, curtains drawn. She should have been snug beneath blankets, warmer upon awakening than any recent morning, not cold enough to make her teeth chatter. Why was this not how it was?

She opened her eyes. Just a bit. Squinted. She could only see an arm's length or so in front of her face. The rest was blurred. She could see enough to understand that she was lying on her side on a platform of rough-hewn wood. The platform was moving. The predominant sound was sloshing.

Poles in river water.

Her nostrils and upper lip reeked with the anise and mushroom bouquet of rapebrew. Someone must have scavenged through the kit of the quarryfolk's midwife and boiled down a bottle of birthwine to full potency. She couldn't believe she had fallen victim. You could smell rapebrew coming from across a room, yet somehow she had not stirred until an instant before the cloth had been clamped over her nose and mouth.

Her eyes fluttered. Brighter now. She had gone blank again, losing another few minutes. Maybe longer. She thought she heard a fish jump. She saw a pair of booted feet. As she tried to scan higher, the brightness made her close her eyes.

And out she went again.

In the end she wasn't sure how many times she slipped in and out of awareness. Finally she reached a point when she knew she was alert and knew it would last. Once that was true, she chose not to reveal her recovery, hoping that would give her some advantage. Calling upon sounds and smells and the occasional glimpse from between slitted eyelids, she took stock of her predicament.

She was on a barge. It was manned by three young, strong men. She had seen all three of them among the quarryfolk the previous night at supper. One was Ravvo, the son of the headman.

She had no weapons. She was all but naked, clad only in the thin shift she had worn to bed.

A manacle enclosed her right wrist—the uninjured one. Another manacle was locked around her right ankle. The chains were thick, the iron unrusted, the padlocks completely shut.

The pain in her crotch felt like the normal pressure of a full bladder, but she took several deep breaths, fearing the pain might have multiple causes. But no, she had not been raped.

Becoming sure of that fact helped calm her, and once the calm took hold, her mind started to work properly. No rape suggested the trio had not been able to afford the time to abuse her. They had devoted all of their efforts to the kidnap and getaway.

They were on the Knotted River. Had to be. The easiest way for her abductors to put distance between themselves and her warriors was to rush her to the ferrytown—the very place the teamster had been going when he had hauled away the cornerstone. Elenya had thought it prudent to post a man overnight along the wagon road— not so much because she expected anyone to be leaving the quarry outpost during the night, but so that if any Dragon's men approached the hamlet, her group would have a bit of warning. Given that she had not already been rescued, Ravvo and his henchmen must not have taken the wagon road. She concluded they must have slung her over a oeikani and ridden to the ferrytown through the woods. The sore places on her torso matched the sort of bruising she would have sustained while hanging unconscious across a saddle.

The barge was probably stolen. Easy enough to do in the middle of the night. They'd taken an almost empty one containing only a pair of crates and some coils of rope. It rode high in the water and was making good speed. This was the case despite the river's reputation. It was often called The Lazy Muddy. The land from here to the coast was nearly flat. That's what made barge navigation possible. But a current was still a current. Each moment she was getting farther and farther from her potential rescuers, and the water wouldn't get tired the way men or oeikani would. Ravvo and both of the others were doing their best to ensure they reached the Dragon's garrison post before the end of the day. Sweat darkened their stoneworker's frocks as they worked the poles.

She didn't like her chances of remaining unmolested. Later in the day, when they were confident they had bested all pursuit, they would take their ease. She had little doubt what sort of entertainment they would be inclined toward. There was probably good reason the trio was familiar with making rapebrew.

Contemplating all that, she ended up staring hard at Ravvo. When he turned to check on her, he saw at once she was awake.

He sauntered over, tossing the raftpole from hand to hand. "They say you're quite the fighter. Didn't have much struggle in you last night."

"Unlock the manacles and I'll try not to disappoint you," she replied.

"Magic them open, if you can."

He couldn't have mocked her more effectively. If she'd had the Dragonslayer's gauntlet, she could indeed have broken free, but none of the other magic she knew could increase her strength.

"Your father is quite a convincing liar," she said, if only to change the subject.

Ravvo laughed. "My father? My father is a fool. All that reward money to be had, and he smokes with you and feeds you a good meal?"

So that was it. Elenya's mistake had not been the trust she extended to Thrend, but the assumption he had control of his people.

"My father never wanted to be anything but a stonecutter, living in the same house all his life. Me? I'll have a fine house on the coast. A *wooden* house, soft with carpets, full of servants. I'll never pick up a chisel again in all my days."

He laughed again and returned to his task. The trio weren't taking any chances, Elenya was sorry to see.

Kneeling there captive, she estimated the odds of escape or rescue, and did not like results of her calculation. The only reason she held out hope was that if these three had acted on their own, against the wishes of the headman, then the headman would not try to stop her companions when they set out in pursuit.

To have any chance of catching up, someone would have had to notice her absence right away. Unfortunately Ravvo had known how to get out of the cottage and then out of the outpost without being seen. They had surely drugged Slees as well. Given how early in the night they had taken her, it might have been hours before the abduction was discovered.

Her friends had not caught up so far. That meant they had not reached the ferrytown until well after Ravvo and the others had cast off. They would never catch up now unless the barge ran aground. Small hope of that. The trio kept studying the water ahead, alert for sand bars and snags.

She was truly caught. She shivered again, but this time it was not just the exposure to the elements. She had never been in a position like this. Even in Zyraii, surrounded on every side by T'lil warriors, it had been her choice to lower her sword.

She pulled on the chains, but they proved just as sturdy as they looked, and all the effort accomplished was to chafe her wrist and ankle. She lay back down on her side.

Ravvo noticed her there, crumpled. He snorted.

The barge continued along. They passed an otterman's hut and later a rotting dock where a footpath led off into overgrown mounds of dangleberry; otherwise they saw no evidence of civilization. Few locals wanted to live right near the estuaries and trickle ponds where the midges and mosquitoes and fever flies grew thick every summer. Eventually the river course transformed into a long, lazy snake bend, turning first one way and then back. The three men all shifted toward the prow, making sure the current didn't induce the barge to run aground.

Elenya caught an iridescent flutter out of the corner of her eyes. She managed not to jump or cry out, but she could not have been more startled.

A pair of rythni landed only half an arm's length in front of her. They held the heavy key to the padlocks. Where had they found it? How had they taken possession? No matter. She didn't care how. All she knew is that they had managed to ferry it to her, and now were lowering it softly to the deck.

The little creatures were gone as quickly as they had come. But the key remained.

Elenya moved as efficiently as she could in silence. She managed to free her ankle without making a click. She wasn't so lucky when she unshackled her wrist.

The man closest to her heard the noise. As she rose to her feet, he pulled out his knife and charged her.

He was a head taller than she, and heavy-set. He expected her to retreat. His type so often did. So she met his charge with one of her own. He wasn't yet committed to his knife thrust. She was able to divert the blade off-line with her rear hand as she plunged the stiff fingers of her forward hand into his throat. She grabbed his windpipe and twisted.

She had taken a risk. Had he recognized a moment earlier what she was up to, he would have clamped his chin down. Stunned and choking, the man fell backward, his grip on the knife slackening. She took the weapon from him and turned to meet the remaining pair.

Now it was her turn to be surprised. Any typical pair of

opponents, untrained in combat skills as these stonecutters surely were, would have hesitated after seeing how fast she had delivered a mortal injury to their companion. She was counting on that hesitation.

But they both rushed her. What's more, they did it without getting in each other's way.

Ravvo was wielding a dirk. The other had only a workman's knife. She dodged to the side that kept her away from the longer blade. She dropped into a deep squat, diverting the knife thrust over her shoulder while her steel dug into his upper thigh, opening his femoral artery.

Fierce pain stung her in the left knee. Ravvo's dirk. It had been long enough to reach her even though he'd had to jab at her around the bulk of his companion.

The dying man dropped his knife, seized her by the neck, and surged forward, driving her backward. They careened together completely off the edge of the barge. Water closed over them.

She had never been buoyant in water. Not enough fat on her body. And the man was solid and heavy. Despite the cushioning effect of the water, they hit the river bottom hard, Elenya on the keel side.

She wriggled, but he had her trapped in the mud. His strong thumbs probed at the base of her jaw, trying to do to her windpipe what she had so recently done to her first opponent.

The murkiness of the water reduced her visual world to his face, inches above hers. He may have been only a stonecutter but the murder in his eyes resembled the kind she had seen in men whose lives had been dedicated to killing.

The impact had knocked the knife from her grip. She struggled to find where it had fallen in the mud, but no matter where she reached, the only solid objects she touched were pebbles and silt clams.

She hadn't fully inhaled before being submerged, and his weight on top of her was suffocating. Even if she kept his thumbs at bay, he could still succeed in drowning her.

Suddenly he went slack.

The murderousness was gone from his expression. His eyes

stared blankly. He had succumbed to blood loss.

She pushed and kicked. Inert, his body slipped off her.

She peeled herself out of the depression in the river bottom. Quite by chance, as she put her hand down to push off, it came down on the handle of the knife she had dropped. She clasped it as she launched upward.

She reached air. She inhaled. Her lungs throbbed as they refilled, the tissues still in shock. But the panic of not breathing went away at once, leaving her ready to defend herself.

Flipping her hair from her eyes, she spotted Ravvo. He was still on the barge, kneeling by the man with the crushed windpipe, who was still twitching but had gone limp. The barge was already a long stone's throw away, having been carried away by the current while she was caught in place.

He looked up and saw her. His grip tightened on the handle of his dirk. He looked ready to jump in the river and skewer her.

She wanted him to try. She kept the knife down in the water so that he might assume she was unarmed, hoping that would bolster his courage.

But he stayed where he was. When she grabbed hold of a submerged log and held on, the barge receded. Gradually it floated past the next river bend and was lost to view.

Only then, with the fight truly done, did she acknowledge how excruciating the pain in her knee was.

She half-clambered and half-swam along the submerged log to the western bank. Finally she pulled herself free of the silt and up onto a grassy bank, where she sat down and examined her injury.

When she pressed on the wound with her palm, the bleeding nearly stopped. That at least was a good sign. She made sure no mud had slipped into the cut, then bound it with strips she carved off the hem of her shift.

The rythni were nowhere to be seen.

"Thank you," she called to the woods. She felt she ought to do that even though she suspected none of the tiny people would be left within hearing, not when killing had just taken place. She doubted any were within a league of this spot by now. They could fly faster than hummingbirds.

She shivered again, worse than she had when she had awakened. It occurred to her that it wasn't just a consequence of anger, nor of the pain. It was the shift clinging to her skin, still drenched and made colder yet by the light breeze coming up the river. She peeled it off, wrung it out, and hung it from a branch.

Goose pimples rose all over her body but she placed herself where the sun would shine full upon her. Its touch — along with the overdue emptying of her bladder — began to restore her equilibrium.

She contemplated her circumstances.

Ravvo was still a problem. He would tell the Dragon's men where she was, and that she was alone and injured. Perhaps the information would earn him part of the reward money and perhaps it would not; he would do it anyway just to punish her for killing his cronies.

She filled her lungs and slowly exhaled, dosing herself with calm. She did this a second and a third time. Then she deliberately took a stride.

The pain in her knee flared. She gritted her teeth and suppressed it. She took another stride. More pain.

Three more strides. Equally careful. Equally painful.

She stopped, panting. She checked the binding over her wound. Blood was still seeping into the cloth, but slowly. Ravvo's dirk had missed the major blood vessels. She would not die of blood loss, and could probably avoid infection. But the jab had damaged something structural. No matter how much Elenya suppressed the anguish, she would not be able to run. She would not even be able to walk properly. Not until it healed. Perhaps not even then.

Her progress had taken her to the riparian fringe of the woods. She found a broken branch — driftwood that had been caught in the tangle of exposed tree roots — and made a crutch. The knife was a blessing in that regard. It was a poor weapon, made for utilitarian purposes, not battle, but at the moment it was just what she needed to shape the wood so that her armpit could rest comfortably upon the thicker end of the staff.

She put the shift back on. It was still damp, but whatever chill was left would soon be overcome by her body heat. She felt just as naked with it on than without it, though, because she had no sword, no demonblades, no weapon she had trained with. She couldn't remember the last time that had been the case. Even yesterday during her bath her rapier had been close enough to seize if need be.

What to do now? Where to go?

The quarry outpost was on the other side of the river. To head back to where her people were right now, she would have to swim across and make her way northward. But that route was where the men of the Dragon's garrison would look for her first.

The only other choice that held any value was west. The woods were largely free of human settlements in that direction. She would be less likely to be seen by chance. She might even find a good hiding place. But it would be just as hard for Dalih and Slees and all the rest of her companions to locate her. Save possibly for one thing.

The rythni had helped her.

The rythni had helped *her*.

Despite the vital contribution the little people had made to the defeat of Puriel and of Omril, Elenya was surprised they had come to her rescue this day. The rythni loved Alemar, but Cyfee was the only one of them who had ever taken a personal interest in her. Neither of the pair who had brought the padlock key to her today was Cyfee. They'd had wings. Cyfee's wings had been burned off during the sack of the governor's castle.

Was it too much to suppose they would help again? If she set off into the wilds, would the rythni let her companions know which way she had gone, perhaps even go so far as to guide them to her?

She decided to put it to the test. She was due for an improvement in her luck.

—o—

Days later, Elenya was still limping through the forest.

She came to a fallen log and sat upon it to rest her swollen knee. Perhaps it had been the wrong move to abandon the tree notch where she had spent the previous night. She had already journeyed far from the river. A little more distance didn't matter that much. Up in the tree, she had been high enough not to worry about chance encounters with fang boars or lurk bears. More important, if she stayed in a tree she would not be making new footprints for her pursuers to find.

But she had to eat, even if eating meant overturning rotting sheaves of bark and gulping down the grubs she disturbed, or downing raw eggs scavenged from a greenjay's nest, as she had the previous afternoon.

Her knee, though. Rest was the only thing that would help it to heal. She knew that. As soon as she found even one thing to eat, she would select a refuge and tuck herself away for the rest of the day, even if she reached the spot many hours before sunset.

She hauled herself upright and went on. A dozen paces or so later, a parrot fluttered onto a branch up ahead.

Cilendrodel had its parrots. Some were yellow, as this one was. Some were as large. But she knew this was no Cilendri parrot. She had glimpsed this very bird in the chaos of Omril's memories when she had delved into him.

She threw the knife.

The parrot was ready—as no ordinary bird would be ready. It waited until her aim was defined, and dodged only when it was too late for her to alter what trajectory the projectile would take. The knife whisked past, claiming only one feather, and even that was dislodged not by the blade, but by the bird's own movement.

"Ha ha," cackled the parrot.

Deliberately, almost mockingly, it restored its plumage to a state of order, though always keeping Elenya under observation. Elenya did not even bother looking for a stone to pick up. It was all she could do to stand there, the agony in her knee surging to a new level. Unthinking, she had settled her weight upon her bad leg when she had made the throw.

The parrot launched into the air. It scribed a half-circle around her and headed off toward the east.

Elenya debated whether to stay there, gathering her strength and fighting as best she could when the pursuit caught up to her. The younger version of herself would have done that. Instead she located the knife. It had proven to be a poor substitute for a demonblade, but that didn't mean it was useless.

She made another crutch.

It wouldn't help much, but it would help some. She cursed herself for not doing so sooner. She could have argued she had not done so because speed would not have made a difference earlier, but she knew the real reason: She was used to toughing things out. A second crutch was an admission of frailty.

Much as it burned to acknowledge it, she *was* frail right now.

She set off, wondering just how far ahead of its master the parrot had ranged.

CHAPTER SIXTEEN

NEARLY EVERYONE AGREED, of all the sectors of Dragonsdeep, the Dowsers Quarter was the least beautiful. It had the fewest parks, the fewest mansions, the least prestige. Quandai was not among the "nearly everyone." His spirits always rose when he found himself striding along between the warehouses and staging depots. The breezes flowed easily down avenues built wide and kept clear of vendors' tables and street performers' stalls in order to accommodate the regular passage of loaded wagons. Here, people didn't use the streets to try to sell you things.

Most of all, when he visited the place, Quandai remembered being a young man in love with a young woman. Brikka was not a native of the Dowsers Quarter, but she had been employed there throughout their courtship.

He smiled. Even today, even as he kept an eye out to be sure he was not being followed, even as he fretted he was not the right man for the task he was undertaking, nostalgia brushed his cheek and made him feel as though he belonged.

Down the lane, he spotted his destination. The guildhouse had not changed much in the past few decades. Why should it? Dragonsdeep would always need such institutions, carrying on as they had for centuries, no matter if the sovereign who occupied the palace was a dragon or a wizard or a bag stuffed with driftwood and barnacles.

The front door was wide open, as he knew it would be at this hour, and the guard gave him a friendly nod.

"Your business?" the guard asked.

"To see Matron Norassa. A social call."

The guard waved him on in. "In the kitchens at this hour."

"Quite so," Quandai said.

A dozen steps more took him through the antechamber into the main study hall. Nearly thirty boys and girls, ages ranging from eight to ten, sat on stools at work benches. A pair of tutors were ambling down the aisles between the benches, observing.

Each pupil was positioned well apart from the others so that their zones of magic would not overlap. All were concentrating upon the nodules that had been set in front of them — grey, coarse oblongs of what looked to be pumice or some other porous rock. Some left the objects on the trays atop the benches, touching them only lightly. Some gripped them. Some shifted their nodules from one hand to the other. The emotions they exuded ranged even more widely, from weariness to excitement, from listlessness to joy, from frustration to confidence.

Just as he was ambling past, Quandai saw one of the older girls achieve her goal. A drop of silvery metal oozed from the nodule she was holding and fell onto the tray. Not silver, Quandai guessed. Something less common. More ductile. He was not expert enough to know what element had lured out into the open. He only knew it was valuable, and was now in its pure state.

The tutor examined the bright speck of metal, which had already hardened on the tray. He smiled and waved the child off to the corner where the refreshments and cushioned divans awaited her.

Quandai knew the girl might need the remainder of the day just to generate a second drop, but at this stage of training, even that much was a promising yield. The most adroit members of groups like these would graduate to more elite teams of adolescent novices. In the end, as adults, the best of the best would be masters and could seduce a desired ingredient from its matrix so well the limit of the city's production was not their skill, but the amount of raw material that could be harvested, and how fast the detritus could be hauled away.

Ore dowsers. As mages went, they were almost charlatans, capable of only one trick. But when it was that particular trick, no one felt cheated.

Every city needed a backbone of prosperity. When the Dragonslayer turned his attention to the construction of a new capital city, he had not chosen a random spot. He put it in easy range of the magma vents of The Deeps. The mines of other realms had enjoyed their booms and become sapped, but Elandris had been able to supply precious metals for over a thousand years at a constant rate, and did it without the use of quicksilver and its deadly fumes. Not everyone enjoyed the rewards the dowsers received, but even the lowliest menial in the trade knew they were lucky. Even the ore-gatherers, for all the dangers they faced, understood they had been spared constant trips deep into mine shafts where the dust and stale air would eventually give them black lung, or cave-ins steal the breath from them in more immediate fashion.

Nearly every child of Dragonsdeep was brought to the guildhouses at age seven to put in a session or two handling the nodules in order to determine if they had any trace of the talent. Quandai's mother had dutifully delivered him there one morning. He had squirmed on his bench, scratched his itchy spots until they were numb, and nearly fainted from boredom. At the end of the day, when his parents arrived to fetch him, the supervising adept told them they needn't bring him back, saying there was no point.

He'd actually been jealous of those who stayed longer, even though nearly all of them were rejected as well, often after only a few more days of evaluation.

When he reached the kitchen, he found Matron Norassa in the midst of inspecting a kettle. She was frowning at the crustiness along the rim, and Quandai understood at once a scullery drudge would be getting an earful before the day was over.

Norassa looked up, and the frown transformed into one of her classic smiles, so familiar to him from decades gone by, even if the wrinkles involved had tripled in quantity.

"The pickle thief himself! How's my Brikka girl doing?"

Quandai patted his belly. "Still allowing me to worship her, unfit wretch that I am."

"So you're not here to steal another of my best pie-makers away from me?"

"Nothing as pleasant as that."

Norassa set down the kettle. "You're here to see *him*, I suppose?"

"I'm afraid so."

She sighed. "There was a time when all I had to do was give you a bowl of soup and a heel of bread."

"I know. But we both have different roles to play now," Quandai said. "I wouldn't have come if I could have avoided it. I don't expect to be here long."

"It's not the length of the visit that worries me, young man."

Sighing again, she indicated the archway at the back of the room—the one he knew led to the kitchen staff's own mess hall.

"Thank you, Matron," he said, and proceeded down the passageway, a long one bracketted by the lavatories and the alcoves where the young mothers who worked here could change diapers or nurse babies in comparative seclusion. The facilities were empty of occupants at the moment.

The mess hall was ample. Thirty paces square. A high ceiling. The man Quandai had sought out was sprawled in a chair at the table in the farthest corner, alone and yet somehow managing to claim a quarter of the space with his presence.

Tollvar frowned. "How did you know where I was?"

"I believe we've already established that my niece knows how to find you, more often than not."

Tollvar hesitated to such a degree it was almost a blush. "I don't encourage her."

"Neither do I."

Tollvar stood. Quandai had assumed that would happen, sooner rather than later. The fellow eased back against the wall behind his table, arms folded, projecting an unthreatened air but nevertheless going beyond what was strictly necessary just to demonstrate that he was half a head taller than Quandai. "Why are you here? Has the king's by-blow already got you running his errands?"

Quandai nodded.

Tollvar apparently wanted more of a reaction. When it didn't come, he stopped leaning on the wall and loomed closer. "What is it, then?"

"You told Prince Alemar when the two of you next saw each other, he should be ready to show how he might help you free Elandris. He is prepared to do that."

"With him as the leader, you mean."

"No. When I say he's ready to help you, I mean he's ready to help you. You'll determine how. Are you willing to speak with him?"

Tollvar gazed steadily at Quandai, as if testing to see whether he'd look away. Quandai simply gazed back.

"I'll not go traipsing across half the city again," Tollvar warned. "I'll meet with him here."

"We felt you might prefer that. He and his companions are waiting not far away, at the home of a friend of mine. I can be back with them in a quarter of an hour."

"Bring them, then. I'll have Norassa cut some slices of her braidbread."

Tollvar said it as though he was still disinterested and not inclined to listen, but Quandai knew that wasn't entirely the case. No one could sit down to a platter of Norassa's braidbread and maintain a hostile mood.

—o—

Alemar couldn't help feel exposed as he and Toren strode behind Quandai along the impressively broad streets. They had earlier taken a route that kept them out of public view at nearly every juncture, but this last part of the journey could be done no better way than for them to behave as though they belonged out and about where they were, just normal denizens of Dragonsdeep doing what such folk did of a forenoon in the Dowsers Quarter.

For what it was worth, Toren's make-up had been applied flawlessly, Solia having turned out to have an adept touch in that regard. The false beard could have fit better, but it didn't look as much unnatural as merely unkempt.

Hair rose on the nape of his neck as they passed through the room of pupils trying to summon metals from their natural prisons. So many practitioners of magic in the same room, all devoted to the full use of their powers. Modest as those powers were, the effect was unlike anything Alemar had encountered before. It was as though he were trapped in a perfume factory when all he wanted was a clean breath. He picked up the pace until they had made it several steps into the kitchen.

They found Tollvar in the rear room, pacing back and forth. He kept doing so even after Alemar and Toren had reached the middle of the space. Quandai lingered at the threshold to serve as their lookout.

Alemar said nothing. Just waited for Tollvar to acknowledge their presence. Eventually he had no choice but to do so. His glance lingered longest on Toren.

"I'm told there was concern you wouldn't survive," Tollvar said. "You're looking well enough now."

"Yes. In fact, I feel more alive than I've been in quite some time," Toren responded.

Tollvar gestured at a set of chairs and chose one for himself on the opposite side of the table.

"I'm also told you're ready to join me."

Alemar had not seen a man so sure of himself since he had first become acquainted with Lonal. The war-leader of the T'lil had good reason to be sure of himself, but Tollvar? Alemar's palms were itching to slap the fellow. He wished he were wearing the gauntlet, the better to do that slapping. It took an elbow nudge from Toren—no, from Polk—to remind him they had agreed he was to maintain his composure throughout the parley.

"A wise man once told me to do what I can," Alemar said. "I lost sight of that. I've been trying to do too much, and it turned me into someone I'm not suited to be. You claim to know what to do to help the people of Dragonsdeep. Very well, then. Whatever it is, I will help you do it."

Tollvar chuckled. "So, you claim you agree with me?"

"Not at all," Alemar stated. "I'm saying I won't stand in your way, and I will help you with your plans. It's not the same as agreement. It's certainly not the same as obedience."

Tollvar finally seemed interested. He leaned onto his elbows, bringing his face much closer to Alemar's. "I'd never trust a royal. Not even a bastard."

"Then don't. Trust what we have in common. We both want to bring down the Dragon's regime. Any time you engage in action that furthers that goal, I will assist in whatever ways I can."

"I suppose you want to start by offering me advice? Discussing strategy?"

"If that's useful to you."

"I doubt it will be. Tell me, what would the gist of your sage counsel be?"

Alemar reflected upon all he and Polk had been discussing from the time they had stood in the oracle chamber, to the moment Quandai had come back that morning to fetch them. "Proceed with caution. Small goals. Effective ones. Meaningful ones. But low risk. You want successes. Get enough of those, and support will grow."

Tollvar laughed. "Low risk? Were the risks low when you tried to kill Gloroc in his own throne room? Do you know how two-faced you sound right now?"

"What we did in the Dragon's palace was the end result of long and careful planning. Centuries of planning, you might say. The options in front of us right now are not on that scale."

Tollvar shook his head. "This is why I am the man to lead the resistance, and you are not. For fifty years, the rebels inside Dragonsdeep have 'proceeded with caution.' What has it achieved? Whatever I do next, rest assured it will be bold."

"Even if the enemy is on the alert for that very thing?"

"If I spent my days weighing risks, I'd never get out of bed."

Alemar was surprised. He still considered Tollvar a fool. Nevertheless, he was beginning to like the man.

"With all of that," Tollvar added, "are you still offering to help me?"

Gast's voice whispered in Alemar's ear. *Do what you can.*

What he couldn't do was change a man's nature. So be it.

"Yes," he replied.

CHAPTER SEVENTEEN

AUNTIE FLUTTERED FROM branch to branch, guiding Enril and his squad of armed men unerringly through the thick growth, indicating by her position when the group need not follow the route their quarry had, but could take a shortcut.

Enril did not need the nag parrot to know the one they pursued was close at hand. He could now sense her directly. As soon as he could actually see her, he would set loose the snare charm he had prepared. His hands were shaking with the anticipation. In his mind, she was already captured.

He spotted another drop of blood on a frond of bracken that hung across the trail. Disturbed soil revealed where her crutches and one good foot had come down. Her pace was flagging. Even with the second crutch, she could not overcome the limitation of her injury — certainly not enough to keep her lead.

The point man halted in a small clearing just ahead. Two others flanked him, taking up guard positions so that Enril could advance and see what had been discovered.

The woman's spoor vanished in the center of the clearing. Two more drops of blood, vibrantly fresh, showed where she had stood. The makeshift crutches lay against a rotted log. Abandoned.

The signs made it clear that three oeikani had recently been there and had headed off at speed, one beast carrying a double load judging by the depth of the impressions left by its cloven hooves. The tracks led in a direction where the trees were not as closely crowded, and where the terrain was flatter and less ensnarled by shrubs and briar. In that sort of forest, oeikani could make good time.

The rebel princess was as yet no more than a few arrow-flights away. Alas, she was already beyond the reach of the snare spell, and was growing farther off with each passing moment.

Enril refused to lose control of his temper in front of his men. Even so, they eased back, leaving it to Lhan to come forward and quietly wait for the wizard to speak.

Enril reminded himself he still had resources.

He knelt down and picked up a leaf that had been struck by one of the falling drops of her blood. He cradled the leaf in his palm.

Straightening up, he said to the grey sergeant. "We go back and collect our oeikani."

— o —

Well before they reached the ravine where they had left their mounts, they heard the inarticulate cries Enril had come to know too well. They sounded more animal than ever — the mewling of a pup that has lost its mother, or of a steer outside the slaughterhouse, smelling the blood of others already hanging from the hooks.

Enril clambered down the bank and up the vines and roots of the other side ahead of his patrol. He went at once to the spot were a pair of attendants were trying to get their charge to take a dose of dream tea.

"Never mind that," Enril said. "I am here now."

At the sound of Enril's voice, Omril's moaning ceased. At the sight of him, he grew calm.

Calm. But not happy. At some level Omril understood that Enril had *chosen* to be separated from him, if only for a fraction of an afternoon. He did not like that it had happened; moreover, he did not like that it *could* happen.

Auntie fluttered onto Omril's shoulder and nuzzled his ear.

Enril took his beloved's hands in his and held them until the trembling stopped.

"I need your help," Enril murmured.

As usual, Omril gave no outward indication he had heard or that he would cooperate, but Auntie grew very still and turned her left eye to regard Enril. That was enough to let the younger wizard know he could proceed.

From a pocket of his fine quarn mage tunic, Enril removed the leaf he had retrieved. He dabbed the little finger of his right hand against the bloodstain. The tip came away crimsoned, the blood still sticky and wet enough to transfer from leaf to flesh.

Omril opened his mouth. Enril put his finger in, and Omril licked.

Omril nodded. He pressed his own finger down upon the bloodied leaf, and fed the resulting trace to Enril.

Enril slipped into a light trance. All distractions—the filtered light of the forest, the humid clutch of the air, the aroma of danglevine blossom—faded away.

While in that altered state, all that mattered was the flavor. It was growing fainter, diluted by saliva, now little more than an echo of saltiness and metallic astringency. He might have lost the memory of it before he could cast his spell. He almost certainly *would* have lost it, if not for Omril. But his beloved knew the trick well. He had taught it to Enril back in happier days, in the final year of Enril's apprenticeship. Omril knew how to read that trace, how to strengthen the familiarity and fashion a link back to its origin. Omril did not let the flavor escape. His mind might be too tangled to cast the spell all on his own, but he reinforced what Enril was doing.

There. It was done. Elenya of Garthmorron could flee a hundred leagues off and Enril would know where to hunt.

He stood and turned to Lhan, who as usual was waiting near at hand, wearing his typical alert-but-humorless expression.

"Do not worry so, Grey Sergeant," Enril said. "Today was a good day after all."

—o—

When Elenya spotted the rythni standing on a log on the far side of the clearing, she thought at first she was imagining it. Why would one appear now, so many days after she had escaped the raft, and not earlier? Surely this one was a mirage, sprung from her state of desperation.

But no. There really was a rythni perched on the log. And even at that distance, Elenya made out the glint of a gold chain around the little creature's neck. This was a rythni she knew.

Hiephora.

Elenya stayed where she was. She had seldom been able to approach Hiephora in the past without frightening her away. She certainly did not want that to happen here and now.

In her softest, least intimidating tone, she said, "Your Majesty, it is so good to see you. If you can help me in any way, I would very much appreciate whatever you can do."

Hiephora was standing right where Elenya had been heading, that is, almost straight to the west. The little being pointed to her left. North.

"I'm quite happy to go that way," Elenya responded, again keeping her voice at little more than a whisper. "But I'm afraid I won't get much farther on my own." She wasn't even sure how she was managing to stay upright.

Hiephora placed her hand against the center of her chest, nodded, and flew off in the direction she had pointed.

Elenya sighed. "You'll fly my dead boyfriend's body from a village square. You'll carry my brother all the way across a *lake*! But me? You leave me to hobble on until I fall over."

She tested the strength of her good knee, and of her wrists — any body part that she'd need to start moving again. Every joint and muscle said the attempt would be a disaster, but she set out anyway, somehow negotiating the right-angle turn and making it another half-dozen "steps."

The foliage parted not far from where Hiephora had disappeared. Three oeikani bounded into the clearing, their riders taking care to shape their movement and render it as quiet as possible, yet still swift.

Dalih was off his mount almost before Elenya realized what she was seeing. He lifted her up and deposited her behind Slees. The beast she found herself on was sturdy and bore the weight of two small women quite well. Elenya wrapped her arms around her friend's torso and away they went.

—o—

They rode for hours, joined early on by the main party of their confederates. They rested only once, and only for a few minutes, mostly in order to shift to fresher mounts. Elenya continued to be a passenger. She was too spent to take the reins. She dozed during the journey, chin resting on Slees's shoulder.

Finally the oeikani began to flag. The animals needed to be fed, cooled down, and rubbed down, or they would be unable to be ridden again any time soon. And in any case, the forest was thickening and was growing less suitable for travelling in the saddle. They stopped and began making their camp.

Elenya didn't try to dismount by herself. She let Dalih lift her down while others smoothed a spot and laid a blanket upon it to receive her.

She realized she must have passed out as soon as she was horizontal, because suddenly, even though the camp was still in the grip of daylight, no sunbeams were penetrating as far as the forest floor. A bucket of water had appeared at the edge of the blanket. Dalih was carefully washing her wounded knee with a moistened cloth. Meanwhile Slees was lightly wrapping a strip of bandage around her right armpit so as to anchor a poultice of soft moss and herbs against the area that had become raw from the abrasion of the crutch.

"Ow," Elenya said, her distress made all the worse knowing it was the *good* armpit being cared for. She did not look forward to the moment when Slees moved on to the other one.

Dalih studied the spot where Ravvo's dirk had penetrated. He rested his fingers over the knee, checking the temperature of the flesh around the wound.

"I do not think it will fester. That danger is past."

"But the knee will not be the same," she said.

He met her gaze full on, and sighed. "I have seen this sort of thing. For the next several months, the pain alone will hobble you. That will eventually resolve itself, but the joint will never again serve you as it did before the blade struck."

Elenya thought she had already accepted the degree of her injury, yet now that someone else had made the pronouncement, she found herself unable to quell the shudder in her eyelids and her jaw.

She did not weep. But Slees did.

None of them stated the obvious. Sorcery could have made a difference. But she wasn't that sort of adept, and while there were a number of members of the rebel band who were skilled in basic tending of wounds, none could repair this damage.

She knew she had been lucky to last as long as she had. Alemar had brought her back from the brink of death after Enns's betrayal, and on a number of other occasions had reversed damage that would otherwise have left her maimed. She had no right to expect better fortune than that.

And yet now, in addition to the trembling, there was an ache in her gut that a hundred meals would fail to banish.

Lost in her thoughts, she only halfway noticed as Dalih and Slees both slipped away. She thought they were simply granting her a period of solitude to feel sorry for herself. Gradually she realized what was going on. Dalih strung a rope between a pair of tree trunks. He tossed a section of tent canvas over it, creating a partition that separated Elenya from the area where the main group of her cohort were occupied ministering to the oeikani or preparing the campsite.

Once the barrier was in place, Dalih stepped behind it and vanished from her view. Meanwhile Slees reappeared with a second bucket of water, a small brick of soap, and a set of clothes.

Elenya couldn't find the words sufficient to convey her gratitude; she made do with a beseeching murmur. Slees pulled off the shift Elenya had worn to bed all those nights ago back at the quarryfolk outpost. Torn and bloodstained and mud-spattered, it was not worth keeping. Slees tossed it into the brush.

Armpits bandaged as they were, Elenya did no more than tend to her private areas, then left it to Slees to wash everything else. Her friend treated the job as a profound mission, scrubbing away every bit of grime, digging out every speck of embedded leaf litter, and then washing Elenya's hair twice over. When that was done, she freshened the armpit poultices and re-wrapped the bindings.

Elenya wanted to savor the nurturance and the comfort it brought. She needed to do so. But the last time she had allowed herself a taste of ease had been at the stone quarry. She would not—could not—let her guard down again as she had done that night.

Slees helped her to put on the clothes, and then took the bucket of filthy water away to dump it. Elenya stretched out on the blanket again, recognizing that being bathed, no matter how little labor she had contributed, had exhausted her all over again. She closed her eyes.

—o—

And opened them to find twilight had settled. Overhead, the half-disc of Motherworld was soon to encroach upon the only open patch of sky, but even so, two large stars blazed brightly enough to snare her attention.

She lifted her head and saw what had made her stir. Dalih was standing not far away, his form outlined by the glow of the nearest cookfire—the partition of tent cloth had been removed while she was sleeping. He was holding a bowl. Wisps of steam were rising over its brim.

"Soup?"

"Please, yes." She rearranged herself until she could lean her back against a log. Getting into position took far more effort than it should, but she was determined to do so on her own, and in the end she succeeded.

Once she had taken the bowl, Dalih handed her a spoon. He showed no sign he might have considered serving her each mouthful.

She appreciated that.

Hungry as she was, she ate at a pace, knowing her stomach would have to get used to having more in it than grubs or mushrooms or the occasional berry. She savored every bit of barley, every nibble of carrot.

Dalih remained not far beyond the edge of her blanket, biding his time in a relaxed squat, a pose she would not have found restful. He apparently did, to the extent that it almost characterized how he would maintain himself when not engaged in any particular activity.

He said nothing. He seemed to be elsewhere, no matter that he observed her each time the spoon rose to her lips.

"What will you do now?" she asked. She used Zyraii, knowing that might generate a substantive answer.

"What do you mean?"

"I won't be much of a training partner anymore."

He was silent for such a long while, she began to wonder if he had heard the comment. Or rather, she wondered if she had actually said the words out loud.

Finally Dalih said, "It is true I study the sword. And I hope to keep doing so. But that is not all I am. Did you think I was so simple a man?"

Elenya felt a blush rise up her cheeks. "If I have offended you, I'm sorry."

He shrugged. "You are forgiven. I have not spoken much of my-self."

"No. Not really," she agreed.

The next pause was even longer than the first one. Elenya was wise enough to know she needn't ask questions; he would get to it when he was ready.

"I was born a slave," he said at last.

"Oh." That had not been what Elenya expected him to say at all.

"My father was a guard for a wealthy merchant. He died when I was very small; I do not remember him. I went on living in the slave quarters with my mother, helping her scrub floors or tend the milk goats. When I was seven or eight years old, I began to be sent along on the supply runs to the market square in order to help carry back melons or sacks of beans or what-have-you. My mother was never allowed to go even as far as that. She died when I was twelve. She had never once in her life stepped outside the perimeter walls of the master's compound."

"You wanted...more?"

"Yes." Dalih drew his sword and tilted it so that it caught a flicker of firelight. He directed the brightness at the trunk of the nearest tree, revealing a bark moth. The insect immediately crawled around the tree to hide from them. "When I was eleven years old, the merchant told the commander-at-arms to have me trained in weaponry, so that I could serve as my father had. The sword became my latchkey. It took me out of the life I was born into. Over the years it has allowed me to pay for my passage to get to the places I've been, and to leave those places when the time came. Nonetheless, I have always known that long before I am forty, even if I remain alive and remain healthy, I will set the sword down for good."

"Just like *that*?"

"No, not just like that. I will come to it gradually. Soberly. But when I have reached that point, I know my mother will visit me, as she does every day, just before I wake. And she will ask me, 'Is this the last day, or the first?'"

Elenya hesitated. "Is that a saying?"

"Yes. My mother used it. Her mother before her. Her mother before that. It means, do you have enough to look forward to? Can you bear the ordeal of your life or have you slipped into regret? If it is the latter, kill yourself and be done with it. If it is the former, seek the happiness. Look forward to the future."

"And you would be happy to put down your sword?"

"Happy? I am not sure that is the word. But I am determined to accept it as I have accepted other good-byes in my life. Wherever I have roamed, I have come to know good people. The places have contained beauty, comfort—and opportunities. Whenever I set down my blade, I know I will be surrounded by ways to find my fulfillment. It will be the first day, not the last. Because the sword is not all I am."

He rose, took her bowl, and left to fetch her another serving, sparing her the awkwardness of having to say anything.

Elenya was astonished to realize that somehow she had failed until now to regard Dalih as a friend. Certainly they had been on friendly terms. She had liked him from the start. Even so, she had categorized him as an ally, a comrade, a student. But he *was* a friend. And as a friend — to her and to others in the camp — he would not be leaving Cilendrodel any time soon. This was a thing she could depend upon.

"Good soup," she said when he returned.

—o—

When the meal was over and Dalih had left her again, Elenya nearly drifted off again, soothed by the soft, busy sounds of the camp, the comfort of a nourished body, the warmth of the blankets atop her. But her eyes remained open. She had finally recovered to the extent that her thoughts were coherent and her level of alertness was trustworthy.

A surreptitious rustling in the leaf litter came to her attention. It was the opposite of sinister, too consequential to betoken the approach of a bracken leech or sweat roach, and yet too slight to represent more than the smallest and least threatening of rodents.

"Welcome, Your Majesty," Elenya said, keeping her volume low, as if she were singing a baby to sleep.

A spherical nimbus of werelight blossomed a footstep or so to the side of her left hip, revealing on the forest floor a slender, androgynous human figure, less than a foot high, head wreathed in an abundance of blue hair, body naked save for a gold necklace of a simple but elegant design.

"Greetings, Your Highness. It is good to be here with you."

Hiephora's command of the High Speech was smooth, if somewhat formal in character, but in her weariness, Elenya had to concentrate to deal with the faintness and the accent.

"I would have asked you to visit me tonight," Elenya continued, "if I had any control over such a thing."

"So you are glad to see me now? Or not?"

"I owe you my life," Elenya said. "I know that, and I'm grateful."

"And yet you saw no sign of us for days as you fled in great pain through the woods."

"Yes. Was that...necessary?"

"Ah," the queen said. "You *do* understand."

Elenya took in a deep breath rather than raise her voice. "No. I don't understand. My brother's the one with that ability. Have you forgotten?"

"I dared not help you more often than I did."

"What do you mean?"

"For those of us with the foresight, inaction is as important as action. If we disturb the course of events, it creates new possibilities — and it takes away possibilities that may have come to pass. I had thought I was careful, but I failed you before."

"You failed me?"

"I let Cyfee influence me. I and my subjects helped you and your brother sack Puriel's fortress. We should not have done so. I see that now."

"You should not have done it? The attack was successful."

"The success brought new enemies to our shores, led by a mage more capable than the one you had faced before. A mage who should have fallen in battle in the west a fortnight ago, but instead is here in Cilendrodel."

"A mistake." Elenya wished the handle of her rapier was in her hand, so she could squeeze it. A mistake to exact vengeance for Milec? A mistake to burn down the castle of a tyrant?

"Yes. A mistake."

"Then how can you be sure you are choosing the right moment this time? You've just pointed out, you're fallible."

"I am. It's true. But this time I did not let my feelings intrude. Feelings are a rythni's greatest weakness. But this time, I have strived to keep the visions pure. I tried not to shape them into versions that pleased me better or that saved me from anguish. I saw that if I dispatched emissaries with a certain key to a certain stretch of the Knotted River on a certain morning, you would be able to rescue yourself. I saw that if I led your coterie to a certain grove on a certain day, they would carry you to safety. If I had done more than that, I fear I would have ruined the chance to do something far more important. I am sorry you suffered, but have no doubt that everything that happened to you in these recent months, good and bad, had to happen. I believe things are now as they must be."

"For what?"

"Tomorrow I will lead you and your companions to a refuge. All may yet be well. How well will depend on you, and upon the sorcerer who pursues you. You must play a role you have never played, and so must he."

"That sounds like a seer's riddle."

"Do not be vexed with me. I will explain in as much detail as you like once we get to the refuge. It is a special place. You will need its influence. For now all I can tell you is this: For years now, in so many ways, you have been a daughter of Keron. Tomorrow, for a few hours—for a day—you must be a daughter of Lerina."

CHAPTER EIGHTEEN

AS SHE OFTEN did after her evening meal, Leyaril ventured out onto the high terrace of the palace. It was an area reserved for the Ril or for Gloroc himself. Not a little of her rise to a position of influence could be credited to the words spoken here while she tarried with one colleague or another or several. She might offer them her latest concoctions of the recreational kind. They might bring out one of their favorite vintages of a traditional—but always very fine—pedigree. Oh, the conversations! They had shaped her into what she was, even the ones that brought her pain or caused a setback in her ambitions.

Tonight it was the view for which she came. The crescent shape of the balcony and the twenty-story-high vantage revealed nearly every part of Dragonsdeep depending on where she stood.

The far side of the city was nearly lost in the night mists. Above, the dome was nearly opaque, the glow of the moons and Motherworld blocked by the clouds that had consolidated across the sky that afternoon. They were not storm clouds, and more was the pity, because there would be no lightning to enjoy. Leyaril contented herself with the reflections of the city's own lights—the glows of the cafés, the watchlights at the major intersections, the circle of illumination from the palace's clock tower.

It all belonged to her.

Strictly speaking it belonged to Gloroc, of course, and any authority she had was no greater than the other high mages and supreme generals. But she was the only one of that echelon in the city this night. For the moment, she need not share the claim.

Two of her three bodyguards were manning the doorway through which she had come. The other was at the railing. They were keeping silent and were avoiding eye contact with her. That was as it should be. A shame, though. When one is glowing, one should have someone at hand to bask in the radiance. Perhaps she should have invited Guestis to come out with her.

She sauntered from one point of the crescent to the other and returned to the center. She was just about to head to her quarters when she sensed something that transformed her mood from contemplative to wholly engaged.

Dragonsdeep had an aroma, a rhythmic murmur, a touch. It was always a complex thing. No site enriched with so many spells and talismans could ever give off straightforward tidings, not to an adept of her sort. Tonight, there was an additional component. She couldn't determine what the cause might be, but whatever it was, it was something that didn't belong.

She shuffled a few steps to her right, then a few to her left. She turned in a circle. Her men began to glance her way, their self-control faltering. She ignored them. She continued until she had calibrated her senses into a sort of compass.

The compass pointed toward a sprawling neighborhood of the city sometimes known as the Supply District. The generals called it the Quartermaster's Tangle, sometimes in mocking tones, more often in complaint. The district was a maze of warehouses containing all manner of goods consigned to the Dragon's service, meant variously to replenish the palace, the record houses, the guard stations. All manner of material could be requisitioned. Rations, furnishings, equipment, uniforms, medical gear. Even such oddities as spare street lamps and ships' anchors. Things had a tendency to be delivered with maddening timing — either so soon the requestors were not ready to receive them, or long after any reasonable waiting period had expired.

She beckoned the highest-ranking of her bodyguards. "Fetram, how keen is your hearing?"

"Never had reason to complain of it, m'lady."

She placed her hands over his ears and wove a spell she had cast upon her own hearing once too often. Fetram would be fine, though. She could probably use it on him eight or ten times before it went sour.

She breathed slowly in and out three times, and the process was done. She released Fetram's head and gestured toward the streets. "Do you hear any unusual noises out there?"

He cocked his head, eyes widening as the spell took effect. Suddenly he moved to the rail, attention focussed upon the supply district. He listened again.

"I hear swords clashing. Men shouting."

An open skirmish? In *Dragonsdeep*?!

She pressed her palms together, shuttering the enchantment. Fetram swayed a moment, but steadied as his senses returned to normal.

"Follow," she said. She spun about and marched back into the palace. Fetram and the others fell in behind. She headed down the grand promenade of the magician's level. Her companions almost needed to scamper to keep up with her long strides.

Before she had made it even halfway to her goal, a palace courier appeared at the top of the staircase, running at his top speed.

"Revered Mage!" he puffed. "The central armory is under attack!"

"I know," she said, but tempting as it was to wave him away, she added, "Stop. Take a breath. Tell me everything you know."

"Two hundred men. Led by Tollvar. They've breached the building. They had battering rams."

"Two hundred? Are you sure?"

The courier hesitated. "So the informant said."

Fetram lifted his left hand and tapped the tips of his fingers with his thumb, the way he often did when he was calculating. "Could be true. Wouldn't be worth trying unless you had that many."

She nodded. To the courier she said, "Tell your commander I have been alerted and will do what I can."

The young man bowed and ran back the way he had come.

Two hundred. That was hard to credit. Only a dozen or so had helped Tollvar when he had made his assault on the dungeons. Over the course of the past year, nearly all of those aside from Tollvar himself had been apprehended or killed. She would have thought that would have stifled any recruiting he might have attempted. Everyone knew there was little hope of sustained resistance within Dragons-deep. The best that conspirators against Gloroc might aspire to? Getting away with small bits of sabotage, arson, or smuggling. Two hundred rebels coming together for one operation? Completely foolhardy. With that many perpetrators involved, she would have so very many chances to root them out, no matter how well they scurried back to their hiding places on this particular night.

Was she missing some angle?

She was still mulling it over as she arrived at the suite of rooms that had once belonged to Danril, the only member of the Ril thus far who could be said to have died in his sleep at the end of a natural decline. His peaceful demise was only one of the many accomplishments of his that Leyaril was determined she would equal.

She held up a hand to her escort.

"See that I'm not disturbed," she said. "Not even if there's another courier."

"Yes, m'lady," Fetram replied.

She placed her hand on the door in front of her. It murmured, recognizing her as one who was permitted to enter, and swung open. She proceeded into the darkness. The door swung itself shut behind her.

The cramped and windowless confines of the observation gallery still reeked with vestiges of Vanril's rotting-fruit body odor despite the spiced candles she had left burning a few days ago. She would have ordered the housekeeping staff to air out the chamber, but the vault was a resource that could never be left unsecured. Intricate wards ensured that only a mage of the Ril could enter. Even Gloroc did not come here, if only because he would never fit inside.

She did not miss Vanril. Altering his sweat so that it smelled of dragon? That was not a sane thing. There were better ways to curry their master's favor. But her colleague's presence and participation would certainly have been useful just then. Though she knew how to make the apparatus function, it was Vanril who had logged the most hours here since Danril had succumbed. Vanril had enjoyed lurking. He had been a creature of observation rather than engagement, and this chamber represented the ultimate peephole.

She turned the valve on the wall to her left and the lights awakened. The interior's two main features unfurled to her view: the circular pedestal in the center of the floor, and the immense mirror on the far wall, encased in its frame of wrought electrum.

The pedestal's slanted top was a topographic of Dragonsdeep, the streets portrayed by a grid of carved grooves in the surface, the parks and major edifices indicated by tiny symbols. Pinpricks of serene blue light scattered throughout the grid revealed where Gloroc's signpost trophies had been installed.

How many were there? Leyaril seldom gave it much thought. A thousand? Two thousand? Enough for the purposes at hand—that's what mattered.

She stepped to the array and set a finger on a dot. Unfortunately she could not start with a signpost in the Quartermaster's Tangle. She had to start with one close to her own position and move from one to the next. The device was a cat, not a dog. She couldn't simply order it to do as she wished; she had to trick it into believing it wanted to go there of its own accord.

The mirror stirred and she was no longer looking at a reflection of herself standing at the pedestal. Instead she saw the main antechamber of the palace. People were bustling in and out as guards, servants, bureaucrats, and couriers reacted to the news of the violence at the armory.

The particular glass eye she was seeing out of was embedded in the skull of her old acquaintance, Marnus. Finally he was managing to do something worthwhile.

She made contact with the next dot. The mirror's view evolved sluggishly, the apparatus accommodating to her by degrees. She adjusted both the pressure of her finger and the way the energies flowed, and at once, the new scene filled the mirror, the focus sharp. The colors were still off-kilter, but that was of no consequence.

Danril had been compatible enough with his talisman to extend his spying to any part of the city within moments. But by her own standard, she soon was doing well. She traced out her route station by station and the views shifted with increasing promptness, taking her past the depot of the funicular through the merchants' storefronts and into the supply district. Barely more than a minute after she had begun, she was close to the precinct that contained the armory.

And then the mirror went black.

"No!" she blurted.

She reversed her progression. When her finger returned to the previous station, the mirror lit up once again, showing her the intersection she had seen moments earlier. Two boys ran past, their body language manifesting their eagerness to get a glimpse of what was happening down the street ahead of them.

Leyaril moved her finger back to the dot that would begin to show her what she needed to see.

And again, the mirror went black.

The sorceress tasted the flavors of the magic that flowed from her hand to the pedestal top, and from one part of the apparatus to another. She listened to the hum of the ethereal conduit that was bringing the visions from the signposts into the palace and into the vault in which she stood. All was well. The enchantment was pure and uncompromised from a magical standpoint. Nor was the fault with her.

There could only be one explanation. The mannequins had been blinded. The pupils of the charmed eyes may have been turned toward the backs of the sockets, or had been painted over. Or blindfolds had been wrapped around the heads. Any number of mundane measures would have been sufficient.

Only one person could be responsible. The existence of a spy array embedded within the eyes of the mannequins was a secret known only to Gloroc and the members of the Ril order. With one exception.

She did not waste her efforts determining the extent to which the array had been compromised. She already knew the answer. Enough mannequins had been disabled that the attackers at the armory, once their goal had been achieved, would be able to vanish into the warrens of the city. She would not see their faces. She would not be able to witness the paths they took, nor see the doorways into which they darted.

She shut down the apparatus and the lights and burst out of the chamber so abruptly it startled all three guards.

"Assemble a squad and go to the house of Quandai the taxidermist," she commanded Fetram. "Assume anyone you find there is a traitor."

"Taken alive for questioning?" Fetram asked.

"If possible. But taken, one way or another."

"Yes, m'lady," he said, speeding away as if his life depended upon the efficiency he demonstrated. Clearly he had taken to heart the lamentable example of his predecessor.

The remaining attendants fell in line behind her as she hurried back to her quarters. The rebels had denied her an advantage she had assumed was hers to exploit, but she had resources to spare.

—o—

Earlier in the evening, though he had not shared his feelings with his comrades, Alemar had put the odds of surviving to see the morning light at no better than even. Now? Hope was a palpable thing, flowing into him like air into his lungs. It seemed possible Tollvar was *not* going to get them all killed.

Another small team of co-conspirators, eight this time, poured out of the armory laden with weapons and gear of all sort, some items tied to belts and strapped to backs, some loaded into bags, some placed inside the coffinlike chest that four of the group were lugging between them. The party fanned out across the square toward their rehearsed routes of escape and concealment.

"Two more crews and we're done," said Nechtuss, the eager but all-too-young comrade Tollvar had assigned to oversee the twenty men whose job it was to safeguard the building's one and only means of access and egress.

None of the nineteen who stood with him had as much actual battle experience as Alemar. Not all nineteen put together. Yet allowing Alemar have authority over any citizens of Dragonsdeep was not a concession Tollvar had been willing to make. In that sense, the man was as much of a scrotum wart as ever.

In other senses, Alemar was willing to credit Tollvar with a shred of insight, a passing acquaintance with strategy.

And more surprising, a capacity to channel his boldness.

Judging by a comment that Clavos had let slip, Tollvar had actually been planning the attack on the armory for two years, and had been astute enough to wait until the right moment to put words to action. So much for the claims he had made of being a decisive leader, always ready to leap into confrontation. He had even held back in the aftermath of his arrest and momentary imprisonment, had swallowed his pride, had chosen not to waste lives and liberty in a fruitless premature effort. Instead, he had studied and planned and rehearsed, and finally he had found himself at a point when the Dragon and most of the Ril were occupied at the battlefront, and fresh assistance had come his way. Assistance for example in the person of Quandai, who had revealed that the spy eyes in the mannequin signposts could be blinded.

So far tonight, Alemar's own sword had not even been blooded. The two hundred had pushed forward in a flawlessly coordinated charge designed to overwhelm the sentries before they could drop the steel-plate portcullis. The defenders had been so stunned most had surrendered rather than be chopped down, and were now tied up in a side chamber.

The battering rams had been helpful, but in truth, the raiders had abandoned them early, leaving many of the sealed rooms intact because they found more than enough plunder within the initial crates and cases and vaults they breached. The operation had only been underway for a small fraction of an hour before the first spoils had been removed and sent off in the keeping of a support corps of women and juveniles.

Alemar had to admit, he was impressed. His main complaint was his deliberately minimized role, but perhaps that was too much to quibble over, because for all Tollvar's dismissive attitude toward him, the man had granted him a role no one else in their company could fill, and his contribution might well be meaningful.

A squad of ten armed men appeared some distance down the main thoroughfare that led to the armory. They were just near enough that Alemar could make out the white-upon-scarlet insignias on their livery when they passed below the nimbus of a large street lamp. They were a contingent from the city watch precinct over by the boundary of the Dowsers Quarter. That barracks lay closer to the armory than any other. Alemar and the others had been expecting them, though not quite as soon as this.

Six of the new arrivals were carrying bows, already strung. The quivers on their backs were stuffed with as many arrows as they could hold.

They arranged themselves in formation and charged at once. Alemar knew their bravery could only mean one thing: Reinforcements were soon to arrive. These men meant to keep the remnant of Tollvar's forces in place too long to complete their getaway.

At Nechtuss's command, half of the twenty guardians countercharged, swords and axes brandished. Alemar saw that they would not get there soon enough. The opposing squad reached arrow range. Four sword-and-shield guardians arrayed themselves in front of their fellows. The archers formed up behind and nocked their first arrows.

Alemar's moment had come. The purple gem on the back of the gauntlet surged to life, emitting not only a glow, but a faint hum as well. A spherical envelope of force, visible only to him, grew until it completely surrounded him. He exerted control, taming it to his command, and it grew further still. By the time it reached its fullest extent, it was so huge it surrounded not only the allies standing beside him, but those scampering across the square.

It was not the sort of ward a magician would brag of, because it was as penetrable as a bubble of sea foam newly laid on a beach. But what he had done would let him hoard his power to use when and where it would be most effective. The barrier was just substantial enough to reveal to him the course and speed of incoming arrows.

The first volley arced up toward them. Alemar felt the sting as the shroud was breached....

And he formed six tiny but stout wards directly in front of each arrow. The effect was momentary, requiring little power, but was enough interference to cheat the missiles of their velocity. The entire volley fell harmlessly onto the square's broad paving stones.

Nechtuss laughed. He raised his arm to clap Alemar on the shoulder, but had the presence of mind to abort the gesture before he disturbed Alemar's focus.

A second volley soared upward. Alemar dealt with it as he had the first. He didn't let himself become over-confident, though. Six arrows at a time was already a challenge, not so much to his magical strength but to his coordination. If the number of archers rose into the dozens? While he still had the luxury of doing so, he studied his own actions carefully, noting where his control was marginal, and where it was certain, and estimating how many of the flickers of resistance he could summon at the same time.

The counterattackers reached the squad. The archers dropped their bows in order to defend themselves.

Alemar turned away as soon as he saw how it was going. Tollvar had chosen some of his best warriors to defend the door. The city watch, on the other hand, was made up largely of men who, if they had been more capable, would have been part of Gloroc's armies of invasion. Their blades and shields served them almost as poorly as their arrows had.

The second-to-the-last crew of plunderers reached the armory exit just as the clash was ending. The sentries made way for them, Nechtuss directing their flight in directions other than down the thoroughfare.

With any luck, thought Alemar, every last member of Tollvar's band, himself included, would be able to reach cover before any further enemies came in sight, and no more blood would flow. But he knew better than to count on luck.

−o−

"Fetch my Irigion longbow," Leyaril commanded her footman as soon as she reached her set of rooms. "And the arrow with the blue obsidian tip."

Her servant hurried off in the direction of her trophy gallery. Meanwhile she continued on into her inquisition vault.

"Where is it, where is it?" she mumbled to herself as she rummaged through cubby after box after bin of the midden of articles left from the interrogations she had conducted here, and the ones she had anticipated conducting.

She forced herself into a state of calm. She had a system. One that only made sense to her, but a system nonetheless.

There. Suddenly the jumble, though as chaotic to the eye as ever, made sense to her. She picked up a small rack of tiny, stoppered vials, and chose one. She smiled as she saw the name TOLLVAR on the wrapping.

As she left the vault, her footman appeared and held out the bow and the arrow. She took the latter, but left the larger item in his grip.

"String it and wait by the door. I'll be there shortly," she said.

She carried the arrow to her workbench and laid it down. From her wall of apothecary supplies she took down a jar of infused beeswax marked with a symbol only she understood. She opened it and was greeted by an aroma of swamp orchid and beetle dust that confirmed the ingredients were still potent.

She dipped her fingers into the wax and applied a coating to the shaft of the arrow near its tip. When she was satisfied she had enough, she removed the stopper from the vial and upended it.

Several small hairs fell onto the workbench: Beard hairs, torn from Tollvar's chin during the rebellious buck's brief stay in the dungeons. Her apprentice had also collected some fingernail shavings, and made him bleed into a few strips of witch gauze. Thanks to Tollvar's escape the next day, Leyaril had never put the samples to their intended use, but she never threw such things away.

She pressed the hairs into the wax until they became thoroughly embedded. And then, just to be certain, she applied a little more wax all around.

There. She was satisfied. She marched out of the workroom. The footman and the bodyguards by the door gave way. They then gathered in her wake as she exited her suite and made her way to the terrace.

Once out in the open, she took the bow from the footman and approached the railing. She nocked the arrow, for the moment pointing it toward the tiles while she took a long, slow breath and cleared her mind of everything other than the sorcery she needed to invoke.

Not many women had the upper body strength to use an Irigion longbow, but she exhaled, tugged the string back, raised the weapon high, and released in one smooth motion. Her tutor would have praised her, had he been there to see it.

The arrow streaked into the air high above the city and disappeared save for the blue radiance of the enchantment. Just as it was beginning to heed the entreaties of gravity, Leyaril succeeded in establishing the link. The arrow's trajectory levelled out into a soaring-eagle glide unlike any flight an archer's arm could have bestowed.

If Tollvar happened to be indoors at that moment, her measures might come to nothing, but she stayed right where she was, bow down and riding idle in her grip, letting nothing disturb the conduit of sorcery between herself and the spark embedded within the blue obsidian.

There! The arrow had scented its quarry.

−o−

No more city watchmen appeared. The last of the salvage teams emerged from the armory, Tollvar and Clavos bringing up the rear. Most of the entrance guards, including Nechtuss, were ordered to escort those who were carrying the heaviest loads. Alemar accompanied a smaller contingent that remained with the leader and his right-hand man.

Alemar wondered if his inclusion with the head group was for no better reason than to ensure he was a direct witness to Tollvar's success. Perhaps it was simply that Tollvar was too suspicious to let Alemar off-leash.

They raced along through the shadowy sides of the streets, swords out, checking for observers and enemies and seeing none. They soon made the final turn and entered a long gap between a pair of warehouses. Toward the far end waited the brick steps that led down to a basement where they were to hide for a day or so. The operation was nearly over. It had gone very much as Tollvar had predicted.

So close to sanctuary, Alemar was about to cancel the shroud of watchfulness he had maintained, but he had not yet done so when he sensed danger coming fast from behind and above.

He whirled around and flung his blade upward, not knowing yet why he did so. The weapon spun as it rose. The hilt struck an incoming arrow, knocking it from its intended path.

But the arrow behaved as no arrow should. It arced back and had almost fully adjusted to the change in trajectory by the time it slammed into Tollvar. Alemar's actions did however cause the missile to drive into the back of his left upper arm rather than his kidney.

Tollvar's reaction was a combination of a blurt of pain and a yell of anger.

Alemar's sword clanged down on a rain barrel and tumbled to the ground. He scooped it up and scanned the rooflines of the warehouses, but neither his eyes nor his magical senses indicated any additional arrows were headed their way.

When he turned back, Tollvar was glaring not at the heights, but at him.

"You had *one job*," he spat. He brandished his arm. The arrow had fully skewered it. The point was jutting out the front side.

The urge to raise his own voice — to defend himself, to explain — burned like hiccupped bile. Instead Alemar said in an insistent but thoroughly calm tone, "I need to examine that arrow."

"By all means." Tollvar seized the fletched end of the arrow in his right fist, snapped the shaft in twain, and threw the fragment at Alemar. Then he grabbed the remainder and pulled it out along the hole it had made.

Tollvar knew Alemar was a healer, but it was to one of his own men he turned. The latter pulled out a bandage from his kit and began binding the arm.

Again, Alemar refused to react to the insult. He tossed aside the butt end of the arrow and said calmly, this time to Clavos, "I need to examine the tip."

Clavos arched an eyebrow at him, but in the end, shrugged and tossed the other fragment toward him.

It landed at Alemar's feet. As he bent to study it, he felt the murmurs of active magic.

—o—

When the arrow punched through flesh, a pulse raced back through the ethereal conduit, sweet as a mouthful of fine liquor. Leyaril swayed.

The emanations lacked the crescendo that would have signalled a lethal strike. Her smile did not fade, though. Tollvar needn't be dead to be defeated, and a living version of him might be of more use.

She raised her hand and beckoned.

"To me," she said aloud.

—o—

Just as his man tied off the bandage, Tollvar suddenly turned and staggered away from the others. The stagger evolved into a run.

The magic was powerful and in no way subtle. The filament of enchantment pulling Tollvar in the direction of the palace was so radiant Alemar could "see" it as if it were an actual — albeit glowing — rope.

"Clavos! Stop him!" Alemar shouted.

Clavos had instinctively jogged after Tollvar and was the only one who had a realistic hope of catching up. And catch up he did. Whether he had accepted that Alemar's advice might be valid, or whether he had judged on his own that he had to do something to counter his comrade's unnatural behavior, he did not hesitate. His long strides chewed up the distance. Tollvar had not yet reached the end of the gap between the warehouses when Clavos grabbed him by the collar and flung him to the pavement.

Tollvar rolled, regained his feet, and swiped across in front of him with his sword. Had he been caught even slightly off-guard, Clavos would have been badly cut. As it was, he stumbled back. Tollvar's subsequent charge nearly overwhelmed him.

Alemar and the others were hurrying up, but for five heartbeats, the clash was a matter of two players, one attempting to kill, the other trying not to die. In that span, brief as it was in retrospect and endless as it was while happening, Alemar finally understood how so many adherents might have been inspired to follow Tollvar and his cause. His swordplay was fluid, refined, and confident. Even Troy of Calinin South would have called him promising. Few men so tall and rangy as Tollvar could move as efficiently as he did.

Clavos was saved by three things. First, he was a gifted swordsman himself. Second, Tollvar apparently was not fully gripped by the enchantment. Twice his performance ebbed, transforming potential deadly thrusts into lunges that Clavos knocked aside. And third, a pair of Tollvar's companions tackled him from behind. His sword clattered from his grip.

"Let me go, let me go," Tollvar murmured, struggling to free himself, trying to squirm in the direction he had been headed.

"Can you help him?" Clavos asked Alemar.

Alemar realized he was still clutching the piece of arrow. He had picked it up just before joining the chase. He held it up in the palm of the gauntlet. He understood all too clearly how the traces of hair embedded in the wax near the tip anchored the spell to its victim.

He called upon one of the first tricks he'd learned to perform with the Dragonslayer's talisman. Energy gathered in the space just above the gauntlet. He focussed it upon the arrow fragment. The wood and wax and hair burst into flame and were consumed. The obsidian head melted into a dollop of glass. He flicked it away.

As Leyaril's working became nothing more than fumes rising toward the dome above, Tollvar ceased struggling against the grip of his men. After four or five blinks and a deep breath, his normal alertness reasserted itself.

His men let go. Tollvar rolled over, wincing as he jostled his wounded arm.

He chuckled. "Well, Bastard. It seems you're not entirely useless after all."

Kneeling, Alemar extended his hand down near Tollvar's arm, not actually touching it, but close enough to decipher his aura. Tollvar did not resist or interfere.

Alemar detected what he had feared. Stifling a curse, he dug into his apothecary bag, pulled out a tiny ruby-red bottle, and freed the stopper.

"Drink this," he told Tollvar.

Tollvar obeyed.

"We need to get that wound rinsed out as quickly as possible."

The Ril sorceress clearly did not operate by partial measures. The arrow's menace had already been thwarted in at least two ways and yet it still might manage to kill its target.

Tollvar cooperated without demands for further explanation. Something in the category of respect was finally exuding out of him and wafting in Alemar's direction. Clavos helped him up, and the whole party fled toward the basement they had earlier been so close to reaching.

— o —

The link evaporated. Leyaril swayed again, and this time she found nothing to smile about.

She opened her mouth and tasted the vestiges of magic the wind brought, rolling the flavors on her tongue.

Within moments, she understood what manner of opponent had thwarted her. The palace, the city, and so many of the things within them had been crafted with magic that exuded a similar sort of piquancy.

"Child of the Dragonslayer," she murmured.

Tonight she had failed, but that could be corrected, and once she did so, her victory would be far grander than bringing down a common saboteur.

CHAPTER NINETEEN

THE CLOUDS DARKENED to a bruised grey. Keron knew luck was no longer on his side.

He and his allies had driven into Simorilia, disrupting Gloroc's forces so effectively the opposing generals had struggled to maintain discipline among the retreating ranks. The port of T'jet was not yet in play, but soon could be. They were *winning*.

But the gains had come while the weather remained dry. That season was about to end.

The dragons would no longer be constrained. Keron had seen what Gloroc could do when he was able to call upon his water magic. Logic said the other dragon—Aroc, a captured officer had named him—could do as much.

Rain was not actually falling yet. Keron had no doubt that was the only thing holding back the appearance of the great beasts over the battlefield.

The Elandri king stalked between the tents, between the wagons, between the farriers dave fletchers and cooks. He itched to take real action. Issue orders. Grab a weapon and fight. But what could be done had been done: His forces and the Calinin legions were spread thinly across the plain, leaving no vulnerable concentrations. The men on the front lines were tucked into trenches. Key leaders such as himself were scattered throughout the troop formations and the supply camps, disguised as common soldiers or workmen. Even Enret was far from Keron's side.

All he could do was pace, gradually circling back to his starting point to loop around in the other direction, the only relief from his agitation coming in the form of reports from the couriers, who paused near him to murmur their dispatches and vanished as quickly as they had appeared.

Alas, none of those messengers brought any actual news. All of them simply confirmed what he could see for himself. The situation remained a standoff for both great armies.

The air seemed to sigh, and the temperature dropped. To the north, the undersides of the clouds lost their billowy contours and in moments, a veil of rain obscured the vantage of distant, low-lying hills — the borderlands of Thiagra.

Two winged shapes flew toward the battlefield. Not birds. Already they loomed in the sky, owning it, revealing themselves as creatures unlike any others to be found on Tanagaran, both in size and in form.

Keron's head throbbed. He knew the sensation. It was the mind-speech of the dragons. It should not be detectable while he stood so far from the source. Something was rendering it more intense — *louder*, if something that did not consist of true sound could be described that way.

The message they sent was wordless. Glee. Pure and constant, it was joy so abundant it could not help but spill from them and manifest in the minds of any sentient being present on the landscape below.

The creatures did not glide about, reconnoitering as they often did. They flew with singular purpose, passing the no-man's-land between the armies to hover above the Elandri front line right at its center, where the phalanx might well be if Keron had intended to launch an offensive thrust.

Without swooping down toward ground level as had been the pattern in past engagements, the dragons poised where they were and spat dragonflame. The intensely bright twin bolts streaked down, merging as they reached ground level. A vast sphere of incandescence blossomed. Keron raised his arm to shield his eyes. A moment later, a wall of heated air slammed into him. He staggered back.

Fearing what he would see, he hesitated a moment before lowering his arm from his face, but he did not have the luxury of turning away.

Nearby, dozens and dozens of his comrades were picking themselves up off the ground, unlike him having been knocked down by the shock wave. Others who had been closer to the blast lay unconscious where they had fallen, and some did not appear likely to ever rise again.

A blood-spattered crater occupied the place where the dragonflame had struck. It was a hundred paces across.

This was far beyond anything Keron had seen before. Gloroc and Aroc's magic had combined in a manner that was not a doubling, but something far beyond that. The biggest catapult ever constructed could not have flung a load even a tenth of the distance between his position and the place the dragons had struck, and yet he was wiping dirt and gore from his face.

No army could stand against this. Even assuming the monsters had only the usual limited number of bursts to call upon, the effect of a single day's worth of punishment would be dire. If the storm lasted into a second and third and fourth day, the campaign would be lost.

Keron had thought he understood the enemy. Knew what he faced. But he had not understood at all.

The dragons glided along so casually it was insolent, their buoyant mood radiating for all to "hear."

Keron could do nothing but stand there, hope draining.

Gloroc and Aroc veered into what was clearly another approach. The apparent target lay far from where they had initially struck.

The twin lances of brilliance raced down and merged, obliterating what appeared to be an ordinary supply tent in the rear of the Elandri encampment, some five hundred yards from Keron's position.

Keron dropped to one knee, covered his head, and braced himself. The shock wave pounded him, but he had estimated its impact accurately. He was back on his feet in an instant.

As before, a crater yawned, smoke trailing upward from blackened and reddened mounds of debris. One aspect was different. Shards of ruptured, seared planks of wood jutted from earth, evidence that the tent had hidden an underground bunker. Aside from the planks, which had been stout slabs of hardwood capable of withstanding a hundred ax blows, nothing remained of the feature other than a rectangular area where the crater was somewhat deeper.

Keron let loose a violent puff of breath as he grasped the meaning of what he was seeing. The dragons would not have used up one of their attacks on a strategically worthless target. They had meant to bring their power to bear on that specific part of the battlefield. The tent had contained more than rations, bandages, spare boots. The bunker had sheltered a number of valuable items, including the Dragonslayer's orb of prophecy.

The refuge had therefore been where Keron's cousin, Treynaf, must have been hiding. Treynaf habitually kept the globe within reach, and often actually within his grip.

Keron and his magicians had taken steps to ensure Gloroc would not be able to pinpoint the talismans of the Dragonslayer with any meaningful precision. Clearly those measures no longer mattered. Apparently, as a consequence of the combining of their powers, the dragons knew just where to attack.

The king choked down a curse. Talismans remained at just two locations on the battlefield. The belt of strength was around Val's waist, and Val himself was somewhere out near his cavalry division, disguised as a courier. The other, the scepter, was hidden beneath canvas in a wagon some fifteen paces from where Keron now stood.

Keron was momentarily paralyzed, mired in the prospect of possibly having to witness his son and heir burned out of existence before his eyes. That would have been more than he could have endured. He thanked the gods of fate when he saw the dragons turn not toward the prince's position, but toward his own, Gloroc curving tightly, Aroc looping around less steadily, his flying skills still not as refined as his sibling.

The king sprinted for the wagon where he had hidden his gear. He fetched the scepter of Alemar the Great, awakened it, and planted his feet.

He was no wizard, but for years the talisman had reliably obeyed him. He would use it. Why make it easy for the dragons to kill him?

"Get away!" he yelled at the people nearby. "Run for your lives!"

Many, having seen the dragons' trajectory, were already doing so. More followed suit.

Not all. Some stood in witness. Their choice. Keron gave them a nod of acknowledgment.

The ward formed around him, its blue energies gathering so thickly the bubble became opaque. He did not see the blasts of dragon-flame rush at him.

The next he knew, he was flat on his back on charred stubble and blackened clods of dirt, a distant crater ridge around him in every direction.

As far as he could tell, his skin—even his clothing—was unburnt. He was not bleeding. His bones seemed to be intact. Strangely, even his eardrums seemed unruptured. But he was stunned to the point he could barely make his body move.

The scepter lay on the ground a few inches from his right hand. He reached out, touched it, but when he tried to wrap his fingers around the grip, he failed.

Far over his head, the dragons were circling. Their smugness was muted. It had become apparent to them he was not yet dead. They seemed, if not surprised, at least annoyed.

Keron head footsteps crunching upon the seared earth. Someone was running to the center of the crater.

"No..." Keron murmured. His own death was certain. He did not want to take anyone along with him.

A man loomed over him. It was Fanhar.

"Run, Your Grace," Keron whispered. "Please."

Fanhar shook his head. "I have run for centuries. Today I will stand."

He slid the scepter from beneath Keron's hand and lifted it up. Its energies woke. They woke more fully than they ever had for Keron —so potently the metal did not simply glow. It sang.

Fanhar caressed the talisman like a child's cheek. "I would rather have had the gauntlets, but this will have to do."

Abruptly, the figure standing over Keron was no longer a curly-haired, rakish prince of the Calinin Empire. He was a man of decidedly modest height with straight, dark hair liberally streaked with grey. Anyone who had seen the statues in the palaces of Elandris would know him.

The dragons began to shift their positions into in what was already a too-familiar configuration.

The Dragonslayer squeezed the handle of the scepter. A sphere of magical protection formed, twice as big as needed to enclose himself and Keron. It resembled a traditional ward in only a few basic aspects—the shimmer in the air, the bee-like drone, the way the energy lifted the hair on the back of the necks of those within its influence. In other ways, it was spellcasting of a type Keron had never seen. It was supple. Aggressive.

The top of the ward ejaculated upward, forming a thick, whip-like extension that reached almost as high as the layer of clouds.

The dragons spun, aborting their attack, swooping away as evasively as they could manage.

The Dragonslayer took hold of the scepter handle with both hands and...flicked the whip.

Gloroc folded his wings and plunged clear. Aroc dodged awkwardly. The top of the ward slapped him in the head.

A moment later the ward dissolved. The Dragonslayer sank to his knees, chest heaving, arm falling. The scepter thudded onto the ground.

Keron scarcely noticed his forefather's collapse. His attention was upon the miracle in the sky. Aroc, body slack and neck bent at an angle contrary to life, folded up like a slapped spider and fell toward the earth. His wings fluttered not by design, but like sails tethered only at one corner, the rest given to the tempest. Finally the dragon slammed into the ground a dozen wagon-lengths away.

"Not the one I was aiming for," said the man who had done the deed. "Could have done worse, though."

Keron had felt the tremor of impact. He had heard the crunch. And now as he managed at last to regain his feet, he was left with a direct view of the carcass. It was an inert pile of flesh and jutting bone. And yet he didn't fully believe what had happened until he heard the screech from the sky over the center of the battlefield.

The wizard accepted Keron's hand and likewise managed to stand up, unsteady though he was when he got there.

"I believe I've made him angry," he quipped.

Gloroc was racing along a broad arc, higher than before, gradually turning so that he would be aimed straight at them. Keron knew what it meant. Though any blast of dragonflame he sent at them would be weaker now that it was not reinforced by his brother's contribution, it would still be mighty, and if delivered at the end of a dive, would almost surely overwhelm them. Meanwhile the Dragon-slayer was unable to stand on his own. Sweat was pouring down his face. Only a few moments past, when he had dropped the illusion spell and ceased to be Fanhar, he had seemed to be at most sixty years old. Now anyone would describe him as elderly.

Gloroc began the plunge.

"He is unreasonably hard to kill," Keron complained.

"I'm not done yet," the Dragonslayer replied. "Stand away, please."

Keron did so. To his amazement, the sorcerer picked the scepter up from the ground and created a fresh ward, but this time only he was tucked within its confines. Keron was left on the outside.

Again, the ward geysered upward. But this time the bubble was at the top, the extension serving as a stalk keeping the sphere — and its occupant — up in the heavens.

Gloroc veered off. He flapped his wings hard, endeavoring to recapture altitude and regain the superior position over his enemy.

The Dragonslayer began to *chase him.*

Back on the ground, Keron laughed. "Please let this not be a dream," he murmured to himself.

— o —

It had been centuries since Alemar had practiced this sort of flying, not since he had been young enough to recover from the effects of such monumental spellcasting. Every instant, he could feel the toll it was taking.

But it was so, so sweet to be dogging Gloroc's tail. The latter closed off his mindspeech, trying to conceal his outrage and fear, but the beast's emotions were still detectable in the sudden, urgent twists and loops of his escape attempt.

Alemar had his own fear to overcome. He was trembling with it, and his mouth had gone dry. He had not been in such immediate peril since Triss had held him in her grip, all those centuries long gone. He had no offense. He was too weak to lash out at Gloroc as he had done with Aroc. Inevitably Gloroc would soon recognize the attempt for what it was, and deflect it by summoning his own ward.

In the meantime, what the Dragonslayer had was strategy. He could still set in motion something that Struth had taught him in the vast underground caverns below Headwater during some of the long sessions of tutoring in dragon magic. She had crafted the spell in advance, supplying it with nearly all of the energy it would require to manifest. All he needed was a bit of strength, a bit of courage, and for Gloroc to behave as what he was — an avatar of rage.

They swooped and circled for a hundred pounding beats of his heart, until he was confident he had stoked Gloroc's fury enough. He broke off, pretending that his stamina had failed, that he could no longer fly about, that his magical barrier had become useless except to prop him up at his current altitude and fend off the drops of rain.

Gloroc seized what he thought was an opportunity. He wheeled about and headed straight for the wizard. His maw opened to spout dragonflame.

Alemar waited until the last instant, then uttered one word and touched his thumb to the tip of the ring finger of his empty hand. A portal suddenly formed behind him. In the same instant, he negated his ward, and gravity took him straight down. He fell just fast enough to avoid being struck by the bolt of flame.

Gloroc, his vantage blocked by the vivid glow of his own attack, streaked along the path he had committed to, which took him right through the portal and entirely out of the skies over Simorilia.

The Dragonslayer twisted around and was rewarded by a quick glimpse into the place where Gloroc had gone. It was, as Struth had promised, the void between Tanagaran and Serpent Moon, a blackness leavened only by a few stars and the crescent edge of Motherworld. Gloroc was flapping his wings, but uselessly, because there was no atmosphere to flap against. His mouth was opening and closing, trying to fill lungs that would never fill again.

The portal snapped shut.

—o—

Craning his head, peering through the rain, Keron was able to witness just enough of the altercation to understand what sort of trap Gloroc had been lured into, and that the great adversary he had fought against his entire adult life was not coming back.

He had also seen enough to be confident the last bolt of dragonflame had missed his ancestor. Now, though, the fall would kill him.

Or perhaps not.

The Dragonslayer waved the scepter. The ward formed again. The enchantment never reached full coherency, but the flower stem of support was reestablished, and his downward momentum began to be checked. The effort was not enough to slow him down all the way, though. The wizard hit the ground hard a short distance from the body of Aroc.

Keron rushed over. He waved away the few who had already tentatively gathered around the fallen magician. A quartet of his bannermen, wordlessly understanding he wanted privacy, urged everyone back until no one remained closer than twenty paces.

The Dragonslayer opened his eyes. He winced. From the neck down, his body was limp and, if Keron was guessing correctly, deaf to his commands. His hair was now utterly white, his skin deeply fissured, his fingernails sunken.

Keron knelt down. "Is there anything I can do?"

"I was doomed from the moment I touched the scepter."

"You saved us. Thank you."

"Do not thank me. I am half to blame for this war."

"Fair enough," Keron said. "Can I at least say I will miss Fanhar? That I enjoyed his company?"

"As you wish."

"May I ask what happened to the real Fanhar?"

"Betrayed and killed by Mahosh."

"I am sorry to hear that."

"He was a decent fellow. I'd like to think I served his memory well."

"I believe you did," Keron declared.

The roar of many voices came from the distance, along with other noises the likes of which Keron knew too well. He stood up and gazed across the plain.

Gloroc's army was attacking. Hundreds of men had already crossed the no-man's-land, taking advantage of the place where the crater had destroyed the trenches. Detachments of archers were loosing volleys. A bank of fog suddenly rose over toward the southern flank, a trick one of the Ril wizards had often employed in recent battles to obscure the movement of the Dragon's cavalry.

"They haven't given up," Keron reported. "If anything they're fighting harder than ever."

"I was afraid they'd be stubborn," the Dragonslayer said. "But now it has the makings of a fair fight."

Keron nodded. A fair fight. That was all he had ever needed. So be it, then. He had long ago learned that feeling cheated served no purpose. He would be humble. He would be grateful.

He would earn his victory.

"I know you're there," the Dragonslayer called out. Keron wasn't sure to whom he spoke until he heard boots scuff the dirt off to the left.

"Treynaf!" Keron blurted. There was his cousin, standing not six paces away. His hair was singed and his garments smelled of dragonflame, but he displayed no indication he was in pain. His small pet monkey was perched on his shoulder, trembling.

"I saw your bunker destroyed," Keron said.

"Yes. The bunker. The orb. My copies of Shahera's scrolls. All charcoal and fumes now." He brushed ash off his pet's tail. "But the little one and I escaped, just in time. I had a vision."

"More than one," the Dragonslayer interjected.

Treynaf hesitated. "Yes. There was another vision."

"Oh, spit it out, will you? I've waited thirteen hundred years to hear it."

"How so?" Keron asked.

"That globe belonged to me, once upon a time. Never was good for much. I'm glad it's been destroyed. But in one of the scenes it showed me, I was lying in the rain on a battlefield, feeling very, very old, knowing a fellow with a monkey on his shoulder would tell me how my story ends. Not how *I* end, you understand. We only have to wait a few moments and we'll all know the answer to that. I mean how my *story* ends. What form does it take?"

"I saw six dragons, flying," Treynaf said.

Keron braced himself for the rest.

"They had no heads," Treynaf declared.

"Hah!" The wizard smiled. "Better than some of the endings I pictured. Thank you."

"You're welcome."

The Dragonslayer coughed. He met Keron's glance and the king knew to kneel back down again so that he could make out his ancestor's final few words over the pit-pat of rain, the clamor of catapults flinging their loads, the discordant toll of battle axes striking shields.

"Take my body back to the temple," the magician wheezed. "Put me in the sepulcher next to Struth."

"You want to be buried with a dragon?"

"I want to be buried with my friend. The fact that she was a dragon is just happenstance."

"I vow I will see it done," Keron said.

"Good."

The Dragonslayer's eyes went dry. The skin of his face tightened over his skull. He was dead before the last air escaped his chest.

CHAPTER TWENTY

QUANDAI HAD NOT at any earlier point in life known homelessness. He had moved straight out of his parents' flat above his father's trophy shop and into his first home with Brikka, and later from that home to the residence he had been given as a reward for his service as a minion of the Dragon. He had always treasured the comfort of familiar walls around him. Familiar scents. Familiar tasks. He thought he would be disoriented, scurrying from one safehouse to another, never sure if the bed he slept in would cradle him the next night.

But he was not disoriented. He was not homesick. His step had a lightness as he walked along the avenue. A fugitive he might be, but finally he was his own man.

Brikka accompanied him, her arm snaked into the crook of his elbow as in the days of their courtship, when he made a habit of accompanying her home from the Dowsers Quarter.

No one paid them any mind. Outwardly they were a middle-aged couple anyone might see traipsing through this busy sector of the city. They were far from their former neighborhood. Quandai's features were on the mundane side of ordinary. His one signature aspect, his receding hairline, was hidden beneath his hat. They had ventured out nearly a dozen times in the days since the successful assault on the arsenal. Hiding in basements and attics was, somewhat to his surprise, not something he tolerated — nor Brikka either. And he had things to do.

They drew up, though, at the sound of angry voices. On the other side of the avenue stood a large house set back from the walkway, fronted by a yard of well-trimmed shrubs and a miniature lemon grove. Through the broken door emerged a squad of palace soldiers. The householder was dragged out, his face bruised and swollen. His wife was next, pulled along by her hair. Their adolescent daughter, hands bound behind her, was allowed to shuffle along between a pair of burly escorts whose scrutiny of her implied she might yet have the worst of it, should the pair of them be allowed to take her off to their own sort of interrogation chamber.

The soldiers paid no mind to the witnesses. If anything, witnesses seemed to be part of the point of the exercise, here in the midst of the day when commerce and traffic were at a height. Quandai and Brikka simply stayed where they were on the walkway, and the armed men barely glanced at them as they turned and headed in the direction of the prison.

Brikka said something under her breath. Quandai couldn't make it out, but he was quite sure of the meaning.

The arrests had been going on for days. The targets were chosen at random. Or at least that was how it seemed to Quandai, because so far he had not been among those apprehended, nor had any of the other Watchers been found. Not one of Tollvar's coterie had been taken. Apparently Leyaril was hoping a wide casting of the net would yield at least one conspirator. She had the means to extract information. Everyone knew her reputation in that regard. But she had to have the right prisoner.

A young mother near the seamstress shop, no matter that she had her hands full with a rambunctious toddler, stared hard at the backs of the departing garrison. On a balcony two houses down, an old man glared in the same direction, his fists tight in echo of days past when perhaps he had been the enforcer at a tavern.

In his lifetime, Quandai had seldom witnessed reactions of that sort in public. For half a century, Dragonsdeep had been a whipped dog.

He and Brikka rounded a corner and continued down a short street, soon arriving at an intersection embellished with a cadaver signpost. He recognized the specimen as one he had crafted six or seven years back.

He stopped right in front of the mannequin, directly in the path of its gaze. When he was sure no one on the street was observing him, he thumbed his nose.

His smile lingered as he and Brikka resumed their strolling.

—o—

An hour later — much of that time spent simply confirming that they had not been followed — Quandai and Brikka were welcomed via an unmarked doorway in a certain alley behind a certain restaurant, and made their way along a well-guarded tunnel into the back of a warehouse. Crates and stacks of pallets were arranged along the periphery and were serving as makeshift platforms for weapons seized in the armory raid, for spare gear of other sort, or for platters stocked with bread and cheese and pots of tea. At the center of the open space stood about a dozen individuals surrounding a table at which sat Tollvar. The table contained a street map of Dragonsdeep.

Tollvar's skin gave off none of the pallor it had possessed during the first three days after his poisoning. The animated way he gestured and pointed at the map was ample proof his arm was unhampered by the pain of his arrow wound, livid as the scars still were. Quandai studied him for several moments, confirming this was all true. When he had first seen Tollvar after the armory raid, he had been sure the man would not survive the Poisoner's touch, no matter what measures Alemar brought to bear. Geim had taken Quandai aside and whispered, "I know what the prince looks like when there's nothing he can do. He's still trying. There is hope."

Geim had been correct. Tollvar had rallied. And here he was, back to orchestrating the resistance within the city.

One thing had changed. The Tollvar that had survived was not the same as the old Tollvar. Now the prince of Cilendrodel stood right beside him, as near on one side as Clavos was on the other. When Alemar gestured at a portion of the map and made a brief suggestion, Tollvar nodded. Even at a distance, unable to hear the exchange, Quandai could see the advice was being taken seriously.

In addition, Toren was among those granted a place in the core circle. Quandai knew it was not the first time. Tollvar had yet to concede that the man played host to the consciousness of a revered founder of Elandris. That threatened his authority too much. But he had at least accepted the principle that a warrior of the Far South could see problems that fighting men of civilized lands were blind to, and was willing to listen to what that person had to offer.

Quandai waited along with Brikka to the side among the crates. He did not attempt to insert himself into the strategy session. He would not be part of any ambush or sortie. He would pick up no blade. He would contribute to the discussion only when called upon to answer specific questions. In particular, he would advise about the character and design of any particular part of the city. He had no wish to intrude until he knew his input was relevant.

Geim detached himself from the edge of the gathering. He smiled as he approached.

"Shouldn't be too much longer. It's down to only two options, I think."

"I am in no hurry," Quandai assured him.

They stood silently for a time, watching.

"It's remarkable, don't you think?" Quandai added. "Gives a person hope."

"It does," Geim agreed. "I find myself actually giving thought to what I might do with myself after the war."

"You sound as though you never expected to reach that point."

"No. I did not."

"I take it you will go home."

Geim shook his head.

Quandai realized his mistake. "I'm sorry. I have said something stupid. I don't know your history."

"No offense is taken," Geim responded. "My past need not trouble me, not in a future that grants me the grace to make new ties, settle in a new place."

"Do you know where that might be?" Brikka interjected.

"I find Dragonsdeep strangely pleasing," Geim answered. "Who knows? When the city is cleansed of dragon taint, I believe I'd enjoy lingering here indefinitely."

"Would your attitude have anything to do with all those conversations you've been having with our niece?" Brikka asked.

If Geim blushed, the reaction was concealed by the deep gold of his complexion.

"She is easy to talk to," Geim answered in what was on the surface a neutral tone.

Quandai envied the Vanihr's ability to see beyond their current ordeal. Quandai could not yet manage that. He was happy for Geim, though. And he conceded, with some satisfaction, that Solia might finally have found, in this much-travelled and extraordinarily even-tempered stranger who had witnessed so much of the world outside the dome, a person who would not run out of responses for the endless questions that bubbled out of her.

Brikka stood up. "I believe I'll fetch some tea."

"That would be nice," Quandai answered.

Alone with Geim, Quandai found himself unable to continue the conversation. They dealt with the awkward silence by turning back to the other side of the room.

And...

"Something just happened," Geim declared.

"I believe you're right," Quandai echoed.

Alemar was holding his right hand up and contemplating the gauntlet as if seeing it for the first time in his life.

The jewels glinted as any jewels would, facets redirecting the light of the room. A passive function. They were no longer lit from within. No longer alive.

Toren reached out. Alemar took off the armored glove and

handed it over.

Quandai held his breath. He had been in the room when the prince had told Toren he could never make use of either of the great talismans again, at the possible cost of his life.

Toren slid his hand into the gauntlet. He closed his fist. Opened the fingers again. And then, unaffected, slid it back off and set it on the table.

Alemar and Toren's glances met.

Something had happened indeed.

— o —

Leyaril regarded the fellow hanging from the dungeon chains. He had confessed to enough wrongdoing to justify the lashes he'd been given, but not to the sort of treason for which he'd been arrested. Given the dose of elixir and the other measures she'd applied, she would know if he were one of the conspirators in league with Tollvar.

"Tell me again why this one was brought in?" she demanded of her deputy inquisitor.

"Neighbors implicated him."

"I can see why they would want to be rid of him," Leyaril granted, "but their maneuver is of no use to me. Let the flies crawl on him for a few more hours, then let him go. We'll give him the chance to show what he thinks of those who turned him in."

A small flicker of animation reappeared in the wretch's eyes, as she suspected it might.

She exited the chamber. Her armed escorts fell into formation behind her. They did not ask how it had gone. They had served her long enough to interpret her mood at a glance.

She had hoped for better. Three times in the past five days the city had endured sabotage or ambushes by Tollvar and his band of traitors, the last in the South Plaza, where among other acts of defiance a statue of Gloroc had been knocked down. As freely as the rebel had been operating, someone should have been found who could say where he was hiding.

Tollvar. He shouldn't even be alive, much less in good health.

That vexed her as nothing had in years. She had done everything right on the night of the raid of the arsenal. Her arrow had hit Tollvar. She had no doubt of that. Yet he had neither died nor been brought to heel by her summoning charm.

The Cilendri prince was to blame, of course. He, too, should have been contained by now, if not captured or killed. And then there was Quandai. She had actually *liked* Quandai, the few times she'd met him. A mild man. Always did what he was told, and did it well, never disturbing the order of things. She would have thought it impossible that someone like *that* could represent a threat, and yet the damage he had done was the worst she had suffered.

"The Dragon's eyes are everywhere in Dragonsdeep." So the saying went. The populace had all understood the Ril had some means to learn of treasonous activity within the city, even if they failed to grasp the mechanism. Thanks to the spy eyes in the mannequins, the Dragon had not needed to maintain the same number of armsmen as in the other cities of Elandris.

But now? The last time Leyaril had checked, only one in twenty of the eyes remained functional, mostly those near or within the palace, such as the one in Marnus's skull. She was reduced to apprehending useless suspects, antagonizing the faceless masses of citizenry, a strategy she knew was unsustainable, that she had only resorted to because *by now* it should have yielded an advantage!

She reached her suite. She told her escorts to wait outside the door. Their silence was no longer enough. She needed them out of sight as well.

She proceeded into her reading room and pulled down a grimoire, giving no particular thought to which one she selected. The volume she ended up with was ancient, its leather cover laced with cracks, the threads of its binding frayed nearly to uselessness. The embossed title was still legible, though: *Viper in a Bottle*. It was one of her favorites, a compendium of formulae created by generations of poisoners of the Great Desert west of Aleoth. She had studied it many times, particularly when the virulence of the concoction she was attempting to brew was secondary to the reliability of the antidote.

She set the book on the podium and began turning pages. She nodded as she recognized in certain entries the inspiration she had drawn from them, and how effective her refinements of those base recipes had ultimately been.

Most important, she relaxed. Eventually she was barely invested in the text in front of her eyes. What mattered was the creative state of being. More than once the solution to a current problem had come while reviewing the details of past challenges. Past *successes*.

Before any insight could blossom, a spasm turned her knees to wax. She collapsed into a fetal position, beads of sweat popping from her brow, mouth wide as a baby bird's, breath impossible to draw in. The podium, nudged by her as she fell, finished tipping over and clattered onto the tile.

The pain vanished as suddenly as it had struck, but she lay on the floor limp from the echo of it for a hundred or more beats of her pounding heart. Gradually air leaked into her lungs. She opened her eyes.

Fetram was looming over her. The noises of collapse — of her, of the podium, of the book — must have brought him. That was as it should be, but it made matters worse.

Panic was in his eyes, but steadiness in his posture. "Revered Mage," he whispered. "What should I do?"

"Go back to your station," she replied. She meant it as a strict command, but the words came out more like a plea. "Pretend you never saw me like this. Speak of it to no one."

He slipped away in the direction of the entrance to her suite. She knew he would do precisely as she directed. Nevertheless he would carry the memory of what he had seen within him. She would have to weigh that, and decide in due course whether that was something she needed to resolve.

She tried to move her left arm, intending to wipe the strand of drool from her chin, but she abandoned the effort. The arm was where the agony had come from. More precisely, it had come from her Ril tattoo. Normally the serpentine form flowed up from her wrist to her elbow, wrought in pigments that evoked the sheen and colors of a living dragon. Now the whole rendering was livid red.

Even as she absorbed the meaning of what she was seeing, the redness waned, leaving behind a single hue: the color of ashes.

She could not have been more taken by surprise. Yet she could not have been more certain of what she should do next.

When she was able to make it to her feet and hold herself steady, when she had straightened her disarrayed robes and washed her face, she went to the door, opened it, and addressed her guards as if she were her usual self.

"Send word to the kitchen, wafers and tea for two. Then go and tell the chamberlain he is to come to my quarters at once."

$-$o$-$

Guestis did not ask for an explanation. He was in the midst of reading reports. If anyone in the palace but Leyaril had tried to interrupt, he would have put them off. As it was, he paused only to wipe the worst of the inkstains from his fingers.

He found the sorceress at her small dining table by the window when he arrived, a basket of thinbreads and pot of steaming tea waiting between the place settings, along with a dish of butter, a cruet of infused olive oil, and small jars of jam. Apricot and pomegranate.

His host gestured for him to sit down. She was already chewing. She had that vague, preoccupied look he had seen so often on the faces of every Ril wizard he had ever known. They often delved into their meditations and spellcasting for hour after hour, only to emerge from their fugues in a ravenous condition. He assumed she had just done so.

Guestis was reassured to see her in this sort of context. Such troubled times they had seen lately. He knew how frustrated she had been by it all. He had been afraid of what he might confront. But she seemed to be at ease.

Best to keep her in that mood. Though he was not hungry, he put a dollop of pale amber jam on a wafer and nibbled at it, just to be companionable.

"How may I help you, Revered Mage?" he asked.

"Things have taken an unexpected turn," she replied. "Share a glass or two with me. It will take some time to explain."

She set a pair of goblets midway between them and poured generous servings of dark red wine.

Guestis knew she could drink him under the table. He calculated the limit of what he would drink before he lifted his glass, vowing to stay well under that threshold. Meanwhile the aroma was enticing. He placed the goblet below his nose, swirled the liquid, and inhaled.

Later he could not recall whether he took a sip or not. He knew he managed to set the goblet down without spilling the beverage, and then his chin subsided in the direction of his chest and his whole body began tilting leftward. He was aware that Leyaril's hand reached out to slow his momentum as he keeled over, but at that point everything went black.

—o—

Guestis awakened by degrees, his body thrashing, gnarling up the bedding on which he lay. Finally he bolted into a sitting position, and only then opened his eyes.

"Steady," Leyaril said. "Don't move too quickly."

She waited for him to take in his circumstances: supine on her wide bed in her stateroom aboard her ship, still arrayed in the robes of his office, gently deposited there by her attendants. Unhurt.

He did not ask what she had dosed him with. After all, he was alive.

She took a cool washcloth and pressed it to his forehead. "A quarter hour or so, and you'll be good as new." She lifted one of his hands and kissed a knuckle. "Truly."

He began to relax. It pleased her more than she could say. So few people in her life were capable of being soothed by her promises.

Inevitably, his gaze was drawn toward the view through the stern windows. His eyes widened as he recognized the towers of Dragonsdeep. They were growing hazy with distance.

"What have you done?"

"Gloroc is dead," she told him.

The ship teetered on a swell. Guestis grabbed the bed's corner post to steady himself. He left the hand there, gripping so firmly Leyaril was inclined to think he was trying to dent the wood.

"Are you certain?"

"Yes."

"Then...all the more reason to have stayed!"

"Tadpole." She laid her hand gently on his knee. "Dragonsdeep is no longer high ground."

"How can you say that?"

"I say it because it's true. Without the dragons, with no other members of my order beside me, with the best fighting men at the battlefront, I could not have held out. Not long enough. Our enemies are...resourceful."

How it burned to say it aloud. She had accepted it. Still — it burned.

Guestis turned back to the view through the window, new anguish wrinkling his brow as another tower of the city dipped below the horizon.

"I never took you to be the sort to run," the chamberlain murmured.

Leyaril lifted her hand off his knee. Blood rushed to her cheeks.

"Shall I lower you into a dinghy and let you paddle your way back?"

"No," he answered at once. He wouldn't meet her gaze. "It's just...it's just..."

"I know."

Poor pet. He did not know what to do with himself outside his usual place and usual role. In a few hours, he would appreciate the favor she had done him — the fondness she was showing him.

"I am not running." She said it calmly, but forcefully. "I am *repositioning*."

"Where will we go?"

"To Firsthold. I left things in good order there. While the rebels remain occupied in Dragonsdeep and in the West, I will create a rally-ing point. I mean to fight. I am simply choosing a better place from which to do that."

"Is it a fight we can win?"

"If I didn't believe that, I would remove this pill case I keep here..." She plucked out the tiny nacre-and-gold container from the hidden pocket near her heart. "And I would ask you to share its contents with me."

Guestis held his breath until she had tucked the case back in its place.

"I have no master now," she declared. "My ambitions are not diminished. They are liberated."

— o —

Alemar raised the spyglass to his eye.

It was true. The vessel on the horizon was Leyaril's transport. The fine accouterments, the state cabin's breadth, and even the design of the craft itself—made for stability and comfort on journeys across the waves, not for speed or military advantage—were enough in themselves to make it obvious. Any slight doubt that remained was wiped away as he made out the Ril emblem on the flag.

"She's tucked her tail!" Tollvar crowed, almost boyish in his giddiness. "She's running!"

Alemar was thankful the man at least avoided raising his voice. For the moment the resistance had control of the tower they had just climbed, but they needed to avoid calling attention to themselves. If the city garrison forces realized how many of their prime targets were gathered at the top of the spire, they might close in, overwhelming the small contingent of allies currently securing the lower level.

Alemar handed the spyglass to Clavos and drifted away from Tollvar and his gaggle of sidekicks. He joined Toren on the other side of the observation deck. In the distance in that direction stood the palace ventilation tower down which the two of them, along with Geim, had infiltrated the city. How long ago had that been? He could probably count the number of days and nights if he tried, but it felt like years.

"Gloroc would never tolerate her abandoning her post," Alemar said, softly enough that only his immediate companion would hear. "He would execute her."

"He would. Therefore it is safe to assume Gloroc is no longer around to be feared."

"Yes."

Toren lifted his right hand and curled his fingers, as if gripping a hilt. Alemar wondered if the modhiv were imagining the moment when he had held the dagger steeped in dragonsbane, and had been cheated of the chance to plunge it into Gloroc's flesh. Now the mission had been completed.

By whom? Surely it was the Dragonslayer himself. And at the cost of his life, apparently, judging by the utter quiescence of his talismans. Alemar hoped he would one day hear the tale of that confrontation.

"Fifteen centuries is a long time to wait."

The surfacing of Polk's consciousness was so natural Alemar could almost believe the legendary First Steward had always been a co-occupant of the tall, golden-skinned body.

"You say it as if you are still waiting," Alemar responded.

"I believe I am. I have known moments of resolution. This does not feel like one."

By now all of Tollvar's coterie had had a turn at the spyglass. The back-slapping began. Alemar made out the fragments "afraid to face us" and "We've won!" before individual comments became lost in a babble of congratulations, boasts, and comparisons of Leyaril's body odor to various creatures of the sea. The group had yet to resort to alcohol, but it was as though they had been partaking for hours.

Polk raised his hand toward them, the classic gesture of a man of mature years about to counsel those too young to grasp the complexities — and the dangers — they were failing to acknowledge.

Alemar extended his arm, gently discouraging his companion from stepping forward to tender his advice.

Polk barely needed the hint. He stopped. Glanced at Alemar. Nodded.

Let the Dragonsdeep boys have their moment of triumph, Alemar thought. Their success might not be as complete as it could be, but it was still success.

He lifted his chin in the direction of the fleeing transport. "That's not the retreat of a broken enemy," he murmured to Polk. "You see it and I see it. But she *is* wounded."

The wind kissed Alemar's brow and played with his hair, a lively breeze from the direction of Cilendrodel. He inhaled until his chest could hold no more.

He smiled.

CHAPTER TWENTY-ONE

"Be alert for an ambush," Enril told the grey sergeant.

Sunlight dappled the landscape, banishing shadows, leaving few hiding places in the open woodland—at most a shrub here, a narrow bole of a tree there. It did not seem like potential ambush territory, but the rebel princess was holding in place no more than an hour's march ahead. Why would she do so in this main part of the day if not to stand and fight?

Lhan absorbed the news with his usual calm. He veered away to the flanks of the formation and relayed the information along with whatever specific instructions he judged necessary.

Was it to be today? Enril wondered. Would the chase be done? The delays, the near misses—he was weary of it. And being whisked along through untracked forest was doing nothing for his beloved. Omril needed a familiar environment. A routine.

Enril nudged his oeikani even closer to the wagon in which his comrade sat, Auntie on his shoulder. Enril set his hand on the side rail. The attendants reflexively retreated to the bench.

Omril continued to stare at his own knees, but he laid his hand atop Enril's.

Enril smiled. It was the second sign that day of Omril's on-going improvement.

A sudden, searing pain coiled around Enril's arm. The Ril tattoo blazed, its hue evolving through shades of red and orange and yellow into searing white.

Auntie squawked and took flight. Enril seized the pommel of his saddle with his free hand and even that was barely enough to keep him from tumbling to the ground. Sweat beaded on his forehead, trickled down the center of his back, slickened his groin.

—And then it was done. The shutting of a door.

Omril moaned. He stared at his own arm. His tattoo was just as livid. It appeared to be fashioned not with ink, but with scar tissue. He kept blinking at the limb, as if not able to interpret what had happened to him. Tears began to seep from the inner corners of his eyes.

Enril inhaled as deeply as he could. He forced himself to a state of equilibrium, ignoring the stink of burnt flesh.

Lhan was beside him, holding the bridle of his mount.

"Gloroc is dead," Enril told him.

Here at last was something that could perturb the grey sergeant. His brows rose. His mouth flattened from the tension.

"Our mission is unchanged," Enril said.

At once, Lhan was his usual self. He released the bridle, returned to his own oeikani, and swung himself back into the saddle. He nodded.

"Continue on," Enril commanded the cadre.

—o—

As they went along, the stony-soil terrain of the past few leagues gave way to a broad valley of rich loam—the sort of land that in any realm but Cilendrodel would be cleared and farmed. The forest became more verdant, the canopy more contiguous. The joyous pirouettes of butterflies were replaced by the purposeful lurking of mosquitoes.

The soldiers around Enril surveyed right and left and upward with increasing fervor. The wizard left that sort of vigilance to them. He devoted his own attention to the tidings of his magical senses. That process took more concentration now that he was receiving no contribution from his link to the Dragon, but the impressions were vivid enough about the thing that mattered: Elenya of Garthmorron still had not moved, and was now no more than a few bowshots away.

Apparent as well was the peculiar aroma of sorcery he had not known until coming to this vexing province of silk farms and loomhouses. Never had he smelled it so keenly. Rythni were not simply here, present for an individual moment in time. The place itself was of them. It had been shaped by them.

Not one glimpse of an enemy warrior appeared, not in the gaps of the foliage, not behind the fallen logs. The sorrel and kickfern betrayed no indications of the recent passage of any creature as large as humans or oeikani. No arrows flew at Auntie as she made a brief circle through the upper branches, to settle once more on Omril's shoulder.

His prey was so near, Enril knew if he were to cup his hands around his mouth and shout at highest volume, she would hear the outburst.

The forest was visibly different just ahead. The species of trees were the same as those between which they had been navigating, but the specimens were grander, thicker of trunk and more profusely flocked. The smooth-barked varieties even seemed to glisten. The grove could not possibly take up more than a small fraction of the valley—they would have detected that sort of presence on their way down from the higher elevation—but it dominated in a way that had nothing to do with its extent.

Enril raised his hand to signal a halt. The group dismounted.

Abruptly Lhan yawned. Whereupon his face reddened. It was possibly the first time Enril had seen him display embarrassment.

"You couldn't help yourself," Enril explained. "Have you heard the tale of the warrior who slept for a thousand years?"

"Everybody has heard that story," Lhan replied.

"Here is the bower in which that warrior slept," Enril said.

The grey sergeant turned and gestured for the cadre to take

several steps back.

"I recommend another stone's throw, or even two," Enril advised. "And if you decide to make camp, retreat even more."

"You're going in there?" Lhan asked.

"The rebel princess is in there. So—yes, I am going in. I can keep the spell at bay with the help of my colleague. Unfortunately I can't extend the protection to you."

Lhan did not debate the wisdom of Enril abandoning the security of numbers, though the wizard could see the man did not like the idea. "What are my orders if you do not return?"

"Take my disappearance as proof there is more here than you can deal with, and look to your own safety. Return to the coast. The news of the Dragon's death may not have reached Admiral Handett. If that's the case, be the one to disclose it to him. Help him to compose himself. Help him strategize. He's not a complete idiot as long as he has competent men around him."

Lhan saluted.

With the help of the attendants, Enril fetched Omril from the wagon. The latter was unusually composed and attentive. He immediately copied the spell of protection as soon as Enril cast it. Enril intertwined their efforts and secured the result; the magic would require no further conscious effort on either of their parts.

Enril began carefully marching forward. Omril did the same.

A pair of nearly identical trees loomed, both ancient, trunks rising from burled knees up a hundred feet or more to lichen-slung umbrellas of branches and fronds. The ground between them was smooth, as if pressed down by the passage of a hundred men a day for a hundred days. It was, in its unmarked way, the stoop of an entrance, demarcating what was enchanted space, and what was simply forest.

Once the two wizards proceeded past the threshold, the soporific effect manifested in full, as if they had stepped into a fog of poppy and lotus and vanilla essence.

"No no. No no," Auntie complained from her perch on Omril's

left shoulder. "Bad kiss. Bad kiss."

The nag parrot's eyelids drooped. Her body began to slouch. Shaking herself, she sidestepped until her shoulder rested against Omril's ear. Once that direct contact was established, her limpness vanished. She stared forward with an intensity, beak slightly open as if to spout an entire series of criticisms. She did not launch herself into the air and reconnoiter the surroundings, as she would have done upon venturing into almost any other place.

Enril could sense individual rythni now. He had the impression of limited numbers, but even so that amounted to several dozen, if not a hundred—enough to enliven the potential of the grove with their singing.

And oh, how they were singing. Soft their voices were, almost beneath the cusp of audibility, and yet the sound was pervasive. Their chorus was a seduction. A pillow. Enril could well understand why it could lull a listener into slumber, but insulated from its full effect, he understood the purpose of the grove was not to dull the senses, but to inspire tranquility. When rythni came here, they did so to meditate, to contemplate, to be restored.

He and Omril proceeded on until they arrived at a clearing. Above, the leaves gave way to an oblong of blue sky. The increased brightness made it difficult to scan into the shadows along the periphery. He did not like that.

At the center of the clearing, stretched on its side, lay a massive, moss-draped column of petrified wood, the remains of a fallen tree trunk from a time when the only creatures inhabiting the continents of Tanagaran were those that wriggled or slithered or tumbled, none that walked. No trees grew so large now, not even the giants here in Cilendrodel.

On the stone log was a small, winged woman, naked except for a thin necklace of gold links but nevertheless cloaked in authority.

"I am Hiephora."

Her voice was not faint, as he might have expected from so small a being. The sound was amplified somehow.

"I did not come for you," Enril said.

"And yet I am here."

"To fight me?"

"No."

"Is there some other way you will stop me?"

"I am not here to *stop* you, Enesthar of Elandris, son of Artin. Son of Faeya. I am here to speak of where it is you will go."

"It has been years since I was known as Enesthar."

"There can be no Order of the Ril without the Dragon at the center. Only individual magicians who may or may not act in concert. You are Enesthar again, whether you acknowledge it or not."

He chuckled. "You're bold for one of your race, I'll give you that."

"Boldness is my curse. Or so say the other queens."

"I have heard of you. You are the seeress."

"Yes."

"I suppose you will tell me you've known for some time that this was the day my master would die."

"This very day? No. That he would die before we met here in this grove? Yes. That became a certainty as soon as the Dragonslayer abandoned his sanctuary and committed himself to the field."

Enril chose not to react to the mention of the sorcerer. "Did you expect that if the Dragon died, we would all give up? That we would let the empire he built evaporate?"

"On the contrary. I saw that many would fight on," the rythni queen stated. "But you? Perhaps not."

"What would I do instead?"

"You might go north."

This time his laugh was full-throated, almost boisterous. "Go north? And do what? Brew ale for the shepherds and trappers? Dredge the bogs for mammoth ivory?"

"If you like," Hiephora said. "The North is vast. Few live there, and only a tiny fraction of that few would care what side of the struggle for Elandris a man had taken. You could do any number of things."

"I chose my course long ago."

"You have never chosen a course," Hiephora argued. "You wanted power and you went along the path that gave it to you, never weighing what else you might have done. Are you still a boy? Still stupid?"

Enril smirked. "Not the most persuasive way you could put it. I suppose next you will tell me if I continue to pursue the war, my side will be defeated and I will die a miserable death."

"I would not tell you that. I cannot see that far. But if you touch my hand, I can show you things you will want to know."

"And while I'm distracted, your ally will attack? I can feel her eyes on me. She wants my death. And even if she did not, I would want hers."

Hiephora nodded. "You hate her for what she did to your lover."

Enril would not have been able to contain the violence of his reaction if the queen's tone had not been so matter-of-fact. Or even compassionate. She was not goading him.

"Strangely," Hiephora continued, "you do not blame Prince Alemar for damaging Omril's mind. That you see as the consequence of a fair fight, which your comrade lost. What outraged you was Elenya's manipulation of him, damaged as he was, as a tool to fight you at the harbor, to interfere with the arrival of the fleet, and to set a trap."

"Yes. That, I cannot forgive."

"Is he the worse for it?"

"What? Of course he is."

"Think on it," Hiephora said with calm.

Enril was brought up short by the turn in the conversation. His gaze shifted to Omril. His beloved had knelt down and was monitoring a caterpillar as it crawled up a stalk of deer wheat. Each time the caterpillar stretched, bands of vermillion widened across a body otherwise as dark as char. Omril smiled whenever it happened. When the caterpillar paused, he tickled the cilia on its rear end with a blade of grass until it began moving again.

Omril was at peace. Enril could not claim otherwise. All the man needed was sunshine and grass and a simple source of entertainment.

"The princess could not make use of Omril as he was," Hiephora explained. "So she repaired some of the damage done to him."

"She did not do so out of affection," Enril protested.

"Granted. But if he is better now than he was, it is nevertheless her doing."

Enril hesitated. Hiephora held her hand out. He contemplated the offer.

Surely it was a trick. It had to be.

"The question you need to answer is simpler and smaller than armies and allegiances. If you continue to be a part of the war, can you protect *him*?" She pointed to Omril.

Enril tried to resist the urge to trust the queen. Surely that was weakness. Was the sorcery of the grove diluting his rage, leaving him pliable? In the end he nudged his suspicions to the side, because he had to know the answer to the question she had posed.

He extended his hand. Hiephora pressed her own tiny palm into his.

The visions were not like those of a dream or even of an enchantment. His awareness of his current surroundings and of the moment remained, but it was as though his mind contained memories that had not been there before, some dim, some compelling, some trivial, some essential.

The glimpses were not in order. There were many gaps. The only theme he could discern was that the clearest represented the immediate future, things that were almost certain to happen. Others were dim and malleable, circumstances that would come to pass only if events flowed in a particular sequence.

The earliest and sharpest scene was of the wharf at Hole Bay, where he was about to step onto a sleek, swift schooner in order to rush back to Elandris.

The most expected tableau placed him at the grand council

chamber in the old palace at Firsthold, where the surviving powerful figures of the Dragon's empire convened to hammer out a governance accord. He saw different versions of this, not always with the same cast of participants, but the end result was consistent. The question of who might become the supreme authority — Gloroc's successor — was set aside. Instead a coalition was forged, avoiding the disunity that would have doomed their cause. Command of the military forces was given to General Beherrig, but wealth and influence and rule was divided among a dozen or more individuals, Enril among them. A situation that might otherwise have turned into a rapid reconquest of Elandris by Keron and his forces became a continuation of the struggle that had been playing out for over half a century.

Enril glimpsed many of the crisis moments he would face in the years beyond that: He saw himself wielding spells from the deck of a burning ship. He throttled an assassin in a palace corridor. He stood beside Leyaril in a tower watching as their navy clashed with a fleet of mingled Tamisanese and royalist vessels. Sometimes he suffered injuries. Sometimes he lost companions. But one way or another, he survived.

Grey appeared in his beard. The creases beneath his eyes deepened. His body ached every morning when he rose from his bed, even when he had not exerted himself the day before. A third of Elandris remained under the rule of himself and his confederates, and no one was speaking of surrender, but still, the war went on.

One vision came to him more than once. He understood eventually that it was not an incident, but a series of them, experienced over a period of years or even decades, conflated down to one. In it, he was sitting in his private chambers, sipping tea, body a shadow of its old self but his spirit unbroken.

He was undefeated, but there at his table staring at the steaming cup in its saucer, he was alone. Had been alone for decades. The only vision in which Omril had appeared was the one at Hole Bay, standing beside him on the wharf with the nag parrot on his shoulder. Omril had not died in Cilendrodel. He had made the return journey. And then?

Enril pulled back his hand, rejecting whatever else the magic might show him.

His shoulders slumped. He let out a breath that took with it all the drawn-bow tightness he had been hoarding.

"I never imagined facing an opponent such as you," the wizard told Hiephora. "You did not even brandish a weapon, and yet I must do as you say."

"I am not asking you to do one thing or another," Hiephora responded. "I am only wondering what matters to you most, and what you will do to have it."

"You are the seeress," Enril said. "Was it ever a question what I would do?"

"It was. It is. Will you go north, Enesthar of Elandris?"

"I will."

— o —

Elenya remained quiet and hidden, high on a branch of a tree along the north edge of the clearing, screened by greenery and shade.

She had listened from beginning to end to the exchange between Hiephora and Enril, but she brimmed with the urge to reject what her ears had conveyed. The queen had told her of the outcomes that might unfold, but this one had seemed impossible. It still did.

"I will," Enril had said. And now he was taking Omril by the hand and walking onward. Toward the north. Away from his detachment of soldiers, from the wagons and tents and gear.

Away from the war.

Elenya was certain his nature would reassert itself, if not within minutes, then within the next day or two. And even if he perhaps had been turned away from personal vengeance toward Elenya, he would still be the enemy. Surely it would be so.

In a few moments, the wizard would pass near the base of the tree in which Elenya perched. Finally she understood what Hiephora had meant when she evoked the memory of Lerina, the parent she was least like, the one who had never picked up a sword. But how could she be that person?

Elenya had no weapon. No rock, no bow, no blade. Hiephora would not permit them in the grove. But she did have her vertical advantage. Gravity could be her weapon.

Perhaps Enril would recognize the danger and throw up a ward in time. Perhaps he would not. Perhaps the impact, even if it succeeded in killing Enril, would kill Elenya as well. She had faced life-threatening choices before. She had always been willing to die if that's what it took.

The sword was what she knew.

She became conscious of Hiephora, still standing on the stone log. The queen was watching her intently. Visionary or not, she did not know what was to happen. How could she? Elenya herself did not know what she would do.

And then the moment was in the past. Enril and Omril and the nag parrot continued past the base of the tree. The moment when Elenya could have flung herself from her branch was gone.

Elsewhere, the war continued. Here, it was done.

EPILOGUE

OBO WAITED IN his favorite gazebo in the heart of the gardens of the Temple of Struth, rereading the latest dispatch from Elandris, smiling again at the personal addendum the king had written, with its inside joke meant just for him.

At last his visitors approached, the golden-skinned Vanihr even taller and more lithe than Obo remembered, but his beloved Deena looking quite herself despite the obvious indications that her pregnancy had reached its final month.

He rose spryly from his chair and pulled them into his embrace, one and then the other and then both at once.

"Here at last, here at last." He beamed. "What news from Cilendrodel?"

"Alemar has returned from his retreat," Toren answered. "His healing magic was completely restored."

"Excellent," the wizard said. "And was there anything he could do for Elenya?"

"Quite a bit, I would say. She no longer feels any pain. But it is clear she will never be able to depend on the knee the way she could in the past."

"And with that, how are her spirits?"

"Genuinely good," Deena interjected. "I think she appreciates another reason not to slip into old habits. She claims she no longer needs to be a warrior, and I believe her."

Toren nodded his agreement.

"Good, good," Obo said.

"She still teaches swordwork, though."

Obo smiled. "I would never have expected any different."

Deena gave a start, and put her hand on her belly. "She's kicking again."

"She?"

"So the rythni queen implied, though I wonder if she was teasing. She's getting a reputation for being..." She turned to Toren, shrugging.

"Playful," Toren supplied.

"Yes," Deena confirmed.

"That is the best kind of seeress," Obo said. He waved his guests toward the divan, gesturing at the refreshments on the little center table. Deena took advantage and was off her feet at once. Obo almost chuckled at her eagerness.

"Geim chose not to journey with you?" he asked.

"Geim is still in Dragonsdeep," Toren answered. "The more he stays the more he seems to like it."

"I am happy to hear it," Obo said. "If a wanderer decides to stop wandering, it means something, I would say."

Toren gestured at the letter Obo had set aside. "Speaking of news, have you any to share?"

Obo nodded. "The coalition is continuing to fall apart, this time in the form of a rift between General Beherrig and Leyaril the Poisoner. And Keron's navy just won a key victory north of the Lost Isles. That will do it, I think. The enemy is now surrounded. No access to supply lines and trade partners. When the common people get hungry enough, they'll tie the last of the leaders to the sea bottom, bloody them up a bit, and leave them for the sharks."

"Let's hope that happens sooner rather than later."

"Indeed."

Obo settled back on the cushion. Force of habit made him do so gradually and carefully, but the fact was, he felt no strain and his motion was steady throughout.

Deena cocked her head. "You're looking well, Master Obo. I would even say vibrant. I was worried for you when we stepped through that portal. I was convinced that was the last I would see of you."

"I had the same fear, child. But I am restored. It could be I have another five years to go. Or seven. Or ten."

"What happened?"

"Miranda found one last forgotten vial of a youth elixir she and her brother had once developed. She had become immune to it centuries ago, but she gave it to me. She had just enough strength at that point to cast the spell that would activate it and, well, here I am as you see me — able to sleep through the night, eat a proper meal. Sometimes I walk by the river, and I am able to hear the crickets and songbirds."

"I can't think of anyone who deserves it more," Deena said.

"I don't know that I am as worthy as that, but I welcome the reprieve. I have books I must finish reading and messages I must write. I expect to get to hold that baby of yours on my lap when it arrives. And in due course, once my lad Keron is sitting on the throne he's worked so hard to win, I may just be hale enough to make my way to Elandris and see that sight with my own eyes."

"I have faith you'll get to do all those things."

"Still have a responsibility here, though," Obo said, the good cheer draining from him. "For a little while longer."

"How much time does she have?" Toren asked.

"Not much. A season. A month."

"The magic is not holding back her aging at all now?"

"A little. If not, she would have died as quickly as her brother did."

"And nothing can be done?" Deena asked.

"No. She and her brother made it through these last several centuries only by means of frequent hibernation in the rejuvenation caskets, along with infusions of a kind of power source only dragons can tap. Once Struth died, the connection to that source became unreliable. A few years ago the amount Miranda could draw directly became inadequate. She became dependent on her brother. He shared his portion with her."

"And now that he's dead..."

"She's been subsisting on dregs. Frankly, I think the only reason she hasn't slipped away already is that her body's so used to being alive, it has to teach itself how to stop. I know it must have been uncomfortable travelling in your condition, but you two were wise not to wait until after the baby was born."

"Have you told her we were coming?" Toren asked.

"Yes. She's expecting you." He waved at the sundial in the nearest of the goldfish ponds. "Now would be good, if you like. She's at her most alert at this time of day."

Toren dipped his head. He seemed to have taken a sudden interest in the pattern of the tiles of the gazebo floor.

"You did say *he* wanted to say good-by?" Obo prompted.

"He does want it," Toren confirmed. "But he's dreading it, too."

"I expect so. If you'd prefer, I'll go with you. Her mind is not always all there. Good days and bad. I've learned some tricks that help keep her in the here and now. Unless he'd prefer to do it alone?"

"With all the ancestors I carry in my head, it's not as though either of us knows real privacy anymore. Your company would be welcome."

"It's settled, then." Obo stood up. "It's this way." He pointed at a blue door in the shadow of an archway in the building to the south.

"Very well. Just give me a moment to...call him."

Toren glanced at Deena. She nodded and got up from the divan. She gave Obo a squeeze on the upper arm and left the gazebo, heading out into the grounds.

"That was unexpected," Obo said.

"She doesn't like being present when he manifests," Toren said.

"I can see how she would find it disturbing. I hope it's not often an issue?"

"Not often, no. The First Steward lived a full life. He's good about not trying to borrow mine. But today...today it's necessary."

Toren set his hands on his thighs and relaxed. He closed his eyes. When he opened them again, he was still golden-skinned and blond of hair. Still beardless. Still a young man—especially from Obo's perspective. And yet Obo could easily sense he was looking at a person as experienced in the world as he, shaped like a stone on a beach by things endured and things witnessed.

He stood and straightened up in a deliberate manner, as if he was finding it hard to believe his back didn't ache.

"Extraordinary," Obo said.

His visitor bowed his head. "Pleased to meet you, Master Obo. I have heard nothing but good about you."

The archaic intonations were nothing like the way Toren rendered the High Speech—as Obo knew better than anyone, having been responsible for providing Toren with that suite of pronunciation, accent, and rhythm.

"I have my flaws," Obo replied. "But decades ago I learned how to disguise them, and then I outlived anyone who knew me before that time."

"I never learned that trick. I never stopped making a pest of my-self."

A pity they would not have more chances to converse, Obo thought. He was certain he would quickly grow to like Polk. But he wouldn't ask that of Toren. Too much had already been asked of Toren.

"Let's see to the matter at hand," the old wizard said, and they made their way beneath the archway, through the blue door, and up to the second level. They did not speak as they went. The tapping of his staff on the planks was the sound that marked their progress.

Miranda preferred light and air and breezes. Obo was not surprised to find she had ordered her attendants to place her in her arm chair on the balcony overlooking her private courtyard with its fountain and its magnificent trees. She noticed them approaching. She waved the servants away.

"So you've come," she said. "I wasn't sure you would."

Obo retreated to a stool off to the side. Polk remained where he was, taking in the sight of Miranda. Her hair was as white as the pillow on which her head rested. Her skin hung slack from her bones. Evidence of her old self lingered, but only to those who had known her well. Polk's gaze drifted from one trace to the next, and Obo felt certain he was recognizing those hints.

"I had to come," he said at last. "I need your opinion."

"Opinion about what?"

"Is it over?" he asked.

She paused so long Obo thought she might have slipped into one of her episodes. But her eyes were focussed. She was gazing steadily back at Polk.

"You know there's never a way to be sure," she replied.

"I did not ask if you know for certain. I asked what you believe. A dragon, new to its wings, was seen crossing the Syril Mountains. It vanished over the Gulf of Therares, heading west. Another dragon recently took up residence on the far side of the Eastern Deserts. A goat-herder claims it hunts in the canyons there, bringing the prey it kills back to a pinnacle of an island in Knife Lake."

"So Obo told me, as soon as the dispatches came."

"And? Could it mean what it seems to mean?"

"What do you think it means?" Miranda asked.

"They are choosing to run away," Polk said.

She nodded. "So it would seem."

"If two have done so, the other four will as well. Or already have."

"Which means the answer to your question is yes. What we did — what you and I and my late brother set in motion — it is resolved."

Polk pressed his lips together, and shook his head.

"I have just agreed with you," Miranda said. "Why do you seem unhappy that I have?"

"Of all the ways it would end, why like this?"

"Why shouldn't it end like this?" Miranda asked.

"Because we killed Faroc and Triss. Because now Gloroc and Beyiss and Aroc are slain as well. Dragons delight in vengeance. Why wouldn't the war go on?"

"Have you not considered who the remaining six hate most? Or should I say, who *did* they hate most?"

"Of course..." Obo murmured, mostly to himself.

Polk's eyes widened. "They hated...Gloroc?"

"You could say that," Miranda said. "He was the master dragon. He dominated his cabal the way his sort do on Serpent Moon—the neuters controlling the breeders. But the six are dragons of Tanagaran. On our world, dragons live in the wild, on their own and delighting in it. I think it pleases them to choose not to further Gloroc's designs. That is the vengeance they take."

Obo watched carefully as Polk absorbed the revelation. In all his many days, he might never have witnessed such an upwelling of relief and peace.

Miranda smiled as she watched him. Then, as Obo had seen so many times in the past few weeks, she blinked and seemed to start over, as if her visitors had just entered the room.

"Look at you," she said to Polk. "So young."

"In a body I have borrowed, and shortly will give back," he answered.

"Ah, but you'll be in there. Noticing things. Being amused by things. Able to whisper a hint of advice if the situation seems urgent enough. And you will be there in centuries to come, assuming Toren passes along his totem and his son passes it along and so forth down the line. It is ironic, don't you think? That you may persist in the world—may have an effect upon the world—for more years than I, despite all the ways I've clutched at immortality."

"I haven't thought that far ahead."

"You should. It could come to pass. Don't say it's impossible."

"Perhaps you're right," Polk said. "But the future belongs to those who will be alive then. If I never witness that world to come, I am untroubled. I am ready for lasting sleep."

"That is one of the things that sets us apart," she responded. "I have never been ready to die, nor am I now. Do you know, that was the reason Alemar and I pursued youth-restoring magic so early and in so many ways? It wasn't so that we would have more time to build an empire. He did it as a way to soothe my fear."

"I know. You confessed that to me, once upon a time."

"Did I? I don't recall." She looked down — the first time she had broken eye contact since the conversation had begun. She fussed with the folds of her coverlet, and seemed to be leagues away.

"I hope you are not here to...watch," she said.

"Watch you die? No. I know you wouldn't want that."

"No. I wouldn't. I'd rather you have as few memories of me as possible looking like *this*." She tugged at the slack flesh on the back of her opposite hand.

"Understood."

"I visited you when you were on your death bed," she told him. "I did it early on, when it was clear you still had a day or two left. That is what I want now. Lately I never have the strength to stay awake past noon. It's almost noon now. Stay with me this little while. By early evening when I wake again, I expect you to be gone."

"I will do as you say," he said.

She held out her hand. "Do you remember the first time we ever spoke?"

"I remember."

She smiled. "Did I not promise you an adventure?"

He offered his hand and let her hold it on her lap. They sat together in silence, watching the fountain and the flowering vines and the hummingbirds. Obo did not know all the thoughts they might be having, but he was quite sure they were untroubled by the subject of dragons and ways to kill them.

A flight of headless dragons. Auspicious.
—*I Ching*, First Hexagram, all nines

AUTHOR'S NOTE

Various supplemental material can be found at davesmeds.com. In particular, at davesmeds.com/trilogy/maps.htm you will find expandable versions of the maps of the world of Tanagaran. And if you would like a little help with unusual terms and names, you can find a glossary at davesmeds.com/trilogy/glossary.htm.

ACKNOWLEDGMENTS

It took so many years to get this book done, I'm not certain I remember every last person I should thank for their contribution, be it in the form of encouragement, collegiality, financial support, or direct feedback on the work-in-progress. Apologies to people who deserve to be mentioned here, but aren't. Sometimes it's hard for this old man to remember where he put his shoes.

First, kudos to the Spellbinders. The group listened to first drafts of every chapter of this at some point along the way. Specific shout-outs go to Bob Fleming, Cherie Kushner, Brent Anderson, Shirley Johnston, Patricia Stillman, Patricia MacEwen, Margaret Raymond, Marian Gibbons, and the late Armando Gomez.

Thanks to my colleagues at BVC, especially Sherwood Smith for the proofreading and Jen Stevenson for the formatting advice.

To the late Alan Rodgers and to Bridget and Marti McKenna, who would have seen this book through the publication process on behalf of Wildside Press and Scorpius Digital, if only I had been capable of finishing it in less than a dragon's lifetime.

To Risa Aratyr, my gratitude for the copyediting.

Finally, my love to my family, Connie, Lerina, and Elliott, for keeping me going.

ABOUT THE AUTHOR

A Nebula Award finalist, Dave Smeds is the author of novels, short fiction, comic book scripts, and screenplays. His writing spans several sub-genres of science fiction and fantasy including contemporary fantasy, hard sf, superhero, martial arts, and horror, as well as imaginary-world fantasy.

His books include The War of the Dragons trilogy (*The Sorcery Within, The Schemes of Dragons,* and *The Wizard's Nemesis*), *X-Men: Law of the Jungle, Piper in the Night,* and the collections *Embracing the Starlight, Raiding the Hoard of Enchantment,* and *Swords, Magic, and Heart.* Those last three volumes include some of the more than one hundred stories of his that have appeared in magazines such as *Asimov's Science Fiction, Realms of Fantasy, The Magazine of Fantasy & Science Fiction, Pulphouse,* and *Dark Regions,* and anthologies such as *Full Spectrum 4, David Copperfield's Tales of the Impossible, Peter S. Beagle's Immortal Unicorn, Return to Avalon, Enchanted Forests, Future Earths: Under African Skies,* and *In the Field of Fire,* along with nineteen installments of the *Sword & Sorceress* series.

In addition to being an author, Dave is a book-cover artist and designer, and from time to time, a karate instructor, having trained in goju-ryu karate-do for almost fifty years. He lives in Santa Rosa, CA with his wife and son.

ABOUT BOOK VIEW CAFÉ

Book View Café is a professional authors' cooperative offering DRM-free ebooks in multiple formats to readers around the world. With authors in a variety of genres including mystery, romance, fantasy, and science fiction, Book View Café has something for everyone.

Book View Café is good for readers because you can enjoy high-quality DRM-free ebooks from your favorite authors at a reasonable price. It is good for writers because 90% of the proceeds goes directly to the book's author.

Authors include New York Times and USA Today bestsellers, Nebula, Hugo, Lambda, Chanticleer, National Reader's Choice, and Philip K. Dick Award winners, World Fantasy, Kirkus, and Rita Award nominees, and winners and nominees of many other publishing awards.

Book View Café's Newsletter includes new releases, specials, author news, and event announcements. Visit the website to sign up.

BOOK VIEW CAFE

www.bookviewcafe.com